THE TRUTH IS
CONTAGIOUS

BOOK IV IN THE CONTAGIUM SERIES

EMILY GOODWIN

A PERMUTED PRESS book

ISBN (trade paperback): 978-1-61868-396-0
ISBN (eBook): 978-1-61868-395-3

The Truth is Contagious (Contagium Book 4) copyright © 2014
by Emily Goodwin
All Rights Reserved.
Cover art by Dean Samed, Conzpiracy Digital Arts

In memory of Kami:
Mother, friend, sister
You will be missed.

PART ONE

CHAPTER ONE

"What?" I asked, my voice shrill, though there was no mistaking what Hayden had said.

"I know how the virus started," he repeated.

"Don't make shit up." I shook my head and leaned away. "There's no way you could know that." I swallowed hard and pressed my lips together.

Hayden's fingers curled around the flash drive. "Fuller knew. He fucking knew all along and never—" He abruptly cut off and closed his eyes. "I have to tell everyone...let them know." He shook his head and let out a deep breath. "We should go. Now." He turned his eyes up to mine.

Suddenly all the air was sucked from my lungs. My head spun. I pushed off of Hayden's lap and backed away. I inhaled and got nothing. Fuller was dead. Hayden and me—of all people—were supposed to take over the role of running the compound. And Hayden was holding some magical flash drive that held all the answers. "No," I said and shook my head, whipping my wet hair over my shoulder. "You need to explain. Now."

Hayden turned the flash drive over in his hand. He set it down on the desk and glared at it. "You might want to sit down."

"Is it that bad?" I asked. My blood ran cold.

Hayden flicked his hazel eyes up at me. "Yes. And it's that long."

"Right," I said and sat on top of Fuller's desk. The back of my purple tank top was soaked from my hair, since I had just showered. When the air conditioner kicked on, I shivered. I rubbed my hands along my arms and stared at Hayden, not sure where we should start. "What's on that?"

"This?" Hayden held up the flash drive again. "Nothing now."

"What do you mean?"

He let the little device drop onto the desk. I picked it up. The plastic and metal was warm from being in Hayden's hand. I turned it over, inspecting it as if it could somehow give me a clue as to what the hell Hayden was talking about.

"It was set up to delete after one view."

I rolled my eyes. "Typical Fuller. And delete what?"

"A video message Fuller recorded of himself, explaining everything."

"Ok, tell me." I put my hands down on the desk to keep them from trembling. With all the shit we had just gone through, this shouldn't scare me. But it did. Finally finding the truth that we had so desperately wanted was terrifying. What it if was worse than what I had imagined? Reality had a nasty habit of doing that.

Hayden put his head in his hands. "It's a mess, Riss. A huge fucking mess."

I pushed aside my feelings of impatience and stood to comfort Hayden. I wanted to scream in anxious frustration and demand Hayden spit out every last detail about the virus and why the hell Fuller wanted me to help him run the compound. But I wanted to help the man I loved even more.

I stepped close to him, leaned over, and wrapped my arms around his shoulders. Hayden reached up and looped his hands through mine, gently pulling me back into his lap.

"You're cold," he said softly.

"And you're still dirty."

He gave me a small smile and nestled his face into my neck. I tightly held onto him, able to feel his rapid heartbeat. "Yeah. I am," he said.

I took in a slow, steady breath and closed my eyes. I needed to stay calm for Hayden's sake. Hayden relaxed just a bit when I ran my fingers through his messy brown hair. "Want to take a shower first? Then we can talk about all this."

He moved his head to the side. "No. I just...I don't even know where to start, Riss." His jaw tightened and he blinked back his emotions. I was mad at Fuller. Really fucking mad. Who was he to put this on Hayden? What on earth possessed him to wait until Hayden was grieving over his loss before he dropped a bomb on us?

"Let's just start with running the compound. Why us? I mean, it doesn't make sense. Hector knows pretty much everything Fuller did." I raised my eyebrows. "With the exception to the whole origin of the virus."

Hayden nodded. "I agree. But in this," Hayden reached over me and picked up the letter, "he said that Hector wouldn't be able to make the necessary sacrifices to keep this place running. You know it's not easy running this place and certain things have to be done for the greater good."

I nodded. And I couldn't disagree. Plus, I knew as well as anyone that Hayden would do whatever it took to keep this place safe.

"And," Hayden continued, "Hector knows it. He's going to stay second in command and help me."

"What about me?"

Hayden's lips pulled into a small half smile. "You're by default."

I raised an eyebrow. "Default? What the hell is that supposed to mean?"

Hayden flicked his eyes to the letter, letting me know he was voicing Fuller's words, not his. "You wouldn't just stand back and let me do this alone, would you?"

"Of course not."

"You're more than just my partner, Riss. I love you and respect you. Though you might be a little...uh, unorthodox sometimes, you know we would do this together, equally. And Fuller knew that too."

"So that's why Fuller was hard on me? He was trying to school me into being a leader?"

"Yeah." Hayden crinkled the paper. "He said that he wants you to know he really respected you as a soldier. And he said he thinks we work well together."

"I have to agree with him there."

"Me too." He set the letter down again. His eyebrows pushed together. He was tired, so tired. "Taking over is going to be...hard."

It suddenly dawned on me that I had no idea what Fuller actually did. My interactions with him were limited to being disciplined and discussing missions. The room spiraled around me. How the hell would we do this?

Hayden shifted his legs. I stood, knowing it wasn't comfortable for him to have me on his lap while sitting in a small desk chair. I perched on the edge of the desk again and realized I was shaking. I looked at Hayden, not even having to say it out loud.

"The virus," he stated and I nodded. "The fucking virus."

"How did Fuller find out the truth?"

"He knew all along. Since the start of it all."

"What?" Nerves prickled though me.

Hayden nodded and ran his hand over his hair. "Ok...ok," he said to himself and bounced his leg up and down. He clasped his hands together and inhaled. "Ok," he said to me and put his hands on his thighs. "The virus was created in a lab."

"Of course it was."

"On purpose."

I leaned back. That wasn't what I was expecting to hear. Ever.

Something this horrible had to be some sort of vaccination research gone wrong. No one would ever *make* a zombie virus. "W-why?"

"To make people crazy." He held up his hand to keep me from firing off another question. "Do you remember how shitty the economy was?"

I moved my head up and down. "Of course. That was why I dropped out of school. I couldn't afford it anymore."

"Did you pay much attention to politics?"

"Not really. I just remember that President Samael drove us deeper into debt than we already were."

"Right. You just need to know that our country was—is—in hot water. And by hot I mean boiling. Other countries didn't want to trade with us, the US dollar was losing value fast, Samael had scattered the troops all over the damn world, and don't even get me started on the health care system...you get it, right? We were losing power. America *wasn't* the greatest place to be anymore."

He narrowed his eyes and shook his head. "I don't think any average citizen realized how close to war we were with more than one other country."

My heart fluttered. "Really?"

Hayden nodded. "Yeah. And Samael wasn't happy about it. So somehow someone came up with the idea to bring the US up by bringing others down."

Something clicked in my head. *Oh my God.* I leaned forward, needing to hear Hayden say it out loud.

"And what better way," he continued, "than to start riots and wars in other countries without having to physically be there?"

I put my hand over my mouth and stared at Hayden with wide eyes. My heart pounded. The air conditioner shut off. The vents shuddered and then silence rang in my ears.

"The virus," Hayden said, "was created just for that purpose. Only no one knew it would turn people into zombies. It was studied in very controlled settings, obviously. The test subjects were executed before the virus could progress further than stage one. No one expected it to have long term effects." Hayden shook his head. "Fuller didn't know the science behind it. He said if he did he would have told Dr. Cara since she's working on a vaccine and all."

Good. If he had withheld information that could have helped us, I wouldn't have ever forgiven him. I extended my arm and took Hayden's hand in mine. He gave it a reassuring squeeze and went on.

"Fuller also didn't know how the virus spread. He just knew it was deliberately planted in more than a dozen countries in the Middle East and a few others in Europe. He thinks basically any country that posed a threat to the US, whether it be a military threat or economic, got hit." He paused and looked around the room. His eyes settled on the picture of Fuller and his son, a son who closely resembled Hayden in looks. "But then something went wrong. The virus worked of course. Too well. It mutated and became contagious, spreading faster than any of the motherfucking scientists could have guessed. International travel couldn't be stopped before it was brought here. Once it was out..."

Hayden closed his eyes and licked his lips, bracing for what he was about to say next. "Samael did nothing to stop it. Fuller said there are shelters—real shelters, built just for this on the east and west coast. He said there is a large number of 'important people' there, riding this out and they had been brought there long before shit hit the fan. Everything was planned out."

I closed my eyes in a long blink. I took my hand back from Hayden and crossed my arms, pressing them against my stomach. The goosebumps turned into chills. "I still don't get how Fuller knew all this."

"He is—was—a commissioned officer in the Marine Corps. He was invited to go to one of the shelters."

"And he said no?"

Hayden nodded. "He said he couldn't sit back in safety while other people—good, innocent people—became infected and killed each other. As soon as he said no, the door was closed on the offer. Fuller knew about this place." Hayden looked up at the ceiling of the compound. "And he swore to do what he had always done: protect the American people."

I bit the inside of my cheek and looked at Fuller's picture on his desk. A new respect for the man built up inside of me. I blinked back tears and turned to Hayden. "I still don't get why he didn't say anything to you before."

The color had drained from Hayden's face. "That's not all, Riss." His words sent another chill through me. "None of us were meant to survive."

I pushed my eyebrows together. "What?"

"The virus wasn't supposed to have long term effects, remember? What is set up on the coasts will keep the infected out for sure, but they're not set up to fight a war against almost an entire country of undead. Fuller thought that it was assumed the entire population would be wiped out in just a few months. No survivors."

I opened my mouth only to close it, at a loss for words. I shook my head and looked at Hayden. "So that's why Fuller never wanted us to go to California."

Hayden nodded. "And the worst—"

"There's something worse than creating a horrible, crazy-making virus?"

Hayden tipped his head to the side. "Maybe."

I swallowed and watched Hayden. "What was done next?"

"When it was discovered that we—the average citizen—weren't dying off like it was predicted, we were hit with another dose of the virus."

The words were like a punch to the stomach. It was awful to think that the place we called home, had been proud to come from, would do that. All in the name of power. My breath left me. I grabbed a handful of wet hair and tugged on it.

"But why didn't Fuller have us go to the real shelters?"

Hayden picked at a spot of dried blood on his forearm. "He said he thought we'd be turned away if we're lucky."

"And if we're not lucky?"

"Killed on the spot."

"Oh." I leaned back and traced my eyes over the bookshelf that sat behind Fuller's desk. It was filled with plastic binders, notebooks, and manila files. Hanging on the wall next to the bookshelf was a map of the compound and hand-drawn blueprints for the cabins that were being built on the land around our shelter. Taped to the blueprints was a list of needed construction supplies. I recognized the handwriting at once to belong to Raeya. The familiarity of my best friend's obsessive list making brought a small amount of comfort to the scary new information. "Wait, why would they kill us?"

Hayden shook his head. "This is where things got complicated. Fuller doesn't think that everyone in the shelters knows the truth about the virus...or that the government left thousands of people to die. The goal is to restart the country, remember? Would you be willing to stand by your leaders if you knew the truth?"

I pulled on my hair again. "No. I wouldn't. I would...oh shit. I would riot." I let my hair fall to my back. "It makes sense now. In a really twisted, fucked up way." I shook my head. "Still, can't we play it off like we don't know the truth? Like we are what we really are: a group of survivors. No one can blame the government for that, right?"

Hayden brushed the crusty blood onto the floor. "Maybe. Hell, I don't know. It would have been real fucking nice to discuss this with Fuller." Anger clouded his eyes.

"So what are we supposed to do?" I stood and paced to the back of the office. The room was small, crowded with the large desk, chairs, and a table. I stopped at the table and drummed my fingers on the surface. "Just keep going like we don't know the truth?"

"That's what Fuller wanted."

"It doesn't make sense." I whirled around and faced Hayden. "You just said it: this is going to end. Someday. Somehow. But if it does...then what? What will happen when everyone in hiding comes out to rebuild the country? We can't stay hidden forever. They will find us. And if they don't want to share supplies with us now, they're not going to want to then."

"He hadn't gotten that far," Hayden spat. "Maybe...maybe he didn't think *anyone* would get that far."

"Way to have faith," I mumbled.

"He did," Hayden said. His muscles stiffened. "He had faith is us. Just not in them."

"And by 'them' you mean the asshats who built shelters before anything even happened."

"Exactly." Hayden leaned forward with his elbows on his knees.

My eyes settled on the picture of Fuller with his son. "Why didn't he tell you before? I get not telling everyone because it would upset them for no reason, but why not you?"

Hayden looked at the letter. "He didn't want me to have to know until it was absolutely necessary." He sighed. "He thought it would be too much to put on me." Hayden shook his head. "And he was right."

I strode over and knelt down in front of Hayden. Taking his hands in mine, I said, "Don't say that, Hayden. You're strong, one of the strongest people I know."

Hayden pulled his hands back. "I'm no leader."

"Yes you are and you don't even realize it. The people here look up to you, respect you. *Like* you." I took a deep breath and shook my head. "Before I met you I was so close to giving up. I didn't want to keep fighting. I did it because I had to, because no one else I was with could. I was tired. I didn't see a way out of this...I didn't think it was even worth it. And then I met you and you showed me that I was wrong, so wrong. You gave me hope, gave me something to live for. I *wanted* to fight." I put my hands on Hayden's thighs. "If you can change my stubborn mind, then you can do anything." I gave him a small smile. "And everyone here already loves you. You're kind and fair and very, very good looking."

Hayden smiled. "Because that matters."

"It doesn't hurt."

His smile grew. "Riss," he started and flicked his eyes to mine. "Thanks."

"Of course Hayden. Like you said, we're a team. Even though we both know I'm the brains of the operation."

He smiled again and pulled me to him. "Then you can tell the guys the truth."

I tensed. "No one else knows, right? Not even Hector?"

"Just you and me for now." Hayden slid his hands down my waist. "And I don't know if we should tell everyone. Fuller kept it a secret for a reason and I think he was right. There is nothing we can do about it, so why upset people?"

"Right." I put my hands over his.

"And don't tell Ray. Not yet, ok?"

I pressed my lips together and didn't respond.

"Riss?"

"Fine. I never keep anything from her, though. Ever."

Hayden parted his legs and drew me in. "Why upset her?"

"She'll be pissed when she knows I kept something that huge from her."

Hayden rested his head on my stomach. "We should get back to the quarantine room. The guys are probably wondering."

I raked my fingers through Hayden's hair. "They probably think we went upstairs and are having wild sex or something." It was a lie. The guys knew something was wrong. We all did as soon as we got home from the mission. "We'll get through this," I promised. "I'd be lying if I said I knew how but I do know that together we're awesome. We're the best, remember?"

Suddenly, boots pounded on the tile floor just outside in the hall. Hayden and I both turned our attention to the door.

* * *

"We've got one!" someone shouted, their voice muffled. "Remember, she wants it alive. Do *not* kill it!"

"What the hell?" Hayden mumbled and strode to the door, pulling it open. Several A2s ran down the hall, heading to the stairs. "Hey!" Hayden shouted.

A young woman with short black hair spun around. Her face went blank when she saw Hayden. Like me, Hayden was an A1. A1s went on missions while A2s guarded the farms and the compound. She turned her head and called to the other A2s.

"What's going on?" Hayden asked.

"Sir," she said nervously. "The trap is full of zombies."

"Trap?" Hayden asked.

"Yes, sir," the A2 answered. She smoothed her shirt and took a tentative step toward us. "For S1s."

S1s were infected, but hadn't yet crossed the threshold to zombie or S2, as they were "properly" called. They were insane, but not yet undead. S3s—gummies as I called them—were late stage zombies who were gummy, gooey, and the easiest to kill.

"Why are we setting traps for S1s?" Hayden asked.

"F-for Dr. Cara." She moved closer. "I'm sorry. We should have asked you, right?"

"It's ok, Jenny," Hayden said, reading her name tag. "Uh, what are you going to do with the S1 once you have it?"

"Put it in a stall in the quarantine barn. That's what Dr. Cara wanted," she explained. "She's studying it or something." She shook her head, causing her short hair to become untucked from behind her ear. When she reached up to push it back, I noticed the colorful tattoos on her arms. The skull threw me at first. The image of the Imperial Lords' logo flashed in my mind—a group we had just defeated. I blinked and took another look at Jenny. The skulls on her arms were pretty, decorated with flowers and swirls. I thought they were Mexican sugar skulls, but I wasn't sure.

"How are you going to safely get it there?" Hayden asked. "Crazies—S1s are dangerous. Probably more than you realize."

"We've done it before," she said meekly. "Only with zombies. They keep getting stuck in the trap." She shook her head again. "There's a net in the trap. We can wrap it around the S1 without touching it. Then we drag it into the barn."

That was an awful plan. I blinked, dumbfounded by the casualness of Jenny's words. What if the crazy got out? It would be loose inside our fences. I rolled my eyes. Fucking Dr. Cara. I had to give her credit. She was determined.

"Uh..." Hayden started. "Can it wait until morning?"

Jenny's eyebrows pushed together. "It is morning. It's a little past six AM."

"Oh," Hayden rubbed his forehead. "Right. Uh, just get Alex to go with you. Shoot the S1 if it gets out of hand. No life is worth a little research."

"Yes, sir," she said and turned on her heel.

"Be careful," he added, consternation growing.

"You did good," I told him. "See, you're a great leader already."

He widened his eyes. "Thanks for lying."

"I'm not," I pressed.

"I do not have time for this," he mumbled and went back into the office. He picked up the letter, folded it in half, and stuck it in the top drawer of Fuller's desk. He added the flash drive and slammed the drawer shut. Then he bent down and reached under the desk, retrieving a small hidden key to lock the drawer.

"Ready?" he asked me.

"If you are." I put my hand on the doorknob. "We can take a few minutes if you need them," I reminded him. "Go upstairs. Shower. Lay down for a bit."

Hayden nodded. "Ok. A shower would be nice." He walked over to me and abruptly stopped. "I don't want to talk to anyone," he blurted.

I smiled. "Welcome to my world. Just keep your head down and walk fast. It seems to work for me."

"You're so social," he teased and flipped the lock on the inside of the door. I held my hand out for him. He laced his fingers through mine and we sped through the hall, reaching the stairs before anyone could stop and talk to us.

While Hayden showered, I plopped back onto the bed with a bag of cheese puffs and a can of Sprite. I shoveled a handful of puffs into my mouth and gazed at the window. A nice breeze blew through our room and I dreaded going back into quarantine. Even though it had plenty of entertainment, being underground made me uneasy. I didn't like feeling trapped.

A headache was starting to form. It was one that brought a horrible stabbing pain right behind my eyes. I straightened my back, closed my eyes, and took a deep breath. I counted as I slowly let it out. I repeated the breathing technique until Hayden came into the room wearing only a towel. He closed the door behind himself and let the towel drop. I ran my eyes over him. It had been a while since I could leisurely gaze upon his naked body.

He was tall and muscular, since all the A1s had to work out on a regular basis. We had to stay in shape, since A1s went out on dangerous missions. Tattoos covered the right side of Hayden's upper body, going over his shoulder and down his arm. There was scar tissue along the side of his abdomen on the opposite side. I knew he had acquired the injury while overseas, but I didn't know exactly what had happened. Assuming he'd been burned in the same explosion that killed his childhood best friend, Ben, I never asked.

My eyes focused on the other large section of scar tissue along his left shoulder. I still thought Hayden shouldn't have taken the bullet for me, that I would have been ok, somehow. But his willingness to sacrifice himself on my behalf made me finally admit that I was completely in love with him.

"I told Hannah she was coming to a safe place." He stepped into a pair of blue boxers.

"She is." I uncrossed my legs and stood. I stretched my arms above my head and slowly bent over, touching my toes. Hannah was Hayden's sister.

"Ok, it's safe, but it's not going to be well run anymore."

I popped up. "What's with all the self doubt all of the sudden?"

Hayden slammed the dresser drawer shut so hard the TV that sat on top shook. Then he sighed. "I don't know. I just...I don't want to do this, Riss. I don't want to be the leader."

"Then don't."

He put his hands in the air. "How can I not be? It was Fuller's dying wish—his last order. I have to do this, Riss."

"No, you don't. Yes, it was his dying wish, but he's dead!" I internally winced at how insensitive that sounded. "What I mean," I added quickly, "is that you can't disappoint him." Damn. That wasn't any better. "Fuller cared about you like a son, Hayden. If he knew you didn't want to take over, he wouldn't force you. We both know that's true."

"Maybe." He ran his hand over his wet hair. "Who will take over?"

I shrugged. "We vote?"

Hayden tipped his head to the side for a second. "That could work. And it would be fair."

I smiled, ignoring the churning ball of anxiety in my stomach. "It would be very fair." I walked over to him and wrapped my arms around his shoulders. His skin was still warm from the shower. "We're both tired. Let's go downstairs and rest, ok?"

He slipped his hands around my waist and kissed me. "Ok." He quickly dressed. "Ready to go tell the guys some really shitty news?"

* * *

"Can't sleep?"

I rolled over and faced Hayden. "No. You can't either?"

He shook his head and pulled the blankets over my shoulders. Ten hours had passed since Hayden repeated to the guys what he had learned. It was a lot to take in: Fuller's death, Hayden's new role, and—most of all—the truth about the virus. The six of us had sat in silence, all too shocked to speak. Now we were all lying down trying to get some sleep.

"Not at all." He heavily sighed. "And I'm tired."

I draped my arm over Hayden's waist and scooted closer. He embraced me and pulled me in, hooking his leg over me. I ran my fingers through his hair until I was so tired I could barely move my hands anymore. Hayden's breathing deepened and slowed. I assumed he was asleep. My hands fell to the mattress and I passed out.

When I woke up, Hayden wasn't in bed with me anymore. I pushed myself up and brushed my messy hair back. I was thirsty and had to pee. I caught a glimpse of the clock as I made my way to the bathroom and was surprised to see that I had slept for a full eight hours. I put my arms over my head and stretched. I needed that eight hours. I could have slept for another few hours too.

I studied my refection in the bathroom mirror as I washed my hands. My shoulders and cheeks were sunburned. And despite all the sleep, there were still purple circles under my eyes. I flicked the excess water from my hands and ran my fingers through my brunette mane, smoothing the bumps caused by sleeping with damp hair. I flicked off the light and left the bathroom.

Ivan, Brock, and Wade sat around the little kitchen table playing cards. Jason was still asleep on the couch. And Hayden...I looked around the quarantine room. He was nowhere to be found.

"Where's Hayden?" I asked and walked into the kitchenette. I opened the fridge and inspected the small selection of food. My stomach grumbled, but nothing looked appetizing. Knowing I had to eat, I pulled out a plastic pitcher of juice and a bowl of pasta.

"He left about an hour ago," Ivan said.

I reached up into the cabinet above the sink to get a plate. "Did he say where he was going?"

"No. I assumed it was to check on his sister," Ivan replied.

"Probably." I stuck my food in the microwave and turned around, leaning against the counter. Wade flicked his eyes up at me.

"How are you dealing?" he asked.

"Fine," I said right away. Though I wasn't fine, not at all. But he didn't need to know that.

"Ok," Wade said and raised an eyebrow. He looked back at the cards in his hand but didn't say anything. He was becoming more perceptive to my lies and could see through them to the truth. I wasn't a fan of that. I turned around, watching the plate slowly turn inside the microwave.

"So," Ivan started. "Underwood told us he asked you to marry him."

I spun around, hating that my cheeks were growing warm. "Yeah, he did."

"That's so sweet," Brock teased.

I narrowed my eyes. "Shut up."

Ivan set a card down and picked up another from the stack in the middle of the table. He made a face when he saw which one he got. "So when's the big day? Do we need to throw an emergency wedding planning mission together?"

"Seriously, shut up," I said but was unable to keep from smiling. Joking around was a good way to keep their mind off what Hayden and I had shared with them as well as the loss of Fuller. "It's not gonna happen like that. Or ever." I shook my head. "I don't know." I whirled around, happy to see there was only seven seconds left on my food.

"You know everyone here would go batshit crazy over a wedding," Brock said.

"Dude they would," Wade agreed. "Just think of all the handmade paper decorations you could have, Riss."

I rolled my eyes. "Raeya wouldn't allow it. That girl's been planning my wedding since we were kids. She has a very clear picture in her mind of how it's going to happen." I opened the microwave with one second remaining.

"Speaking of Raeya," Ivan began. "Has she moved on yet?"

He was talking about the death of her long-term boyfriend, Seth. Raeya was with him at a Halloween party when the virus struck. Seth got infected and was dead in a matter of hours.

"I think so," I said and pulled the hot plate out. I set it on the table. "It's been…uh, I don't know what day it is," I admitted.

"The end of June." Brock said. "The twenty-eighth, maybe?"

"Shit." I picked up my fork and stabbed at the limp noodles on my plate. "Has it really been that long?"

"It doesn't feel like it," Wade said. "But then sometimes it feels like it's been longer. Ya know?"

I nodded and stuck a forkful of pasta in my mouth and looked at Ivan. Once I was done chewing I said, "She hasn't brought him up in a while. And I haven't mentioned it either."

"So I can swoop in and sweep her off her feet?" he asked and wiggled his eyebrows.

"You can try." I shrugged.

"You say that like you don't think I can do it." Ivan put his hand over his heart. "That hurts, Penwell. Have a little faith."

I laughed and took another bite of pasta.

"Oh shit," Ivan suddenly stated.

"What?"

"I just realized that if something *did* start between Raeya and me, I'd have you to answer to. You'd be worse than the overprotective father who likes to clean the guns on the first date."

Brock and Wade laughed.

I glared at Ivan. "How am I worse?"

Ivan waved his hand in the air. "Nah, I'm just kidding with you,

Penwell. It'd be fun. You and Underwood can double date with us. We could have wild Friday nights in the theater room!"

I smiled at Ivan and twirled more noodles around my fork. Everyone was acting normal: joking, talking, and playing cards. But an unsaid tension hung in the air, the kind of tension that made my stomach twist into knots. Too many times those I cared about died, and I'd had no choice but to move on. But that was the world we lived in, right? Always running, never stopping. If I didn't stop moving, I would die.

* * *

Hayden hadn't returned when our time in the quarantine room was up. I went upstairs and changed into a loose fitting brown tank top, shorts, and boots. I brushed my hair and pulled it over my left shoulder, braiding it as I hurried back downstairs to find Raeya.

I punched in the passcode and pushed open the doors to open the C level that housed residents' rooms, the cafeteria, and activity rooms. Anyone in the C category did everyday jobs around the compound—cooking, cleaning, and laundry.

"Hi, Orissa!" someone called as soon as I stepped foot into the hall. I turned to see a group of girls coming toward me. I recognized one of them but couldn't recall her name. We had saved her group from being eaten alive a while back. I resisted the urge to pretend I didn't hear her and hurry past. Pressing a fake smile to my lips, I turned my head.

"Hi," I replied.

"We heard that the mission was a success. We wanted to thank you," she told me and ran her hand over her blonde hair, which fell in a braid over her left shoulder. She was wearing a red plaid shirt with the sleeves rolled up. "All of you, really, for going out there and keeping us safe."

I had to admit it was nice to hear and even better to know that the residents appreciated what we did. It was dangerous every time we went out.

"Yeah," one of the other girls agreed. "You guys are so brave."

I nodded. "Thanks. We do what we gotta do, right?"

They agreed in unison.

"I have important mission business to attend to. See ya later." I didn't wait for them to say bye. Like I had told Hayden earlier, I usually looked at the floor to avoid eye contact and speed walked down the halls of the compound.

I stopped outside Raeya's door and knocked. A few seconds later,

Lisa opened it.

"Orissa!" she exclaimed and threw her arms around me. I leaned over and hugged her back. It might be wrong, but I definitely favored the small group of people who had been with me from the start. Except Lauren. I hated that bitch.

"Hey, Lisa, how are you?" I ran my hand over Lisa's tight braids. "Oh you got your hair done. It looks nice."

"Thanks. Olivia did it." She beamed.

I smiled back at her. Olivia fit into my small group of favorites as well. "Is Ray in here?"

Lisa looked behind her and shook her head. "She's in the shower, I think. She should be back soon. Want to wait with me?"

"Sure." I went in and sat on Raeya's bed. The rooms down here looked like tiny windowless dorm rooms. I admired the effort that Ray had put in to make this place look comfortably and homey.

Lisa told me about the new crops that had been planted in the garden, and that she heard someone say they were pretty sure one of the cows was going to have her calf soon. It was great news, but it felt wrong to share in her excitement when I knew that there was a large number of people living in safety and comfort on each side of the country.

"Rissy!" Raeya squealed as she rushed in. She was dressed, but her hair was in a towel. She dropped her bag of shower supplies and ran over.

I stood and hugged my best friend.

"Oh my God. You have no idea how much we were worried! And shut up, I know I always worry but this time was worse!" Raeya said.

I turned my head down and blinked back the emotion that my best friend was always able to bring out of me. There was so much I wanted to tell her. "I know. We're back—all of us. And we brought more people with us."

"I heard!" She released me and stepped back, fixing the towel. "I had the A3s in the guard tower radio me when you guys came home. And I heard about the horse! Now I have to hear that story!"

"Me too!" Lisa said. "Sonja and Olivia will want to too!" She jumped off the bed.

"Hey," I started, "why don't you go find them? Tell them I'll be in the cafeteria for breakfast soon."

"Ok! I can do that." She smiled and raced out of the room.

Raeya closed the room, knowing that I only had Lisa leave so we could talk in private. She picked up her shower bag and put it away in the top drawer of her dresser. We sat on her bed, angled toward each other.

Leaving the compound seemed so long ago, but a lot had happened in just days. I took a deep breath. "We found Hayden's sister, Hayden got bitten again, I killed Eric Sutton, Hayden asked me to marry him, I killed a bunch of uninfected people at that mental hospital, Fuller wants Hayden to take over running the compound, and the virus was released on purpose." The last part of my sentence slipped from my mouth before I had time to think about it. I had to tell someone, and I wasn't used to keeping secrets from Raeya.

Raeya's mouth fell open. She blinked. "You're engaged?" She grabbed my left hand, pulling it toward her so she could look for a ring.

"That's what you took out of all of this?"

She let my hand go. "How'd he ask?"

I smiled and shook my head. "It's kinda funny, really." I didn't realize that my heart was racing. Thinking about the mission...all the blood and fire at Eastmoore. I shuddered. So much had changed that day.

"Wait," Raeya said. "Let's start from the beginning. How in the world did you find Hayden's sister?"

"We were in Texas." I blinked and remembered crawling through the woods. "We ran into another group. And Hannah just happened to be in it."

"Oh my God," she said slowly. "What are the odds? No really, there are how many people in the world? And then how many of those are infected or dead?" She tensed and grabbed my arm. "You did find her alive, right? I just assumed."

"Yes, she's alive and well. Sorta, not completely well. Her arm is broken from a car accident."

"Car accident?"

"Yep. She was driving and swerved to avoid hitting the horse. He was in the road. I brought him back with us."

Raeya stared at me for a few seconds before shaking her head. "I bet Hayden was ecstatic to see her."

"Yeah, they both were pretty happy. He was kinda in shock for a while."

"That's great, though. She's lucky to have him as a brother."

"I know, right?"

Raeya frowned. "And you said he got bitten again?"

I sighed. "Ugh, yes."

"How?"

"Being stupid by trying to protect me."

"That's not stupid, Riss." She took the towel off her head and rubbed her hair. "What else did you say happened?"

I quickly recapped everything that happened on that mission. "Ok," I started and glanced at the door. "Hayden doesn't want me to tell anyone so *don't* say anything. Promise?"

"Promise," she said and clasped her hands together.

"Fuller left Hayden a file that explained everything he knew about the virus. It still leaves a lot of questions of course. But..." I launched into the detail of everything I knew. When I was done, Raeya stared at me, her brown eyes wide and unblinking.

"I-I...really...oh my God," she stumbled over her words. She leaned back and shook her head. "Are you serious?"

"Yeah and it makes sense if you think about it. Why else would Fuller—holy shit!"

"What, Rissy?"

"The greenhouses." I stood, curling my fingers into my palms. "The motherfucking greenhouses!"

Raeya nervously folded and smoothed her towel. "Not following you, Riss."

I turned to the door my heart pounding. I wanted to race upstairs and find Hayden, get in the truck and drive like crazy to the greenhouses. "We found that greenhouse farm, remember?"

"Of course I remember. You guys brought back a ton of—holy shit!" She jumped up. "You really think so?"

My head moved up and down. "It would have to be for them, right?"

Raeya wrapped her arms around her torso. "Who else could it be for? It has to be for the protected people on the east coast. You said it was set up and running like it would have been before the virus hit, right?"

"Yeah. It was completely functional." I thought back of the industrial-sized greenhouses. The constant supply and low prices put traditional farmers out of business fast. It was one of the main reasons that the small farming communities turned into ghost towns.

We had discovered the greenhouse farm on accident during one of our missions. The road that lead to the farm hadn't even been marked on the map we were using. When I happened to see a fresh set of footprints leading into one of the houses, Hayden and I went in on a whim and discovered the farm to be fully functional with a shit ton of fresh fruit and vegetables. We knew someone was taking care of them, but we didn't know who. Now I was pretty certain I knew.

Raeya sank down on the bed and put her head in her hands. "This...this is just too much, Rissy. Knowing that our own government abandoned its people when we needed them most..." she trailed off and shook her head.

I sat next to her and put my hand on her shoulder. "I know. It's awful."

"Tell me about it," Raeya agreed. Someone knocked on the door. I jumped up and opened it, smiling right away when a set of blue eyes locked with mine.

"Hey, Orissa," Padraic said with a broad smile. He stepped into the room and opened his arms. I hugged him. "Glad you're back in one piece." His hands slid down my arms. "When I was told someone had a broken arm, I thought it was you."

"Have a little faith, Padraic," I said. "I stayed relatively unharmed this time around. Wade and Jason on the other hand..." I shook my head. "They did come see you, right?"

"No, why?"

"Wade had heat stroke and Jason got shot."

Raeya stood, her arms out to her side. "Jason got shot!"

"Grazed," I said and turned around. "He was lucky. I assumed he would go to the hospital ward just to make sure everything was healing ok." And Hayden needed to go as well to have his bite checked out. I made a mental note to drag him down to the B level once I found him. "How is Hannah, anyway?"

"Without being able to see the breaks with an X-ray, it's hard to say how good or bad something is, but I don't doubt she will be fine." He raised his eyebrows. "She sure is talkative."

"Try being in the car with her for eight hours. If she wasn't Hayden's sister I would have gagged her."

"I can't believe you guys found someone you not only knew, but who was family." Padraic ran his hand over his dark hair. "It's very hopeful."

"It is," Raeya agreed. "Who knows who else is out there, right?"

I internally cringed. *Good question, Ray. Just exactly who was lucky enough to get picked for the ultimate protection against the zombies?*

* * *

I sat with Raeya and Padraic at their usual table in the cafeteria, digging into a bowl of cinnamon oatmeal. Halfway through our meal, Hannah's group entered the cafeteria. They were being given a tour of the compound, lead by an older woman named Esther.

Hannah said something to Esther and she looked a bit nervous to be around so many people. Her eyes met mine and I stood, meeting her halfway.

"Is Hayden with you?" she asked.

I shook my head. "No," I said; it was pretty obvious that Hayden wasn't with me since she couldn't see him.

"He said he's come see me in the morning. So typical of him," she huffed and cradled her arm to her chest. Padraic had done a good job rewrapping it, making it look like an actual cast instead of the crappy cardboard contraption I had come up with.

"He never came?" Nerves prickled along my spine.

She shook her head. "No. Why do you look so surprised?"

I took a breath, not caring that my carefully practiced poker face gave way to my emotions. It didn't matter. What mattered was finding out where the hell Hayden had disappeared to. "I don't," I flatly lied.

"Then do you know where he is?"

"Not at the moment." I flicked my eyes to Esther. "I'll tell him to see you when I find him. Go back to the tour."

"Yes ma'am," she said under her breath and turned around, leaving the cafeteria. I went back to my seat, slowly letting out a breath to hide my nerves.

"Hannah?" Raeya asked.

"Yep," I answered.

"The broken arm gave it away." She smiled. "What did she want?"

"She was looking for Hayden," I said and pushed my spoon into my oatmeal. I was so incredibly sick of oatmeal. It was going on my list of things I never wanted to eat again once this was over. "He wasn't in the quarantine room when I got up this morning."

"You don't know where he is?" Raeya asked.

I shook my head.

"Maybe he's in Fuller's office," Padraic suggested. My blank stare prompted him to continue. "I know that Fuller wanted him to take over." His blue eyes clouded. "I was with him when he died."

My heart skipped a beat when I thought about Fuller. "Oh, I didn't know that."

Padraic sighed. "He told me he left Hayden a letter. Even I thought it was bad taste to tell him something so important that way."

"Yeah," I agreed and was surprised at how relieved I felt that Padraic knew. I was more than used to keeping things to myself. I just hadn't realized how tiring it was.

* * *

I finished breakfast and checked out Fuller's office. The door was locked. I knocked and got no answer. I pressed my ear to the wood and heard nothing. Hayden wasn't in there. I turned, ready to go upstairs and see if maybe he had crashed in our room. He hadn't slept well last night so I was sure he was tired.

"Orissa!" someone called. Her voice was high pitched and annoying. Great, it was Scarlet Procter. "Hey, Orissa!"

Damn it. I hesitated. I couldn't pretend that I didn't see her now. I dropped my hand and turned to her. "Scarlet, hi."

She had been one of the first people to arrive at the compound. Hayden rescued her and her family right when shit hit the fan. She had no idea what it was really like out there. Her heels clacked against the hard tile floor as she hurried to me. She was wearing a gray pencil skirt and a white blouse, looking ridiculously out of place.

"I heard you all made it back," she said and pushed her blonde hair back into place. A string of pearls slid down her arm when she put her hand at her side. "I'm sure you heard about my idea for a paper."

"Uh, no. I haven't."

"Oh, my. Well, it was *all* my idea." She smiled.

"Ok." I impatiently shifted my weight. I had important things to do, lady. *Hurry the fuck up.*

"I'm putting together a little newspaper for everyone! It will have updates on the construction, crops, little tidbits of info on some of our interesting residents, and interviews with the A1s. Brilliant, I know!"

I gave her a blank stare. "Sure."

"Speaking of interesting people," she started, "you're one of them. You should know everyone is curious about you." She leaned in, as if she was telling me a juicy secret. "We don't know you, Orissa. Not a darn thing."

"Yeah, there's a reason for that." I put my hand on the key pad.

"Of course there is." She waved her hand in the air. "Want to tell me about the latest mission?"

"Not now," I stated and punched in the code. "I have something important to do," I rolled my eyes and rushed through the door, closing it behind me and started my search for Hayden.

Hayden wasn't in our room, and his bed was untouched.

Something was wrong...

CHAPTER TWO

I felt stupid for not thinking of it before since Hayden loved his truck almost as much as he loved me. I jogged down the stairs and walked through the first level of the old brick house.

I nodded and said hello to the A3 who stood guard by the back door. It had to be so boring standing there all day. I would end up wishing for zombies to attack just to give me something to freaking do.

Once outside, I held my hand up to my face, shielding my eyes from the bright sun. The air was hot and humid and smelled wonderfully like clover. The scent brought back an unwelcome memory of a summer spent on my grandparent's farm. I shook my head. Thinking about my grandpa teaching me how to shoot a bow and arrows wouldn't do me any good. I had no time for nostalgia now.

I walked through the overgrown front lawn, swatting a swarm of gnats and stepped over a clump of dandelions. I abruptly stopped and scanned the line of cars.

Hayden's truck wasn't there. I pushed my hair out of my face and continued walking. Maybe he had taken it around back by the quarantine barn so he could hose off the muck. Squinting in the sun, I cast my eyes down to avoid getting a headache. The tall grass itched my exposed legs, which was one of the reasons I always wore pants when out on missions.

The quarantine barn came into view. It was a large barn, newly built and looked like something that would house expensive horses. The interior had been reconfigured to safely keep anyone recently infected under control by using high voltage wires that wrapped around the metal fronts to the stalls.

I ducked around it. The black Silverado was still nowhere in sight. I spun on my heel, ready to run to the front gate and ask if Hayden had left when a snarling growl came from inside the barn.

I froze. *Shit.* I hadn't brought any weapons with me. I suddenly felt naked without a gun on my hip or my quiver hanging down my back. My eyes darted around as I looked for a makeshift bludgeon. A metal rain gauge was stuck in the ground next to the barn. In a pinch, it would work as a hand-held spear.

I whirled around, ready to dive to the ground and yank the gauge free. I looked into the barn. Nothing came running at me. I silently moved forward.

"Hey," I called.

Still nothing.

Curious, I stepped into the barn. My eyes didn't adjust right away and for a split second, I was blind. But no one attacked me.

The growl floated down the barn's center. And then something rammed into a stall door.

"Right," I said to myself. "The trap." I pushed my shoulders back and walked down the barn. It was narrow like an aisle. Dr. Cara was catching crazies. I didn't know why, but I didn't know why she did half of what she did.

The scent of horse lingered in the air, covered up by the heavy smell of bleach that was used to clean the stalls. Each was set up with a cot and a blanket, and sheets hung up along each side to give its occupant some privacy. I stopped at the second to last stall. A red-headed child flew to the front. Her small hands clasped around the iron bars. Electricity clicked and sparked from the hot wire, but she didn't let go.

I inhaled slowly, pushing away the sick feeling in the pit of my stomach that always formed when I saw an infected child.

"Let go, dummy," I said under my breath. Finally, the charge built up and her head flopped back and she fell to the ground, twitching. I stepped closer to the stall and looked inside. A fluffy comforter was wrinkled at the foot of the cot. Two stuffed animals had fallen to the ground. There was an overturned table, broken dishes, a smashed tomato, and a dog bowl filled with the bloody remnants of some sort of meat.

I leaned closer. The toys, table, and dishes weren't supposed to be there, even if she wasn't crazy. Why the hell did she have this stuff?

She groaned and pushed herself up. I shook my head and stepped away, moving down to another stall. This one housed a tall adult male. Like the child, he thrashed against the bars in a desperate attempt to pull me in and rip my stomach out with his teeth.

I stood just an inch out of his grasp and stared into his eyes. He precariously stuck his arms through the gaps in the iron bars, avoiding the hot wire. The burn marks on his arms told me that he had learned to avoid the electricity. Crazies weren't supposed to figure shit out.

My stomach twisted again. I couldn't accept that as truth anymore, not from all we had seen while out on missions. Was that what Dr. Cara was trying to figure out?

I peered into the stall. There was only a sleeping bag and a bucket of water. I stepped back, even more curious now. I'd hunt down Dr. Cara later and have her give me answers.

With both crazies banging against the stalls, snarling and growling. I left the barn, blinking in the bright sunlight again. I made my way to the front of the estate, jogging down the driveway. The compound was lined with double fences and trees. Outside of that was 'the moat.' Really, it was a deep and wide ditch that worked as zombie sink holes, preventing the undead from pushing on the fences—like they had done once before.

"Hey," I called as I approached the guard tower. The sun was almost directly overhead, making it impossible to keep my eyes open as I looked up.

"Hi, Orissa," someone answered and came out of the stone structure.

"Did you happen to see Hayden leave?"

"Yeah," he answered and I recognized the voice to belong to an A3 named Jones. "He left just around sunrise."

"You have got to be fucking kidding me," I muttered to myself. "Did he say where he was going?"

"Yeah, the farms."

"Sure he did," I muttered again. "Ok, thanks." I turned on my heel and went back into the house, going directly downstairs. I detoured to the weapons room so I could get my bow and arrows. I punched in the code to open the door and stepped in.

Right away I noticed the shelves were scary low on ammo. We had dozens of rifles, shotguns, pistols, and machine guns. All had been cleaned to the point of gleaming. But what good would they do when we had no bullets?

I unbuckled my belt and slid the sheath of a knife through it so that the blade rested on my hip. I picked up my bow and held it in front of me, making sure nothing had been messed up when it had been cleaned. I liked not having to scrape the zombie goo from my weapons, but it bothered me to have someone else messing with my bow. I drew the string back, testing the pull. Satisfied, I set it down and picked up my quiver, filled it with arrows, and slung it over my head. I grabbed the bow again and went to the back of the room.

The tunnel door stuck when it opened. I yanked it hard and got hit with a blast of stale air. A path had been worn on the dust and dirt covered floor from people walking in and out of the tunnel. It wasn't used very often. It was dingy and creepy and full of spiders. But it was a direct—and safe—route to the farms. If Hayden really did take over, I'd have him enforce the use of the tunnel. Why waste the gas driving to the barns and fields?

I turned around, stepping back into the weapons storage room and grabbed a flashlight. Then I went back into the tunnel and closed the door behind me. I clicked the flashlight on and made my way down the dark hall.

There was a steep and narrow stair case at the end of the tunnel. I hooked my arm through the bow so that it hung on my shoulder and climbed up the stone steps. There was a small platform at the top of the stairs. Double doors guarded the entrance to the tunnel and could only be unlocked from the inside. I twisted the heavy wheel lock and the metal bars that held the door banged into place, echoing down the long hall.

The steel door creaked and slowly opened. Holding the flashlight in my mouth, I pulled it closed and opened the second door. Spiderwebs crackled when I pushed the door open. Refusing to let myself be bothered by them, I stepped through that door and flipped the lock to the exterior door, which looked like an old fashioned root cellar.

I turned off the flashlight and looked out, making sure the coast was clear. The exit to the tunnel was outside of the fences near where the cars were parked. A shed had been built around the trap doors. Sunlight filtered through the slats in the wood and the little building smelled like hay and grain. I stepped out and closed the doors, brushing dust from my shirt. I stood perfectly still and listened.

Birds chirruped and I heard voices in the distance. I closed the door and stepped out of the shed to see our small herd of cows lazily grazing under the warm sun. I hiked up a small hill, looking for the people who were patrolling the field.

"Hey!" I called and held up my hand. I didn't feel like getting shot at today.

An A2 with buzzed dark hair turned around, gun in hand, and squinted. He was standing under the shade of an oak tree with a rifle held loose in his hands. "Oh, hi Orissa." He smiled and slid his eyes up and down my body when I came near. I set my face and glared. He cleared his throat and looked away. I walked over, looking at his name tag. I hadn't bothered to learn the names of most of the people here.

"What are you doing out here?" *Brian* asked. He was very tan and had red areas of sunburn on his cheeks and arms.

I unhooked the bow from around my shoulder. "I wanted to see the horse," I lied and stole a glance over his shoulder. Cars were parked a ways down by the main barn. Hayden's truck wasn't among them.

"Oh. He's out here somewhere." He turned, sweeping his hand over the pasture. "Sundance, right?"

"Yeah."

"He was scared of the cows," he said with a laugh. "But he got used to them quick. Nice looking horse." He tipped his head and raised his eyebrows. "I don't know anything about horses, though. Do you?"

"Yeah. I used to ride. My grandparents always had horses."

"I figured you would." He took a breath, puffing out his chest a bit and held the gun up. "You're so athletic you look like you can do anything."

"Pretty much," I agreed and turned around, holding my hand to my face. I spotted Sundance at the opposite end of the pasture. His head was down, busy grazing.

"So, I, uh, hear you're pretty good with that thing."

"What?" I whirled around and caught Brian checking me out again.

"The bow," Brian said and flicked his eyes to my face.

"Oh, yeah. I am. I've been into archery for years."

"I can tell by your muscles." He leaned against the tree. "I've always wanted to learn."

"Mh-hm," I said and scanned the rest of the farmland, still not spotting Hayden or his truck.

"So," he started. "What are you doing tonight?"

Nothing with you, that's for sure. "Training." I readjusted the quiver and turned around.

"Oh, well, if you have time and want to watch the Friday night movie with me…" he trailed off, running a hand over his short hair.

"Yeah, no," I said then heard Raeya's voice in my head telling me to be nice. "We have a lot to sort out from our mission. But thanks." I forced a smile. Maybe I *should* let Hayden get me an obnoxiously large engagement ring. "Well, I'm gonna go." I spun around and went into the shed, climbing back into the tunnel. I swatted away another dangling spiderweb and locked the doors behind me as I passed through.

* * *

I went directly upstairs, not in the mood to talk to anyone. I wanted to sulk in my room and think of what I was going to yell—I mean *say*—at Hayden when he finally came home. A little voice in the back if my head wanted to question that 'when' with an 'if.' I yanked on my braid and took a steadying breath. Hayden might be stressed beyond his limits but he wasn't stupid. He would come home.

"Hey, Riss," Jason called from inside Wade's room. I opened my mouth to ask him what he was doing upstairs and quickly snapped it shut when I saw the boxes.

"Welcome to the official A club," I told him with a slight smile.

"I have a window." He turned behind him. "An actual window. And TV. And a bathroom that doesn't have stalls and is shared with thirty people."

"Feels good to be this close to normal, doesn't it?"

His smile grew. "Heck yes."

"Have fun unpacking."

"I'm almost done. Luckily I don't have much to move." His brow furrowed as he thought about what he just said. Shaking his head, he turned back to me. "And the guys have video game parties?"

I rolled my eyes. "All the damn time."

"You don't like video games?"

"Not really my thing."

"Huh, interesting. You're so *not* a typical girl with a lot of other things, I figured you'd like them."

I shrugged. "I think they're boring." And I majorly sucked at them. I couldn't get my video game characters to walk straight let alone run and fire a gun at the same time. I hated losing.

"So you don't go?"

"I usually sit with Hayden and end up falling asleep," I admitted.

Jason laughed.

"But have fun. See ya later." I walked down the hall and into my room, slamming the door shut on accident behind me. I strode to the window, drumming my fingers along the sill. Where the hell was he? My heart started beating faster. I grabbed the end of my braid and pulled on my hair.

My anxiety was reaching the point where I couldn't breathe. I moved to the center of the room and stood still. I closed my eyes and reached over my head, inhaling deep. Then I bent forward and placed my palms flat on the floor.

I repeated the Sun Salutation six times. My muscles were relaxed but my head still spun. Going for the next best thing, I opened the closet and pulled out a bottle of Captain Morgan. I unscrewed the lid and took a swig, making a face from the strong flavor. I took another drink and waited for the fuzzy feeling to take over. Once it did, I went back downstairs. Finding Raeya seemed like a good idea. I needed a distraction.

* * *

"I'm going after him." I set my cup down so hard on the nightstand that water sloshed out. "And when I find him, I'm going to kill him."

"You're not going out there," Raeya said calmly. "It's late."

"Exactly. Hayden should have been home hours ago."

"I agree with Ray," Ivan said. "You're not going out there. Not alone. I'm going with you."

I smiled and sat up, throwing the blankets off my legs. Raeya, who was sitting on my bed next to me, frantically snatched them and yanked them into place, as if the material would keep me from springing up and going out into the dangerous unknown.

"No," she said. "Neither of you should go anywhere!"

I whipped around. "You think Hayden should fend for himself?"

"Of course not, Rissy. But how in the world are you going to find him? It's dark. It's late. He left in a car. You can't track him and find him," she said, being the voice of logic. "He's my friend too," she told us. "And I want him back here safe and sound, but leaving right now isn't a good idea." She smoothed out the blankets. "What if he comes back right when you leave?"

"Then I'd be happy he was home safe," I said and looked at Ivan. "Right?"

His brown eyes clouded with worry. "Yeah, I'm with Penwell on this." He looked at the floor.

"What?" I asked.

"Nothing," he said quickly.

"Bullshit."

He took a breath, his muscular shoulders rising. "What if he, uh, freaked out again and is seeing things that aren't really there?"

My stomach dropped. I hadn't even thought about Hayden's PTSD and how it could affect him. I swung my legs over the bed. "We have to look."

"No need," Brock said from the hall and held up a walkie-talkie. "He's back."

The biggest wave of relief washed over me. And then I felt anger.

Brock stepped aside. "Tell that future husband of yours he's an ass for leaving like that."

"Trust me," I said and shoved my feet into boots. "I will." I stormed out of the room and jogged down the hall, flying down the stairs. I had just burst through the front doors of the brick estate when Hayden turned off his truck. I broke into a run. Hayden opened the driver's side door and got out.

His eyes met mine, sending a jolt right through me. I stopped just inches from him, not knowing if I should slap him or kiss him. I chose the latter and pressed my lips to his. Hayden wrapped his arms around me, crushing me against his sweaty body. My hands flew to his waist. He dipped me back and pushed his tongue into my mouth. His lips were salty and warm and felt good. So good. My body went rigid. I moved my hands onto his chest, pushing him off of me.

"What the hell, Hayden?" I twisted out of his embrace. "You take off and are gone all day and don't have the decency to fucking tell me a damn thing!"

He extended his arm, reaching for me. "Riss, I—"

I ducked out of the way "No! I don't want to hear it! I can't believe you did that to me—to all of us! Do you have any idea how worried I was?" My hands flew out in front of me as I spoke. "Your sister is freaking out, Ivan thinks you went crazy and we're not even married yet, and you're already pissing me off!"

Hayden took a step back from my seething anger. Dark purple circles hung under his hazel eyes. A line formed between his eyebrows and he pressed his lips together.

I dropped my hands to the side and sighed, shaking my head. "Why did you do that?" My voice cracked at the end of my question, the emotion I was holding back spilling out.

Hayden looked at the ground. "I'm sorry, Orissa." He took a small step forward, hesitating as he reached for me. When I didn't flinch away he put his arms back around me. "I'm really sorry. As soon as I got out there I realized what I jerk I was for leaving."

"Then why didn't you come home?" I rested my head against his chest. His shirt was slightly damp from sweat.

"I didn't think it would take me so long."

"What?" I looked up at him.

He tipped his head behind him, motioning to the truck. "I fixed the window."

"Oh my God." I pushed him away again. "All this was over your stupid truck?" My hands balled into fists and my ears were hot.

"The truck's not stupid," he said calmly. "It has the—"

"Machine gun, I know. I fucking know." I wanted to hit

something. Repeatedly. The hood of the truck seemed like a good punching bag. I whirled around and started to storm off before I lost control. Hayden grabbed my wrist.

"Riss, wait, I'm really sorry."

I pulled my arm out of his grasp. "Do not talk to me right now. I am so mad at you!"

"You have every right to be. And I really am sorry, ok?"

I kept walking.

"Would it help if you took out your anger sexually?"

I turned around and glowered at my fiancé. Though throwing Hayden down and slapping him more than once sounded very appealing.

"Riss," he said, his face softening. "It kills me to know I upset you. I didn't want you to worry."

"Then why did you take off like that?"

He shook his head. "I don't know… I just needed some time away from everything." He moved closer. "I was wrong. I'm sorry." He outstretched his arms. "I won't do it again."

I stepped into his embrace. My anger melted almost instantly when his arms wrapped around my body. "That was easy," I said with a smile and hugged him.

Hayden kissed my neck. "I don't want to fight with you. I need you. I wished you were with me the whole time."

"I would have come."

"I know." He rested his head against mine.

"You smell," I told him, breathing in the scent of sweat and dirt. "And you have blood on your face."

He loosened his hold on me and wiped his face. "Oh. It's not mine."

"I can tell. It's brown. How many zombies did you kill?"

He shrugged. "A dozen, maybe. I didn't count this time."

I nodded and stepped back. "Really. You need to shower."

"Will you shower with me this time?"

"Of course."

* * *

"I hate bothering you," Raeya said quietly as she sat across the table from Hayden. "But we need supplies." She pushed her lunch to the side and opened a notebook. "Babies need an alarming amount of stuff."

Hayden finished chewing. "Do you have a list?"

Raeya looked at me, amusement sparkling in her eyes. "A list? Do

I have a list?" She carefully tore out a piece of paper from the notebook. "There's a printed copy in Fuller's office. Well, your office now. I slid it under the door." She gave the paper to Hayden. I leaned over his shoulder, staring at the list. "That's what I did before if he wasn't in there. There's a binder on the shelf behind his desk, third one in, labeled 'supplies.' You can't miss it. Fuller kept the lists of everything we needed, crossing off anything you guys brought back."

"Thanks," Hayden said and set the list on the table in front of him. I took my eyes away from the paper to study Hayden. After his excursion yesterday, Hayden was a lot calmer. The dark circles under his eyes had faded but were still there, though it wasn't exactly like we went straight to bed last night. Well, we had gone to bed. We just didn't get much sleep.

"You're not going out, right?" Raeya asked and flipped a page in the notebook. She pulled a pen out of the metal spiral and clicked it. "Since your group was out last. It's the others' turn."

"Yeah," I told her. "They'll go out." I took the list from Hayden. "Text books?" I asked, raising an eyebrow. "How's that gonna help us survive?"

"It won't, not entirely," she answered. "But it will help keep things normal. There are a lot of kids here. Kids who need some sort of school."

I hadn't thought of that before. "Shouldn't we be teaching them survival skills? Learning American History isn't going to help us." I eyed the last book on the list.

"Someday this will be in a history book," Hayden said. He looked up from his plate of tuna casserole.

"That's assuming we make it through this," I mumbled and pushed noodles around on my plate.

"We will," Hayden and Raeya said at the same time.

Raeya nervously clicked her pen. "It's an odd thought, isn't it? That we are living history."

"We were always living history," I told her.

"Well, yeah, technically. But before our lives weren't book-worthy. Now they are. We are trailblazers in a sea of undead. Oh! Maybe my name will be in there once or twice."

Hayden chuckled. "I'm sure you'll have a paragraph or two. Raeya Kingsley: the woman who kept us organized."

Raeya smiled. She set the pen down and leaned forward. "Maybe there will be questions about me on a history test!"

I laughed, shaking my head. "I'm sure there will be, Ray. We couldn't run this place without you."

"Thanks, Rissy. Same goes for you guys. Really, everyone here is important." She put her hands on the table. "So, Hayden, do you approve the list?"

Hayden picked up his cup of water. "Uh, sure."

"Great!"

I stabbed a noodle with my fork. "You mean he could not approve something?"

"Yeah. That's how it worked before. You do want to keep things the same, right?"

Hayden flicked his eyes to mine. I pressed my lips together and tipped my head in Raeya's direction. "Actually..." Hayden began, trailing off when Ivan and Brock took their seats. Ivan winked at me and sat next to Raeya.

"What?" Raeya asked, picking up the pen again.

Hayden sighed and straightened up. "I might as well tell everyone." I put my hand on his thigh for reassurance. "Riss and I talked and..." He shook his head. "I don't want to run the compound. It's not fair to just have someone be appointed the new leader. We," he looked at me, "thought it would be better to let everyone vote."

Ivan nodded. "Very democratic. I like it."

"Me too," Brock agreed. "But what if someone wins who would really suck at running this place?"

Raeya flipped to a new page. "Technically Hayden is in charge now. He gets final veto power."

"Should we let people campaign?" he asked her.

Raeya shook her head. "No. That's too political. I say we make up forms tonight and have everyone vote tomorrow. Ya know, give them some time to think about it but not enough time to be persuaded."

"That's a brilliant idea," Brock said, smiling.

"Thanks." She started jotting down notes. Hayden put his hand on mine and let out a breath. His shoulders relaxed. I looked around the cafeteria, wondering who would want to run the place. Whoever it was needed to be level headed and fair. Though Fuller and I never saw eye to eye, he did a good job. When the world was falling apart all around us, he provided stability and safety. Granted he felt a huge amount of guilt for knowing the truth, but he didn't have to do this. He didn't have to unearth this old bomb shelter and fill it with survivors.

* * *

After lunch, Hayden and I went upstairs and into our room. A warm breeze blew in from the open windows. I kicked off my boots and lay down on my bed, stretching my arms over my head. Hayden turned on the TV and pressed 'play,' starting the same movie we had watched last night. He grabbed the remote, turned the volume down, and climbed into bed with me.

We resituated, cuddling together. I turned on my side and wiggled close to him, resting my head on his chest. I draped my leg over his. Hayden enveloped me in his arms.

"Love you," I whispered.

"Love you too." He turned his head and kissed me. I closed my eyes. I was tired and wanted to nap. Listening to Hayden's steady heartbeat was comforting and lulled me to sleep in no time.

My dream twisted into a nightmare. I was back at Eastmoore, running through billowing black smoke, frantically searching for Hayden. A zombie staggered from the rubble. I reached behind me to grab an arrow but my fingers touched nothing but air. My quiver was empty.

Suddenly the zombie was in front of me, pushing me down. My limbs were too heavy to move. I couldn't fight back. And then I saw his face, wrinkled and decaying. Yellow teeth snapped at me and rancid breath burned my nose. Dre moved over me, brown saliva dripping onto my neck.

"Riss." Hayden shook me. "You ok?"

I opened my eyes. I was on the edge of the bed. My hair was a messy web over my face and cold sweat had dampened my skin. "Yeah," I breathed. I pushed my hair out of my face and sat up. "Just a nightmare."

Hayden gave me a wry smile "I know how those go." He put his arms around me. "What was it about?"

"Eastmoore."

"Oh." He picked me up, setting me back down on his lap. "Riss," he said gently. "We never talked about what happened back there."

He didn't have to explain any further. I knew what he was referring to. Both he and Wade warned me about it. I knew what I was getting myself into. "I'm fine."

"Are you sure? You killed people, Riss. People who weren't infected."

I looked up into his eyes. "We did what we had to do. I didn't kill anybody innocent."

He turned away, looking out the window. "It's ok, Riss, to admit you're not fine."

I rested my head against him. "I know it is. And you'll be the first person to know I'm not. It's just...I don't know. It's like I haven't even had time to process it all, ya know?"

"I do. And a lot of shit happened."

"Yeah. I need a fucking vacation," I laughed.

"Seriously. Me too." He sighed and leaned back against the pillows, bringing me with him. "We deserve one, that's for sure."

"Tell me about it."

"Then let's take one."

I looked up, raising an eyebrow. "And go where?"

"Anywhere." He flipped me over so that his body was on top of mine. He propped himself up on his elbows and kissed me. "Anywhere away from here. Just for a day."

I wrapped my arms around his neck. "We will never get away with it."

"I'm in charge now." Hayden grinned. "What I say goes." He lowered his head until our nose touched. "And I say tomorrow morning we go on a hunting trip."

"We could actually use some meat too."

He pressed his lips to mine. "Exactly."

"We have shit to take care of," I reminded him. "We should do it now if you want to leave in the morning."

"Dammit. I promised Hannah I'd hang out with her."

"Go. I'll go over everything with Raeya and talk to Alex."

"No, you don't have to, Riss," he said.

"I know I don't. But Hannah is your sister and family is important now more than ever. Think of all the families that have been torn apart." My mind wandered to my grandpa and Aunt Jenny. I'd give anything to know what had happened to them. "It's more than a little amazing you found Hannah."

He nuzzled his head against my breasts. "It's more than a little amazing I found you, too," he mumbled and kept his head down, as if he was embarrassed to say that out loud. I ran my fingers through his hair.

"I'm glad you did. Mostly because I'm not certain I would be alive."

"I like that you're alive," he said with a smile.

"Me too." I dropped my hands onto the mattress. "I'll go get started on everything. I'm looking forward to telling Alex what to do."

Hayden rolled off of me and smiled. "You still haven't forgiven him for deserting you either?"

"No, I have. It's a waste of time and energy to hold that grudge. I generally don't like him as a person."

"That's my girl," he said with a smile.

I ran my hands over my hair in a lazy attempt to smooth away the bed head. I put my boots back on and headed downstairs to find Raeya.

I crossed paths with Dr. Cara on my way down the stairs. She was wearing a pink Hello Kitty t-shirt and men's khaki shorts that were several sizes too big for her. Instead of a belt, they were being held in place by a scarlet and gold scarf. Her hair was in a tight bun at the very top of her head.

"Hello Orissa," she said with a curt nod. "Has Hayden's semen infected you yet?"

My jaw dropped. There were few times when I was left speechless, and this was one of them. "Uh...uh...no." I blinked and recovered, thankful no one was around to hear her. "I think you'd know if I became infected."

She smiled and shook her head. "Of course I would." She leaned close to me. "If you do get infected, can I experiment on you?"

"Sure, have at it." I smiled back, leaning against the wall. "What are you doing with those crazies out there?" I asked before she could scuttle off.

"Experimenting."

"Obviously."

"If it was obvious then why did you ask?"

I sighed. "What kind of experiment are you doing? Why does one have decor and the other doesn't?"

"The decor doesn't matter so much." She took another step closer to me. "Not as much as the food. The younger one with the food has been in there for several days. And she's not deteriorating."

"Really?"

"Yes, really. My current theory is that being fed and staying generally healthy keeps the virus from taking over. The weaker the body, the faster the transition from S1 to S2."

It made sense. Rider was as weak as he could be and turned into a zombie in just a day. "Does it help with your vaccine research?"

"I don't know yet."

"Oh, ok." We both turned at the same time and walked in opposite directions down the hall.

* * *

Raeya was not happy to hear that Hayden and I were leaving in the morning. When I reminded her that we would get to eat anything I killed, she was rather agreeable. She then helped me get everything together that was needed to brief the other group of A1s about their mission.

Along with the list of supplies, Fuller had a binder full of store names. Thanks to Raeya, it was extremely organized and easy to look through. The list of stores coordinated with a map that showed their location. That was also thanks to Ray. Stores that we had previously been emptied were marked as 'dead' to save us the hassle of going to empty places.

Alex was surprising professional when I went over his mission with him. He took the list and guessed it would take them four days to gather everything we needed. It was odd being on the other end of things. Odd and kinda nice...I felt like I was accomplishing something when really I didn't have to do anything other than hand someone a piece of paper.

I spent the rest of the day with my friends, not seeing Hayden again until I went upstairs for bed. He was packing a bag for our hunting trip tomorrow. We set everything out, ready to grab and go, and climbed into bed. We needed our rest. Who knew what tomorrow could bring?

CHAPTERTHREE

"Where are we going?" I asked Hayden and grabbed a lose strand of hair that was blowing in the breeze from the open truck window. I tucked it behind my ear.

"I don't have a destination in mind," he said and took his eyes off the road for a second. "I am curious to see how much of Highway 7 is blocked. We've avoided it in the past." He reached for his iPod, shuffling through songs.

"On the way back we are *not* listening to country," I told him.

"Driver picks the music."

"Then I'm driving."

He laughed. "Uh, no."

I looked out the window. Cars lined the side of the road. Dust and dirt covered their windows, too thick to see through.

"Does it matter where we stop?" Hayden asked.

"I suppose not anymore. I think anywhere around here is ok for hunting. Animals have free rein over the land. Well, sort of. If we find a water source, it will up our chances of finding deer."

Hayden nodded. "I haven't been hunting in years."

"You used to hunt?" I asked. He hadn't told me that.

He looked sideways at me. "I grew up in North Dakota. You weren't a man if you didn't know how to hunt."

I laughed. "Then should I let you be in charge of this?"

He shook his head. "I hunted with guns."

"Oh, you're admitting I'm better with the bow than you are."

"Hardly." He gripped the steering wheel and stared straight ahead.

"Then how about a little friendly competition? Winner gets a massage."

"That's lame."

I turned toward Hayden. "You only think that because you know you will be the one rubbing *my* back."

"I did enough rubbing last night to make up for the whole year."

"Doesn't count." I put my hand on Hayden's thigh and leaned back in the seat. I closed my eyes, trying to enjoy the breeze. I couldn't relax, not when we were out here. The morning was bright and warm. It was perfect. But I knew it would soon be ruined by zombies.

I took my hand off of Hayden and leaned forward in the seat, keeping my eyes peeled. I constantly looked back and forth, inspecting everything we were passing. I noticed a patch of weeds that were bent and stomped down. I straightened up to get a better look.

"What?" Hayden asked and let off the gas.

"Nothing," I said and shook my head. There was no direction or order. The path was wide, as it would be from a herd blundering through. "Just a zombie trail. An old one at that."

"Oh, ok." Hayden sped up. Several miles went by without us passing any cars and only a few zombies, which enabled us to keep a steady pace and make good time down the highway.

"Riss," Hayden said and pointed out his window. "What about that?"

I looked through the dense trees. Sunlight reflected off of slow moving water. "Perfect."

Hayden pulled the truck over on the side of the road. We rolled up the windows and got out, going around to the bed to get our weapons. I put my hand on the side of the truck only to snatch it back. The black metal was hot from the sun already. Hayden jumped in and handed me the quiver. I filled it with arrows and put the strap over my shoulder, situating it evenly on my back before buckling the strap around my waist. I tugged my shirt down.

Along with my bow and arrows, I had a knife on my ankle and a gun on my hip along with two extra clips filled with ammo. Hayden had a rifle, a pistol, a knife, and extra ammo as well. Though our plan was to avoid zombies, we wanted to be well prepared.

"Want to take the food with us?" I asked.

"No. We can eat now and come back when we're hungry. I'll just bring the water."

"Sounds good to me."

Hayden grabbed our bag of food and put the tailgate down. The bullet holes along the back of the truck had been smoothed over and polished. I climbed up in the bed and sat next to Hayden and pulled out two peanut butter and jelly sandwiches. We ate in silence, finishing off the sandwiches with a can of peaches.

I pushed a jar of mixed nuts and two granola bars out of the sun and closed the passenger door. I readjusted my weapons and turned to Hayden. He was already wading through the weeds, eager to start the hunt.

He turned, pausing to lock the truck. I silently moved through the tall grass and lowered the bow. Keeping it close to my body I slipped into the trees, ducking under a low hanging branch. Hayden followed suit. I smiled to myself, happy that I didn't have to look back and worry that he would be too noisy or get us seen...by anything.

The thick canopy of leaves blocked out the sun. A fly buzzed around my face. I whipped my head to the side, using my hair to swish it away. Crunchy leaves carpeted the ground, covered up by fresh green growth. I couldn't see all of the dry leaves. If I didn't move my feet carefully, each step would be a dead giveaway of our location.

I shimmied around a tangle of weeds, not making a sound. I stopped, looked back, and waited for Hayden. He was only a few feet behind and was being just as quiet. I looked in front of us, squinting my eyes at the sparkling water. Birds fluttered overhead. We moved around a poison ivy-covered oak tree.

I stopped short, inspecting the ground. It was unnaturally uneven. I carefully kicked away a clump of weeds and dirt.

"What the hell?" I traced my eyes over the wood and metal. "Train tracks?"

Hayden knelt down and touched the rotting wood. "No. Too narrow for a freight train. It looks like..." he trailed off and shook his head.

"What?" I asked.

He stood up. "It looks like tracks for a ride."

My eyebrows pushed together. "A ride?" I looked around. "We're in the middle of the woods."

Hayden shrugged and shook his head. "I have no idea. Come on, let's go."

We edged through the trees and got caught by a rusty chain-link fence. Instead of climbing it, we ventured down a few yards until we found a break. Hayden pulled the metal up, allowing me to pass through untouched. I took it from him, bending the fence out of the way so he could slip through. We continued on.

"That is creepy," Hayden said.

I flicked my head back, expecting to see a zombie or something else that was dead. "Shit," I swore. I wasn't expecting that. "It is." I took a quiet step toward the merry-go-round. The paint on the four little animals was faded and chipped. I walked around it, feeling like their black and white eyes were following me with each step. I turned around. "If that thing moves on its own, we're leaving," I only half joked. It looked likes something straight from a horror movie.

"Agreed," Hayden said and turned. We came to the edge of the trees. There was a small overgrown field to cross before we came to the water. Something snapped behind us.

I reached behind me, grabbing an arrow. Hayden and I both whirled around at the same time, weapons raised. But there was nothing there. We turned back around and moved to the water's edge.

"I don't see any deer trails," I told Hayden as I looked over the water. Algae covered the surface for several feet. "It's kinda sludgy here." I held my hand over my eyes and wished I had remembered to bring sunglasses. "Maybe down there, where the steam narrows. It looks clearer."

We noticed something else out of place as we walked along the small river. I eyed the slimy red plastic. It was shaped like a pool inner tube but made out of hard plastic and with rusting metal handles. I was curious, but it didn't matter.

I hiked the bow up on my shoulder and swatted away the swarm of mosquitoes. The grass gave way to cracked and faded pavement. My gait slowed as I took it in. Where the hell were we?

Hayden and I walked in sync, our boots hitting the hot pavement together. I kept my eyes on the water, looking for any sign that this would be a good place to set up and wait for an unsuspecting animal to cross our path and become our dinner.

Hayden's feet scuffed as he came to a sudden stop. He grabbed my arm. I tensed. If there was a zombie or crazy, why didn't he grab his gun?

"What the fuck?" he asked slowly. I followed his eyes to two large stone statues. Faces had been carved into the rock and each had its lips puckered as if about to offer a kiss.

"What the fuck is right," I muttered. "Those are the ugliest things I've ever seen."

"Yeah," Hayden agreed. He shook his head and looked around. His shoulders tensed. I bet he was feeling the same unease that I was.

"There," I said and used the arrow to point. "We can set up by that bridge and wait."

Hayden nodded and we picked up our pace. A wooden bridge crossed the river. The planks were dark around the edges from being soaked with water. The center was gray and cracked, dried out from the sun. Since I was the lightest, I went first. I hooked the bow around my arm and put my hand on the splintering railing.

Hayden kept a constant vigil. I lifted my foot, carefully moving it onto one of the worn boards. I put my weight on the ball of my foot and slowly rocked my boot back, distributing the weight.

The bridge creaked. I took another step. The whole thing shook. But it didn't crash into the water. I moved as fast as I dared and finally jumped off onto the dry land. I reached behind me for an arrow, stringing it on the bow just in case. I stepped away from the bridge and watched the surrounding area as Hayden made his way across.

He was roughly five inches taller than me and at least fifty pounds heavier. The old bridge groaned under his weight. I flicked my eyes to his feet, watching as he took a tentative step.

Water lapped the bottom of the bridge. I had always like the sound of running water. There was something calming about it. The stream behind my grandparent's farmhouse was the deepest in the spring. On very quiet nights I could hear the rush of water over rocks from my room.

Something blundered through the woods behind us. I whirled around, pulling the arrow back. Low tree limbs swung wildly. Hayden hurried to get off the bridge. He looked up, taking his eyes off the weak boards. A gargling growl came from the trees.

The board broke with a sickening crack. Hayden's foot went through, causing him to fall forward. He dropped the rifle; it landed with a heavy thud on the wooden planks. His hands smacked against the bridge.

The zombie tumbled out of the trees, tripping over broken branches. Her brittle bones audibly snapped and pushed right through her skin. The scent of rotten fat and muscle permeated the air. The broken leg caused her to tumbled forward and roll down the slope that led to the water.

Her spine twisted; her legs and torso faced opposite directions, and one of her arms was tucked behind her body. She reached out with her free hand, eyes latched onto Hayden. I took a step to the side and released the arrow.

"You ok?" I asked Hayden, moving to the bridge. I set the bow down and put my hand on the railing.

"Don't," Hayden said. "It's not strong enough. And yes, I'm fine. Just, uh, stuck."

"If your foot went through it can come back out."

"True." He pushed himself up and sat, looking at the hole. "I don't want my shoe to fall off," he said with a smile. "I hate wearing wet shoes."

I rolled my eyes and smiled back. "Me too. The constant squishing bothers the shit out of me." Hayden pulled his leg up and winced. "What?"

"Got cut. Not a big deal."

"Oh, ok." I turned around, surveying the land. "Do you feel like we're being watched?"

Hayden looked up at me. "Not really, but I'm a little distracted."

I wrinkled my nose at the unease and scanned the forest behind Hayden. The feeling of eyes pressed into me. Were there more zombies?

"Almost free?" I asked.

"Give me a second, will you?"

I didn't mean to come across as impatient. I just didn't like Hayden being stuck while I felt so *watched*. I picked up the bow and strung an arrow just in case.

"Almost got it," Hayden said. His ankle was up to the boards now.

"Good because—" I cut off when something moved through the forest. Hayden looked up at me, reading my eyes. My heart began to beat faster. I raised the bow, holding the arrow back. I let out a breath to steady my aim.

Something moved—fast. It was just a blur of white and light blue through the leaves.

"Hayden," I whispered. "Get out now."

* * *

I could hear my heart beating in my ears. The string groaned when I turned my body ever so slightly, wanting to be released. I swallowed. Something else raced through the trees.

Suddenly, a little girl wearing a white and blue sweater stepped out of the foliage. She came to a halt, eyeing me. I lowered my bow when I saw the gun in her hands.

"Hey," I called to her. "It's ok. We're not infected."

Another person appeared behind her. He put his hand on her shoulder and stared at me. Behind them, leaves rattled and branches shook as at least a dozen more people emerged into the weeds.

"Hey," I called again to the group. But no one responded. The little girl tipped her head. Something was wrong...very wrong. "Hayden. We need to go. Like yesterday."

I ran my eyes over the group that stood across the river. They were dirty and ragged, that was for sure, but who wouldn't be? Almost all of them carried some sort of weapon from the gun to a metal rake. But they had no packs, no bags, or supplies. Half were dressed for much cooler days. And half had blood smeared across their faces.

Nerves tingled along my spine. Fuck.

"Hayden, they're crazies." I swallowed hard. The little girl raised the gun. "Hayden!" I raised the bow and let the arrow go. The string snapped back, flicking the exposed skin on my wrist.

The arrow lodged in the girl's chest. The gun flew from her hands. She stumbled back and fell. The man next to her looked down, confused at what had happened. He wrapped his fingers around the arrow and pulled. The girl's body came up with it. Her head flopped back, dead eyes open and her arms hanging loosely at her sides. He put his foot on her stomach to hold her down and pulled again.

The arrow cracked her sternum as the broadhead point was brought up. Fresh blood dripped onto her body as he raised it to his face. He sniffed it then snarled, turning around to his fellow crazies. Then he raised the arrow and growled.

"Hayden!" I yelled when they charged forward. I reached behind me and pulled another arrow from the quiver, shooting the nearest crazy in the head. "Hayden, now!"

His hazel eyes were wide. He turned around, taking in the horrifying sight of the herd of crazies. Then he pulled his foot free and grabbed the gun.

"There's too many!" he shouted to me as I grabbed another arrow. He was right, and I couldn't retrieve my ammo like I usually did and I couldn't guarantee hitting—and killing—every one of them with one shot. Those fuckers were moving fast. He grabbed my arm and pulled me forward. We took off, racing down a grassy path.

I stole a glance behind me. The crazies were having a difficult time with the bridge and the water. I slowed, watching. One chose to bypass it all together and waded through the knee-deep water.

Shit.

I tightened my grip on the bow and pressed on. Dried grass crunched under our boots. An old building loomed ahead. Its roof was caved in from the weight of wet leaves and moss grew up along the sides. Hayden tipped his head toward it then looked at me.

"Yeah," I breathed. We jumped off the path into waist high weeds and sprinted to the old building. Hayden skidded to a stop and raised his rifle. He ducked inside, scoping out the surroundings.

"Clear," he whispered and stepped into the shade. The sweet smell of rotting leaves mixed with the foul odor of rain-ruined boards.

I let out a breath and relaxed my bow arm. Then something grabbed my hair, yanking me back. It caught me off guard and I tripped as my feet scuffed the ground. Hayden whirled around and jumped into action right as I elbowed the crazy in the ribs. He didn't react to the pain but hesitated when the air whooshed out of his lungs. I brought my arm up and spun, bringing it down on his wrist and breaking his hold on my hair.

Hayden rushed in and, with swift grace, pulled the knife from his hip and shoved it into the crazy's ear. He stepped back and let the crazy slum to the ground. Blood splattered my feet.

"You ok?" he asked and flicked the brain matter from his knife. Fresh brains weren't as sticky as zombie brains. And it didn't smell as putrid.

"Yeah, but the bastard ripped out several strands of hair." I reached back and felt my braid.

Hayden gave me a wry smile. "Well, if that's the worst he did then we're lucky." He put the strap of his rifle over his head and put his hand on my arm. We stepped into the shelter of the old building.

"What the hell," I whispered.

"A herd of S1s?" he asked incredulously. "That isn't supposed to happen. And they're armed. Not well, but..."

"I know. This is bad. Really bad."

"We need to get out of here."

I nodded in agreement. "We need a plan first."

"Right," he said and took a step to the entrance of the old barn. He winced.

"Shit," I swore. "You're bleeding." I swung the bow up and over my shoulder and moved to Hayden's side. I knelt down and pulled up the leg of his jeans. A large splinter had forced its way under his skin. I cringed at the sight of it. That thing had to hurt like a mother.

"Just leave it, Riss."

"No way. It could get lodged in even further."

He looked down at me. "I don't think it works that way."

I shook my head. "Raeya always said so," I muttered. "This is gonna hurt." I pinched his skin with one hand and grabbed the splinter, digging my nails into the shard of wood. I had to brace myself for the pain it would cause Hayden. On a mental count of three, I yanked the sucker out.

"God damn," he swore and turned away, lifting up his leg.

I pushed my eyebrows together and stood, holding up the splinter. "It needed out."

Hayden took in the size of it and shrugged.

"I need to stop the bleeding." I said. I was pissed at myself for leaving the first aid kit in the truck.

"It's not that bad. And it won't matter unless we figure out how to get out of here."

"Good point." I dropped the splinter and looked at Hayden. "I say we run that way," I pointed in the opposite direction that we had come, "and cross the river as soon as we can. Then book it through the trees and get back to the truck. Well, given we don't run into the crazy train again."

"Good enough for me." He peered out once more. "Ready?"

I nodded and we took off. We ran through the long forgotten pasture that surrounded the little barn and jumped over a broken white fence. More trees surrounded the old barn, but they at least weren't as thick as the ones we had come through before.

Using the sound of the river as my guide, we rushed forward. I held my bow out in front of me, pushing away branches to keep them from scratching my face. Sunlight filtered through the thick leaves, creating blinding patches of light. Something snarled and crashed toward us.

"Duck!" I shouted as I pulled an arrow. Hayden bent at the waist. I strung the arrow without looking and pulled it back. Right before I let the arrow go, another crazy leapt out from behind a tree and tackled me.

I was pushed off balance, and my arrow didn't hit its target.

It hit Hayden instead.

CHAPTER FOUR

"Hayden!" I screamed as I fell to the ground. My head hit on a fallen log and the bow bounced out of my hand. The pain radiated, making my ears ring. "Hayden!"

The crazy moved on top of me, pinning my legs down. The arrows in the quiver stabbed into my back. She grabbed my wrists and snarled. Her curly red hair was matted with dirt and blood. One of her blue eyes was clouded over and unmoving. Saliva dripped from her mouth and she bent over me. I twisted my body to the side with enough force to knock her off.

I brought my legs up and kicked her square in the chest, pushing her onto her back. I scrambled to my knees and pulled the knife from the sheath and slashed the blade across her face. I turned my head just in time to avoid the spray of blood.

"Hayden!" I desperately called and turned around. He wasn't dead—thank God—and was fighting off two crazies. I grabbed an arrow and raced forward, driving it into the back of the skull of one of the crazies.

Her body went rigid, arms and legs stiffening. Then she fell, taking the arrow with her. I grabbed the other crazy by the shoulders and yanked him off Hayden. Hayden recovered quickly and shoved his knife into the crazy's open mouth. I dropped the body and looked at Hayden, panting.

"I hit you," I stammered, eyes wide with horror.

Hayden held up his left arm and the cloth of his shirt was torn, but there wasn't much blood. "Clipped me."

"I am so sorry."

"I'm always getting shot when I'm around you," he said with a smile. "It could have been worse."

"Be mad at me, please." I needed him to be mad at me; I was mad enough with myself.

"No time and you didn't mean it," he said and pressed his hand over the sliced open flesh on his arm. "This place is crawling with S1s." He shook his head. "It's like they're gathering together."

I grabbed my bow and arrow from the crazy's neck and flew back to Hayden's side. I carefully peeled his hand off of his wound. The cut wasn't too deep, but paired with the open gash on his leg and Hayden was a walking sponge for infection.

"You have blood on your cheek," he said and used his thumb to wipe it away.

"So do you." I readjusted the quiver and pushed the bow into place on my shoulder. Keeping our knives in hand, we took off again, going slower this time to look for crazies.

The end of the trees couldn't come soon enough. A small bit of relief flowed through me when we stepped back into the tall weeds. Bugs flew around us, attracted to the sweat and the blood that clung to our bodies.

We paused, inspecting our surroundings for crazies. When we didn't see any, we continued on.

"Where are we?" I asked aloud. On the other side of the river was a large plot of pavement. A bunch of dilapidated old buildings sat on the surface. In front of us was an old covered merry-go-round. Beyond that was the rickety skeleton of an old roller-coaster. "You have got to be freaking kidding me. We're in a theme park?"

"An abandoned one by the looks of it," Hayden said.

"Way to pick the destination," I mumbled. "I didn't even know there was a theme park in Arkansas."

"Looks like it was abandoned years ago." Hayden peered into the merry-go-round. "Wait a minute." He sheathed the knife and drew his gun. "Riss, look."

I took a step closer to the merry-go-round. A pile of blankets was gobbled in the center of the sun-faded animals. They were dirty and haphazardly thrown around but one thing was certain...

"It's a nest." I blinked. A tingle of cold fear ran its finger across my spine. "What the hell?" Hayden looked behind us before stepping closer. I followed. "Do you smell that?"

"Ugh, how can I not?" he asked and wrinkled his nose. "It smells like someone microwaved leftover roadkill then shoved it up a dead horse's ass."

"I don't know what that smells like but sure." I rolled an arrow in between my fingers. "There," I said and used the arrow to point to a garbage bag that was half covered by a tattered yellow quilt. "I bet you it's full of stomachs. The last, uh, organized crazy I came up against collected stomachs to eat."

Hayden moved a few paces away and picked up a stick and came back over and poked at the bag full of human remains. Liquid swished around. We both gagged at the smell.

"Yeah...don't need to see it to know that the crazies are keeping snacks for later." Hayden dropped the stick and covered his nose with his arm. "What the hell are they doing, making a nest like this?"

"I don't know, but I don't like it." I shuddered. I pulled my shoulders back and blew a loose strand of hair out of my face.

"Grouping together...carrying weapons...nesting." I shook my head. "Are they getting smarter?" Hayden asked.

"They have to be."

We hurried away from the merry-go-round, taking shelter behind what was left of a food stand. Hayden wiped sweat from his face and leaned against the rotting wood. Though he would never admit it, I knew he was in pain. I put the end of the arrow against the bow string, took a breath, and leaned forward, looking out at the theme park.

The rusty remains of a roller coaster were behind us. Tall, browning grass grew through cracks in the pavement and dilapidated buildings surrounded the section of the park.

Something moved inside the nearest one. I ducked back, out of sight. I looked at Hayden, silently telling him that we weren't alone. He put his finger over the trigger and nodded.

"On three," he mouthed. *One.* I strung the arrow. *Two.* I pulled the string back. *Three.* Together, we jumped around the corner. The crazy from inside the building burst through the door. He screamed and charged at us, holding a broken board above his head.

My arrow hit him in the shoulder. Completely unfazed, he kept running. When Hayden didn't fire, I knew he was waiting for me to grab another arrow so we could avoid the very loud gunshot that would give away our location.

Then another crazy appeared out of nowhere. He barreled down the pavement, spitting and growling and was joined by two others. All three ran toward us, eyes set on a kill. Hayden had no choice but to fire.

As soon as we took down those four, Hayden and I sprinted down the lot. We passed the first building, which was an old restaurant. A crazy inside lunged forward, banging on the dust covered glass windows of a gift shop. I turned, reaching behind me for an arrow at the same time.

Her eyes met mine. The vividness of the green struck me, brought out by the bright red blood that covered her face. Her teeth pulled back in a snarling smile, taunting, as if she knew she would rip me to shreds.

"Riss, look out!" Hayden yelled and reached for me.

But he was a second too late. I whipped my head around just in time to see the trip wire. I tried to jump over it but didn't make it. The bow flew from my hands and I fell. The heels of my palms bit into the pavement, and I caught myself just inches before my chin hit the hard ground.

Reeling in pain, I pushed up onto my knees. Hayden rushed over, swinging the rifle back around. He grabbed me under the arms. The crazy girl from inside the shop laughed. I put my hands on Hayden's arms and stood as he pulled me to my feet.

The girl was in the lot with us...as well as a dozen of her friends. Hayden held onto me as I stepped over the wire. Where was my bow? I knew I had dropped it. My heart pounded and the muscles in my legs ached. We needed to run. We needed to get the hell out of here as fast as we possibly could.

Hayden jumped forward but I didn't move just yet. I needed the bow. Without it, I only had the knife and a gun with limited ammo.

"Leave it!" he shouted over the growling. The crazies were inching toward us. He swung the rifle around and started firing. "Riss, come on!"

The bow was several feet away. I hesitated for a second and then dove for it. My fingers wrapped around the grip. And a crazy took a swing at me. I leaned back and he missed.

I brought the bow up hard, hitting him under the chin. Pain did nothing to hinder his attack. He curled his fingers into fists and let out a harrowing growl. The gun fired and he fell.

"Orissa!" Hayden yelled. "Now!"

I turned on my heel and sprinted away. As soon as I was by his side Hayden picked up the pace. Another crazy stood in the entrance to another ruined building that was labeled the Honey House. She was young, with once pretty curls and big, blue eyes.

She hissed when she caught sight of us. Hunched over with fresh blood streaming down her front, the crazy girl turned away, hiding her stomach—one that she had plucked from a dead or infected body—from view as if she was afraid we would take it.

"This way," Hayden called and dodged off the pavement and back into the weeds. Sweat dripped down my back. We pressed on, racing through the overgrown grass. A patchy area of trees was several yards in front of us. I stole a glance behind me. The crazies were still on our ass and growing in number.

We had to get to the truck. That was the only way out of this. Hayden and I were in excellent shape, but we were human, after all. Noninfected, healthy humans. We would get tired and winded.

Would the crazies?

They had to! They fucking had to. They might not feel it, but their bodies would react to the physical exertion on this hot day. Maybe they would just collapse. It would make for an easy kill.

The weeds gave way to the trees. Once we were in, we would be out of sight of the crazies. It could give us a few yards advantage...I hoped. If not—no, I wasn't going to think about it. Getting caught by crazies would be worse than zombies. Zombies ate you—all of you. You'd be ripped apart and dead in seconds. Crazies, on the other hand, liked organs and other meat. You'd stay alive and feel every bit of agony as they shoved their hands into your abdomen.

I jumped over a dead tree. Prickers caught on the thighs of my jeans. They ripped off, tearing into my flesh before I even realized they were there. I didn't have time to let the pain register. We had to keep moving. Underbrush loudly crunched under our feet as we tore through the trees.

Suddenly, I skidded to a stop. Hayden halted next to me. Panting, we looked at each other, then at the old broken down train. The engine was separated from the open passenger cars. Spiderwebs and moss wove along the rusted metal bars and the smell of animal droppings was heavy in the air. Taking a deep breath, I took off again, going down and around the train. I had just pushed into a run when the air left me.

The zombie's head was down. Crusty black curls hung in her face. The long dress she had on at the time of death was tattered and filthy. Something mental jangled with every shaky step.

A low moan escaped her when she heard the crashing of trees and leaves as Hayden and I came to an abrupt stop. Her movements were jerky and it seemed to take all of her remaining energy to lift her drooping head. Half of her face was gone, eaten away by the maggots that crawled and wriggled around her empty eye socket. Her jaw hung loose, and her tongue flopped out of her mouth.

I didn't consider gummies much of a threat. They were too far gone, too slow to get you in situations like this. But she wasn't alone.

I snapped my head up. My eyes widened. Zombies staggered through the trees. Heart racing, I grabbed an arrow without even thinking about it. Then it hit me. Hayden and I were stuck in between two herds: zombies and crazies.

I whipped around to Hayden. I didn't have to say anything. His wide eyes and blank face said it all. We were royally fucked.

* * *

I curled my fingers around the arrow and struggled to take in air.

One of the zombies let out a gargling growl. His rotting arms were held out in front of him. Not yet in the gummy stage, he was able to quicken his pace when he saw us. His increase in speed caught the others' attention and the whole herd hurried to us.

A crazy climbed through the train, jumping over benches. I backed away, breathing hard. Hayden flicked his eyes at me and swallowed. I moved my head up and down. Then we started running, following the tracks of the train ride. It would lead back into the theme park eventually, but for right now it was the only direction we could go without running into infected human beings who wanted to kill and eat us.

When the tracks started to curve back into the park, we kept going straight, running for our lives.

A zombie, separated from the herd, stumbled toward us. Its body had been burned. Charred flesh flaked off, revealing rotting muscle underneath.

His teeth clicked together as he chomped the air. I slowed, tightening my grip on the arrow. It pushed into his head with ease. I yanked it back and kept going.

The sight of the road was beautiful. Hayden and I stopped, panting. I put my hands on my knees and took a breath before standing and pushing my shoulders back. I slowly walked forward.

"I have no fucking clue where we are," Hayden said, his voice breathy.

I closed my eyes for a second, remembering the position of the sun when we stepped out of the truck. I pointed to my left. "We have to go this way. I don't know how far."

Hayden nodded. "Let's not waste any time." He took a deep breath and pushed into a jog. We didn't stop until the truck came into view.

"Hello, beautiful," Hayden breathed and dug the keys from his pocket. "Aren't you a sight for sore eyes?"

For the first time I couldn't fault Hayden for being so happy to see his truck, since I wanted to hug it too.

* * *

"You're late," Raeya said and leaned against the frame of the open door. Hannah and Ivan stood beside her. Hannah crossed her arms, trying to glower at her brother, but I could see the relief on her face.

"We ran into a few complications," I sighed and trudged toward the front of the compound. It was nearing midnight. After narrowly escaping the crazies, Hayden and I put several miles between us and the amusement park before we felt safe enough to get out and try hunting again. And then it took the rest of the day to bag two deer.

"You could have let us know," Raeya said and pushed off the door frame.

"And how would we have done that?" Hayden asked and shrugged off the rifle. He sounded as tired as I felt. Hannah pushed past Raeya and flung her arms around him.

Raeya crossed her arms. "I don't know," she said and shook her head causing her thick brown hair to fall out of place. She pursed her lips and narrowed her eyes, doing her best to look angry. "But that's two nights in a row you made us worry about you," she added pointedly. "At least you're home." She stepped forward, opening her arms for a hug.

I put the bow and quiver down and moved in to embrace her. Raeya wrinkled her nose and jumped back.

"Ew, Rissy. You're absolutely disgusting!"

"You are always covered in blood, Penwell." Ivan smiled, flashing perfectly straight white teeth. His eyes darted to Hayden. "You too, Underwood."

Hannah dropped her arms when she realized Hayden was dirty. She made a face and stepped back. "Just when I'm finally clean for the first time in months you have to go and get me dirty."

"Uh, you hugged me," Hayden sighed.

Hannah shook her head. "So typical. What happened?"

Hayden held up his left arm. "Riss shot me."

I turned, scowling at him. "Thanks."

He shrugged. "Well, you did."

"Do I want to ask?" Raeya said and held the door open for us to come through. She closed it, checking the locks twice.

"She didn't mean to," Hayden explained. "So I'll let her off easy. This time." He smiled at me. Even with dirt smeared on his cheek and splatters of blood dotting his face, Hayden could be charming when he wanted.

We stopped in the foyer where Hayden and I shrugged off our weapons, leaving them with the A3 who was on duty that night. Everything needed to be disinfected before it went back into the weapons room. I told him about the two dead deer in the bed of the truck. I wasn't the only one who knew how to skin and gut a deer, but I was one of the few who was able to go outside, especially in the dark. I internally cringed. Tonight was going to be a long ass night.

"You said you ran into complications. What kind of complications are we talking about?" Ivan asked quietly.

I raised my eyebrows and shook my head. "I would say you wouldn't believe me if I told you, but at this point I think anything is fair game."

"That bad, huh?"

"Oh yeah." I took a deep breath and flicked my eyes to Hannah. Ivan gave me a small nod, understanding my silent request to wait until she was gone to talk freely about what had just happened.

"Hannah," Hayden began, also wanting to talk to Ivan without his sister around. "It's been a really long day—"

"No!" she interrupted. "I'm not stupid, Hay." She leaned away from him. "And I'm not going to my room. You might be the boss of this place, but you're not the boss of me."

The color drained from Raeya's face. She blinked and smiled. I narrowed my eyes. That girl was covering something up.

"I'm not the boss of this place," Hayden said. "Not really anyway." He scratched his face. Dried blood had a tendency to make you itchy. "But I *do* have something important to discuss, ok? Go downstairs."

"No." Hannah crossed her arms.

I could feel the annoyance rising in me. I pushed it down, reminding myself that she was Hayden's baby sister.

"Hannah," Hayden said, rubbing his eyes. "Please?"

Her face softened when she caught the desperation in his voice. She let out a breath. "Should I be worried?"

"No, not at all," he said with a sigh. "And I will talk to you in the morning, ok? Just please let me have a meeting and get some sleep."

"Fine." She uncrossed her arms and stepped forward. Hayden gave her one more hug before walking her to the basement door. Raeya inspected her bracelet, running her fingers over the brown leather strap and rubbing the metal elephant charm as if she was polishing it.

Bullshit. She was avoiding me. Hannah had said something she wasn't supposed to, and I wanted to know what was going on. Before I had a chance to ask, Ivan bombarded me with questions.

"What did Underwood do to piss you off enough to shoot him?" He flashed me his characteristic toothy smile.

I shook my head. "Nothing...today." I took a deep breath. The memory was right there, fresh in my mind. The scent of the rotting stomachs was so strong I was sure my hair reeked of it. "Crazies," I began, "aren't so crazy anymore."

Ivan's brow furrowed. "Come again?"

Hayden returned. He put his hand on my back. "Is everyone asleep?" he asked, eyeing the stairs.

"Probably," Ivan said. He looked at Raeya and smiled. "I stayed up so Ray wouldn't have to wait for you two alone."

Raeya looked at the ground and smiled. "Sorry," she said quietly. "I know it's late."

"Nah, it's not that late. And besides, I couldn't sleep not knowing if I'd be setting out on a rescue mission in the morning," Ivan said.

Hayden curled his fingers under the hem of my shirt. "It can wait until morning then. We need to have a meeting with all the A's; they need to know this. And Dr. Cara and Padraic would probably want to know too."

"Whoa," Ivan said and put his hand up. "You can't leave us hanging."

Hayden nodded. "Come upstairs then." He tipped his head back, signaling to the A3 who stood a ways behind us. Ivan and Raeya followed us upstairs and into our room. I stopped at the threshold, kicking off my dirty boots. I grabbed the hem of my t-shirt, ready to pull it over my head.

"Uh, I can see you," Ivan said and held up his hands.

"Please," I sighed and pulled the shirt off. I had a tight tank top on underneath. I gobbled up the shirt, keeping it inside out so the grit and grime wouldn't rub off on anything. I went to the closet and tossed it in our hamper.

"Can you close the door?" Hayden asked and bent over to unlace his boots. He winced when he pulled them off. I knew his ankle still hurt.

"What happened? I'm getting scared," Raeya said and sat on my unmade bed.

"We ran into a herd of S1s," Hayden said.

"Crazies don't group in herds," Raeya said. "They kill each other."

Ivan tipped his head. "Not all the time."

I removed the hair tie from the end of my braid and started raking my fingers through my messy locks. Something sticky coated the ends…I didn't want to think about what it could be. "We saw it before," I told her. "When we were in Texas. But this…this was way worse. They were nesting, like with blankets and bags of organs left to bake in the sun."

"It was like they were organized." Hayden took over the explanation. He went on to tell them exactly what we had encountered. Raeya traced her fingers over her collar bone until the skin was red.

"What are you going to do about it?" she asked, her voice hoarse. She cleared her throat and put her hand down, pressing her palm against her thigh. "I mean, if they are grouping together and more or less *planning* how to attack, then that is a really big threat."

"It is," Hayden and I said at the same time. I turned to look at Hayden, reaching inside my shirt for his dog tags. I pressed my thumb against the flat metal.

"We need to go back and kill them," I said, voicing the conclusion Hayden and I already had come to. "A nest of crazies that close to home isn't something we can ignore." I turned my attention to Ivan. "We still have a few Molotov cocktails left over that will come in handy. The six of us will go tomorrow after breakfast and the meeting and take care of business."

"Molotov cocktails?" Raeya asked. "Your idea?"

I raised one shoulder. "What can I say? They're easy to make?"

"Wait..." she began and shook her head. "Why did you— Oh. Never mind. Eastmoore. Bombs. Makes sense now in a dark, disturbing way." She quickly shook her head and fiddled with her bracelet again.

I smiled at her as if it didn't bother me. And it didn't, not on the surface at least. I hadn't had time to process everything that had happened at the state institution just yet. I wasn't sure if I would be bothered knowing that I had killed people—people who weren't infected but who were just as bad if not worse than zombies.

"What time do you want to meet in the morning?" Ivan asked.

Hayden shrugged. "After breakfast is fine."

"All right." He took a step back, shoulders tensing just a bit. Raeya's eyes flitted to his then back down again.

"What are you not telling us?" I asked, nerves fluttering.

"Nothing," Raeya blurted quickly. Too quickly.

"I can tell you're nervous about something."

"Of course I'm nervous, Rissy! You just said there is a flock of crazies not too far from here!"

I pursed my lips. "I saw you acting off before we told you."

"It's nothing bad," she promised. "And you have so much going on right now."

"He needs to know," Ivan said suddenly.

"What do I need to know?" Hayden asked.

Raeya looked up at Ivan again, unsure of whatever she was about to say. Then she smiled and turned to Hayden "You won."

"Won what?" Hayden asked and unclipped his pistol from his side.

"The vote."

My stomach dropped. I had completely forgotten about the compound's election.

"And you won by a lot. Over eighty-five percent of the votes were for you," Raeya continued.

Hayden sank down on his bed. He closed his eyes, slowly exhaling while shaking his head. He looked at me and laughed. "This was supposed to avoid that." He rubbed his forehead. "I don't want to do it, but it seems I have no choice now."

"Yes you do," I told him, heart racing. "Don't do it." I shook my head. "Not if you don't want to. No one will be mad at you."

Ivan stepped forward and held up his hand. "I have to respectfully disagree, Penwell." He brought his hands together. "Underwood was here when this place was just a bare bones operation to save anyone we could find. He has a good reputation and everyone knows he was close to Fuller. And we all know that Hayden is fair but will also do whatever it takes to keep this place safe. There was a reason Fuller picked him all along."

"You want him to do it?" I asked.

"I do," Ivan said and shyly smiled. "I voted for him."

Hayden looked at his friend as if he had just betrayed him. Forgetting my pants were dirty, I sat on the bed next to Hayden, putting my hand on his arm. I bit the inside of my cheek. I couldn't refute Ivan's statement. Hayden *would* make a great leader. This place would be in good hands and I knew that Hayden would have no issue keeping certain types of people out.

Hayden ran his hand through his hair. "Do I have to make a speech or something?"

"I don't think so," Ivan told him with a shrug.

Raeya's eyes widened with excitement. "I'll write it. I love writing speeches!"

"Uh, have at it," Hayden said, looking at her as if she was crazy. His muscles were tense. I wanted to strip him of his clothes and give him a massage. I pressed my hand against his leg and winced when his jeans caught on the fresh scab forming on my palm.

"I feel bad," Raeya said and sat next to me. She linked her arm through mine. "Now that I know what you guys went through today. This is the last thing you need."

"You got that right," Hayden muttered. He slowly inhaled, steadying himself. "First things first. We need to eliminate the threat of the S1s. Then I'll worry about how the hell I'm going to fill Fuller's shoes."

I smiled at him, knowing that he was already worrying about it. There was no putting off the huge weight of taking over. It was just added on to the stress he was already dealing with.

"Holding the meeting is a good way to start," Raeya said. "You're taking action. Fuller would be proud."

Hayden forced a smile. "Sure."

"I'll do what I can to help. I organized Fuller's office so I know where everything is and what binders and lists go to what."

Hayden seemed even more overwhelmed by the thought of going through Fuller's things. "Thanks, Ray."

"But now you two need to rest." She looked at the bloody bandage around Hayden's left arm. "Probably go to the hospital ward first, though."

We all knew she was right. After saying goodnight to Ivan, she went with us downstairs. I opened my mouth to ask her if any feelings had finally sparked between her and Ivan but stopped. I wasn't in the mood to talk. Too much had happened today.

* * *

"And this?" Hayden looked up from the binder that lay open on Fuller's desk.

Raeya turned around. "That is the master list of everyone living here. It has their name, age, room number, category, and any significant info, like a few people have health conditions. It's alphabetized."

Hayden set his jaw and flipped the page. He slowly blinked and looked up. "Fuller knew everyone. How am I supposed to remember their names? I'm horrible with names."

"Everyone wears name tags," Raeya encouraged. "Well, everyone except Riss." She shot me a glare over her shoulder.

"Everyone knows who I am," I said without looking up from the map. I traced my eyes over the black Xs that marked the map. Each was earned after fully exploring a town. It was a reminder for us not to go back and waste time looking for supplies; there was nothing left.

"Right," Hayden said, unsure of himself. He closed the binder and leaned back in the chair. "Name tags."

"We need to talk about the tunnel," I said and stood, picking up the map. I pinned it back to the corkboard that hung on the wall opposite Fuller's desk and turned around. Raeya took the binder from Hayden and put it back on the shelf behind him.

"Right," Hayden repeated. He shuffled through the notebooks and papers on his desk until he found the list Raeya had made, ranking the suggestions the other A1s and I had come up with. "You are right about wasting gas." His eyes scanned the page before he looked up at me. "And it would be safer. The drive from here to the farm isn't protected. We don't want anybody hijacked by crazies. And if a herd came through the same time anyone was driving…" he trailed off, shaking his head. We all knew the outcome of that situation.

"You're going to make people use the tunnel instead, right?" I asked.

"Yes." He nodded. "But, there is one issue."

"Oh," I said as it hit me. "The weapons room."

Raeya waved her hand in the air. "Easy fix. The storage room across the hall is twice as big and has better lighting. There'd be a place to set up a table for cleaning the weapons so you don't have to do it in another room and then drag everything in."

Hayden smiled. "You're a genius."

Raeya beamed. "Thanks. I'm just good at organizing stuff." She picked up her 'to do' list and jotted something down. "You'll want the hall blocked off while we transfer everything, right? And probably only have those authorized to use weapons do the moving?"

"Yes," Hayden said, his shoulders relaxing considerably.

"It'll be done by tomorrow," Raeya said with a smile.

"Thank you," he said slowly. "Really."

Raeya held up her hand. "No need to thank me. It's my job to keep things organized."

"I never realized how much you did," I confessed. "I'm impressed."

Raeya tried—and failed—not to smile at the compliment. She looked up, blinking. "It's nothing. I make lists and alphabetize stuff."

"You're keeping me sane," Hayden told her. She brushed off the compliment.

Hayden eyed the clock.

"Anxious for our meeting, sir?" I asked him with a half smile. I was, though most of the anxiety had to do with going back and killing the crazies before they killed us. I wanted to get it over with without any of us getting hurt. And then I wanted to come back and rest. We had been on the go since Eastmoore, and I was tired.

"Yeah," he said. "Go get breakfast while you still can. I'll meet up with you later. I want to go through the files once more."

"I'll have them save something for you," I said. He flicked his eyes up and smiled. Raeya and I left Fuller's office. I made a mental note to stop referring to it as Fuller's office. It wasn't his anymore.

* * *

Raeya took Hayden's spot at our table in the back of the cafeteria. Alex, Mac, Noah, José, and Gabby—the soldiers who made up the other A1 group were eager to sit in on Hayden's meeting. They wanted to know about the new information we had learned and they wanted to know their assignment for the next mission.

I noticed Padraic sitting close to a woman named Maya. She was pretty with flowing hair and flawless, pale skin. But she was also weird in a way that made Dr. Cara seem normal. I still remembered her throwing salt into the air saying it would keep the zombies away. She was the only person I had yet encountered who thought that the virus was really caused by demons.

Padraic leaned in, laughing at something she said. A subconscious smile pulled the corners of my lips up. It was nice to see the blue-eyed doctor happy.

Olivia approached me when I stood to dump my tray.

"Hey, Orissa," she said shyly.

"Hey, Liv," I said and put the plastic tray on the stack of dirty dishes. I was *very* glad I didn't have to wash the dishes of over 300 people. "How are you?"

Her green eyes sparkled and her cheeks flushed. "I'm good...for real. But can I talk to you?"

"Of course you can." I waved goodbye to my friends and followed Olivia out of the cafeteria. The hall was buzzing with people. I had to turn my shoulders and shimmy my way through.

When we pushed past the bulk of the crowd, Olivia turned, looking up at me. She pressed her full lips together and smiled. "My birthday is in two days," she blurted, avoiding the subject. "I can legally drive...not that it matters, right?" she said with a laugh.

"I know you didn't come to me for driving lessons," I said.

She let out a nervous laugh. "No. But if you wanted to give them to me you can. I'd love to get out of here." Her smile instantly faded. "Maybe not. Not when there's still zombies and bad people out there."

"I'd keep ya safe."

Her smile returned "I know you would. I trust you." A group of teenage girls passed us. They waved and said hello to Olivia. "Can we go somewhere less crowded?"

I nodded and led her toward the staircase that took us down to the B level. The air conditioner rattled as it kicked on. "What's going on?" I asked her and slowed my pace.

"Remember how I told you that I kinda liked someone?"

"I do. Did you tell him?"

Her cheeks flushed. "No." She shook her head. "Not yet," she corrected, looking up at me. She stopped and ran her hand over her hair, which was in a side braid. "I'm pretty sure he likes me too."

I smiled. "That's great. But, uh, how do you know?"

"His sister—"

"Jason," I interrupted.

Her eyes widened and the slight red in her cheeks brightened. "How did you know?"

I raised an eyebrow. "How many guys in your age group have sisters you're friends with?"

"Damn you're good." She took a breath. "Anyway. Sonja thinks that—"

"Wait," I interrupted again. *Did I just hear...?* I tipped my head, listening. Yes, there was definitely something going on below us. I sprang forward, moving down the hall. I heard it again...a high pitched scream followed by a long, harrowing growl.

CHAPTER FIVE

I pushed into a run, skidding to a stop at the top of the stairs. The scream resonated off the cement walls.

"Go get Hayden!" I called to Olivia before I realized she had no idea he was in Fuller's office. I threw the door open and jumped down the stairs, taking two at a time. Something metal clattered to the floor. I rounded the landing, my feet flying as I ran. I burst through the door, heart racing.

The screaming got louder. I ran down the hall, pushing past a small crowd of people who had come out of their rooms to dumbly stare in the direction of the commotion. Suddenly, someone burst through the hospital ward doors.

The crazy was sputtering, madly pulling at his arms, which were in restraints behind his back. He saw me, snarled, and took off. I slowed and pulled my shoulders back, ready. He pitched forward, opening his mouth as he prepared to sink his teeth into my flesh.

I brought my arm back, sending my fist into his throat. While the pain did nothing, the inability to breathe caused the crazy to stop and take in a rattling breath. I reached out, planting my hands on his head. I closed my eyes and twisted.

His body collapsed onto the floor, face first, head loudly thumping on the tile. His nose was broken and blood splattered out.

"Son of a bitch," I muttered. I stepped away from the body and looked up. The few residents who had watched the exchange stared at me in awe and horror. I swallowed and shrugged before shaking myself. "Everyone all right?" I asked.

Hands slapped the glass of the hospital ward door, leaving a bloody streak. My heart skipped a beat and I jumped. At first I thought it was another crazy.

"Don't kill him," Dr. Cara panted, pushing through the doors. Blood slowly dripped from a gash on her forehead, above her right eyebrow. She looked at me then eyed the lifeless body at my feet. Her eyes widened and the color drained from her face. She stared at the dead crazy looking heartbroken and terrified at the same time.

What the fuck was going on?

"Are there any more?" I demanded.

She blinked and tipped her head up, her eyes settling on me. She tucked her left arm close to her body. "No. He was the only one." She reached up, gently touching the cut on her forehead with her fingers. She flinched then wiped the blood away.

"Did he get anyone in there?" I asked.

Dr. Cara wiped her hands on her shirt, smearing red over a preexisting stain. She shook her head, and I stared daggers at her. "What the fuck were you doing with that thing?"

If looks could kill, Dr. Cara would also be dead on the floor.

She turned her head up, blinking. "I was close to a breakthrough," she said.

Footsteps pounded on the stairs, and Ivan and Brock burst through the doors and into the hall. Ivan's dark eyes were wide. "What's going on?" he panted.

"That's a good question," I spat, whirling around to glare at Dr. Cara again.

"Shit!" Brock said when he saw the body on the floor.

"It's a crazy," I said quickly before he raced over and dropped to the floor to perform CPR on what looked like a resident. His eyes lingered on the blood that was seeping from the crazy's nose. Then he turned, squaring his shoulders.

"Is anyone hurt?" he asked, scanning the crowd. He and Ivan moved down the hall, stopping at the body. Brock nudged it with the toe of his boot. I realized I was clenching my hands into fists. I flattened my palms against my thighs, and tried to let go of the anger.

"Go back to your rooms and close the doors," Ivan calmly ordered. "We will deal with this." He stood over the body while the dozen or so compound residents scattered. The closing doors echoed down the long hall. "What the fuck?" Ivan asked, looking at me.

I shook my head. "She's freaking lucky I was here. He could have gotten anyone—really. None of us are armed and it's the *last* thing I expect to happen."

Brock knelt down, rolling the crazy over. "We need to get this cleaned up. Now."

I nodded, taking another breath to calm my temper. The door flew open again, hitting the wall with force. Hayden rush down, eyes open wide. He looked at the three of us then at the crazy, taking in the zip-tie handcuffs that were tightly wrapped around the crazy's wrists.

"What is going on?" he finally asked.

"Heard screams and came down here to find this guy running through the hall," I explained.

"You killed him?"

I nodded. "Snapped his neck. Then Dr. Cara comes out asking me to spare him."

Hayden opened his mouth to say something but stopped, shaking his head. He closed his eyes in a long blink. "Is everyone ok?"

"It appears so," Ivan said, looking around. "But she's bleeding."

Dr. Cara put her hand over the cut. "It isn't a deep wound," she stated.

"Did he bite you?" Hayden asked as he strode over.

Dr. Cara pressed her arm into her stomach. "No. He pushed me and I hit my head on the counter. You can look at the blood splatter if you'd like."

Hayden shook his head "I believe you." He turned away from her. "Uh, we should take the body out and away from here before burning it. Then bleach the hell out of the floor.

"Wait," Dr. Cara said suddenly. Her face, which was usually blank, showed fear. "Can you bring him into the lab?" She closed her eyes and bit her lip, looking vulnerable and as if she actually was capable of feeling emotions. "I need to test something."

All eyes fell on Hayden. He swallowed, looked at the body, and then at me.

"Hell no," I said, anger rising again. "That *thing* is bleeding. It's a huge infection risk."

"I at least need the head," she stated, earning incredulous stares from the four of us. "For research."

Hayden held up his hand to keep me from protesting. "It's dead and isn't posing a threat anymore. However, he's still full of all his, uh, juices so he needs to go."

"But my—" Dr. Cara started.

"Just the head, right?" Hayden asked.

"Yes."

Hayden looked and shook his head, as if he couldn't believe what he was about to say. "Fine. Take him outside first. Then remove the head."

Dr. Cara relaxed. "Thank you."

Hayden's lips pressed into a tight line. "We need to have a word."

Dr. Cara nodded.

"In Fuller's—my office. Now." Leaving Ivan and Brock to clean up the mess, Hayden, Dr. Cara, and I went down the hall.

"What the hell?" Hayden asked before I could even close the

door.

Dr. Cara stood in the middle of the room, slightly dejected.

"You brought an S1 *inside*! What were you thinking? It could have bitten someone!" His hands flew around when he spoke. "They are dangerous. The virus is doing something to their brains, something different—which you would have found out if you didn't bring that thing in here and we were having the meeting like I planned." He stopped, chest rapidly rising and falling.

I knew Hayden and understood that he was shouldering some of the responsibility for what had happened. He felt that since he was in charge, anything that went wrong fell on him.

"How did you sneak it in?" I asked and crossed the room to be next to Hayden. My ears were hot and my temper was rising again.

"Drugged it. Had it carried in," she stated and cast her eyes to the ground. She kept her arm close to her body. It was obvious she was hurt; maybe she twisted her wrist when the crazy pushed her. I figured it wasn't that bad since she hadn't mentioned it.

"Why?" Hayden asked, completely exasperated. His eyebrows pushed together and little lines of worry formed around his mouth.

"Research," she stated as if it was obvious.

"Oh good, Hayden," I said sarcastically. "It was in the name of research. Which makes endangering every-fucking-one totally worth it!"

"He wasn't supposed to get away," she told me, her voice level.

"I would hope not!" I spat back. I shook my head.

Hayden put his hand on my shoulder. He took a step in between Dr. Cara and me. "Cara," he said directly. "You cannot bring the infected inside. It's enough of a risk bringing in blood and tissue samples. You know I support your research, but I can't allow this."

I narrowed my eyes. "What about your crazies in the barn? Why not go out there and inject them with whatever the hell you've come up with?"

She pressed her lips together. "I wasn't going to inject that particular subject with anything."

"Then what, pray tell, the hell were you going to do with your *subject*?" I crossed my arms.

"Open his skull and dissect his brain." Her eyes met mine.

"You—" I cut off, eyebrows furrowing. Typically, dissecting happened on *dead* subjects. And that crazy was very much alive until I snapped his neck. "You wanted to poke at his brain while he was still alive?"

Hayden twisted his head to look at me. He blinked, realized the truth in my statement and turned to Dr. Cara. "Is that true?"

Her eyes flew to the floor for a second. Then she looked straight at Hayden. "Yes."

Hayden leaned back. "Doesn't that seem, uh, a little crude?"

"You kill them."

I shook my head. "Yeah but we don't strap them down to a table and slice open their skulls." I didn't want to admit it, but the thought made me curious. It wasn't like the crazy could feel pain, anyway. "What good would that do, being alive?"

She turned her face to me. "I want to stimulate parts of the brain to see if it has an effect."

"Like a cure?"

"No. You cannot reverse permanent brain damage."

I waited for her to explain what exactly she was hoping to accomplish by stimulating parts of the brain, but Dr. Cara wasn't one for conversation. Her direct, to-the-point answer usually didn't bother me. But now I wanted information.

Hayden ran his hand over the back of his head. "From now on I need you to run all experiments and research by me." He sighed. "And never, *ever* are you to bring in anything that's infected. Got that?"

Dr. Cara nodded.

"Now," Hayden said. "I need the names of the people who helped you bring it in. We need to have a lesson on safety."

"Safety?" I scoffed. "How about fucking common sense?"

Hayden cast his eyes in my direction. His forehead wrinkled and his shoulders were tense. He scribbled down the names Dr. Cara gave him. He told her to get her forehead cleaned up before the meeting.

"One hell of a first day on the job," he said once Dr. Cara left the room. He leaned against the desk. I moved over to him, putting my hands on his waist.

"You're doing fine." I stepped closer so that my hips brushed against his.

"She said something about the traps. And I forgot to look into it." Hayden wrapped his arms around me. I pressed my lips to his.

"There was a lot going on," I whispered and moved my mouth to his neck. He exhaled when I sucked at his skin. His hands went under the fabric of my shirt. And then he suddenly spun us around, bending me over the desk. He put himself in between my legs. My arms moved to his neck, pulling him onto me. He leaned forward, kissing me and pushing his hardness against my core. Warm desire pulsed and I wanted Hayden. Now.

I reached up, rounding my back so I could unbutton his jeans. My fingers tightened around the metal button. I yanked it loose.

"Riss," Hayden breathed, moving his mouth to my collar bone. "We have the meeting."

"Postpone it." I stuck my hand inside his pants, curling my fingers around his erection. He softly moaned and kissed me, working his way to my breasts. He took my hard nipple between his fingers, turning me on even more. "You are the boss after all."

He stopped and moved his face back to mine. "I am." He kissed me once more before stiffly leaning away. "I wish we could spend the day together, naked and in bed."

I wrapped my legs around him, not ready to stop just yet. "We can."

"Tomorrow."

"I don't like you being responsible."

"I don't like it either." Grudgingly, he straightened up. "Not one bit." I took my hand out of his pants and sighed. He looked at the clock the smiled deviously. "We have twenty minutes."

* * *

Hayden stood. His first official meeting was over. Since the room we had previously used for meeting had been converted into a bedroom, everyone had crowded around the dining room on the rarely used first level of the estate. Hayden had sat at the head of the table, with Hector to his left and me on the right.

He discussed the S1s' scary new behavior, went over using the tunnel, stressed that everyone was to be twice as cautious as before. Everyone was settling in here and getting comfortable. And bad things were more likely to happen when you let your guard down.

We were going after the nest of crazies today. Assuming everything went all right, Alex and his group would leave for a mission tomorrow, gathering the supplies we needed. Ivan, Brock, Wade, Jason, and I hung back while the others shuffled out of the room and back downstairs.

"Are we leaving right away?" Jason asked. His brown eyes were wide with excitement.

"Yeah," Hayden closed the folder that lay in front of him. "I don't want to be out there after the sun sets."

Hector, who stayed behind as well, shot Hayden a surprised glance. "You're going?"

"I was planning on it," Hayden answered. "Riss and I know the layout. Besides, these guys need me." He flashed a grin at Ivan.

"Why wouldn't he go?" I asked, sensing Hector's opposition.

"It makes perfect sense," he answered. "But Fuller never went on missions. He stayed here to keep an eye on everything."

Suddenly, I felt trapped. Hector was right; Fuller never left. He gave us assignments and then went back into his windowless office, back to making plans but never leaving, never setting foot outside the fenced in protection of the compound.

Sweat broke out along my spine. I didn't want to go on a mission without Hayden, and more so, I knew Hayden wouldn't want me to go on a mission without him. Would he ask me to stay here with him? A lump formed in my throat. I couldn't. I couldn't do it. I'd feel like I was stuck in a cage, pointlessly living out the days while someone else risked everything to keep me safe.

"No," I said aloud. "Hayden has to come with. It would throw off the vibe of our group."

Hector's face softened. "I didn't want to say it, but the reason Fuller didn't go on missions was because it's dangerous. If something happened to Hayden while he was out there, we'd be back in the position we were just in. This place, these people, need a leader."

Hayden's expression was tight. He thought Hector was right but he also didn't want to be stuck here for the rest of the apocalypse. I ran my fingers along the chain that held his dog tags. Everyone waited for Hayden's decision.

"You'll be fine without me," he said as if he was addressing our entire group. Really, he was talking to me. Hayden was so much more than my assigned partner and I had a feeling Hector was catching onto that.

"Of course we will be." I forced a smile and nodded. I turned, scanning the faces of my friends. "Ready?"

* * *

The Range Rover bumped along the long forgotten road that led into the entrance of the park. Clouds muted the bright sun and lowered the temperature a few degrees. I was sitting in the middle in the back seat, wedged between Jason and Wade. My quiver full or arrows and bow sat uncomfortably between my feet and the butt of Jason's rifle was poking me in the side.

The back of the SUV was full of more weapons along with the Molotov cocktails we hadn't used in Eastmoore. It had been a quiet ride. While we roughly knew what we were getting into, the thought of willingly walking into a herd of crazies made us nervous. Ivan slowed, passing by a faded blue and yellow sign that read 'Welcome to Dogpatch USA.'

"You would come to an abandoned theme park to hunt," he said and let the SUV coast to a stop. He looked at me through the rearview mirror.

"Hayden picked it," I reminded him. Ivan cut the engine. In silence, we got out and suited up, strapping weapons to our bodies and shoving ammo into our pockets.

"After the last mission," Jason started and held his rifle to his face, checking the scope, "this doesn't seem too bad."

"It doesn't," Wade agreed. "But don't go into this thinking it will be easy." He opened the back of the Range Rover. "S1s aren't scared of death or pain. That makes them very dangerous."

Jason nodded. "Which way?" he asked me.

I turned around, looking at the parking lot. "I'm not sure. We didn't come through this way at all." I pushed my braid over my shoulder and wrapped my fingers around my bow. "Once we get in I'll be able to figure it out."

"Ok," he said. I watched him load his pistol and stick it in the holster on his hip. He was so enthusiastic to be out here, so excited to have the chance to run with us and make a difference. It made me worried he would do something I would do…something so reckless he'd get himself hurt. Jason had grown on me as if he was the younger brother I never had. I didn't want him out here. I didn't want him getting hurt.

"Got your radio?" Ivan asked me.

It hung from my belt. I patted it. "Yep."

"Good." He turned his on. We weren't planning on splitting up but brought the walkie-talkies just in case. He locked the Range Rover and tucked the keys into his pocket.

I took the lead. Jason sped up to get next to me. Dry weeds crunched against the broken pavement as we walked through the lot. I darted my eyes back and forth, watching for any sign of movement. My heart sped up. I slowly inhaled. The air smelled faintly of rotting filth.

We were getting close.

The path that led from the parking lot into the park was long and wound through trees. At one point I was sure it was pretty. I imagined kids tugging on their parents' hands, excited to get inside and on a ride. Now moss and weeds covered most of the pavement. The trees on either side of us crept up, branches almost touching each other.

Jason slapped his neck, squishing a mosquito. "How do you stand hunting?" he asked quietly. "Don't you sit still for hours?"

"Sometimes." I scanned the trees. "And hunting was always more than just *hunting*."

"What do you mean?"

"It was something my grandpa and I did together. Being out in the woods was just...just relaxing." I turned to look at Jason. "Although sometimes I hated it and wanted to be inside on the computer like a normal kid."

"You hunted when you were a kid?"

"Oh yeah," I said and remembered Jason knew very little about my childhood despite the fact that he had stayed at my grandparents' farmhouse with me for several weeks. "My grandpa wanted me to know how to take care of myself. He, uh, was a little obsessed with teaching me how to survive."

"I'm glad." He smiled. "If you didn't know how to do all that stuff, we wouldn't have made it." He ran his hand down the barrel of the rifle and laughed. "Do you remember when you attacked Padraic in the basement?"

"What? I never attacked him."

Jason nodded. "You said you thought he was keeping us down there on purpose."

"He *was* keeping us down there on purpose," I teased. "But yeah, I do." We both laughed and Jason explained the whole story to Ivan, Brock, and Wade. Suddenly, our laughter ended.

"There's something over there," Brock said, pointing to a dilapidated structure that was barely visible through the trees. We moved into formation with our weapons raised. "Keep it quiet if possible." He gripped a knife in one hand and kept the other on his pistol.

"Riss," Wade whispered. "You got this?"

I pulled the arrow back and nodded. Jason let out a shaky breath. Eastmoore was fading from his mind and he was getting scared. Good. I hoped it would keep him rational.

I swallowed and took another step toward the old ticket booth. My heart was in my throat and nerves tingled along my spine. I wanted to turn and go back to the car. Something was wrong. I could feel it.

I squeezed my fingers around the arrow. Leaves crunched. Whoever was in the ticket booth was moving. Seeing Brock out of the corner of my eye was reassuring. Each heartbeat pounded in my ears as I waited.

The screen door creaked open and the crazy stepped out. He was tall and thin, looking to be in his mid thirties. His sandy blonde hair was a horrible mess and blood and dirt streaked his face. Wild eyes took us in and he tipped his head, curious. Then he held up his hands.

"Uh, guys?" I asked and lined the arrow up with his chest. "Should we take his gesture of good will?"

"Doubt it," Brock whispered.

Ivan lowered his gun. "Cover me," he said and stepped forward. He put one hand up, showing the crazy he wasn't going to hurt him." We come in peace," he said. I kept a steady hold of the arrow. The crazy tipped his head up and sniffed. Then he turned around and made a strange strangled cry five times.

Ivan took another step. I sucked in air and held my breath, muscles aching to release the arrow. The crazy leaned forward and pulled his lips back, showing his teeth. In a flash, he reached behind him, pulling a gun from his waist band.

I let the arrow go. It hit him in the shoulder. The crazy stumbled back and the gun fell from his hands. I strung another arrow and hit him in the throat.

"The fuck?" Ivan asked, spinning around to look at us.

Brock shook his head and holstered his pistol. Carefully, he edged forward. I grabbed another arrow, expecting another crazy to pop out of the booth. He bent down and picked up the crazy's gun, grimacing at the filth that covered the grip.

"It's not even loaded," he said and turned it around.

"So they have enough sense left to know what guns are but not how to use them," Wade said as he surveyed our surroundings.

"Looks like it," Brock said and tossed the gun onto the crazy's chest. He yanked the arrows from the body, flicked off the blood, and handed them back to me. I shoved them back in the quiver. "Does this unnerve anyone else?"

"Yes," Ivan and I said at the same time.

"It's good it wasn't loaded, right?" Jason asked.

"Yeah," Wade answered. "But I'm not going to bank on the next S1 we run into to *not* have a loaded weapon."

"How do they know who's infected and who's not infected?" I asked. "Like can they sense it or something?"

"Good question," Ivan said.

We regrouped and moved deeper into the park.

"Maybe we can bring a few back and let Dr. Cara do more experiments." Ivan turned and grinned. "And then you can snap more necks in front of children and give them nightmares."

I scowled at him. "Shut up."

He laughed. "Too soon?"

"What choice did I have?"

Brock held up his hand.

We stopped and looked in the direction he was pointing. A large building sat surrounded by pavement. It was in fairly decent shape with the exception of the broken windows and missing front door.

Someone was watching us from the second story window. I narrowed my eyes, focusing on her face. The old woman stared at us, unmoving.

"That is creepy," Jason said with a shudder. "Why is she doing that?"

"I don't know," I whispered. The hair on the back of my neck prickled like it did when I was being watched. I felt the eyes drilling into my back. Shit. The old woman was in front of me. I whirled around.

"Guys!" I shouted and grabbed an arrow. The second my fingers grazed the fletching, I knew it wouldn't be enough. A herd of crazies emerged from the trees. There had to be at least thirty. Thirty fast moving, armed, crazies who feared neither death nor pain. And there were five of us.

Fuck.

I let the arrow go, hitting a crazy in the stomach, and reached for my gun. The guys were firing away. I watched the front line of crazies drop, only to be replaced by more. I yanked the gun and flicked off the safety. I held it up and started shooting. I fired three rounds, aiming for the head, before I remembered that almost any gunshot wound could be fatal to a crazy. I could fire more rapidly if I wasn't aiming for the head.

Suddenly, Jason screamed. I flicked my eyes to the side just in time to see a crazy lunge through the air and land on his back.

"Jason!" I screamed and ran to him.

Jason fell, face first, onto the pavement. His face smacked and his gun was trapped under his body. The crazy dug his fingernails into Jason's shoulder.

"No!" I cried.

She tipped her head up and howled before sinking her teeth into his neck.

CHAPTER SIX

The gun fell from my hand. I gripped the bow and thrashed it through the air. It collided with the crazy's head. She fell sideways off of Jason, blood dripping from her ear. She scrambled up, snarling. Ivan turned and shot her in the forehead. Blood sprayed in the air and she fell.

"Jason!" I cried and dropped to the ground, hurting my knees. He was perfectly still with his hands clamped around his neck. "Jason!"

I reached for him with shaky hands. My fingers wrapped around his wrist and pulled his hand away. There was no blood. He turned, his face grinding against the rough pavement. His lip had split open and his cheek and forehead were scratched to all hell.

I put my hand on his neck and felt a bubble of laughter rise in me. Teeth marks were scored into the leather strap of his rifle. The laugh that had escaped as relief rapidly changed my emotions. He was ok. I jumped to my feet and helped Jason up.

He moved his hand to his neck, rubbing the skin in disbelief. His eyes, wide with fear, turned from me to the dead crazy. He swallowed hard and shook his head.

"We need to get out of here," Brock said as he reloaded his gun. He stretched out his arm and fired, hitting a crazy that was running at full speed toward us. I snatched my gun and pulled the trigger.

It was empty. Shit. I didn't have time to reload. I grabbed Jason's arm and ran. We raced over dry weeds, our boots pounding on the sun-warmed pavement. With the bow in one hand and my empty M9 in the other, I had no way to shoot at the crazies that charged at us. A young crazy jumped from a patch of tall weeds. His hands were out to his sides, fingers curled in.

A gun blasted next to me. The crazy looked down at his stomach, confused at why his shirt was getting soaked in blood. He pressed his hand to his abdomen and then brought it to his face. He sniffed the blood and then licked it.

"Come on!" I shouted to Jason, who had slowed to shoot the crazy. He lowered his rifle and ran after me. We jumped into tall grass. The smell of pond scum mixed with the metallic scent of blood. Soggy earth gave way. I threw out my arms to keep my balance. Shit, I had led us into a swamp.

We crossed through several inches of murky water. I turned around to make sure everyone was ok, but I only saw Jason. Had we gotten separated? Or were we the only ones who got away?

Something grabbed my ankle. My body tensed and I yanked my foot up, careful not to knock myself off balance. A zombie lay hidden in the weeds and water. His lower body had been torn away. Intestines spilled out, strewn across the swamp. What was left of the skin on his face was transparent.

Too weak to hold on, his fingers slipped off my boot. I wrinkled my nose. No wonder it smelled horrible. Swamp water was bad enough on its own. A decaying zombie soaking in it was even worse. I stomped my heel on its face. His weak skull cracked easily and browning brain matter oozed out.

Jason and I ran without slowing until we were out of the swamp. An old roller coaster loomed ahead. Jason looked at me in question; I nodded and we pressed on, stopping when we were under the rickety frame. Parts of the wooden tracks were rotted and covered in moss. Broken tree limbs balanced dangerously above us.

Panting, I put the gun under my arm and pressed it to the side of my body and grabbed a loaded clip from my pocket. I changed it out in just seconds, shoved the weapon into the holster, and picked up the walkie-talkie.

"Guys?" I asked.

Jason moved closer, gasping in air.

"Guys?" I asked again but heard nothing but silence. My heart thumped and I felt dizzy. We needed to go back and help them.

"Riss, you ok?" Brock's voice came over the radio. I cradled the walkie and closed my eyes for a long blink. Thank God.

"Yeah. Jason is with me. You?"

"We got away. Wade got sliced pretty bad."

"Sliced?" I backed under the shadows. My heart plummeted again.

"An S1 had a saw blade. Got his arm. Ivan's stopping the bleeding now. I saw Jason get bitten. Is he…"

"Didn't break the skin," I answered and exhaled. Sweat rolled down my face. "Where are you guys?"

"In the woods. You?"

"By the roller coaster."

"All right. We will—" he abruptly cut off and loud gunfire sounded over the radio. My heart sped up. I held the radio closer to my face. My fingers tightened around the plastic.

"Brock?" I said into it.

Jason leaned in, his arm brushing mine. Heat radiated off of him.

"Brock?" I said again, desperate. All I heard was static.

I clipped the walkie back to my belt and turned up the volume. "We have to go to them," I said and looked at Jason. I cringed. His face was a bloody mess with bits of pavement and dirt stuck inside the cuts. The scab that had formed over the spot where the bullet grazed his forehead hung limply on his face.

"You look horrible," I said.

Jason gave me a half smile and shrugged. "It's nothing."

"Bullshit."

His smiled faded. "Yes. It hurts like hell and I feel sick from swallowing blood." He dabbed at his lip with the back of his hand. "But this beats a crazy bite any day, right?"

I nodded and hooked the bow over my shoulder. I opened my leather bag and pulled out two glass bottles and handed one to Jason. "Time to start blowing shit up."

A broad smile broke out on his face, flashing bloody teeth. He patted his pocket, checking for his lighter. I loosened the cap on my bottle just enough to make it easy to remove in case of an emergency...which we were more than likely to run into.

"What's our plan?"

"No fucking clue," I sighed. "I don't know this place. Hayden and I ran through so fast I didn't get a chance to remember the lay out. Ugh! I wish I had a way to look..." my eyes went to the old roller coaster. "...around." I couldn't help the smile that pulled my lips up.

Jason grabbed my arm. "Orissa, no. No way. That thing is one splinter away from falling!"

"It's fine," I said and put my hand on a board. I gave it a tug and it snapped in half. "Damn it."

"Riss, it's suicide."

"It's kind of my style."

He shook his head. Jason wasn't going to argue with me, not the way Hayden would have.

"If I can get up there, I can see where the guys are *and* where the crazies are hiding out." I moved down and tested another board. "Cover me. And watch your own ass. If anything happens, get out of here, ok?"

"Riss, I can't."

"Jason," I said sternly. "You have family! You're going back to the

THE TRUTH IS CONTAGIOUS

compound alive, got it?"

"Got it." He stuck his finger over the trigger on his rifle and turned around. "You have family too, you know. Just 'cuz they're not related doesn't mean they're not family."

I hesitated, my foot hovering a few feet from the ground. "I know." I hoisted myself up. The frame creaked under my weight. "That's why I have to do this. You guys are my family now." I moved up another few feet.

"You'll have a husband soon," Jason said. I could tell he was smiling.

"Shut up." I pushed the bow back and edged over, finding a board strong enough to hold me.

"Can I ask you something, Riss?"

"Sure," I called and kept going, resisting the urge to look down and see how high I was. I kept my eyes focused on what was in front of me, calculating my next move.

"You and Hayden...how did it start?"

"What?" My hair stuck to my sweaty neck. I moved my hand, sticking it in a spiderweb. I instantly recoiled and lost my balance. My foot slipped and I thrashed my arms, wrapping my hands around a soft board. I swallowed my pounding heart. Holy shit that was close.

"I mean starting a relationship after so much bad stuff has happened. It makes some things seem unimportant, ya know?"

I steadied myself and moved up. "I thought that too," I called. "That it was pointless. But being with him makes the bad stuff not seem so bad."

A cloud rolled over the sun. The air seemed staler the higher I climbed, but it was probably just the wooden roller coaster. The boards had some serious weather damage from years of neglect.

"So things started like normal?" he called.

"Can we talk about this later? This really isn't the time to talk about this." I flicked my eyes down. Fuck. The ground was far away. I hadn't realized how high I'd gotten. My hands still hurt from falling on the ground yesterday, but I didn't stop.

I ducked under a railing and stepped onto the tracks. I bent down, keeping a hold of the metal, and climbed my way up an incline. The coaster swayed in the wind. The boards creaked and groaned with each step I took. Maybe this was a bad idea. A plank rattled, threatening to give way. Yes. This was a horrible idea.

But it worked. I was above the trees. I straightened, clinging to the railing for dear life. I hated wooden roller coasters even when they were in good condition. There was just something about them...something too old fashioned that made me think the beams would snap and break.

Across from the swamp was a cluster of shops and buildings. That was where Hayden and I encountered the bulk of the herd. The river curved along it. I traced my eyes over the water until I found the bridge we had crossed, the one that Hayden's foot fell through.

Static came through the radio. Apprehensively, I let go of the railing and unclipped it from my belt.

"Brock?" I spoke into the radio. It was hard to make out what he was saying, but I knew I heard my name. "I can't hear you," I said. "But we are fine. I'm scouting out the area. Hang on." I scanned the park, memorizing the layout. It looked so small from way up here. "Crazies. I see them." I watched as little bodies zoomed in and out of the buildings. What the hell were they doing? "They are in the center of the park," I said and then realized that the guys had no idea what the center of the park was.

"Where are you?" Brock's voice came through clear as day.

"On the roller coaster."

The breeze picked up again. My stomach dropped when the old coaster swayed. A group of crazies went into one of the buildings.

"On it?"

"Uh, yeah."

"How can you...shit, you're literally on it."

"It's a great vantage point," I said and stole a glance down at Jason. Fuck. I shouldn't have done that. I wanted down, off this godforsaken piece-of-crap ride. "I can't see you."

"We're in the building that's at the end of what used to be a tram...if that helps."

I slowly turned. "See it. Stay there if you can and we will meet you." I turned around and eyed the cluster of shops. "The crazies went inside. I think we can come up with some sort of plan and attack the nest from the outside."

"Sounds good to me, though I say we set this place on fire."

I couldn't help but smile. "Deal."

"Be safe, Riss."

"I will. You too." I clipped the walkie back onto my belt. I pulled on my braid while looking down. It was going to take a while to safely descend this thing. .I pushed the bow up and ducked under the railing. I concentrated on my breathing as I climbed down. When I finally dared to look, I was twenty feet or so from the ground. Relief flooded over me. I took a few seconds to look around. Jason held his weapon up, looking through the scope. I moved down another section of scaffolding. Then I smelled him.

"Jason, zombie!" I shouted. Jason turned, still holding his rifle up. The end of his gun smacked against the zombie, pushing the scope back into his face. Already injured, Jason reeled from pain. He stepped back and tripped over his own feet.

I hooked my legs over a plank and leaned forward, removing the bow from my shoulder. I grabbed an arrow, pulled it back, and let it go. The arrow went right through the zombie's head and it fell just feet away from Jason.

"Thanks, Hawkeye," he breathed and pushed himself up.

"Don't mention it." I stuck my arm through the bow and hurried down. I recapped what I had talked about with Brock. After Jason reloaded his rifle, we took off, silently slipping through the weeds that surrounded the swamp.

"There," I mouthed and pointed to a small building. We dropped to our knees to stay hidden. I picked up the radio and told the guys we were just yards away.

On the count of three, Jason and I dashed across an open section of pavement and into the building. It was nothing more than a break room for the workers who manned the tram. A table with a broken leg was pushed into a corner and the floor was covered in old papers and garbage.

"I'm glad to see you, Penwell," Ivan said.

"Same here." I took the bow off my shoulder and rubbed at my skin. It was sore from the string rubbing against it. "You ok?" I asked Wade. A makeshift bandage had been tied around his left arm. Blood seeped through the material.

"Good enough," he said and held up his arm to show me he was still capable of fighting. "You seriously climbed that old roller coaster?"

"She did," Jason answered for me.

"I'm telling Hayden," Wade teased.

"Good," I shot back with a smile. "Maybe he'll spank me."

"Tell us what you saw," Ivan said, looking through a dirty window.

"There's a narrow river that cuts through the middle of this place. It's shallow from the drought. It was only waist high in one part that we saw. There's a bridge behind that office. Hayden and I went over a bridge before and it wasn't strong enough to hold his weight." I shook my head. "I have no idea if the other bridge will be strong enough either. But we need to get across somehow. There's a building shaped like a T. I saw the crazies going into it. They didn't come out."

"Yet," Brock added. "There's no guarantee they're still there."

"It's worth a shot," Ivan said. "If we can attack the nest from the outside, it's our best—and easiest—bet."

"How are we gonna do it?" Jason asked.

All eyes fell on me. I recalled the layout of this place and gazed out the window. Everything looked different on the ground. "There should be another bridge that way," I said and pointed. "If we can cross it and stay in the tall grass along the river, we might be able to get by unseen."

"But *we* won't be able to see anything," Wade reminded me.

"Damn. You're right." I bit my lip, thinking.

"Let's just do it," Ivan suggested. "We are sitting ducks in here." He cocked his gun. "We don't have to take them all out," he reminded us. "Just enough to make them not as big of a threat."

"Everyone got their cocktail?" Brock asked.

We nodded. "Ok. Let's do this."

Ivan went first, making sure the coast was clear.

And it was clear...eerily clear.

* * *

I couldn't help the sick feeling that the crazies were planning something. We ran across the lot and into the woods, bypassing the old two story office building all together.

The calming sound of running water echoed off the trees. Anxiety balled in my stomach and my eyes involuntarily flicked to Wade's arm. Would the smell of blood draw in the crazies?

"You're the lightest," Ivan said, casting a glance at me. I nodded and moved forward. I made it across without an issue. Jason crossed next, followed by Wade and Brock. Ivan was last and jumped off the old wooden structure. We took a second to collect ourselves before pushing on.

"There," I whispered and moved a branch back to peer through the trees. I had been happily surprised at how quietly Jason moved behind me. I could tell he was really trying. "The fourth building."

"That's where you saw them?" Ivan whispered.

"Yep."

"You two go around, catch the stragglers. The three of us will light it up." He pulled his lighter from his pocket and held up a wine bottle filled with explosives. "Showtime."

Nervous excitement rippled through me. I unlatched my back, getting my own Molotov cocktail ready. Jason and I slipped through the trees, racing to the nearest building. I ducked behind it, pressing my back to the wall. I wrapped my fingers around an arrow, just in case. Jason had traded his rifle for a pistol, which was better for shooting when the crazies were right in our fucking faces.

"Do you hear that?" Jason whispered. His knuckles were white from gripping his gun.

"Yeah," I whispered back. Weird chatter spilled from the building full of crazies. Real words weren't being said, but there was a definite tone to the clicking and growling.

"They're talking."

"We'll be ok," I assured him. He didn't have to tell me he was terrified. I knew he was because I was too. I felt like we were walking into Eastmoore again, but this time we had a piss poor plan.

"On three," Brock's voice came over the walkie. There were a few seconds of silence before he came back, tapping on the walkie three times. I closed my eyes and braced for the explosion.

Jason jumped when the bottle smashed into pieces and the fire ripped along the wall of the building. Two more blasted after that.

And then chaos broke loose.

The crazies tore out of the burning structure. Some were on fire. Jason and I pushed off the wall, running into the street. Black smoke billowed around us, making it hard to see the crazies until they emerged from the thick cloud.

My ears rang from the loud shots that blasted from Jason's gun. I fired arrow after arrow, each one getting lost as the crazies fell. We dodged around another building, trying to stay on the sidelines and out of a direct fight.

The smoke choked me. My eyes watered, making it hard to see what was in front of me. Jason doubled over, coughing. I fired one more arrow before I lowered my bow.

"Jason," I said and went to him. I hooked my arm under his. "Hold on." I helped him up and dragged him around another building. He was panicking, gasping for air. "Hey, Jason," I said and put my hands on his shoulders. "Stand up straight. It will help you get more air."

His eyes widened even more and he made a strangled noise of surprise. I whirled around. A crazy barreled at us. One of his arms was on fire and, instead of reacting to the pain or trying to put out the flames, he used the fire as a weapon, waving his arm in the air.

Flakes of charred skin fluttered to the ground and the smell of burned flesh made me sick. He was too close to shoot with the bow. I grabbed the knife from my hip and threw it, hitting the crazy in the neck. He sputtered, not giving up the pursuit just yet.

I grabbed Jason under the arms, ready to haul him off to safety. And then the crazy fell. Jason clung to me, still unable to breath. Had he inhaled hot smoke? Had his lungs burned on the inside?

He let go of me, falling to the ground. I bent to pick him up but he pushed me away and threw up.

"I have to get you out of here," I said over the crackling flames and screams. Jason wiped his mouth and stood, still coughing. "You inhaled too much smoke."

"I'm fine," he said between coughs.

"No, no you're not." We moved around another building and away from the smoke. Jason leaned against it, wheezing. I reached for my walkie and walked a few yards away, looking around the corner for crazies. I pressed the button and raised it to my mouth.

"Riss!" Wade shouted. I looked up and saw a crazy running toward me. He was holding something, something that looked familiar. Oh shit. The crazy cradled the Molotov cocktail against his chest. Fire burned on the cloth stuffed into the jar. "Look out!"

But it was too late. The cocktail exploded before I had a chance to get away.

CHAPTER SEVEN

Blood and guts splattered over me. I closed my eyes. Something warm and thick dripped down my face. I held my arms out, horrified. Had bits of glass torn open my skin? If they had, I was infected for sure.

"Orissa," I heard Jason pant. The bow slid down my arm and clattered to the ground.

"Fuck," Wade said. Boots pounded on the pavement. I hoped it was him running over and not a crazy. I couldn't open my eyes without getting some sort of crazy juice in them. "You ok?" he asked, just inches from me.

I nodded.

"Hang on." He moved closer and wiped my face with the hem of his shirt. "That's as good as it's gonna get."

I opened my eyes. My eyelashes stuck together. I looked down at myself. My entire front was covered head to toe in red. I picked part of, what looked like, an ear off my arm.

"She ok?" Jason wheezed and made his way over.

I nodded again, still not wanting to open my mouth and risk tasting a crazy.

"Let's get out of here," Wade said.

I didn't object. He took the walkie from my belt, grimacing when his fingers became covered in blood, and radioed to Ivan and Brock. They were still fighting off crazies and said they would meet us at the bridge.

I picked up my bow, the grip slippery with blood. The three of us took off, not stopping until we go to the bridge. A crazy stood in the water, putting out the flames that spread across her back. Wade shot her in the chest. She fell and blood washed out, staining the water. We crossed the bridge and turned, waiting for Ivan and Brock.

I looked into the water. The bank wasn't steep. I hurried down it, going a few feet upstream from the dead crazy. I knelt down and cupped my hands, splashing water on my face.

It smelled like dead fish. But it was better than having liquefied human parts on my lips. I rubbed water on my arms, washing away some of the splatter.

"They're coming," Wade said.

I hurried back up to the bridge. We didn't hesitate. As soon as Ivan and Brock set foot on the wooden bridge, we took off, racing through the woods and not stopping until we were in the parking lot by the SUV. Ivan unlocked it and in a jumbled mess, we piled in.

"Everyone ok?" Brock asked from the front seat. Two rifles sat awkwardly in between his legs. He turned around, mouth falling open when he saw me.

"Not sure how it happened," I started.

"An S1 caught a cocktail I threw," Wade filled in. "And ran straight for her."

"Like a suicide bombing?" Jason asked, leaning forward. His cheeks were bright red from coughing.

"I don't know," Wade said, shaking his head. "I couldn't tell if he knew what it was. He caught it like a football and ran."

"And exploded all over me," I huffed.

"Did it get in you?" Ivan asked.

"I don't know." I looked at my boots. A molar was stuck in the laces. I shuddered.

His question hung in the air. Was I infected?

* * *

"Jesus, Riss." Hayden's eyes slid down my body. "What the fuck happened?" He had been waiting at the guard tower for us to arrive back home. I got out of the Range Rover as soon as I saw him. He put his hands on my arms, which were crusted in crazy goo.

"Ever wonder what happens if a crazy holds a Molotov cocktail when it goes off?" I gave him a wry smile, but inside I was panicked.

"Are you ok?" Worry aged his handsome face.

I shook my head. "I want to shower. Like yesterday."

Hayden stared at me. "Yeah. Of course. Go," he said, looking at the SUV. "I'll catch up."

"Bring me clothes?" I asked. "I don't want to go in our room like this."

"I don't want you to either." Hayden wrinkled his nose. "Yeah I will."

I got back into the Range Rover, squeezing in next to Jason. Ivan stopped in front of the brick house. I went straight inside and down to the quarantine room.

"Sick," I said when I took off my boots. The laces were gooped to the leather. I put them inside a garbage bag. I shoved my clothes into a bag as well, tying it shut. I should take them out back to be burned.

I pulled the drain stop on the sink and began filling it with hot water. I took Hayden's dog tags off and dropped them in the water and then undid the clasp to a delicate chain. A single silver leaf hung from it. Belonging to my grandma, the charm had great sentimental value. I swished the necklaces around in the water until the dried blood softened. Then I scrubbed them clean and got in the shower.

Hayden brought me yoga pants and a t-shirt but forgot a bra and underwear. I sat on the closed toilet wrapped in a towel—inspecting my body one more time for open wounds and waiting for him to come back with underwear. Thankfully, I found no cuts or gashes in my skin. Once dressed, I sat on the couch.

"Are you staying?" I asked Hayden, who sat next to me. He wrapped his arms around me and pulled me in, lying down so that I was resting on top of him.

"Yes," he said softly and kissed me. I moved my wet hair over my shoulder and put my head on his chest. "That was awful," he told me. "I'm not doing it again."

I lifted my head up. "You freaked out, didn't you? Not knowing what we were doing or what danger we were in caused you to panic, right?" I smiled and Hayden laughed.

He hugged me tight. "You know damn well I go crazy without you."

"Maybe you'll go crazy with me," I mumbled. It still scared me to think that I had been covered head to foot in pureed crazy. "I should probably have Dr. Cara test me."

Hayden sat us up. "You should. Now."

* * *

He went with me to the hospital ward. Jason and Wade were still there, getting treated. Olivia was taking care of Jason and I couldn't help but smile. Though we had never had a chance to finish our conversation, I knew what Jason had been getting at back at the coaster. He caught my gaze. I wiggled my eyebrows and pointed to Olivia, whose back was to me. Jason flushed.

Dr. Cara was off today so Karen, another one of our nurses, tested my blood. She said she didn't see any traces of the virus but would have Padraic or Dr. Cara go over it later that day to be sure.

Hayden and I headed back to the quarantine room along with

Wade and Jason.

When we got there, Ivan was in the shower and Brock stood in the small kitchen area warming up a bowl of pasta that had been put in the mini fridge for us. He dished it out in bowls; I grabbed one and plopped down on the couch.

"Is anyone gonna wonder why you're in here?" I asked Hayden and put a spoonful of pasta in my mouth. I didn't care if anyone did, but I assumed Hayden would.

He shrugged. "Maybe. It's getting late," he said and looked at the clock. "So it's not like I'd be doing anything, uh, official anyway."

I bent my legs up so that they rested on Hayden and smiled. Jason put in a movie and the six of us eventually settled on the couches.

"Tired?" Hayden asked me half way throughout the movie. His arms were around my waist. I tipped my head up.

"Yeah. And sore. My hands still hurt."

He put his hands around mine, bringing them up. "They're scabbed over already." They had scabbed over before the crazy had thrown the cocktail, so I hoped that would be good enough. I hoped Padraic or Doctor Cara would give me good news.

Hayden laced his fingers through mine and nestled his head into my neck, gently nipping at my skin. I closed my eyes and arched my back, leaning into his chest. I twisted and wrapped my arms around him. "Lay down," he suggested and stretched his legs out in front of him. The couch wasn't comfortable. We moved to one of the twin beds in the back of the room.

"I'm glad you're with me," I said to Hayden as we climbed under the covers. He put his arm around my waist again, spooning me.

"I wouldn't be anywhere else." He brushed my damp hair over my shoulder and kissed my neck. "I love you, Orissa."

"I love you, too," I whispered and closed my eyes. It only took a few minutes for me to fall asleep.

I woke up several hours later and was uncomfortably hot from being snuggled next to Hayden and under a thick comforter. I wasn't going to move away from my Marine, so I kicked the comforter down and exposed my arms to the cool air.

I wiggled closer to Hayden. Even in sleep, he held me tight. I could feel his chest rising and falling with each breath. Just the sound of him breathing was comforting. I held onto his arms and never wanted a night to go by without Hayden being with me.

* * *

For the next few days, the crazy in the basement was the talk of the compound. It was odd, hearing the residents gossip about one lonely crazy with such fear. They had no idea what we had encountered at the theme park or what we encountered on any of our missions. And Hayden wanted to keep it that way. There was no reason to ignite terror in everyone, he had said more than once during the meetings.

The story of how the crazy burst through the hospital ward doors, running full speed at me, twisted and grew each time it was retold like a game of Chinese telephone. In the end, it was made out to sound like I single handedly took out a giant, super-strong maniac who came at me snarling and swinging with dagger like fingernails and very sharp teeth. It was far from the truth. But I could live with that.

Alex and his group had left three days ago, the day after we came back from Dogpatch. And then things went back to normal. I went to training every morning just like before. It took a lot of convincing—verbally and physically—to get Hayden to change the time and allow us to sleep in an extra hour and a half.

Since Hayden was busy going over the unofficial policies Fuller had written up with Hector, I decided to go outside and have a look at the cabins. The construction had been put on a halt while we were waging a battle on Eastmoore and just recently resumed.

The brick estate was surrounded by tall chain link fences and ditches had been dug on the outside of these fences. I blinked in the sun and scanned my eyes over our defenses. I remembered when I first arrived here; the place looked utterly normal and abandoned. Even the solar panels and the huge wind mills didn't give it away. It was normal for businesses and large houses to switch to natural sources of energy. The price of fuel had risen to a fucking ridiculous price prior to the zombies.

Now it was quite obvious that this old brick estate housed survivors. Still, I doubted anyone would suspect that the house was just a rouse for what laid beneath. I crossed the yard, stopping at a large pen. Almost every dog raced over when they heard the metal latch clinking open. I wedged in, holding up my hands at the jumping dogs. Once the initial excitement was over, only one remained by me, wagging his nub of a tail.

"Hey buddy," I said to Argos and sat on the trampled grass. The Doberman pushed his face against my chest. I wrapped my arms around him in a hug. "I missed you, boy. Want to go for a walk?"

His ears perked up at the sound of the word. I stood, slipping my hands through his collar. I picked up a slobbery tennis ball and threw it. The pack of dogs took off after it, giving Argos and I enough time to slip through the gate.

Happy to be free from the pen and the other dogs, Argos took off, racing away from me and out of sight. It wasn't anything unusual. The dog always came back. And we were still surrounded by fences. Still...it unnerved me to have him out of my sight. I went around the house. The cabins were located in what would have been the backyard. The grass around the construction sites had been hacked away with electric weed whackers. We weren't going to waste gas mowing.

Extension cords snaked through the yard, coming from the side of the compound. A few A3s stood guard, holding rifles and looking bored. They snapped their attention up when they saw me, straightening their shoulders and taking a proper grip on their weapons.

"Hello, Orissa," a teenage boy said to me. He fiddled with the safety on his gun and smiled nervously.

"Hi," I said, looking for his name tag. Hayden could rest easy knowing he wasn't the only one who didn't know anyone's name...though it wasn't as if I had taken the time to try and learn. His badge was flipped around. Damn it. "How's it going?" I asked just to be polite.

"Oh good," he said, his brown eyes glued to mine. "They're almost done with the first one."

I took a step away and nodded. There were bases for six structures. They were small; the cabins would only have the basic necessities and how to install running water was still being worked out.

Raeya had gone over the designs with me plenty of times and promised they would look modern and clean, not old fashioned and dark like I imagined. The cabins had an open floor plan: the kitchen, living room, and dining room were all one large open room. If a bathroom could be added, it would be in the back. The sleeping quarters were in the second story loft. The ladder could be removed in case of a zombie attack, safely stowing away whoever hid inside. Or at least that was the plan.

I ducked under a hanging cord and stepped into the first cabin. The walls and floor were plywood, which took away any feelings of this place being a real home. There was a spot for one window next to the front door. Eventually, it would be barred. I walked to the kitchen, happy to see the counters and stainless steel sink. There was a spot for a stove and a refrigerator. Maybe Raeya was right after all. With a little decor and furniture, these little cabins would be totally livable.

The smell of freshly cut wood filled the air and dust particles floated in front of me, made visible by the streaming sunlight. I slowly turned, taking in the insulation that poked out around the door. I had hoped Hayden and I would move out here, though now I wasn't sure. With his new job, it wouldn't make sense for him to leave the compound.

I chatted with the construction workers for as long as I could stand. I used training as an excuse to leave again and wandered around the yard looking for Argos. Assuming he had gone back to the pen with the other dogs, I wasn't too worried.

I tipped my head up to the sun, wishing for the day when I could spread a towel out on the sand and relax with a drink in my hand. The beach Raeya and I had gone to in our youth was nothing more than a manmade sandbar dumped around a lake. But we had spent many summers there, and each one was as enjoyable as the last.

I closed my eyes, letting my guard down, and rolled my neck. Along with a beach I wanted a massage. I was getting a little tired of being constantly sore, though this time it was my fault for lifting more than I should have while working out that morning.

A soft breeze blew the loose strands of hair that had fallen out of my braid. I tipped my head up, enjoying the day. The distant sound of barking floated around the house. I should have brought a ball. Maybe Argos would have stayed near me to play. I went around the back of the house to find him.

A strangled yell came from the quarantine barn. My heart skipped a beat and my blood ran cold. The crazy erupted in gargling growls that twisted into manic laughter.

And then Argos yelped, the pitiful sound echoing through the narrow halls of the barn.

CHAPTEREIGHT

I raced through the yard. The tall grass painfully whipped at my thighs as I ran. I didn't slow down until I was in the quarantine barn. I blinked, unable to see in the dim hall.

"Argos!" I shouted as my eyes tried to adjust. I squeezed them shut and shook my head, as if that would help somehow. The crazies at the end of the barn thumped against the stall doors, screeching and growling.

And I heard Argos whimper.

I opened my eyes, desperately scanning the aisle. I didn't see the dog. Oh God, had he somehow been pulled into the stall? I flew to the end of the barn, and slid to a stop. The young crazy in the homey stall reached through the bars. Electricity sizzled as it shocked her, and the scent of charred skin filled the air.

"Argos," I called again. My stomach tightened. I was scared to look in the stall but I didn't hesitate. If he was in there, I might still have a chance to get him out, to save him.

But he wasn't there. I pushed my hands off the wooden stall and moved to the next one. The crazy was at the front, snarling. His eyes were gray and clouded over. He was changing as the virus progressed. I didn't have time to think about it. I had to find Argos.

He yelped and barked again. I jerked my head to the side, looking out the door at the end of the barn. Terror rippled down my spine when I realized that the fence was only yards away. I spun and raced out of the barn.

"Shit," I breathed when I caught sight of the black and tan dog. He was against the fence. Literally. One of his paws was through the links and a zombie had a hold of it. She was standing in the moat and her face was level to the ground. Blood dripped down Argos's fur and the zombie bit down harder.

I didn't have any weapons. My heart pounded. I was there, right next to Argos, in just seconds. I wrapped my hand around his leg, hands shaking. I didn't know what to do. If I pulled, the flesh would rip right off his leg. Argos squirmed back.

"Hold on, boy," I panted. Without thinking, I stuck my hand through the fence and grabbed the zombie by the hair. Her tresses were slimy and coated my hand with goo in seconds. But I didn't let go. I curled my fingers, dug my nails into her scalp, and pulled.

She let go of Argos. He scrambled back, holding his right leg up in the air. The zombie turned faster than I expected. I yanked my arm back and my hand caught in the link. I needed to close my fist and tuck my thumb in to fit it through.

The zombie closed her fingers around my hand. Argos bolted forward, fiercely barking at the zombie. I rocked back and put my feet against the fence. She tugged on my hand, trying to pull it to her mouth. Though she was undead, she was strong, and being several feet lower than me gave her an advantage.

"Let go, you undead bitch," I muttered through clenched teeth. Her nails scraped off a layer of skin. Suddenly she stopped pulling me toward her and moved her face closer, bringing her teeth to my skin. Argos lunged at the fence, his nose bumping into the metal. The zombie turned her attention to him.

That was all I needed. I pressed my foot against the fence and pushed off. My hand, slick with blood, slipped from her grasp. I fell back and landed on the ground. Shaking, I sat up. My hand throbbed, but that didn't matter.

"Argos," I said weakly. He was still barking at the zombie. "Argos!" His fur was on end. He kept his right leg tucked close to his body, unable to put weight on it but he was still barking, still showing his fangs and growling. He would protect me to the very end.

I moved over to him, slipping my fingers under his collar. I pulled him back. He snapped his attention away from the zombie, sniffing me. Then he licked my face, his cropped tail wagging.

I wrapped my arms around him, trembling. "Good dog," I whispered and let out a breath. The zombie rattled the fence. I held onto Argos for another few seconds before getting up. I kept a hold of his collar and jogged into the quarantine barn. I needed something—anything—that could be used to kill the zombie. My eyes darted around, settling on a broom.

Hunched over to keep a grip on Argos, and we scurried down the aisle. I grabbed the broom and ran back to the fence.

"Sit," I told Argos. His fur rose when he got sight of the zombie but he listened. I knelt on the ground, lining the handle of the broom up with the zombie's mouth. The blunt end made it difficult to kill her. But luckily she had started to rot from the inside out and after only a few shoves, the handle popped through the back of her throat and into her brain. She instantly went limp and slid down.

"What. The. Fuck," I said slowly. I pulled the broom backwards and out of the fence. I tossed it aside and looked down inside the moat. It was deep, too deep for her to be at ground level. Either she was freakishly tall or...

"There's a body pile," I said out loud and looked at Argos. Three bodies were piled on top of each other like a festering step stool. The ground at the base of the fence had been clawed at. A shiver ran down my spine. The zombie was digging *under* the fence. I leaned back, taking it all in. I blinked and jumped to my feet. "Shit, Argos."

He was still holding his leg up. A steady stream of blood trickled down from the flap of fur and skin that hung lose above his ankle. I turned to the house; it was too far for him to walk. I bent over, wrapping my arms around his body, and gently picked him up.

"Shhh, it's ok," I soothed when he balked at being held. "It's ok, boy." I ground my teeth. Argos was gonna be ok...he had to be. Guilt bubbled in my stomach. I shouldn't have let him wander off. I should have kept a better eye on him.

Argos was heavy. I was in excellent shape, but my arms were tired by the time we got to the house. I put my leg up, balancing Argos against my knee as I punched in the code.

"Get Jack!" I called to the A3 who stood guard inside the foyer. "Now!" I tried to keep my voice steady. I failed. My jean shorts were wet from Argos's blood. He had stopped struggling to be put down. My heart was sinking and the guilt was rising. Argos had to be ok. He just had to.

The A3 looked at us, wide eyed. "What the fuck are you waiting for?" I yelled, my fear slipping through. "Open the goddamn door and get Jack!"

He nodded and sprung from his post. He opened the door for us then scrambled past to fetch the veterinarian.

I didn't even think about it; I took Argos straight to the hospital ward. I used my foot to push open the doors. Olivia was sitting at a desk at the entrance.

"Oh my God," she said and stood, rushing around to us. Her eyes flitted over Argos, wanting to help. She hadn't received any training for tending to animals, but that didn't stop her. "Put him on the bed." She pointed to the first bed before racing into the supply room. I had just laid Argos down when she returned with bandages and alcohol.

Padraic, who was on duty, saw Olivia running out of the medical supply room and ran out of his little office. He must have been thinking a person was injured.

"Orissa," he exclaimed. "Are you—" he cut off when I stepped to the side. "What happened?" He flew to the bed and put his hand on Argos.

"He went to the fence," I rushed out. My hands were still shaking as I held Argos down. "There was a zombie and she bit him."

"He's infected?" Olivia asked, her voice high and full of fear.

"No," Padraic said. His blue eyes were clouded with worry. "The virus doesn't affect animals."

Argos tried to get up. All three of us held him down, soothing him at the same time. The hospital doors thrust open and heavy, shuffling footfalls came from behind us.

"Let me have a look," Jack said, his voice scratchy. Olivia stepped back, letting the vet in. Argos whined and put his head down. Tears pricked the corners of my eyes. I bit my lip and forced them back. "Hold his head," Jack told Padraic. Padraic gently cupped Argos's head in his hands, bringing his muzzle away from his injured leg.

Argos yelped and jumped when Jack inspected the bite. "Please tell me he was in a dog fight," he said without looking up.

"Zombie," was all I managed to say. I took a shaky breath. "Is he going to be all right?"

Jack put Argos's leg back on the bed. "Yes. He needs stitches. I've treated worse," he told me with a small smile. My stomach unclenched a tiny bit. "Keep him still. I have to get my kit to sedate him."

He went into the supply room, returning with a black leather bag. Anxiety coursed through me and I watched him draw something up in a needle and inject it into Argos. In a few seconds, the dog relaxed.

"He's not knocked out," Jack told us. "So you need to hold him." The three of us nodded, arranging ourselves around Argos so that we wouldn't be in the way.

"Need better lighting?" Padraic asked.

Jack looked up at the distantly spaced fluorescent before nodding. We wheeled the bed a few feet into the hall so that it was directly under a rectangle of light.

I felt a little sick when Jack started stitching the wound closed. The same thing had happened when I saw the awful injury getting shot had caused Hayden. There was something about seeing someone I cared about hurt that unsettled me.

Olivia folded a comforter in half and laid it on the floor. She piled another blanket onto that, making a comfortable bed for Argos. Once Jack was done, we carefully moved Argos to the blankets where he would be under observation for the next several hours to monitor for dehydration. He would be given an IV if necessary.

I tightly crossed my arms over my chest and looked at Argos. Although he didn't appear to be in any pain, I felt awful.

"It's not your fault," Padraic said softly.

I turned, unaware that he was behind me. I sighed. "Yeah, it is." I shook my head. "I should never have brought him out."

Padraic put his hand on my shoulder. "Riss, I'm guessing you brought him out of the pen so he could play and run."

I nodded and clenched my jaw.

"You were being nice. I bet he misses the days when he could run in a big open area."

I blinked back tears when the memory of Argos running around my grandparent's farm flashed into my mind. The emotion was only apparent on my face for a second. But Padraic caught it. His blue eyes met mine in concern.

"Hey," he said softly and put his hand on my arm. "He's gonna be just fine. Trust me. I'm a doctor," he added with a smile.

It wasn't just Argos. It was this whole damn thing, with everything going back to the day Zoe died and I let Finicus run away. Had zombies gotten that stupid animal? Or did he starve to death, not knowing how to fend for himself after years of being Aunt Jenny's spoiled house cat.

As hard as I tried, I couldn't return Padraic's smile. He pulled me in for a hug. I had forgotten how slender yet firm he was. I rested my head on his shoulder and put my hands on his back.

"Orissa," he said softly. "Don't blame yourself."

I closed my eyes and tried to let go of all the shit that had built up inside of me. I had been so concerned with Hayden and his happiness that I hadn't realized I was stressed as well.

The hospital ward doors opened. I looked over Padraic's shoulder to see Hayden rushing in. He slowed, taking in the sight of my arms around Padraic. Was that jealousy that flashed across his handsome face?

"Are you all right?" he asked, the question sounding forced. Padraic let me go, sliding his hands down my arms. His eyes met mine and he gave me one more reassuring smile before he let his hands fall to the side.

"I am," I said and stepped over to Hayden. "This isn't my blood." I waved my hands at the front of my shorts and then motioned to Argos.

Hayden put his arms around me, shaking his head. "I just heard you ran to the hospital ward covered in blood...again. They didn't say anything about a dog." He crushed me against him, and I couldn't help but wonder if his enveloping embrace was overdone for show.

"Who told you?" I asked, my lips brushing against his neck.

"I don't remember their names," Hayden confessed. "Some teenage girls." He leaned back, looking into my eyes. "I should have known they were being dramatic." He smiled, his hazel eyes brightening.

Being this close to Hayden, even in the company of others, made my heart skip a beat. I wanted to tell him he had nothing to be jealous of. There was no one for me but him. Hayden flicked his eyes to Jack, who was busy pretending not to notice our intimate greeting. Olivia, who was sitting on the floor with Argos, already knew about our couple status.

"How did he get attacked?" Hayden asked and took a step back, letting go of me. I subconsciously reached up and pulled on the chain that his dog tags hung from.

"Zombie."

"What?" Hayden was completely taken aback. He must have assumed it was a dog fight.

"It was by the fence," I said softly.

Hayden's eyes narrowed in question.

"It freaking stood on a pile of dead zombies and was clawing at the ground like it was going to tunnel its way in here." The words sent a chill down my spine. "Don't worry, I killed it.

I could feel his stress level go through the roof. I took his hand, giving it a squeeze. For several seconds, Hayden didn't move. He just looked into my eyes and held onto my hand. Then he blinked. His body tensed and his nostrils flared, just like they do when he's having a flashback from his days in the war.

"Hayden," I said and gave his hand a tug.

"You're all right?" he asked again.

"Yes. Perfectly fine."

His fingers moved over the new scratches on my hand. He frowned and lifted it up, inspecting the torn skin. "So fine."

I yanked my hand back. "It's no big deal."

"Have it looked at?" he asked.

Padraic, having heard, came over and took my hand from Hayden. "It's not deep," he stated. "But this needs to be cleaned." He moved my hand closer to his face. "This is from fingernail scratches, right?"

"Yes," I sighed, knowing both he and Hayden were going to make a bigger deal out of it than necessary. It wasn't like I hadn't been scratched by zombies before. Nevertheless, I didn't object when Padraic scrubbed it with soap, slathered ointment on, and then bandaged my hand.

"Where was the zombie?" Hayden asked.

I knelt down to pet Argos. "Inside the moat."

"I know that, I mean where along the fence."

"Oh." I ran my hand over Argo's muzzle. "By the quarantine barn." I stood. "Like literally parallel to it." My eyes met Hayden's. "There are crazies in the barn."

"You think it was trying to get to them?"

I nodded. "Why else would it be so determined to get under the fence?"

"But the step stool made out of zombies..." he trailed off shaking his head. "Zombies can't do that. There's just no way."

"Maybe it wasn't a zombie when it fell in," Olivia said shyly.

I looked at her, a smile forming on my face. "You're brilliant."

Her cheeks turned red and she looked away.

"And it makes sense." I said. "A crazy would be able to pick up and move shit. It would be alive enough to think of something like that. But it wasn't able to get fresh meat, or stomachs, or water, or whatever Dr. Cara said they need to keep from turning into zombies."

"So it stacked the bodies and then turned." Hayden ran a hand through his hair. "We got lucky."

"Argos didn't," I mumbled.

Hayden looked away from me and at the dog. "If he hadn't discovered that zombie, we probably wouldn't have until it was too late." He sat on the floor to pet Argos. "Kids go outside, Riss. That could have ended horribly."

I bit my lip and felt oddly emotional. Argos opened his eyes, looking up at me. I scratched under his chin. "We need to have people patrol the moats every day." It had been done only a few times a week. "And whatever is killed needs to be taken out and burned. No more leaving it in there."

Hayden nodded. "I can arrange for that to happen." He sighed. "It makes me nervous for our animals."

A lump formed in my throat. Just when things seemed to be going smoothly, giving us hope that we were going to survive this, we hit a setback. Hayden put his hand on mine.

We would get through this. Somehow, someway, we would make it work.

* * *

Padraic brought Argos into his room every night. It was the

normal routine for the dog, but with him being injured and me feeling horribly guilty about it, I wanted him upstairs with me.

I carried him up the stairs and through the house. My arms were tired and sore by the time we reached my room. I set him down on the bed, trying to get him to stay put. Jack had told me there was no reason Argos couldn't put weight on his leg; it was a skin tear that hadn't even gone into the muscle. Still, I was babying the dog.

Around eight that night, Argos started pawing at the door. I had just taken him out, so I knew that wasn't what he wanted. I shook his food bowl; he wasn't hungry. He didn't want water and wouldn't play fetch. He pawed at the door again.

"You want to go to your normal bed?" I asked and opened the door. Argos walked out of the room, sniffing the floor in the hall. "I'll take you," I told him and let him walk to the stairs. I picked him up and carried him down.

The halls were dimmed, and many of the residents were turning in for the night. Argos's nails ticked as he jogged along. Light spilled out from under the door of Hayden's office. I hesitated. He said he was going to go over Fuller's notes again. I didn't want to bother him, but I couldn't just pass him up, could I?

I stopped and put my ear to the door. "Hayden?" I softly called. A chair scooted on the tile.

"Riss?" he said.

"Yeah."

After a second he opened the door.

"Late night?" I asked.

Hayden frowned and put his head in his hands. "Again. Want to help?"

"Of course." I smiled. "And by help do you mean bend me over the desk and have your way with me again?"

Hayden only half smiled and tipped his head back. I looked past him and saw Hannah sitting at the desk. Her arms were folded on the surface, cradling her head. She had fallen asleep. I stepped in, Argos following close behind, and closed the door, turning the knob so as not to wake up Hannah. Argos immediately started sniffing everything he could in the new room.

Hayden was tense. His hair was rumbled and black ink stained his fingertips.

"What's wrong?" I asked.

Hayden went back to the desk and sunk heavily into the chair. With a sigh he leaned forward, putting his head in his hands again. "I've been doing some math."

"Math gives me a headache too."

He shook his head and looked up. He hadn't shaved in a few days and purple circles hung under his eyes. "There are a lot of people here, Riss."

I perched on the edge of the desk. "And that's bad?"

"No, not at all. But it makes it hard to keep everyone fed."

"The gardens aren't really gardens anymore. They're more like fields. And Ray said everything is growing as well as we could hope, even in this drought."

"She's right." Hayden picked up a pen and turned it over between his fingers. "They are doing well, really well."

"But?"

"But plants only grow for so long. What are we going to do in the winter? We can't count on scavenging; it's not sure enough to have that be our only plan."

It hit me like a punch to the stomach. I remembered learning about some of the first settlers way back when I was in middle school. As a kid growing up in a modern world, I found it hard to believe that they spent the summer preparing for winter. But it had to be done.

And though our world was technically still modern, we were living just like those first settlers. Well, with zombies.

"We start canning stuff?" I tried.

Hayden shook his head. "We could do that and have enough for the winter. And not have anything now. There are just too many people."

Being hungry and not knowing where the next meal was coming from was awful. I had to endure it for several weeks before Hayden saved me. I crossed my arms. Goosebumps broke out along my skin. "And Sally—Sarah maybe—I don't know her name, is due in a few weeks. What if Alex can't get enough formula or baby food?"

"Breastfeed?" I said seriously. "It's healthier anyway, right?"

Hayden looked at me like he hadn't even thought about it. "Oh, right. And yeah." He nodded and crossed something off his list. I looked at it. He had messy handwriting. Ink was smeared over the paper. Words were scrawled across the page, some scratched out with the correction written above it. He had arrows going to the side of the page, pointing to more notes. It was nothing like the insanely organized and neat lists I was used to seeing from Raeya.

"I don't want to be the one to say we can't take in more people." He turned his head up to me. "Fuller never would have turned anyone away."

"That's why he picked you," I said carefully. "He knew you would do whatever it takes to keep this place safe."

Hayden's eyebrows pushed together. "Think of it Riss: we go out on a mission and find people. We help them, save them from zombies. And then leave them? No." He put his hands on the desk and shook his head. "No. I couldn't do it."

"Then we will bring them back."

"Back here to starve."

"Hey," I said gently and moved behind him. I put my hands on his shoulders. "No one is going to starve. We'll figure it out. We always have."

He put his hand on mine and then swiveled the chair around, reaching for me. His hands settled on the curves in my waist. "What would I do without you?"

"You'll never have to know." I stepped in closer.

"Get a room," Hannah mumbled, lifting her head off her arms. Crease marks indented her face. She leaned back, running her hands over her hair. It struck me just how much she looked like her brother.

"This *is* my room," Hayden said and let his hands fall onto his lap. He spun the chair around. "You can go to bed," he told her.

She shook her head. "I said I'd help you."

Hayden put his elbows on the desk and cupped his face in his hands. "I think I'm done for the night."

She stood. Argos got up from where he had settled to sniff her. Hannah bent down to pet him. "I met all the dogs," she said, flicking her eyes to me. "I like that people are allowed to bring their pets here." Then her face broke, tears welling in her eyes. "I miss Snowball."

Hayden rushed over to his sister and awkwardly put an arm around her. "Me too," he said softly, his hazel eyes going misty.

"Who's Snowball?" I asked.

"Our dog," Hayden told me. "Hannah, what happened to him?"

She wiped her eyes with the back of her hand. "Heather brought him with and...and..." she started crying and turned to Hayden, wrapping her arms around him. Hayden hesitated for a split second then hugged his sister, pulling her close. "After she..." Hannah couldn't say it, but I knew what she meant. Their sister had died from the virus. "Zombies got him."

I closed my eyes, abhorrence making me dizzy. I crossed the room and knelt down next to Hayden and Hannah. Argos moved to lick my face. "I'm really sorry," I said to both of them.

"Hayden got Snowball for our mom on Mother's Day," Hannah said between sobs. I put my hand on Hannah's shoulder. She let go of Hayden and turned to me. "He was really old. He didn't stand a chance against them."

Hayden rocked back and sat on the tile floor. His eyebrows pushed together and he ground his teeth, trying so hard to remain stoic. Keeping her broken arm close to her body, Hannah gave Argos a one armed hug.

"Hayden put him in a box," she said. "It was a surprise so we kept him hidden." A smile crept onto her face. "We tried to get our mom downstairs to open her presents, but it took her forever, remember?"

Hayden nodded. "What was she doing? Her makeup or hair or something." He put his arm around his sister's shoulders. She leaned on him. He looked past her to me. "By the time she came downstairs, Snowball was covered in poop."

Hannah laughed. "It smelled so bad! I can still see the look on Mom's face when she took the lid off the box."

Hayden smiled. "And I was the one who had to clean him up. It took days to get the brown out of his fur," he laughed.

My heart broke for them. I hated seeing Hayden upset; seeing him hurt was even worse. I put my hand on Hayden's thigh. Argos, feeling left out, weaseled his way onto my lap. Careful not to bump his stitches, I lugged him onto my legs. His nubby tail thumped against me.

"What happened to your family?" Hannah asked me.

I shook my head. "I don't know."

"It sucks, doesn't it?" She wiped her eyes again, blinking hard to get rid of the tears. "It was like I didn't have a chance to be sad before, ya know? We were too busy running, too busy being scared."

I knew exactly what she meant. "Yeah."

She inhaled. "And now that I'm here..." She shook her head and turned to Hayden. "It still scares me that this isn't real, that you never found me."

Hayden squeezed her hand. "It's real, Hannah." Then guilt clouded his face. "I looked for you. You, Mom, and Heather. I was there; I was home."

"Hay," she started, "we were gone before you got there."

He only nodded. I wanted to tell him that she was right, that there was no way he could have saved everyone. He shouldn't blame himself. I kept my mouth shut because I felt the same way. What if I had left the hospital sooner? Would I have found Aunt Jenny? Maybe we could have gotten Raeya and gone to Kentucky before my grandpa left.

But then I wouldn't have met Hayden and Padraic, Jason, and the rest of the people from the basement...would they still be alive?

"So when are you two getting married?" Hannah asked, changing the subject. Hayden's eyes met mine and he shrugged. "What, you haven't picked a date yet?"

"It's not like we have to reserve a venue," I told her.

"I know. But it's something to look forward to, ya know? And it would be fun to plan a wedding, like a happy distraction for us."

I looked at Hayden again. We were worried about making it through the winter. I wanted to marry Hayden. I didn't need a special day or decorations to prove it. "Maybe," Hayden said to humor her. "You can start thinking about it."

Hannah smiled. "Ok!" She looked at me. "I don't know you well enough—yet."

Oh joy...she wanted to spend more time with me. But I smiled anyway. One way or another Hannah would become my family. "Just talk to my friend Raeya about it. She's had my wedding planned for years."

"I will! Our mom was always worried Hayden would never get married," she whispered to me, loud enough for Hayden to hear. "She was waiting for grandchildren. And let's face it, Hay, you weren't getting any younger."

"I'm twenty-eight. That's not old," he balked.

Hannah rolled her eyes and put her hands on Argos's neck, scratching him.

Hayden's stomach grumbled.

"Hungry?" I asked. He had skipped dinner and I was confident he hadn't gone into the cafeteria and gotten himself a snack.

"Yeah," he answered.

"I'll get you something," I offered.

"That'd be nice." He stood and stretched before holding out a hand to help Hannah to her feet.

I slowly got up, my muscles a bit sore from working out.

"I'm going to finish here. I'll meet you upstairs," Hayden said.

I nodded and went to the door, patting my leg so Argos would follow. Hannah said goodnight to Hayden and left, walking with me down the hall.

"I think that was the longest we've gone without fighting," she said softly.

I looked at her. "How come you two never got along?"

She crossed her arms, pressing them into her chest. "I don't know." She sighed. "Yes, I do. I do know why. Hayden was always an overachiever. Looking back now, I know he didn't mean to be. He did whatever he could to help us. After our dad left, Hayden took over. I never realized until pretty recently how much he gave up for us. I'm six years younger than him. When we were kids all I saw was my older brother bossing me around, telling me what I can and can't do. And he could do no wrong. Hayden got away with murder and our mom was constantly bragging about him and everything he did."

Then she let her arms drop, her casted wrist swinging at her side. "And then he left. As much as I thought I hated him, I hated him being gone even more. I felt so...so abandoned if that makes sense. I really regret being so mean to him. All he ever did was try to help."

Well, shit. Hannah and I were more alike than I imagined. The way she felt about Hayden was pretty much the way I felt about my stepdad, Ted, and my own mother. All they wanted was to make my life better, to give me chances to help others and in turn, myself. But in my youth all I saw was my mom leaving me for someone she loved more, using mission trips as an excuse to get away from her only daughter.

"Yeah," I said. "I get it."

"You do?" she asked incredulously. We turned the corner.

"I do."

"You're not mad at me for being mean to Hayden?"

I shook my head. "I haven't seen you be mean to him. The past is the past, right?"

Her hazel eyes were wide. "Yeah, gosh, you're right. I guess this mess gives me a clean slate somehow, right?"

I wanted to think so. I regretted my past too. "Why not?" We stopped at a corner. Hannah hugged me goodbye and went down the hall to her room and I went the opposite way to Padraic's room.

* * *

Argos trotted ahead, knowing exactly where to go. He pawed at the door and pressed his nose along the crack. I leaned over him and knocked. Thirty seconds went by. I knocked again. Maybe Padraic was asleep.

"Padraic?" I said softly, putting my face near the door. "It's Orissa. I brought Argos."

Still, there was no answer. I put my fingers around the door knob and twisted. It wasn't locked and the door slowly opened. Dim light from a small lamp spilled across the room. And Padraic was nowhere in sight. His bed was still made; he was still up.

Argos pushed past me and jumped onto the bed, turning around in a circle before he lay down.

"Night, boy," I whispered and closed the door, wondering where Padraic was. I knew he wasn't working tonight and wouldn't be in the hospital ward unless there was an emergency. We needed to rescue another doctor. Poor Padraic was the only one we had.

I turned to go to the cafeteria and find something for Hayden to eat. Then I stopped. I had to check the hospital ward...just in case. I hurried through the quiet hall, stopping only when I pushed through the ward doors.

The B3 who was working tonight shot up from the desk near the door. His eyes ran over my body. I was about to tell him off for so blatantly checking me out when I realized he was looking for injuries. I guess I couldn't blame him...it wasn't uncommon for me to be bleeding.

"Is Padraic in here?" I asked.

"Yeah, he's in the back," he answered. I didn't remember his name, but I recalled his face. He had taken care of Hayden when he was healing from being shot. I quickly scanned him. He looked tired and bored. That was not the face of someone who had dealt with an emergency. Still, I wanted to know what Padraic was doing.

"Thanks," I said and hurried through the row of beds. There were two exam rooms, both with doors leading into the lab. Beyond that was a large room Padraic had set up for surgery, though I had heard him grumble about the non-sterile environment more than once.

I entered the first exam room not expecting to see Padraic. I crossed right through and opened the door to get into the lab. Right away, I was hit with a nasty odor.

"You have got to be freaking kidding me," I said under my breath and held my hand over my nose. Disembodied slices of zombie were set out on a table with a desk lamp pulled overhead, warming them up. I looked them over. Most of the samples were dissected to the point of being unrecognizable, though I was sure that one chunk of gray was a brain slice.

I moved around the table, repulsed by the smell. It was something I would never get used to no matter how many times I was exposed to it. How could Dr. Cara work like this? I suppose she had to...it wasn't like we had bottles of formaldehyde or anything.

I came to a sudden halt. Little speckles of blood dotted the tile and a scalpel with blood and blobs of thickened goo lay on the floor. A turned over tray lay on the floor, its contents strewn everywhere.

My chest tightened with unease. I stepped around the blood splatter. The harsh artificial light reflected off of some sort of body slice. It was dark red and moist. A few strands of Dr. Cara's hair stuck to it, at least it looked like her hair based on the texture, color, and length.

"What the...?" I shook my head. Maybe it was nothing. Dr. Cara was always spilling food on herself—and then not cleaning it up.

Maybe that's all this was: some sort of mishap where she'd dropped a tray full of crazy entrails.

I went to the surgery room and stopped at the door. People were in there, talking. Their voices were muffled, and I couldn't tell what was being said, but there was no mistaking that Irish accent.

"Padraic," I said and knocked.

"Riss?" he asked.

"Yeah."

"Good," he said and opened the door. His attractive face was muddled with worry. A prickly web of fear crept over me. "I'm glad you're here. I was just going to send someone to get you and Hayden."

"Get us? Why, what's going on?" I looked past him. Shante, a nurse, sat next to Dr. Cara, looking utterly pale. Dr. Cara's back was to me, but it looked like she was holding something.

"Cara," Padraic said and put his hand on the back of his neck, "she's infected."

CHAPTER NINE

"What?" I blinked and leaned away from Padraic, not wanting to believe his words. "How?"

Padraic looked behind me. "Come in," he said softly. I hurried in and shut the door. It took everything in me not to storm over to Dr. Cara and interrogate her. Though if she was crazy it wouldn't do any good.

Padraic, who knew me and my quick temper well enough, put his hand on my shoulder.

"She's like Hayden," he rushed out.

"What?" I asked, my voice shrill. I pulled my shoulder back and moved past him. I didn't even think about what he had said. Hearing Hayden's name and knowing Dr. Cara was infected was enough to make me angry.

"She's infected but not contagious," he said quickly. "Just like Hayden."

I whirled around, looking at Padraic. His blue eyes met mine and he nodded. Dr. Cara turned around in the chair she was sitting in. Her arm was bandaged. I looked next to her. Shante, who was shaking and pale, was wearing gloves. She tossed a bloody bandage in the trash.

"You!" I yelled, pushing past Padraic. Anger seared through me. "You brought that crazy in here and it bit you! Then you didn't say anything!" Padraic ran over, putting himself between Dr. Cara and me.

"How fucking stupid are you?" I shouted.

"Riss," Padraic said and held up his hands.

"No!" I said. "I can't believe you would do that! What if you were infected, *really* infected. And then went crazy and tore this place up? But you don't care, do you? All your care about is your fucking research!"

Shante stared at me, wide eyed. With trembling hands, she took off her gloves. Then she looked like she wanted to run out of the room as fast as she could. Dr. Cara cradled her injured arm close to her body.

"I needed to test the vaccine," she said.

"The vaccine?" I asked.

"Yes. I told you I was coming close to a breakthrough."

I opened my mouth, set on continuing to yell, but was at a loss for words. She tested the vaccine? On herself? Wait...it worked?

"Riss," Padraic said. "Let her explain."

I took a step back and crossed my arms. "This better be good," I muttered.

Dr. Cara stood. She had on a pair of candy cane striped pajama pants and an oversized t-shirt with a print screen wolf howling at a full moon. Her hair was in a twisted messy bun on the side of her head.

"Like I said, I was coming close to a breakthrough. I inactivated the virus and injected it intramuscularly. I waited forty eight hours then let the S1 bite me."

"But you're infected," I said pointedly.

"As is Hayden," she reminded me. Her eyes met mine. "He's not insane. The virus is in his body, but his body doesn't react to it," she said slowly, making sure I was following along. My heart sped up. Yes, Hayden was infected. He had been since the day he received his first bite. But nothing had happened to him.

"So this vaccine...it will keep people from turning into zombies?" I asked, feeling dizzy. I subconsciously fiddled with Hayden's dog tags.

"Theoretically," she answered.

"What's that supposed to mean?"

"I tailored this vaccine specifically to my body. And I took the virus from the same subject that bit me." Her gray eyes clouded over with disappointment. "I don't have the means to test this any further."

"What do you need?" I blurted. If she was this close to finding a vaccine, we couldn't stop now. This could be our saving grace.

"A proper lab," she stated. "And people to test the vaccine on."

"Oh." I let go of the dog tags. "Yeah, that's not gonna happen." I crossed my arms and inhaled. It killed me, being so close to an answer.

"We should tell Hayden," Padraic said.

I wanted to tell him no, that Hayden had enough to deal with right now. "I'll get him," I said, knowing it would be impossible for me to keep this from him. Besides, it was almost good news. Hayden could use some right now.

I left the hospital ward and sped down the hall to Hayden's office. There was no light spilling out from the crack under the door. Still, I tested the knob; it was locked. I hurried into the cafeteria, thinking Hayden might have stopped to get something to eat. He wasn't there either.

Great, he was upstairs and I was going to have to make him come back down here again. Cringing at the idea of bringing more stress to him, I walked through the halls and jogged up the stairs and into our room.

"Get lost?" Hayden said when I opened the door. He had taken his shirt off. The sight of him, half naked and tattooed, sent a tingle through my core. He unbuttoned his jeans. "Uh, forget something?"

I shook my head and crossed the room. "Stop," I said.

"Stop what?"

"Getting undressed. I have to tell you something."

Hayden pushed the button back. "What's wrong?"

"Nothing," I said quickly. "Dr. Cara tested the vaccine on herself and it worked."

Hayden inhaled, holding his breath. "Are you sure?"

I nodded and held out my hand. "She's in the hospital ward with Padraic right now."

Hayden picked up his shirt and yanked it over his head, not noticing that it was inside out until I told him. He fixed it then took my hand. We rushed out of the room together.

Shante had left the surgery room by the time we arrived. Padraic was sitting on a wooden stool with his arms crossed. His dark hair was rumpled and his shoulders sagged forward. He straightened up as soon as he saw Hayden and some of the tiredness in his eyes disappeared.

Dr. Cara, on the other hand, looked as if she was ready to fall asleep. She was leaning back in the chair, holding her right arm close to her body. Hayden stopped short. I didn't know what he had been imagining, but this wasn't it.

"Uh, I heard you found a vaccine," he said, eyes darting back and forth between Dr. Cara and Padraic.

"Yes," Dr. Cara said with a curt nod.

"And?" Hayden asked when she said no more.

"It worked."

"Yeah, I kinda got that." He moved closer to Dr. Cara. "Explain."

Dr. Cara took a deep breath. "I inactivated the virus from that S1 that I brought in here."

Hayden held up his hand. "How did you even do that?"

A smile crept across Dr. Cara's face. "It took some time." Then she launched into details of how she did it.

Hayden nodded. Was he following along? I was lost and getting bored. I looked around the surgery room. It was a mix of modern and old fashioned. We had scavenged equipment from hospitals, but obviously we hadn't been able to get anything big. The operating table was a refurbished exam bed and the lights that hung overhead were nothing more than hanging bulbs and a few fluorescents. The sterile surgical tools were wrapped in blue towels, stashed in a cabinet with glass doors. Strips of tape were across it, letting Padraic know when if it had been opened.

"So this *isn't* going to protect everyone from getting infected?" Hayden asked and rubbed his eyes. I felt so bad for him. He had to be fucking exhausted.

"No," Dr. Cara told him. "As I told Orissa, I have no way of testing this for mass production."

Hayden bit his lip and ran a hand through his hair, not knowing how good he looked when he did that. "Oh, ok." His hand fell and he pushed off the wall he had been leaning against. "Wait a minute." His eyes narrowed. "If you let that S1 bite you a few days ago, why are you bleeding?"

Shit, he was right. I hadn't even thought about that.

Shante came back in and sat next to her. The gloves the nurse wore were covered in blood.

"Since she was hiding her bite," Padraic answered. "The wound got infected."

"Of course it would," I mumbled. "Did you think to wash it? You're supposed to be a doctor."

Dr. Cara pressed her lips together. "I did clean it."

I raised my eyebrows. "Not very well."

"I didn't want to wash out the virus. I waited a day."

Padraic sighed. "The infection—the bacterial infection I mean—had gotten sealed in by that point. I gave her antibiotics and a pain pill. She should rest," he added and looked at Hayden. "But I wanted to make sure you were informed first."

Hayden nodded. "Good thinking. Uh, Cara, you can go back to your room."

She got up and scuttled out of the surgery room. Padraic let out a heavy sigh.

"That's it?" I asked, my arms going up. "You just let her go to her room as if nothing happened?"

"Riss," Hayden started. "Nothing—"

"Bullshit!" I interrupted. "She brought that thing in here and *let* it bite her! Don't you realize how stupid that was? What if she went crazy?" I whirled around and stared at Padraic. "What if you were in here? Or Olivia? We could have had two crazies on our hands. We all know that the crazies are evolving somehow. This could have ended so very badly and you just let her go to her room?" My voice was high and shrill. My ears grew hot and my heart raced.

"Riss," Hayden said, stepping close to me. He took one of my hands into his. "You're right." His fingers curled around mine. His words shocked me. Again, his understanding dissolved my argument in just seconds and he didn't try to tell me I was wrong. "She was reckless, so incredibly reckless. And trust me, every bad scenario has gone through my head. Even one involving you..." he trailed off, closing his eyes in a long blink. He shook his head. "But it didn't happen. And what can we do? Ground her to her room and ban her from the lab?"

I raised one shoulder in a shrug. "Sounds like a good idea to me."

Hayden pulled his arm back, moving me closer. I suddenly was very aware of Padraic's eyes on us. "Enough is going on right now," he said quietly. "I will try to monitor her better." He looked past me to Padraic. "You're her boss, technically. You are in charge of all the Bs."

I turned around to look at Padraic. His face was blank and I knew he didn't want to have to tell Dr. Cara what she could and couldn't do. "Yeah," he said. "I will ask her to run everything by me from now on."

"Thank you," Hayden said.

I tightened my hand on Hayden's and outstretched my other arm toward Padraic. His eyes flitted from me to Hayden and he hesitated before he stepped in, taking my hand. "I don't want anything bad to happen to you guys. It's so bad out there. In here...this is my safe place. And the thought of somebody making it anything but that pisses me off." I forced a smile.

Padraic smiled back. "It still is safe," he said right away. His voice was calm and he sounded so sure of himself that I almost believed him. There was something about Padraic that was so serene, so trusting, that he made me feel better just by talking to me. "You guys made it this way," he added softly. "You'll keep it safe."

Hayden's hand squeezed mine. "We will, Riss."

I nodded. "Good, because if this place goes..." I shook my head.

"It won't," Hayden and Padraic said at the same time. Padraic pulled his hand out of my grasp and took a step back.

"Get some sleep," he said to both of us. "You look like you could use it."

Hayden laughed. "Yeah, I could." His eyes moved to the mess of bandages and bloody gauze on the operating table.

"Go," Padraic said. "I'll clean up." He winked at me. "I have high standards when it comes to this room, anyway."

"All right. Night, Padraic," I said. Keeping ahold of my hand, Hayden said bye to Padraic and moved to the door. "Oh," I said when we got in the threshold. "I put Argos in your room."

"Thanks," Padraic said with a smile.

Hayden didn't let go of my hand when we walked through the hospital ward. The B3 at the desk eyed our fingers laced together and smiled politely as we left. We detoured to the cafeteria for food and then went up to our room for the night.

* * *

"Good morning." Hayden rolled over and put his arms around me.

I blinked open my eyes and smiled. My arms were already above my head; I stretched them out until my fingers hit the wall behind the bed. Hayden pulled me close and pressed his lips to my neck. I put my hands on his back, sticking my fingers under his shirt. He lifted his arms up, letting me pull it over his head. I threw it on the floor.

"You're so warm," he whispered, pressing his body against mine. I grabbed the hem on the back of his boxers and pulled him between my legs. I ran my fingernails up his back and through his hair. I arched my neck when he nipped at my skin. A shiver ran through me.

Hayden propped himself on his elbows and reached down, sticking his hand inside my panties, and pressed them against me. I softly moaned when his fingers started moving in slow circles. I could feel Hayden's desire start to grow, pressing hard against me. I grabbed the top of his boxers and tugged them down. I wrapped my fingers around his erection, slowly pumping my hand up and down. Hayden pushed my tank top up and moved his mouth to my breasts, his tongue circling my nipple.

Then the door burst open and Hannah jumped in "Surprise!" she exclaimed, arms open.

I froze. Did that really just happen?

Hannah's jaw dropped as if she couldn't believe what she had walked in on either. Her hands went to her face, covering her eyes. Hayden grabbed the blanket and pulled it over us.

"Jesus fucking Christ, Hannah!" he yelled. "Don't you know how to knock?" He flattened himself against me.

"Oh my God, oh my God," she muttered and turned around.

Hayden yanked his boxers on.

"I am so sorry!" She stepped out of the room.

"Close the door!" Hayden called after her.

Hannah still had her hands over her eyes. She bumped into the doorframe twice before she found the knob. "I just wanted to tell you happy birthday," she muttered. "You really should lock this next time." Then she slammed the door.

Hayden stared at the closed door for a few seconds before turning to me. He shook his head, hazel eyes flashing.

"Well that was awkward," he huffed.

"I didn't even realize it was your birthday," I blurted. Guilt grasped at my chest. "I stopped keeping track of days."

Hayden rolled off me, heavily plopping down on the mattress. "I did too," he confessed. "And I'm not exactly excited to be twenty-nine."

I straightened my top and turned onto my side. "You're old." I wrinkled my nose at him.

"You're only four years behind," he teased.

I stretched again and put my hand on Hayden's hip. "Still in the mood?"

Hayden snorted a laugh. "Not anymore. And knowing Hannah," he said and sat up and grabbed his boxers, "she's still in the hall, waiting for me."

"Then you should go," I said, pulling the blankets up to my chin. "She told me last night she's sorry for not getting along with you in the past. Take her horribly-timed happy birthday as an olive branch."

"You're awfully calm about all of this," he said, smirking as he put his pants back on.

I shrugged. "It's not the first time someone walked in on me during sex." I tried to say it casually but struggled to keep the smile off my face.

The smirk instantly faded. "That's not funny. I don't want to know about anyone else. Maybe. No, no I don't. I like to pretend you've only been with me."

I rolled my eyes. "Yeah, 'cuz I'm such an innocent virgin."

"You are. Well, were. Stop it. It's not funny," he repeated.

I laughed and reached for him, wrapping my hand around his arm. "Are you jealous of my ex-boyfriends?"

"Kinda," he said and scooped me up into his lap. "I wish we met a long time ago. So much time was wasted not being with you."

I pressed my head against his chest. His words stirred emotions in me and my heart swelled. I loved him so fucking much.

"I know," I said. "But then I wonder how different we'd be if we had met years ago."

"I'd be happy," he whispered. I turned my head up and kissed him.

"Ugh!" Hannah said as she opened the door. "Don't you people ever stop?"

Hayden and I broke apart. I moved off his lap and got out of bed. I was only wearing a tank top and underwear. I had never been shy about people seeing my body and I rarely stopped to think if others would be offended by it. Hannah's eyes ran down my legs.

"You are so muscular," she said flatly. "I'm kinda jealous."

"I work out a lot." I opened the bottom drawer of the dresser and pulled out a pair of shorts and tossed pajama pants to Hayden.

"How did you get up here?" he asked Hannah as he pulled on the pants.

"Ivan let me up. He didn't know it was your birthday either. Why didn't you tell people it was your birthday? Are you really that ashamed of your age? You shouldn't be since you don't look that old. Though you're way more covered in scars since I last saw you but that doesn't age you and I guess it doesn't matter as long as Orissa doesn't care since she's the only one who your appearance should matter to, ya know?"

Good lord that girl talked fast. I don't think she even stopped for air while she spoke. I pressed my lips together in a reminder to keep my mouth shut and be nice to her. How the hell did she remind me of a younger version of myself last night?

She sat on the other bed, bouncing on the mattress as she looked around the room. "I like your room. It's so normal. Except the bars on the window. It looks like a real room, though. Not that I'm complaining." She whipped her head back and forth in a manic shake. It was the first time I had seen her with her hair down. It fell a little past her shoulders and had a slight wave to it. I wondered if Hayden's hair would be wavy if it was longer.

"It's safer downstairs," I said and opened the closet, pulling out my bag of toiletries.

"I know," she said. "I can handle myself. Remember I survived a lot longer out there than you guys did." She shot Hayden a look.

He inhaled slowly, steadying his nerves. Hannah was on his last one. "Now you can relax."

"Right," she said, meeting my eyes. I tipped my head down just a bit, giving her a please-don't-start glare. "And I have been relaxing. It's so freaking nice to watch TV again!"

"The little things," Hayden sighed and straightened the blankets over our bed. I yanked the hair tie from the bottom of my braid. Several strands of hair snapped and broke. I raked my fingers through it, carefully working out a few big knots before brushing it.

"When is your breakfast time again?" Hannah asked. "Mine is the first session."

"We don't have a time," Hayden told her.

She raised her eyebrows. "Oh, since you're the boss and all, right?"

"I'm not the boss," Hayden told her. The stress that had slipped away overnight came crashing down on him. Little lines of worry appeared around his eyes and his shoulders suddenly became tense.

"Well whatever, hurry up and come with me."

"We still have forty-five minutes until breakfast," I said, looking at the clock. "Why are you up so early?" Our bed was calling my name. Resentment built up inside me. I was tired, stressed, and wanted nothing more than lazy morning sex with the man of my dreams and then to pass out naked and sweaty in his arms.

"I couldn't sleep. Well I could but only for a few hours. Then I woke up and couldn't fall back asleep and then I realized what day it was and had to come up and say happy birthday to my big brother."

"You could have waited," I said under my breath.

"Have you been sleeping?" Hayden asked, concerned.

Hannah shrugged. "Yeah enough."

Hayden didn't press. I flipped my head over and gathered my hair into a messy bun, too lazy to braid it again. I sorted through my pile of dirty clothes that I had discarded on the floor last night, looking for my bra.

"I want to shower before I go down," Hayden said, running a hand over his messy hair. It needed to be cut.

"Ok," Hannah said, jumping up. "I'll wait here." She strode over to the bookshelf and picked up a book. "You're such a nerd," she said to Hayden, looking at the cover of a fantasy novel.

Hayden sighed again and grabbed clean clothes from the closet. Taking his lead, I did the same and joined him in the shower.

* * *

"Do you think Padraic knows much about psych meds?" he asked me while he washed his hair.

"Probably. Why?"

He shook his head. "Hannah needs something."

"She's a little hyper, but she's not *that* bad."

"Little?" He raised an eyebrow.

"She's been calmer since she got here," I pointed out.

"She's bipolar," he stated. "She's manic right now and handles this phase pretty well...until the no sleeping thing starts."

"Oh, shit." My stomach did a little drop. I was so worried about finding food for the winter and fighting off crazies that I forgot about normal problems that we had to deal with. It felt insignificant when compared to life and death situations. "I think we can manage her," I assured Hayden.

"The mania only gets worse until she's talking nonsense and not sleeping for days. Literally. Then she'll bottom out and get depressed." He turned the water up as hot as it could go and stepped aside, letting me rinse the conditioner out of my hair. "She gets suicidal, Riss."

My stomach dropped even further. "We will get her meds." There. A simple solution. Go out and find the medications Hannah needed to gain stability. But it wasn't that simple, not at all. Nothing was simple anymore. There was no just going out anymore. Every move, every action had to be thought out and carefully planned. We had to be prepared for anything. One step forward and two steps back. Hayden's head drooped. I put my hands on his shoulders. "Hey. We're going to take care of everything. I have no freaking idea how, but we will. We have to."

Hayden just nodded, wanting to believe my easy fix. The water temperature dropped. I quickly rinsed and cut the water before it became icy. We got out, dressing in silence. Before Hayden opened the bathroom door he paused, taking a moment to put on a happy face and hide the stress that was weighing on him.

With two very forced smiles, we joined Hannah and went down to the cafeteria.

* * *

"It's been a week," Ivan said, turning around from the map that hung on the wall in Hayden's office. "And they're still not back."

"Should we go after them?" Jason asked. He leaned forward in the metal folding chair, putting his elbows on his knees. His eyes met mine for a second before looked at Hayden, who was sitting behind the desk. Wade and Brock were crowded behind him. I was perched on the edge of the desk and Hector sat to Hayden's right with his hands tightly clasped together, pressing against his chin. His daughter, Gabby, was among Alex's group who had yet to return.

"Maybe they had to take a detour," Hayden said. His words sounded more like a question than a statement. "It's happened to us before."

Ivan held a narrow strip of paper to the map, measuring the distance from the compound to the farthest town the group was assigned. "They should have been back by now."

Hayden looked down at his to do list, hoping for a magical solution to pop up. He bounced his leg up and down and drummed his fingers on the dark wooden desk. "If we go, there will be no one left to defend the compound in place of an attack."

"Are we expecting an attack?" Jason asked, straightening up. "Everyone from Eastmoore is dead, right?"

"I assume so," Haydn answered. "And attacks can happen when you least expect it." An uneasy silence fell over the office. Hayden looked around at all of us. "But we can't do nothing."

"What about the A2s?" Brock asked. "Most of them have been guarding the perimeters for months now. You don't think they can handle it?"

"Zombies, yes. That's what they were trained for," Hayden said. "Anyone who fights back..." He shook his head. "I hope they can."

"No one can get inside," Brock reminded him.

"But anyone can get to the fields," I said. "Which is why we pulled some of the A2s from the house to go there. We don't have many left inside these fences."

Hector leaned forward. If it were up to him he would have sent us out moments after the allotted four days was up. I hadn't worried when the fifth day came and passed. We had overstayed our estimated return plenty of times.

When day number six came to a close, the unwelcome feeling that something was wrong crept up. And now it was late in the evening on day seven. Hayden called a meeting after dinner to discuss our best option.

"What if just two of us went out?" Brock suggested. "And we keep this strictly a search mission, only get out of our vehicles if necessary."

Hayden considered it. Before he could reach a decision I said, "If they ran into something bad enough to take all five of them down, we should send out more than two."

"Herds disperse," Wade reminded me. "It that's what they ran into..." he trailed off, eyes flicking to Hector. He pressed his hands against his legs and shook his head. "If it was, the herd could be long gone by now."

"This place," Hayden said and jammed his finger onto the desk. "Has to be our priority. If this place falls or if we lose our farm, we will not make it through the winter."

His words hung heavy in the air. Then he leaned forward, rubbing his eyes. "There are more than enough people here capable of handling a weapon. I know Fuller wanted to let the people make their own choices but, maybe it's time for a draft." He looked up, taking in our reactions.

"You're right," I said. There were plenty of residents here, young, healthy, and able to stand in the watchtowers. They chose to stay underground where it was safe. Fuller had allowed that without even batting an eye. Truth be told, his valuing free will weighed heavily on my decision to stay at this place.

"We can bump everyone up," Ivan suggested. "New A1s, A1s to A2s. Then there would be enough to guard the estate."

Hayden nodded and turned to Hector. "What do you think?" he asked.

Besides looking like he wanted to burst into tears over the potential loss of his daughter, Hector agreed. "It's a good idea; one that could work."

"We need to implement this now," Hayden said.

"Call an assembly," Hector started. "Explain the situation and ask for volunteers first."

"What if no one wants to?" Jason asked. After losing Jessica and then Rider, Fuller opened up a position for an A2 to move up. Jason was the only one who applied. Another man named Mike volunteered at first, but backed out after realizing the danger we were in every single mission.

"Then I'll do what I have to do," Hayden said, hating the words that were coming out of his mouth. It would kill him to force someone to do something they didn't want to do, especially when it was dangerous. "We have to keep this place going." His eyes flitted to the list in front of him. "We're in need of quite a bit of supplies."

"So let's go," I said and pushed off the desk. "Round everyone up."

* * *

Bands of dark clouds stretched across the red morning sunrise. The air was electrified, as if a distant storm was brewing. I walked along the quiet pasture, carefully stepping over the many divots created by the cows. The grass was chewed down to the dirt, unable to grow before it was eaten again. I cast my eyes to the clouds. The lack of rain wasn't helping either.

I stopped outside a barn to lay a plank down over the moat. A small cloud of dusty dirt poofed around it when it thudded to the earth. I hopped across it and began unlatching the multiple locks on the barn door.

"Hey sweetie," I called softly when Sundance whined a hello. I reached inside a bin of sweet feed, taking only a small handful. The dozen or so cows in the barn heard the clanking of the metal lid and pushed to the front of the large stall. "Sorry, guys. There's not enough to give everyone a treat."

Since he was our only horse, Sundance had his own stall at the end of the barn. The cows were jammed in a large, open stall that took up most of the barn. They were put away every night since it was too difficult to see in the dark and guarantee their safety. I went into the horse stall, holding my hand out to the brown and white horse.

After Sundance ate the feed, I ducked out of the stall and pushed my way through the cattle, unlocking the end door. Then I had to go out and walk around, opening the back door from the outside where I could press my body up against the barn's wall and avoid being trampled to death.

The moat went around three sides of the barn. It was four feet wide and close to six feet deep. The backside of the barn didn't have a ditch, allowing the animals safe passage in and out. It was protected by three metal gates and several hot wires. I cut the power to the wires and opened the gates before sliding the barn door open.

The sound of thundering hoofs sparked something inside of me and suddenly I was there, standing at the base of the stairs in my grandparent's house. I closed my eyes, pressing my sweaty palms into my legs.

I leaned against the barn. My heart thumped in my chest. Dammit. We didn't have time for this. Only a few A2s and myself were out here this morning. The rest were meeting with Hayden.

I closed the barn and walked through the pasture, keeping a look out for zombies. I was on edge, the same way I felt when after a zombie close call. Shit. It was just a memory. Why did it affect me so deeply?

"Be realistic," I muttered to myself. With all we'd been through, I was lucky I wasn't a freaking basket case. I reached up, pulling on the nylon strap of my quiver that was rubbing uncomfortably on my shoulder.

I stepped over a pile of cow manure and continued my hike across the pasture. I had just gotten to the bottom of a hill when a voice came over the radio. Adrenaline shot through me, firing my muscles to sprint back to the barn.

"I saw something," one of the A2s said to me. She held her gun at her waist, waiting for my instruction. I was too distracted to tell her this world waited for no one. Neither should she.

"Where?" I unhooked my bow from my shoulder and pulled back an arrow.

"In the trees." She raised her gun, quickly putting her left hand under the weapon for support...and to stop her fingers from shaking. I cast a sideways glance at her. Maybe Hayden's speech about the crazies getting smarter had a bigger impact that I thought.

"Take a breath," I told her. "We're behind the wire." I pulled back on the arrow. "And you have me," I added with a grin. She turned her head, staring at me with wide eyes. I missed Hayden. He at least understood my dry sense of humor.

She listened, at least, and took a deep breath, pushing the air out immediately. I was about to tell her to do it again but slower when I saw movement.

"Should we fire?"

"No, not yet." Something was off. I narrowed my eyes, damming the dim morning light. All I could see was a silhouette. It was hunched over and...holding its side as if it was in pain. Something echoed across the trees. Was it crying? "Go and get backup, but make sure they stay behind the fence unless I call out," I said and dropped to the ground.

"Orissa!" the A2 called. "What are you doing?"

"Crazies don't feel pain." I rolled under the fence, being careful not to touch the live wire. I hiked the quiver into place as I stood and took off, silently slipping into the waist high grass. Several yards were put between the wire and me when I heard it again. Yes, it was crying.

I tightened my grip on the arrow. The hair on the back of my neck stood up when I thought back. A crazy had tricked us once before...

I shook my head. No. I couldn't think like that, not when I was already out here.

The crying grew louder. I ducked behind a tree and out of sight. It sounded like a female. I peered around and saw her fall, tripping over uneven ground. A cry escaped her lips as she hit the ground.

I lowered the bow and dashed out from behind the tree. Holy shit. She looked awful, dirty and covered in blood. I rushed to her, dropping to my knees. "Oh my God, Gabby!"

She looked up, dirt stuck to fresh cuts on her face. "Riss?" she sobbed.

"Yes," I said and put the bow down and took a hold of her arm, prepared to help her to her feet. She winced and I let go, taking my hand away. My palm was covered in blood. I grabbed the walkie-talkie from my belt. "Hello," I said into it. "I found Gabby!"

The reply was nothing but static. "Gabby is here," I said slowly and only got static again. I shook my head and clipped the walkie back to my belt loop. "I need to get you inside."

She sucked in air and wrapped blood crusted fingers around my wrist. "They're all dead," she cried. "I s-saw them." She broke down in sobs. I hooked my arm under her, which was hard to do with the bow poking her in the face.

"It's ok, Gabby," I soothed.

"No it's not!" She doubled over, sobbing.

"You're right," I said flatly. "It's not ok at all. None of this is." I blinked away another memory, recoiling at the way I could still feel the blade pushing into Rider's skull. "But right now you need to get inside."

She was hysterical, gripping onto me, unable to walk from the force of her tears. I stopped moving forward and hugged her. She melted into me, sobbing. My chest tightened. Here we were, struggling to get by on a daily basis. We had lost so much, seen so much death. And there were people living along the coast in perfect comfort and safety, completely prepared for all this.

It wasn't right.

We stood there for a few seconds, holding onto each other in an awkward hug. Gabby's hands rested on the quiver and the bow pressed into her chest. "Come on," I encouraged, putting my arm around her for support. She leaned on me, eyes swollen from crying so hard.

It was slow going through the grass and weeds. My pants became wet with dew and a chill set deep in my bones. Gabby gripped me a little tighter and sniffled.

Something moved behind us. I came to a sudden halt. "Be quiet," I whispered and turned around, leaning to see past Gabby. "There's nothing—"

I didn't get to finish my sentence. Zombies stumbled out of the weeds, arms out, reaching for us. I let go of Gabby and grabbed an arrow, stringing it up in the bow. But then hands grasped my shoulders.

The zombie's nails dug into my skin as I twisted to get away. He was tall and had been muscular at one point. His once colorful tattoos were fading and wrinkled on his rotting flesh. Gray mold covered half of his face. He advanced on me, mouth open and moaning.

I brought the bow up, hitting him under the chin. His head flopped back. I kicked his knee and his leg bucked. I brought my arm up, raising the bow and kicked him again. I grabbed an arrow, stringing it in the bow. I lifted my foot and brought my heel down on the tattooed zombie's face and let the arrow go, hitting a zombie that was several feet away.

"Gabby!" I screamed. She had fallen to the ground. A zombie was advancing on her. Fast. "Gabby look out!"

I snatched another arrow and rammed it into the eye of another zombie. Her long blonde hair was clumped together. Streaks of bird poop dripped down her face. I pulled the arrow back, bringing up my foot to push off her chest.

The zombie was over Gabby. She turned her head and closed her eyes. She was waiting to die.

"No!" I shouted when the zombie opened his mouth. Thick mucus dripped off his tongue. I didn't even think or take time to steady myself. I just fired the arrow.

The zombie collapsed onto Gabby, arrow sticking out of the back of his skull. My heart raced. I whirled around, looking for more zombies.

"Gabby," I said and hurried over. She wasn't moving and panic took over. Had the arrow gone through his head? I bent over, dropping the bow, and put my hands on the zombie's shoulders. Despite being dead and dehydrated, the bastard was heavy.

"What the hell was that?" I spat out, not meaning to sound angry. "You were going to let him bite you, weren't you?"

"I saw them all die," she whispered, lip quivering. "Ripped apart...eaten. All of them. Except me." She rolled onto her side, bringing her legs up to her chest.

I closed my eyes, forcing away tears. I put my hand on her shoulder. "I'm sorry," I said softly.

"I just ran," she cried. "I thought they were behind me. T-then I turned around and saw I was alone." She took a shaky breath. "So I went back. I went back for them!" She squeezed her eyes shut. Fat tears dripped off her face. "I can still hear the screaming." She brought her hands to her face. "I tried. I tried to save them but I didn't."

"Gabby," I repeated, looking around nervously. "I'm so, so sorry. But we need to go."

"I-I can't," she cried. "I want to die too."

"No you don't. You wouldn't have come back here if you did. Your dad...the rest of us...we want you to come back. Please, Gabby." I bent over her, trying to get my hands under her arms. Hayden's dog tags came untucked and swung free, dangling in Gabby's face.

She didn't flinch when the metal hit her. Shit, she was in shock. I pulled her up only to have her slump down again.

"Gabby!" I said. "I don't want to die out here!" I let her go and rocked back. "And I'm not leaving without you." I sat on the ground, crossing my legs. My heart continued to hammer and my muscles twitched, wanting to run and carry me to safety.

Gabby swallowed a sob and opened her eyes. "Go," she said hoarsely. "I'm not worth it."

I wasn't going to argue with her. Though it had been a while, I had been in a mind frame like that more than once. No amount of convincing or telling her she in fact *was* worth it would mean anything to her right now. She wasn't thinking logically, and I couldn't blame her. Seeing Rider stagger through the darkness as a zombie was horrifying and still haunted me. Seeing everyone in our group ripped apart...I shuddered.

Dew seeped through my pants. I tucked the dog tags back into my shirt and looked behind us. The weeds were too tall to see the barn, but I knew it wouldn't be long before someone came out here looking for me.

"You survived for a reason," I started. I shook my head. The words sounded forced and lame. I wished Ray was here. She could talk me off a ledge. I wasn't good at stuff like that. "Please, Gabby," I said, sounding more desperate than I meant to. "There are people that love you and will really miss you. We already have to deal with the loss of four people. Don't add to it."

Gabby started crying harder. Dammit. I sucked at this. I bit my lip. "There are people back there that I love and want to get back to, and I'm not going there without you."

She didn't so much as look at me. I tightened the strap of the quiver and bent over, hooking my arms under hers. "You've left me no choice," I huffed and brought Gabby to her feet.

"Put me down," she said and feebly pushed against me.

"We're not staying out here. It's not safe. At all." I strained under her weight as I flipped her over my shoulder. Between the loaded quiver on my back, Gabby, and the bow, it was slow going back to the barn.

"Put me down," she said again, getting some fire back. "Orissa."

"Do me a favor," I panted. "And shut up." The barn loomed ahead of us.

"I'll walk," she said.

I stopped. "You better or I'm dragging you in." I put her on the ground.

"Don't tell them," she said when we drew close enough to the barn for the others to see us. "Don't tell them that I watched."

"I won't," I promised and squeezed her hand. My heart sank when I saw the crowd of A2s gathered at the fence. I had to tell them about the others, that they were torn apart and scattered inside the stomachs of zombies, that there was nothing left but bits of torn clothing and hair.

CHAPTER TEN

Rain fell from thick gray clouds, pattering down on us. Drops hit my face, splashing into my eyes and rolling down my cheeks. I kept a steady hold on Hayden's hand. Hannah stood on his other side, keeping her casted arm dry inside her jacket. We stood in front of a group of people gathered for the memorial service. Pastor Jim was to our side, reading a passage from the *Bible* and not caring that the thin pages were getting wet. We didn't have any umbrellas, which was as odd as much as it made sense. They weren't something anyone thought to bring with them while running for their lives.

Gabby was still in the hospital ward. Her wounds were superficial but the mental trauma was deep. Once she stopped hysterically crying, she became quiet...too quiet. She didn't talk to anyone and wouldn't eat. Worried, Padraic gave her a shot of something that helped her relax and Hector was able to get her to take few bites of her dinner. She was a little better today than yesterday. Padraic told me she talked to her father and ate lunch.

I bit the inside of my cheek. I could only assume that she felt the same way about the guys in her group as I did in mine. If anything happened to my friends...no. I didn't want to think about it.

Pastor Jim closed the *Bible* and bowed his head, reciting a prayer my mother used to say with me every night when I was a child. The crowd murmured "amen" and then dispersed, some going back into the shelter to get out of the rain while others went to the wooden memorial plaques and said their own words of prayer.

Hayden and I stayed until the last of the residents went inside. Ivan and Brock came up to us, stopping by the plaque. Raeya, Sonja, Jason, and Olivia were a few steps behind them.

"What's going to happen?" Sonja asked, voice shaking. Her eyes fell on Hayden.

His hand trembled ever so slightly and I didn't think it was from the chilly rain. I moved in closer, slipping my hand from his and wrapping my arm around his waist. Hayden pulled me close, leaning into me.

"We'll rebuild our groups. A lot of the A2s are getting really good with weapons." Hayden looked at Jason. "The formal training helped the others, but your brother's doing just fine without it. He fits in with us."

Normally, Jason would be grinning ear to ear from the compliment. But today he just nodded.

"But nobody wants to go out on missions," Sonja said quietly. Her eyes were the same dark shade of brown as Jason's. She crossed her arms and stepped closer to her brother, shivering from the rain. "They said it wasn't safe before. And now...now no one will go."

Thunder crackled as it rolled through distant clouds. I turned my head up, studying the sky. "We will tell them they can stay here where it's safe and starve or they can go out and get supplies." I looked at Sonja. "Someone will step up. They've got to or we can't keep going. Our supplies will run out, and I'm not just talking about food. This place has become as close to normal as we can get it: movie nights, hot water, washing machines...that will be the first to go when we're scraping for supplies."

Sonja took a shaky breath and turned to Olivia, who was equally as shocked. "I never thought about that, but you're right." She moved her eyes up to mine. "I'll do it. I'll go out with you guys on missions."

"No freaking way," Jason objected.

Hannah huffed. "Older brothers are the worst."

Hayden's hand tightened on mine. The wind picked up and the rain fell harder. Wanting to avoid another session of pointless family drama between brothers and sisters, I suggested we all go inside. Brock defused the tension by reminding both Sonja and Hannah that they could start as A3s and work their way up. I knew there was no intention of letting them move up.

Maybe we should let them. Hannah was no sharp shooter, but she could handle a gun with confidence and accuracy...most of the time. And Sonja was fast and quiet. During our time running from the zombies, she had come in very useful by sneaking in somewhere and getting what we needed.

We parted ways with our friends and trudged upstairs to our room to change. Hayden took off his wet clothes and sank onto the bed, leaning over with his head in his hands. I pulled my shirt over my head, tossed it in the laundry and shimmied out of my pants. I sat on the bed behind him, massaging his shoulders.

Hayden let out a sigh. His muscles were so tense and his skin cold. I pressed my fingers into him a little harder, working out a knot.

He tipped his head to the side. I pressed my lips against his neck.

"Hayden," I whispered. "I'm sorry." Everyone had been telling Hayden how he'd figure this out, how we'd pull through. But no one stopped to think that Hayden was not only worried about our survival, but he was grieving as well.

He put his hand on mine, his skin was callused and rough. He twisted, sliding his hand up my arm until it hooked around my body. He gently pulled me into his lap, embracing me.

"I love you," he said.

"I love you, too."

* * *

A full tray of food balanced precariously on my forearm as I opened the door to Hayden's office. He, Ivan, Brock, and Jason, were crowded around the desk. Raeya sat cross legged on the floor, scribbling things down in the notebook. Wade had spent the afternoon with Gabby. It was seven in the evening and they were still together. I hoped she found comfort in him.

"I can't believe you gave them the master list," she mumbled, shooting daggers at Hayden. He looked up from the map, dark circles clinging to his eyes. Three days had passed since the memorial service and Hayden was still stressed.

"I didn't know I wasn't supposed to," he said.

Raeya shook her head so fast her thick brown hair fell into her face. She pushed it back. "We have a copy machine," she said pointedly.

"I didn't think we'd need it," Hayden said quietly.

Raeya looked up, guilt pulling down her face. She opened her mouth to apologize when I came in.

"Food," Ivan said, looking up from the map that was spread across the desk. "Thank God."

"Call me Orissa," I said with a smirk. Brock cleared papers off the little table across from the desk. I set the tray down and looked at our dinner.

"I'd do anything for a pizza," Jason mumbled when he picked up a bowl of canned vegetable soup. "And a salad. Never thought I'd say that."

I nodded, crushing saltine crackers and dumping them into my bowl. "I would eat a bag of lettuce plain. I miss it."

"The garden's getting bigger," Brock reminded us. "Maybe you can eat a head of lettuce soon."

"Is it weird that I would totally do that? God I miss fresh fruit and vegetables."

"And cheese," Raeya added. I grabbed another bowl and sat down next to Raeya. She took the soup and winkled her nose. "I used to like canned soup."

"It wouldn't be so bad if it wasn't watered down," Jason said and added salt to his bowl. "I bet the cooks serves themselves a big bowl of condensed soup with barely any water. Then serve us this thinned out crap."

"I should have been a cook," Brock mused and took the salt from Jason.

The office grew quiet except for the clanging of spoons on bowls. I pushed my crackers to the bottom. I liked them extra soggy.

"So," I said after I finished my soup. I set the bowl down and stood. "What's the game plan?"

Raeya flicked her eyes to me and then the map before quickly going back to her list, moving her pen so fast I knew she wasn't really writing. I stared at her, waiting for her to feel my eyes. She ducked her head into her chest. Clearly she wasn't going to give me an answer.

"There are a few decent sized cites we haven't checked out yet a few hours north," Hayden started, "since they were overrun. But now—"

"You think the herds have dispersed," I finished for him.

"Exactly."

I moved to the desk, close to Hayden and looked at the map. "Where are we headed, captain?"

He put his finger on the map. "Kentucky."

Kentucky. The state I grew up in. The place my grandparents lived and the place we had run to, seeking shelter from the horrible world. We had found peace, come to know each other and develop friendships that would last throughout the most harrowing times. It was funny how that one word stirred up so much emotion.

"Ok," I said without missing a beat. "Do you have a specific location?"

"Bowling Green," he said, close to cringing. Raeya must have told him. I know for sure I hadn't.

I nodded. "I'm familiar. We lived close to there." I looked across the desk at Jason. "Do you remember much from when we drove around?"

He lifted his shoulders. "A bit. I watched you, mostly," he admitted. "Was Bowling Green the town you, Padraic, and I were in when those kids hiding under the cars got eaten?"

Shit. I hadn't thought about it since it happened. "No. But it was close."

Raeya narrowed her eyes. "What? Why did I never hear about this?"

Jason and I looked at each other. "Uh..." he started.

"I didn't want you to hear about it," I told her. "They were the first people we had come across since getting you that weren't infected. And they died before our eyes."

She gripped her notebook. "I'm glad I didn't know. Thanks."

I gave her a tight smile, making sure I looked calm and collected. Inside, I was conflicted, confused at why going back to Kentucky seemed so hard. It was just a state. This was a mission. Being only miles away from my grandparent's farm shouldn't matter.

But it did.

"When are we leaving?" I asked.

Hayden looked up, his eyes wide.

"You're going?" he asked.

"Uh, yeah," told him, raising an eyebrow. "Why wouldn't I?"

His cheeks slightly flushed. "I just thought you'd want to stay here." He made a deal of smoothing out the map. "With me," he added quickly. I sucked in a breath. Hayden wasn't going? I blinked, shaking myself. Right. He couldn't go. He had to stay here and keep things running smoothly. Still, I didn't believe that. Somehow he'd find a way to leave, a way to come with me.

Hayden ran his hand through his hair. "I'm not sure how we are going to do this, honestly." He sighed. "If we go as we normally did, who would be left to guard the compound?" We looked at each other, none of us wanting to split up.

"There's really no one else to take over?" Raeya asked.

"There is," Ivan answered. "There are plenty of people who are able to defend the compound."

"They don't want to do it," Brock said bitterly.

Anger built inside of me. "Ugh! This is so frustrating!" I turned, bringing my hands up toward my face. "And complete bullshit! Is anyone else feeling majorly taken for granted? It's time for people to buck up, grab a gun, and stand the fuck by the gate!"

"Yeah," Jason said. "I was an A3. It's not hard. Scary, oh yeah. Very. But I was in the tower, relatively safe. If we saw anything, we called for help, basically keeping our hands clean."

"Remember when the zombies pushed through the fence?" Brock said. "Right after we got back from that mission. Everyone pulled together and we did it. We can do it again."

"If they're forced," I said and rolled my eyes. "People need to realize that we are living on the edge of life and death every single day, that each time that sun rises over that bloody horizon and we're alive to see it is a victory. They need to know that it takes blood and sweat and tears to keep this place going and that we're here, scraping the bottom of the barrel for food and medical supplies while hoity-toity twatwaffles sit safe and sound drinking tea and eating cookies not giving a damn about us!" I let out a breath, heart pounding.

"She's rather inspiring when she gets all fired up," Brock whispered to Raeya loud enough for me to hear.

"Really, she is." She tipped her head at him. "Are you thinking what I'm thinking?"

He beamed, eyes sparkling. "We need to work on her language though."

She shook her head. "I've tried. For years, literally, with little success. I've gotten her to go from unruly drunken sailor to well-educated drunken sailor at least. And by well educated I mean her vocabulary of swear words increased ten fold."

Brock nodded. "Impressive!"

"What are you talking about?" I asked, temper high.

"See what I mean?" Raeya asked, speaking out of the side of her mouth. She turned to me and smiled. "You are right, Rissy. The people here have gotten used to the comfort. I haven't even seen a zombie since we came and I am so, so thankful for that. But I still remember what it's like." She closed her eyes. "The way they smell. I won't ever forget it." She opened her eyes and inhaled. "Each day that goes by makes me feel a little more normal and a little more healed and I can only hope it does the same for everyone else. So yes, maybe they do take you guys for granted. Maybe if they heard what you just told us, they'd feel more inspired to help."

I blinked. "You want me to give an inspirational speech?"

"Yes."

I leaned away, laughing. "That's a horrible idea. Have you met me?"

"Over fifteen years ago." She beamed. "And I don't mean a literal speech. Just talk to everyone, telling them what you told us. But with more detail, perhaps. Your fiery spirit might give off a few sparks. It'd be really nice to have volunteers." Her eyes flicked to Hayden and I knew what she meant. If people volunteered, then Hayden wouldn't have to force anyone.

"Ok," I said. I would do anything to help Hayden. Anything.

* * *

I looked out my bedroom window. Ivan and Brock drove toward the gate, the Range Rover bumping along the long driveway. They were leaving on a mini mission to recover the truck full of baby supplies that had been abandoned and were taking one of the new A1s with them.

Raeya was right. We had spent the next few days talking to the residents. I hadn't realized before that some of them were pretty clueless as to what went on here. I scoffed at that notion at first, saying it was impossible to not know how we operated. But Hayden reminded me of the efforts Fuller had taken to make sure the residents were not only safe but comfortable, living as close to normal as he could provide.

Many residents were moved when they found out about missions. Even more were scared, and rightly so. The notion of leaving the compound generated a slew of responses. One thing was clear: everyone wanted the compound to stay the way it was.

And that meant going out on missions.

At the end of our first day of A roundup, as Raeya called it, we had over a dozen people to add to the A category, allowing those who wanted to move up to do so. We now had three new A1s.

We didn't waste time getting them into training. With our dwindling ammo, Hayden put an emphasis on hand-to hand-combat and knife usage. If we could wrangle up more bows, I would give everyone archery lessons.

Gabby was finally able to speak about what had happened. Her group had gotten everything they needed with little problems. They were on their way home, only forty-five minutes or so from the compound when they came across two girls trudging down the road.

The girls flagged them down, desperately waving for help. They got out, of course. The youngest pointed to a car off the side of the road and then burst into tears. Alex and Mac went to check it out, leaving the others to comfort the girls.

A crazy jumped out of the car, landing on Alex. Gabby said Noah grabbed the girls, taking them to safety. But they were crazy too. The whole thing was a set up. Gabby didn't remember getting out. One minute she was with José, holding his hand, and then next he was dead on the ground. She just ran until I found her.

The Jeep was still there, keys in the ignition and full of supplies. Supplies we needed. Supplies four of our soldiers had died for.

I turned around, wrapping my arms around myself, chilled from the early morning breeze that blew through the open window. Hayden lay sprawled out on his stomach with one leg hanging off the bed. He had had another nightmare last night, one that shook him so deep he woke up thinking he was back in the desert during the war.

I carefully crawled over him, pulling the sheet up to his waist. In his sleep, he reached out for me, wrapping his arm around my side. I wiggled close to him, tracing his tattoos with my finger until I drifted back to sleep.

* * *

"Riss," Hayden said an hour later. "We need to workout." I pretended to be asleep. I was comfortable and didn't want to get up, let alone get up and do physical work. Not yet at least. "Riss," he repeated. The closet door closed. "Get up. We have the new A1s with us today."

Begrudgingly, I opened my eyes. Hayden stood by the bed wearing black athletic shorts and a white t-shirt with the sleeves cut off. He had an iPod in his hand. "I'm up," I grumbled and went to the closet, yanking a tank top off the hanger. I grabbed a pair of shorts and slowly walked into the bathroom to get dressed.

It was weird, being down in the training room with only Hayden, Wade, and Jason. I didn't have to wait to use any equipment at least. Still, I missed Ivan and Brock and couldn't shake my worry about them.

I was only three miles into my run on the treadmill when the new A1s came in. I recognized one as Brian, the guy from the fields who hit on me when I was looking for Hayden. I pushed my finger down on a button, decreasing the speed on the treadmill. He seemed a bit nervous, standing next to the other new recruit, an older man who I guessed to be in his late forties. His gray hair was cropped close to his scalp. He looked familiar but I couldn't place his face. I mentally shook my head, Of course he looked familiar. I had only been living with these people for how long now?

The older man introduced himself as Bryan, flipping his name badge over for us to see. Great. Brian and Bryan. That wasn't going to get confusing at all...

Hayden showed them around and suggested they take it easy today, trying all the equipment while he evaluated them to see what they needed the most improvement on.

Brian—with an 'i'—followed me back to the treadmill, getting on the one next to mine.

"I used to go to the gym six days a week," he said, hitting the speed button. "I miss feeling the burn." He smiled at me. I glanced over. Brian wasn't bad looking, not at all. He had dark blonde hair, cut short and deep blue eyes. And he was tan, very tan. "I'm guessing you used to work out regularly before this too. You don't get those kind of muscles overnight." He leaned back, flicking his eyes to my behind.

I increased my speed, breaking into a jog. "No, you don't." I kept my eyes straight ahead. I didn't like to be bothered when I was working out, not even by my friends. Brian was getting off on the wrong foot already. He pushed his finger down, matching his speed to mine.

"You should start out slow," I said, looking over.

He waved his hand at me and smiled broadly. "I like to push myself. No pain no gain, right?"

"Right," I said and increased my speed again. "Unless that pain is zombie teeth ripping into your skin."

His face turned a little green. He turned forward, jogging a few paces before increasing his speed again. With his hands moving at his sides he turned to me, watching my breasts bounce as I ran.

Seriously? I tried to ignore him. I looked out across the room. Hayden was busy helping the other Bryan with free weights. Wade was doing pushups and Jason was on the leg press. He caught my eye, looked at Brian, and snickered.

I rolled my eyes and smiled at him. He moved his gaze to Hayden then back at me, raising his eyebrows in question. I shook my head and shrugged then went back to running.

Brian continued to flirt with me for the rest of our workout, dropping lame pickup lines along the way. Hayden finally noticed but instead of being bothered, he was amused by it.

Wade, Jason, and I went with Hayden into his office after our workout. I looked over the list of everyone in the A group. My little speech worked and over thirty people offered to do their part in protecting the compound...but only three wanted to go out on missions with us.

Hayden and Hector had been busy talking with everyone, figuring out their strengths and weaknesses and finding the best place for them in our group. Raeya came up with a schedule for us to follow, one that left little spare time. The next week or two was going to be brutal...and that was true even if things went as planned.

CHAPTERELEVEN

I pushed open the hospital ward doors. It was around ten at night and the young B3 that sat at the desk had fallen asleep. I hesitated, debating if I should wake her up. Not seeing the point, I continued on.

Several of the beds were occupied. About a week into our training with the new A's, an upper respiratory infection broke up. Over a dozen people were sick, Padraic included. And yet here he was, working the midnight shift.

"You're supposed to be in bed," I said quietly, opening the door to the exam room.

Padraic looked up, dark circles under his pretty blue eyes. "Is everything ok, Riss?" He stood and rushed over to me. That was just so *him*. He was sick, still working, and concerned about me.

"I'm fine," I told him. "But you're not."

Padraic waved his hand in the air. "Nah. I have a slight cough." His accent was heavier than normal. He was tired.

"You're just as bad of a liar as Ray." I closed the door behind me.

"What are you doing then?"

"I came to get that list."

Padraic gave me a blank stare then blinked. "Oh, right." He stood from the stool and sifted though the scattered papers on the counter. Due to the breakout of upper respiratory infections, we were low on medicine. Really low. Padraic had written up a very long list of medications we needed along with various medical supplies.

"Here ya go," Padraic said, extending his arm. He quickly turned his head and coughed.

"Oh, yeah, just a little cough," I said. Concerned, I took the list and moved closer to Padraic and pressed my hand on his forehead. "You feel feverish. Go to bed."

He took my hand in his. "I'm all right, Orissa. I gave Karen and Shante the night off anyway. One of us should be here."

"You can be on call, ya know." It still surprised me how soft his skin was. "It's not like you're leaving the building. You're what, thirty seconds away?"

He let go of my hand and sighed. "You're right."

I leaned on the counter. "You need to take care of yourself. What if it were me?"

"I'd tell you to rest before it gets worse," he admitted with a charming smile.

"Exactly."

"But," he countered. "I'm not working physically hard like you do. I'm sitting, reading up on pediatric medicine."

"Sounds thrilling." I raised my eyebrows. "As first lady of this place, I command you to go to your room."

"Command?" he questioned, laughing.

I set my face and crossed my arms. "Go. Now. I will tuck you into bed myself if I have to."

Padraic coughed again. "Yes, your highness." He bowed to me and we both laughed. "I will do rounds then go to bed."

"You better."

He smiled. "Promise. Shouldn't you be sleeping too?"

I raised my shoulders in a shrug. "It's hard to sleep before missions. I'm all antsy."

"I can only imagine." Padraic ran his hand through his dark hair. It had grown out since we first met and fell into his face. On anyone else, it would look unkempt and messy. On Padraic, it looked good. "I hate that you're leaving again."

My stomach flip flopped. I hated it too. "It has to be done."

He nodded. We walked out together. "I will see you off in the morning then. Night, Riss."

I gave him a side hug. "Night, Padraic." I left the hospital ward hoping that he really would get some sleep. I hurried through the halls to Hayden's office. He had been talking with Ivan and Brock for over an hour.

"Dude, you're making a bigger deal than you need to," Brock said. He sat in a chair facing the desk. Ivan stood behind him, arms held behind his back. "We can handle it."

"I know," Hayden said, eyes flicking to me. I closed the door and moved to him. Hayden put his arm out, wrapping it around me when I stepped over.

"If it bothers you that much then stay here," Ivan said, his voice smooth and level.

Hayden shook his head. "I can't...not again." He didn't need to explain it. We all knew that he couldn't stay here if I were to leave.

And I wouldn't have left, not yet, if we had more A1s. But right now our numbers were so low, every person counted. Losing another A1 would be detrimental to our lacking number of soldiers to carry out missions.

So I had no choice but to go out. Wade and Jason would come with me. This was too important of a mission to bring a noob along. Everything was mapped out: where we would go, how long we'd be gone, the roads we'd take to get there.

I didn't want to go without Hayden. He didn't want me to go without him even more. After much debate, he decided he couldn't stay behind. The anxiety would get to him and he'd be distracted. I expected Hector to be surprised when he learned about our relationship. He wasn't, not at all. He said he had known for a while. I guess Hayden and I weren't as good at hiding our feelings for each other as we thought.

"We can handle it," Ivan assured him. Ivan, Brock, and Hector would take over the role of leader while Hayden was away. That was the backup plan if anything—God forbid—happened to Hayden anyway.

"I know," Hayden said. "Probably better than I can."

I put my hands on his shoulders. In a weird way, I hoped going out on a mission would allow Hayden to let go of the extra stress he was holding. He could forget about being in charge and focus on...not dying. I rolled my eyes at myself. There was nothing relaxing about a mission. We needed that beach.

"Want to go over everything again?" Brock asked.

"No," Hayden said with a sigh. "You got it. You're right. You can handle this."

"We got this," Ivan said with a smile. "Take him upstairs," he said to me. "Wear him out so he'll get some sleep."

I massaged Hayden's shoulders. "I think I can do that," I said with a grin.

* * *

"Ready?" Jason asked me as he crossed the yard. The truck was already loaded and we had our lists. He unlocked the Jeep that he and Wade would be taking.

"As ready as I can be," I answered. "I'm still waiting for Hayden, though."

He nodded toward the house. "Wade's still in there too. He's saying bye to Gabby." He wiggled his eyebrows. Wade and Gabby had spent a lot of time together over the last few weeks and had finally confessed their feelings for each other just days ago. Being with him pulled Gabby out of her depression.

"We're gonna have to drag those two apart," I said, wrinkling my nose.

"Hey now." Jason smiled. "You have no room to talk."

"We're not that bad," I said, feeling a little embarrassed. Not wanting Jason to see me flush, I reached into my bag, fishing around for my sunglasses. I put them on and sat in the truck, pointing the air vents at me. I watched Wade leave the house in the rearview mirror. He tossed his stuff into the back of the Jeep and got in. Now we just needed Hayden.

I turned down the air and drummed my fingers on the center console. A minute ticked by. I was bored. For the hell of it, I turned on the radio. Static crackled through the speakers. Not paying specific attention, I cycled through the stations, all just as fuzzy as the last. Then I put my finger over the icon for the satellite radio, expecting to hear the same static.

I had been confused way back when this all started as to why the satellite went out. There weren't zombies in space. It just didn't make sense. I leaned back, holding my finger on the screen, quickly flipping from station to station. Each was fuzzy, with the static louder on some than others.

Then I heard it. Just a quickly little blip. I yanked my hand back, staring at the screen, heart racing. It was a voice. It had to be a voice. There was no music, just talking. I couldn't make out what was said, but I heard it. I leaned forward, breathing fast. What channel was I on? Shit, I didn't know. I had to get back to it. I pushed hard on the screen, desperate to go back. I went too far and started back up. Dammit. Nothing. I knew I heard it. The voice. It was there, wasn't it?

"You know that's not gonna work," Hayden said, opening the driver's door. I looked up, blinking.

"Yeah. It won't. Right." I was thankful for the sunglasses; I knew there was no way I could hide the shock in my eyes. I turned the radio off altogether. Hayden would plug in his iPod later and subject me to horrible country music.

He looked behind him at the compound before getting in. He held his stress in his shoulders; they were tense and stiff.

"It's in good hands," I said before he could object and beg me to stay behind with him.

"I know it is," he said, putting on his seatbelt. "Better than mine, maybe."

I gave him a sympathetic smile. "Don't say that."

He put his hands on the steering wheel and nodded.

"Is it bad I was kinda looking forward to this?" I asked him. "Not so much the mission but being together again outside of the compound. It feels normal."

"Your definition of normal is pretty fucked up," Hayden said with a smile. He slowly pressed on the gas, flicking his eyes to the rearview mirror, watching the compound as we drove down the bumpy driveway. "But I get it."

I turned the air off to conserve gas and took the map out of the glove box. Faded lines ran through it from being folded and refolded so many times. It would take us all day to get to Kentucky and even longer if we ran into trouble.

We drove through the gates and turned onto the road. Once the compound was out of sight, Hayden relaxed considerably. He let out a breath and leaned back into his seat. He put his hand on mine and we rode in comfortable silence for a while. Then he plugged in his iPod, blaring country music.

Our plan was to drive straight to Bowling Green. It would take roughly eight hours, depending on what we did—or didn't—run into. We made it halfway before running into trouble.

CHAPTERTWELVE

"Here?" Wade asked over the radio. Hayden let off the gas. I rolled down the window and surveyed the medical plaza's parking lot. It was empty except for three cars. Had the employees here had time to flee?

"It's worth a shot," Hayden said and turned off the street.

"Do doctor's offices have medicine?" I asked him and pushed the release on my seatbelt. "Every time I've gone they send me out with a prescription."

"That's how it normally works," he said and let the truck coast to a stop. He turned it off and put the keys in the side pocket of his jeans. "There are gloves, and uh, exam tools that we can take."

"Good enough," I said and got out of the truck. I opened the back door and started arming myself, ready in just minutes. Hayden, on the other hand, was still in the truck. "What are you doing?" I asked. He ducked his head down, turning away from me. "Hello? Hayden?" I asked.

Without a word he got out of the car, going to the bed to get his weapons. All righty then...I shook my head. Jason walked over, holding an assault rifle at his side.

"How are we gonna do this?" he asked. A tiny bit of excitement glinted in his eyes. Before I could answer, Wade called him back to the Jeep. Something funny was going on. I narrowed my eyes. Wade turned around.

"Riss," Hayden said. "Ready?"

"Sure." He came around, keeping his hand against his side. He was holding something and he didn't want me to see it. I raised an eyebrow but didn't say anything. Hayden did a great job avoiding eye contact as we moved through the parking lot. Unable to take it any longer, I whirled around, ready to question him.

"Do you see that sign?" he asked before I could get one word out, pointing to a closed sign that hung from a boarded up window across the street from us.

"Yeah."

"Think you can hit it?"

I snorted a laugh. "Of course I can hit it."

"Prove it," he said with a smile and held up an arrow. So *that* was what he was hiding at his side. With my eyebrows raised, I took the arrow, giving Hayden my best what-the-hell-are-you-doing stare. I nocked the arrow without having to think about it. The movements were second nature to me.

But something was different. Sunlight glinted off the arrow point. Wait. That wasn't the arrow that was sparkling in the sun. My eyes widened. I stared at the end of the arrow then looked at Hayden.

"Is that…" I started. A huge smile pulled up my lips. "No, you…" I couldn't stop smiling.

"Want to try it on or just stare at it?" Hayden asked, also smiling ear to ear.

I shook my head, laughing before lowering the bow and holding it out for Hayden to take. The smile hadn't left my face.

"I was worried you'd think it was lame," Hayden confessed.

"It might be." I brought the arrow to me, carefully touching the engagement ring that hung from it. "But I love it."

I unscrewed the arrow point and slid the ring off into my hand and held it up. It was gorgeous, boasting more diamonds than I could count.

"Raeya told me your ring size," Hayden said. "Hopefully it fits."

I turned the ring around, letting the sun shine on the diamonds. A large oval stone sat in the center of two smaller round ones. Tiny diamonds covered the entire band. My heart sped up when I slipped the ring over my finger. It fit perfectly.

I turned to Hayden, wrapping my arms around him. We embraced, pulling apart after a quick kiss. "How?"

"I didn't just fix my truck that day," he told me. "That's why I didn't ask you to come with. I wanted it to be a surprise."

I kept smiling, shaking my head. "I can't believe Ray was in on this."

"Do you like the ring?" He leaned forward, nervous to hear my response.

"Yes!" I looked at my hand again. "I know I said I didn't need one, but I love it; really I do."

"She said you would like something vintage styled. I don't really know what that means so I just picked one I thought was pretty."

"You did good," I said, tearing my eyes away from the sparkles to look at him. The smile disappeared from my face. I grabbed my bow from Hayden and fired an arrow.

The zombie's forehead smacked into the pavement and exploded like someone dropping a water balloon.

"Ew," I said and walked over. The arrow was lying in a puddle of rotting brain slush. "He can keep that one." I nudged it with the toe of my boot. The smell was awful. I turned my head, blinking hard. It was bad enough to cause my eyes to water. Hayden and I went around the truck. Wade was leaning against the brick exterior of the medical plaza, grinning.

"You knew, didn't you?" I asked him.

"Yup. The whole time. Mad at me?"

I couldn't help but smile. "Not at all."

Jason looked back and forth, confused. Then his eyes settled on my left hand and soon he was grinning too. "Ah, I was wondering when he'd give it to you!"

I shook my head, feeling too much like a cliché. "Come on," I started, hiking the strap of the quiver up along my back. "Let's go in. We don't have too many hours of daylight left."

"It's locked," Jason said, eyeing the door. "Can you pick it?"

"Of course I can," I said, seeing the simple lock. "I'll show you. It's really not hard."

"That's kinda scary," Jason said and moved next to the door. Hayden and Wade kept watch while I showed Jason how to bend the bobby pins the right way. It took him a few tries since the weak metal kept bending when he pushed it into the lock but eventually he got it.

The smell hit us like a fist to the face. We were only a few steps in and already I wanted out. Hayden went first, pushing open the second set of doors that led into the waiting room. He stopped short, turning around with his mouth open.

"What?" Wade asked.

Hayden shook his head and looked forward, moving aside so we could get through.

"What the fuck?" Wade muttered. I stepped next to him. Shit. I swallowed hard, the rancid smell so strong I could taste it. Bodies, charred and blackened beyond recognition where lined up throughout the office. Empty cans of gasoline had been tossed to the side. Damage from flames covered the walls. The ugly, floral print wallpaper was curling and hanging off in burned sheets.

Their hands and feet were bound around their bodies. I didn't want to stare but I couldn't look away. The blackened remains were small. Its knees were bent up, head buried into the body next to it. Its head had fallen back, mouth twisted in agony.

They had been burned alive.

Jason stepped closer to me, unnerved. For several seconds we just stood there, frozen in shock. Then Hayden stepped over a body, starting our search. It didn't take us long to discover that this place had already been cleaned out. We left the building, gasping in fresh air.

"It was locked from the inside," I said, removing the quiver from around my neck. "After those bodies were burned."

Wade shook his head. "Maybe they came to the doctor with symptoms?"

"And once it was realized they were infected they were put down," Jason said. "By fire."

"It doesn't matter," Hayden said, unable to take his eyes off the building. "There's nothing here for us." He was as unnerved as the rest of us. Sticking to the mission kept him focused. "Let's go."

We loaded back up in the cars and took off, speeding away from the building full of burned bodies. We drove past a hospital. Zombies stumbled around the parking lot, dead eyes following the moving truck. We didn't stop.

Anxiety wound in me. There were only a few hours of daylight left. We hadn't gotten any supplies and we'd need to find a safe place for the night soon.

"Hey," I said suddenly. "There's a nursing home."

"So?" Hayden asked.

"I didn't even think about it before." I sat up straighter. "That place would be full of medical stuff."

"Really?"

"Yes. My grandma stayed at one for a while to do rehab when she was sick. All sorts of shit goes on there. Wounds, regular sick people, and some crazy people. We might be able to get meds for your sister."

A lightness pulled up on Hayden's face. He radioed to Wade and turned the truck around, driving through a weedy median, and into the nursing home parking lot. We got out, suited up with weapons, and turned to the building.

"I hate these places," Jason grumbled. "They smelled like death and depression before the virus hit."

I tightened the wrist protector and put the quiver over my head, staring at the large sign in the front of the building that read Silver Living Centers. "Yeah," I agreed. "Nursing homes are nasty. I never want to be put in one, though I don't think it's an issue now."

Wade chuckled. "We'll be lucky to make it into old age at this point."

Hayden jumped down from the bed of the truck. Clouds rolled over the sun, darkening his face. "Ready?" he asked, flicking the safety off his gun.

"As we'll ever be," Wade said. The four of us crossed the parking lot. The wind picked up, blowing garbage across the pavement. "You said the medicine was in a big box?" he asked me.

"Kind of," I answered. "It's like a giant vending machine with no glass front. Or at least that's what it looked at that hospital we went to."

"Interesting," Wade said. He was carrying an empty backpack with the hopes of filling it up with medical supplies. We stopped under a brick awning. I held my bow to my side and leaned in toward the front door.

"It's dirty," I mumbled. A thick coat of dust and dirt made it hard to see inside. Hayden spit on the glass and wiped it with his hand. I wrinkled my nose at him.

"What?" he said with a shrug. "Now you can see in."

I shook my head and held up my hand, shielding away the light. "What I can see is empty." I straightened up. "That doesn't mean shit."

"Only one way to find out," Hayden said, putting his hand over the handle. We readied our weapons and moved around Hayden. Our eyes met and he nodded then pulled back the door. I moved in, jumping to the side to allow the guys to follow behind.

Instantly, my eyes watered. The smell of urine mixed with rotting bodies. I turned my head to the side, getting one last breath of fresh air before the door closed. We were standing in a lobby. There was a desk in front of us, tucked behind a half wall. Brown stains streaked the couch that was pushed off to the side, surrounded by dead plants and a god-awful floral print rug. A large staircase led up to an open walkway above. The lobby emptied into intersecting halls and a cafeteria was across from us.

"Oh my God," Jason said, gagging. He covered his nose with his harm. "It is rank in here."

"There's nothing like a building full of rotting old people," Hayden said and took a few steps forward. Blood streaked across the lobby floor. Hayden stepped in it and froze.

"What?" I asked him.

He lifted up his foot. "It's sticky."

My chest tightened with fear. Forcing myself to focus, I pulled back the arrow.

"What?" Jason asked, raising his gun. He looked at the floor then at me. "What does that have to do with anything?"

"Sticky means fresh," Wade said. "Relatively fresh."

The employee entrance was locked. The only way in was through the front doors and I felt confident no one—no one sane at least—had come through here recently. So how the fuck did fresh blood get on the floor?

Hayden wiped the sole of his boot on the carpet. Next to him was a large glass bird cage. Tiny winged skeletons littered the bottom. He crept forward. I was only a step behind him.

Something clattered to the ground. I tensed, pulling back on the arrow. Hayden froze, flattening himself against the wall. Wade and I moved back. Jason's body stiffened. With wide eyes he stared straight ahead.

There was another bang. I tipped my head. Did someone just hit a wall? I held my breath. My heart pounded in my ears. I leaned forward, fingers trembling as they held back the arrow.

Three distinct raps came from deep inside the nursing home. Hayden looked over his shoulder, furrowing his brow. I shook my head, answering his unspoken question. I had no idea what the hell was going on. Hayden held up his hand and bent his fingers, signaling us to continue forward.

I picked up my foot. Every muscle tingled, ready to run or fight. I swallowed hard and took in a breath, slowly blowing it out to steady myself. Hayden was at the corner now. He held his gun up and out of sight, waiting. I watched his chest rise and fall before he sprung around the corner, gun raised.

His shoulders relaxed, and I knew it was clear. I turned around to tell the guys to follow. My heart skipped a beat. There was someone behind Jason! Where the fuck had she come from?

"Jason!" I screamed. But he was fast. The second his crazy eyes took in the sight of me he pounced, leaning off the staircase and landing on Jason's back. Wade whirled around aiming his gun, unable to get a clear shot.

The crazy let out a scream and wrapped his arms around Jason's neck, bringing him back into a choke hold. I lowered my bow. They were moving too much. I could shoot Jason by accident.

"Guys!" Hayden shouted. "We've got company!" I didn't have to turn around to know that more crazies were ascending on our group. The echoing bang of gunfire let me know that there were more than just a few behind us.

I ran to Jason. He was on the floor, wrestling with the crazy. Wade was almost there. Then two S1s leapt off the balcony, landing right in front of us. Wade raised his gun, using the butt to whack a crazy in the face. The female stumbled back, blinking from the blood that dripped into her eye.

The pain didn't even register.

Cold, clammy hands wrapped around my wrist. I twisted my arm and brought it up, breaking the hold. The arrow was still in my hand. In a swift movement, I jammed it into the crazy's eye.

Her face wasn't rotting. It took a considerable amount of effort to shove the broadhead arrow point into her skull. Her body twitched, fingers splayed in a final attempt to claw me to pieces before she fell.

Another took her place.

"We need to get out of here!" Hayden shouted, already shoving a new clip into his gun. He elbowed a crazy in the throat, causing him to wheeze. Hayden grabbed his knife and stabbed the S1 in the side, above the stomach. The blade punctured the crazy's lung. He snarled at Hayden, lips curled over yellowing teeth. Bits of flesh and hair stuck to his chin.

Hayden leaned back and kicked the crazy. He turned, eyes meeting mine for a fleeting second. It was a second too long. A boney fist collided with my jaw. I stumbled back, the pain fueling my rage.

I came back swinging, my knuckles landing on his temple. Dammit. Did he even feel it? My hand hurt, just a bit, and the crazy was still there, foamy saliva running down his face.

I dropped the bow, not wanting to use it like a baseball bat and risk damaging it. I reached out at the sputtering crazy. My hands landed over his ears, flattening his messy hair. Something moved under my palm. Gross. It shouldn't have shocked me that crazy's had bugs in their hair...they were too busy disemboweling living people to shower.

His nails, long, jagged, and dirty tore into the exposed flesh on my chest. Then his eyes diverted to my cleavage and he stopped struggling to kill me. I couldn't help it. I brought my knee up, smashing his testicles as hard as I could even though I'd get no satisfaction from seeing his pain.

His mouth fell open and he reached for me. I snapped his neck. The body collapsed on the ground. I whirled around, completely unnerved from that, and saw Jason on the ground. He was on top of a crazy, punching him in the face.

I knew the feeling: so angry you wanted to break everything in sight. But he was being careless and wasting time. My hand closed around the knife on my belt.

"Jason!" I called. "Just kill him already!" Jason didn't so much as look up. "Jason, goddammit!"

Something wrapped around my neck. I let go of the knife, hands flying up. Whatever was around my neck was thin and hard, like a cable. I had practiced—relentlessly—how to get out of this type of hold with my martial arts instructor. But all our moves, that careful practice...the rules of the art went out the window.

I couldn't inflict pain, couldn't apply counter pressure to make the crazy let go. All I could count on was being stronger than him. Judging by the way he pulled me back off my feet, this fucker was big. Much bigger than me.

I opened my mouth to call for Hayden. Only a strangled cry came out. My vision blurred...I had to do something. The crazy was dragging me back behind the desk.

I grabbed my gun, struggling to get it free from the holster on my thigh. The crazy jerked me back. My feet caught on a body and I fell, my weight pulling down on the cord.

Vomit twisted in my stomach. My eyelids were heavy, so fucking heavy. My body went limp and I passed out.

CHAPTERTHIRTEEN

I woke up to a throbbing pain in my head. The ground was cold and hard beneath me. I was propped up against a post, my hands bound behind my back. Right away I knew the quiver had been taken, and I was sure I had been hit in the head. Dim light flickered from the hall and the hum of the fluorescent bulbs was sure to give me an instant headache. I looked down: the gun and my knife were also gone.

Fucking great. I blinked, still out of it from being nearly choked to death and hit over the head. Pipes wove their way on the ceiling above me. I was in a basement—again. The room was dimly lit. Shelves lined the walls. It took a second for my eyes to focus on the glorious sight of a medical storage room. Bandages, latex gloves, and more. The air was sticky and stale. I could taste the rancid body odor and rotting on my tongue.

I yanked my hands, loosening the knots. Crazies might be homicidal and determined to get their kill, but lacked fine motor skills. I gave the knots another pull. My left hand was almost free. I folded my thumb into my palm and pulled. The coarse rope caught on my knuckles. I braced myself against the pain and continued to pull. The cord slipped over my knuckles only to get caught on my ring.

Fucking hell.

"Hello?" someone called. My blood ran cold. "Hello?" she called again, her voice a shallow whisper. "Is there someone there? Someone sane, I mean?"

"Yeah," I answered, twisting my hand. I didn't want to lose a diamond. Stupid, I know, but the ring was so pretty. Dammit. I'd leave it in the truck next time.

"Did they bite you yet?" she asked feebly.

"No," I said right away then did a mental check. I didn't feel any pain or warm blood dripping down my body. I was good then, right?

"Wait, what do you mean by yet?"

She coughed. "That's what they do. Bite us until we turn."

Holy fucking shit. The crazies were *infecting* people?

"I've been here for days, but I'm not sick. I have so many bites." Her voice wavered as if she was about to burst into tears.

"You're resistant," I blurted. "The virus doesn't infect everyone."

"So I'm gonna stay here forever."

"No." I pulled my hand free. She'd be dead soon. She didn't have the zombie virus but that many bites would get infected with something else. My eyes flew to my ring; all diamonds were accounted for. I rolled my eyes at myself then quickly shook my head and got to work on the other knot. "My friends are upstairs. If I don't get us out of here first, they'll get us." The woman whimpered, not believing me. "What is your name?"

"Megan."

"All right Megan," I said, twisting and reaching for the knot. This one was tied rather tight. "I need you to stay calm, ok? We will get out of here alive, I promise." My nails hooked under it. It would only take a few pulls to get it free. "I'm Orissa."

The door to the storage room was open, allowing just enough light to spill into the room. There were three shelves in here, creating two aisles. Megan was out of eyesight in the other aisle. Someone shuffled their feet outside the room. A rattling breath turned into a growl.

"It's them!" Megan cried. "Oh God, it's them!"

I pulled at the rope to no avail. A shadow fell over me. I whirled around, sticking my left hand behind me to look like I was still tied up. A crazy walked in, her navy blue scrubs stiff with dried blood and other bodily fluids. Curly dark-blonde hair was matted to her face.

"Please!" Megan screamed. "No. No more! She said I can't turn. She said I'm resistant!"

The crazy stopped in the threshold, tipping her head as her eyes ran over me. Her body twitched unnaturally, eyes narrowing at the sound of Megan's cries.

"Shut up," I told her. "You can't reason with them."

"Please," she continued to beg. "Let me go!"

The crazy's lips pulled up in a sneer. Her bloodshot eyes sparked and she laughed. My skin crawled.

"No, no, please!" Megan cried when the crazy moved toward her.

"Hey!" I shouted. "How about some fresh meat? She's obviously not converting into your latest crazy cult member."

The crazy craned her neck around to beyond what was normal. Her body followed her head, twisting until she was facing me. Drool hung from her open mouth.

"Yeah, that's right," I coaxed, struggling to get my right hand free. "Come on Felicia," I said, reading her name from the ID badge that was pinned to her chest. Adrenaline coursed through my veins, speeding up my pulse. My hand was almost free.

Felicia stopped short, sticking her hand out in front of her. Primal growls vibrated deep inside. I didn't think she was even aware of the noise she was making anymore. She leaned forward, grabbing something off of the shelf.

Oh shit.

She held the knife up, sniffing the blood crusted blade. Her eyes closed and she opened her mouth, scraping the dried blood off with her teeth. It crunched when she ate it.

"You are disgusting, you know that, right?" I said, wrinkling my nose. "I've seen a lot of nasty shit these last few months, and I've got to say eating left over blood crust ranks pretty high."

She narrowed her eyes, staring at me. Did she understand my insult? No, she couldn't. Crazies weren't smart. They weren't supposed to understand anything. I slid my left hand back, sticking my fingers under the rope. Crazies weren't supposed to group together, stock up food, or make nests either.

Crap. She turned around, spinning on the heel of her worn out Crocks, and let out a high pitched yelp. Then she lunged at me. My hand wasn't free yet. I twisted my wrist, the rope dug into my skin, tearing off a layer.

I put my left hand on the ground and kicked out, knocking the crazy off her feet. She landed with a heavy thud. Suddenly the room got dark. Two more crazies stood in the doorway, blocking the light.

Megan started screaming.

One of the crazies was huge and wore camo pants and tan boots. His white t-shirt was ripped and stained. In his hand was a human arm. The flesh on the fingers had been gnawed down to the bone.

The other was an elderly woman in a hospital gown. Her lungs crackled with every breath. She was pitched forward, holding onto Camo Pants for support. The flesh on her face was peeling off. She reached up and picked at it, pulling a large flap of skin off her cheek. She put it in her mouth.

Sick.

Felicia rolled onto her stomach and reached for me, swinging dirty hands through the air. She caught my boot, digging her long nails in as hard as she could.

"That," I started and yanked my leg up, "is why I wear leather." I kicked her in the face. Her nose broke with a sharp snap. Blood streamed down. She roared, unaffected by pain. Then she coughed, looking confused by the act. "Not so tough when you can't breathe, are you?" I asked.

My arm was free. I sprang to my feet. Camo Pants rushed forward, raising the bloody stump like a weapon. I ducked when he swung. Growling, he dropped the arm and curled his hands into fists, coming at me.

I caught his fist right before it smacked into my face. Using both hands I twisted his wrist, snapping the bones. He wouldn't be able to hit me with that hand again despite his best efforts.

The old woman weebled in, holding onto the wall for support. She hissed and pointed at Felicia, who was still reeling for breath on the floor. Camo Pants charged again, his good hand finding its way to my throat.

I was still sore from being choked with the cord, and I couldn't breathe. In a panic, my hands flew up, grabbing onto his arm. He was bigger than me; I couldn't pull his off.

I tipped my head up, elongating my neck. I pushed off of him, whipping my body around. His nails tore into my flesh. Felicia spit blood onto the floor and got up, gurgling a low growl.

I needed something—anything. Their lack of response to pain made the crazies seem non-human. I swiped my hand across the shelf, knocking boxes of glove and containers of medicine cups to the floor. I sprinted around the shelf, trying to get to Megan.

Camo Pants tripped. Felicia stepped right on top of him. Her foot pressed hard into his ribcage. He didn't even flinch. Her heel rocked back and she fell, her elbow hitting Camo's teeth. Blood dripped into his mouth. He shot up, taking hold of her arm. A twisted smile lit up his face.

Purring, he stuck out his tongue, lapping up the blood that dripped from Felicia's arm. She hissed and pulled back. Camo was stronger. He flipped her over, pinning her body down with his, groaning as he sucked the wound.

What. The. Fuck. I blinked and turned around. Now was as good of chance as any to grab Megan and get the hell out of here. My foot caught something and I threw my arms out just seconds before I fell.

Another person lay bound on the floor. Bites covered their arms, pus filled and swollen. Cold, dead eyes stared at me. Completely revolted, I jumped over him, rounding the shelf.

Megan sat in an office chair with her hands tied to the plastic arms. Thick brown hair covered her dirty face. Red bite marks dotted her arms and legs. She was a wreck.

She screamed when she saw me. "It's ok," I whispered. "I'm

gonna get you out."

"Kill me, please," she begged. "I won't turn, I won't turn."

"I can get you help. One of my friends is a doctor." I knelt down. She was bound with electrical cords and they were tied fucking tight. "We'll take you to him and he'll make you better."

"No," she cried.

I worked on the knots at her wrists. I had just about loosened one when Felicia threw herself at us. I dodged out of the way. She landed on top of Megan, knocking the poor woman over.

Out of the corner of my eye I saw a stone garden gnome being used as a door stopper. Felicia disentangled herself from Megan. Camo was right behind her, so close I could feel his body heat. His eyes sparkled from getting his fill of fresh blood.

They stood there, staring at me. Felicia tipped her head, leering. I made the first move and jumped back, rolling to the floor. I grabbed the gnome, not expecting it to be heavy cast iron. Felicia raised her hands up, lips curled over teeth. She lunged at me. I was ready.

I swung the gnome, the pointy end of his hat colliding with her forehead. Blood sprayed, warm on my face. I tightened my grip on the gnome, bringing it back. I hit her again and she fell. I raised the gnome up again and smashed it on her as hard as I could.

Her body twitched. Parts of her brain were exposed from her cracked skull. Camo looked at Felicia, writhing on the ground dying of massive head trauma. He screamed, his breath rancid from the fresh blood. His hands flew up to his face before he leapt, unnaturally soaring through the air.

With a well aimed blow, the gnome busted open his head. He fell, knocked out but not dead. I knelt down, ramming the cast iron base into his skull over and over until pink brain matter oozed onto the floor.

Panting, I stood. Blood dripped from my hands. I backed up, looking at the carnage. Then someone grabbed me. I flipped around. The old woman hissed. I pushed her shoulders and she stumbled back, hip cracking when she hit the floor.

Knowing she couldn't get back up on her own, I flew back to Megan, frantically untying the cords.

"Can you stand?" I asked her once she was free.

She stared at me, blinking. "You killed them with a garden gnome."

"Yeah." I put my hand on her arm, ready to pull her up and flinched back. It was impossible to touch her without coming into contact with one of her open wounds.

"You..." She looked at the bodies. "Really? A gnome?"

I shrugged. "Come on, we gotta get out of here. I'm sure there are more."

She grabbed onto me, struggling to her feet. I hooked my arm around her, supporting her weight.

"I really won't turn?" she asked.

"It's been more than twenty-four hours?"

"Yes."

"Then no, you won't." I paused in the doorway, looking out. The hall was long and narrow, with cement walls painted a hideous yellow. A battery powered lantern hung from an overhead pipe. Down the hall and to our right was a door labeled 'soiled utility'. Feet shuffled and dragged inside that room.

Zombies.

Yep...not going in there. Heavy footfalls boomed above us. I held my breath, heart beating so fast it hurt. I moved my head to the left. There was an unmarked door on the same side of the hall that we were on. Then the hall forked. My eyes went to the smears of blood along the floor. I had just found our breadcrumb trail out.

"I don't understand," Megan said. I carefully let her go, ducking back into the supply room to get the gnome. It was the only weapon I had. "Everyone who gets bitten gets infected."

"Not everyone," I whispered and stepped out of the room. "I know two people who are resistant."

"Oh." Her body slumped even more.

"Why do I get the feeling you're disappointed by that news?" We edged down the hall. Someone ran above us. My chest tightened. I forced myself to take even breaths for Megan's sake.

"Why did you come in here?" she asked.

"To get medical supplies." We moved another few feet, just yards away from the door.

"Me too." Her head fell. "Do you have children, Marrisa?"

I opened my mouth to correct her but stopped short. I didn't like where this was going. "No." Sickness rose inside of me.

"I do. Did, I mean."

"I am so sorry." I meant it. I didn't know what it was like to have a child. I loved Hayden more than anything and the thought of losing him was bad enough. Of course, my brain had to conjure the image of us having children together and then watching them get eaten by zombies. "I can't even imagine."

"I was waiting to turn." Tears dripped down her face. "To forget who I was, to forget them and the pain. It hurts so much." She slumped against the wall.

"Megan, please." I tugged on her arm.

She put her hand on the cement. "It was just an ear infection. We didn't have to stop. But when I saw this place…"

Something scuttled in the cross hall. I didn't blink or take a breath. Megan sniffled, wiping her nose with the back of her hand.

"You have friends up there?" she asked.

I nodded.

"You need to go to them, get out of here, and never come back."

"That's my plan." I stood, expecting her to come with. "Megan," I whispered. "Come on."

She shook her head. "No."

The zombies in the spoiled utility room pushed against the door, their rattling death moans muffled. We needed to get out of here. I had no idea how much longer that door would continue to hold.

"There is a room full of zombies behind us. We *have* to leave." I pulled on her arm. Her eyes fastened on the spoiled utility room's door. She stood, looked at me, and nodded. I gave her a small smile and pressed on, taking a few steps before I realized she never followed. I whirled around to see her sprinting down the hall.

"Megan, no!" I called after her, reaching out. I lurched forward but was too late. She was closing in on the door. I skidded to a stop. The metal knob rattled when she twisted it, and then she threw the door open.

Hoarse growls and moans filled the basement. Megan held her arms out to her sides and tipped her head up. She was ready to die, to leave this harrowing world and all the pain it caused.

My heart thumped in my ears. My throat, suddenly dry, hurt when I swallowed. I watched Megan disappear, pulled apart by zombies. I forgot to breathe and I couldn't look away. Her intestines pulled and snapped, flinging blood and digested food into the air. Zombies scrambled for it, shoving it into their festering mouths.

Angry voices upstairs startled me. I jumped, my hand flying back and smacking into the wall. I blinked.

"Where is she?" It was Hayden. Oh, thank God. He was alive. "Where is she?" he screamed.

I wanted to call to him, tell him I was ok, but I couldn't. My eyes flicked to the zombies. They were busy eating…for now. Soon there would be nothing left. I took off, walking as fast as I dared down the hall. I stopped when I got to the fork.

Was that the dim outline of an exit sign or a mirage? Whatever it was, I took my chance. Gripping the heavy gnome, I ducked into the hall. It was hard to see but it was too late to turn around and grab the lantern and risk bringing unnecessary attention to myself.

I held one hand out, feeling my way to the door. I opened it, fingers trembling. Stairs...maybe. I blinked in the dark. Yes, there were stairs in front of me. The door would close and I would be totally blind.

A zombie made its way down the hall, feet dragging. Fuck it. What other option did I have? The door closed behind me. Everything was black. Pitch black. I got a flash of being stuck in the basement of that parking garage. Rider was with me.

Rider.

It still hurt. I could still remember the way he sounded, groaning and swinging his arms. I could still remember the knife puncturing his brain and his body going limp.

"Orissa!" Hayden yelled. His voice was louder. "Riss! Can you hear me?"

I fumbled my way up the stairs. It hurt, keeping my mouth shut. His name was on the tip of my tongue, and I wanted to shout it as loud as I could.

Finally, I reached a landing. I ran my hands along the wall, panic building as each second passed.

"Riss!" Hayden was close, so close. Something else could have been closer. I almost cried out with relief when my fingers grazed the door knob. I needed out. The darkness pressed on me, suffocating.

I turned the knob. The door was locked. I ran my fingers along it, trying to figure out how to get out. Even if I could see, there wasn't a lock to pick. It had to be locked from the outside.

"Hayden!" I called, slapping the door. He didn't answer. Dammit. I waited too long. He was gone. He couldn't hear me. I twisted the knob again, slamming my body against the door. "Hayden!" I screamed.

I couldn't go back down, not when the hall was filling with zombies. I rapped my knuckles against the metal door. "Hayden!"

Seconds ticked by. Nothing. I rested my forehead against the door. He'd come back. He'd hear me. And he'd do it before the zombies stumbled their way up the stairs.

"We already checked in there," Wade said, his voice muffled and distant. I leaned back.

"Guys!" I shouted. "I'm in here! The door's locked!" I banged. "Hurry there are zombies!"

"Riss!" Hayden was frantic. "I'm coming!" He grabbed the door knob, rattling it. "Get back," he told me. I moved away from the knob, turning into the wall. I covered my ears just before the shot rang out.

Hayden swung the door open, reached in and grabbed my arm, pulling me out of the stairwell. I jumped away from the door and slammed it shut. Then I turned to Hayden, our arms flying around each other.

He pulled me in until my breasts crushed against his chest. Panting, I held onto him and never wanted to let go. His heart was racing. He put his hands on the side of my head, and kissed me. He pulled away, wiping blood from his mouth.

"It's not my blood," I said quickly, bringing my hand to my face. The blood hadn't dried yet but was going thick and sticky. Ugh. So nasty. Zombies pounded on the door at the bottom of the stairs.

"We need to get the hell out of here," Jason said and turned around. He had my quiver hooked over his shoulder. Wade had my bow. Hayden took my hand, leading me through a narrow corridor. Faded notes were pinned on a cork-board. Dust covered jackets hung below. A paper skeleton had been tacked to the wall. Right. Halloween. That's when this all started.

Wade went first, gun raised. He motioned for us to follow; we sprinted through the lobby and out the front door, not stopping until we reached our vehicles.

"What the fuck was that?" Jason panted. He whirled around, eyeing the nursing home as if it might jump to life and swallow him whole.

"Let's get out of here first," Hayden said, getting his keys from his pocket. Wade nodded. We got into our trucks and sped out of the parking lot, not stopping until a few miles had been put between us and Silver Living Center.

We pulled over in the middle of the street. A shopping center was next to us. The glass fronts had been smashed in. Carts lay on their sides in the parking lot.

Hayden cut the engine. He turned to me, running his eyes up and down my body. His eyes were misty when he reached out for my hand, pressing it to his lips. I unbuckled and leaned over the center console.

"That was fucking unbearable," he whispered. "I looked over and you were gone."

His pulse picked up again. I put my hand on the back of his neck. "I woke up and you weren't there."

He leaned away. "Woke up? You got knocked out?"

"Yes. I'm getting really tired of getting kidnapped."

The doors to the Jeep closed and Jason and Wade walked down the street, stopping by the truck. Hayden let me go and got out. Clouds rolled over the sun. It was still hot and the promise of rain made the air slightly humid.

Goosebumps broke out on my arms. I closed my eyes, forcing myself to take a steady breath and push the image of Megan surrendering to the zombies out of my mind. I had seen people get eaten, ripped apart until there was nothing left. I had killed countless zombies and crazies. All traces of humanity were gone but I was aware—each and every time—that they were humans who used to have families and relationships. Hell, I'd even killed those bastards at Eastmoore.

None of that bothered me as much as someone committing suicide.

"Riss?"

I startled. Hayden stood next to my door, his hand on the open window. His face showed concern. I gave him a tiny nod, letting him know I was ok. He opened the door and held out his hand, helping me down. How did he know my legs felt like Jell-O?

Wade opened the backpack, pulling out my gun and knife.

"Did you get medicine?" I asked, taking back my weapons.

"No. We looked for you," he told me.

I blinked and in that millisecond of darkness flashed the image of Megan's blood spraying as a zombie bit into her neck. "I met someone," I started.

"Should I be worried?" Hayden joked.

I looked at him, not at all amused.

His face went blank. "In the basement."

I shook my head and held up my hand. "Let me start over from the beginning. A crazy came up behind me, strangled me with a cord until I passed out. I woke up in a storage room with my hands tied behind my back. There was another woman down there." I took in a ragged breath. Hayden put his hand on my waist. "She told me that the crazies were taking people and infecting them."

The buzz of insects was deafening. A grasshopper leapt from a tall weed growing through a crack in the pavement.

"So they're building an army?" Jason asked, rapping his fingers along the side of his assault rifle.

"They're infecting them, not killing them?" Hayden asked.

I nodded. "That's what she told me."

"They *are* building an army," Wade said quietly.

"An army of cannibalistic serial killers. That know no pain or fear." Jason laughed. "Nothing to worry about."

"Fuck this shit." Wade's mouth fell open and he shook his head. "Zombies...we can handle. They're dumb, only want one thing. But these S1s...they can think, plan...attack."

"How is this happening?" Hayden said, looking around us. "Are they getting smarter?"

"I don't think it works that way, right?" I asked. "Maybe the virus isn't, uh, doing what it used to?"

Hayden shuddered. "This is something Dr. Cara can look into. I don't want to think about it."

"Me neither," Wade agreed. He slid his hands down the barrel of his gun. "Riss?" he said gently. "What happened to that woman?"

I bit my lip. "She didn't make it." My instinct was to hide the truth, to keep the guys from knowing something that would upset them. But it felt wrong. I didn't want to keep anything from them. "She told me she had a child that died. The loss was too much..." I wrapped my arms around myself. "She was covered in bites and not crazy. I told her some people are resistant and that she had to be one of them. When she found out she would never turn, she threw herself into a room full of zombies. I couldn't stop her in time."

Jason's face was white. Wade looked like he instantly regretted asking me what had happened. I forced a smile. "It's over now. Her pain is gone and...and maybe she's with her baby."

"I like to think that," Jason said softly. His eyes moved to the sinking sun. "What now?"

"We need to find a safe place for the night," Hayden said. "We have to take more precautions than before to stay safe from crazies."

"The farmhouse..." Jason started. "Nah, never mind."

"What?" Hayden asked.

Jason nervously glanced at me. "Riss's grandparent's house was safe. We left food and weapons there. And it's close."

All eyes fell on me. I shrugged. "We don't know if it's still safe. When we left, a herd was passing through." The thought of home swelled in my heart. I wanted to go so bad it hurt. I wanted to walk through the front door and hear the creaky floorboards. I wanted to sleep in my bed.

My bed.

Jason went on. "There are bars over the windows and the doors are boarded up and reinforced. The place is a fortress."

"I wouldn't go that far," I said. "We left for a reason."

Jason nodded. "It was just an idea."

Hayden's fingers pressed into my side. "We can always drive by. I know it's nice to be somewhere familiar anyway," he added quietly.

"Ok," I said. "Let's go. There are a few places nearby we could stay if the house isn't in good standing anyway." I moved to the back of the truck, pulling my blood soaked shirt over my head. I tossed it on the ground, seeing no point on bringing something so dirty along with us.

"You're sure you're ok with this?" Hayden asked. I pulled a pale yellow tank top over my head.

"Yes. It's just a house."

"We both know that's a bunch of bull," he said, half smiling.

I put the bow and quiver up front and got in. "You're with me so I'll be fine." I looked down at my left hand. A chunk of skull stuck to my diamond. Grimacing, I peeled it off and flicked it out the open window.

Hayden got in the driver's side and started the truck. He reached over, linking his fingers through mine and started the drive to the farmhouse.

CHAPTER FOURTEEN

Just like last time, it was dark when we rounded the curve in the road near my grandparent's farm. Nerves bubbled in my stomach, twisting into painful cramps. I tugged on the end of my braid, preparing myself for the worst.

The images flashed through my mind: the house, burned to the ground. All the bars pried off the windows, zombies stomping around the house, so full of the undead we couldn't get in. I couldn't get another image out of my head, and it frightened me the most.

I closed my eyes and it flashed through my brain. We would pull into the driveway and see the distant yellow glow of lights. My grandpa would open the door, with a gun turned on us of course, with Aunt Jenny behind him holding a pistol of her own.

Hayden reached over, taking my hand so that I couldn't pull on my hair. He linked his fingers through mine, giving them a squeeze. I opened my eyes and looked at him. We would be all right.

"They can go first," he said, meaning Wade and Jason.

"No." I shook my head. "It's just delaying the inevitable. Besides, if it's bad we'll need to move on as soon as possible. It's dark and dense." I cast my eyes to the thick tree line. "Anything could be lurking."

"You sure?"

"It's just a house," I told him, letting go of his hand. "We can find another."

Hayden tightened his grip on the steering wheel. "Right." He knew it wasn't just a house to me. And he also knew that I needed to convince myself it was true. I had to, just in case...

"Turn here," I told him. Hayden cranked the wheel, pressing hard on the brakes. "Shit." Bodies lined the street. The truck lurched to a stop, headlights illuminating the pile. Arms and legs twisted unnaturally.

"What's going on?" Wade asked over the radio.

"Bodies," I answered. "In the way."

"Zombie bodies?" he asked.

I rolled down the window and was immediately hit with rank air, confirming my suspicions. A pile of non-infected bodies wouldn't have lasted much more than a day. They would have been eaten. "Yes."

Hayden put the truck in park and turned to me. "We have to move them."

"Put it in four-wheel?" I questioned.

He shook his head. "I don't want to risk an arm or something getting caught in the wheels."

Grass and weeds crept over the shoulder and onto the road. The foliage was thick on both sides and clouds covered the moon.

"Ok," I said and unbuckled my seatbelt. "Let's be quick about it."

"I should do it," he started. "Since I can't get infected."

"There's gloves in the back," I added.

Hayden's face tightened; he wanted me to stay in the truck where it was relatively safe. I grabbed gloves from the backseat and tied a bandana around my face, covering my mouth and nose. We got out, doubled checked that our guns were loaded, and got to work while Jason and Wade kept watch.

The night was alive with the peaceful hum of crickets and frogs. The gently breeze made tonight's air perfectly tolerable. It was the kind of Kentucky summer night that I loved, the kind of weather for sneaking out my bedroom window and running to Raeya's or meeting a boy that my grandpa would never approve of. Every window in my grandparent's house would have been open, and the heat wouldn't creep in until late the next morning.

I looked up at the cloudy sky. It was so dark. If not for the headlights streaming at us, I wouldn't have been able to see into the trees at all. I pulled on the gloves and moved to the pile of dead zombies. The pungent smell of rotting burned my eyes.

They must have been here a while. Their wrinkled, rotting skin had melted off, sliming off their bones and onto the pavement. I curled my fingers around a zombie's wrist, having to peel her arm off the street. Bits of sticky skin stayed behind. My fingers mushed into a crispy layer of fat that covered muscle. Her ligaments had dried up and hardened and rolled under the fat as I pulled.

Maggots wriggled out of her empty eye socket, sprinkling the road as I dragged her away, dropping her arms when I reached the side of the road. I went back and grabbed the ankles of another zombie. He was piled atop of several other bodies; I had to give him a good tug before he came free. Face dragging along the rough road caused his skin to rub off, leaving a nasty smear of festering flesh.

I picked another that was on top of the pile. I pulled on its arm. The bones cracked and muscles snapped. I stumbled back when the arm ripped off. Melted tissue dripped onto my feet. I wrinkled my nose in disgust and tossed the arm aside. I leaned over, closing my eyes to keep them from watering. The smell of rotting was so strong it seeped into my soul, gagging me. I hoped that we could get the showers working again.

I grabbed the back of its jacket, heaving it up and off the pile. Half of its head was missing, cut clean off by a very sharp blade. The remaining half of the brain was shriveled up to almost nothing. Curious, I turned it into the headlights.

There was a gap—about an inch wide—between the dark, festering coils of brain matter and the skull. I narrowed my eyes, moving my face closer to inspect the black spots that covered the inside of the skull.

Behind me, Hayden was still moving zombies. He picked up a body with ease, tossing it to the side. I tipped my nearly headless zombie down and carefully stuck a gloved finger inside the skull, rubbing the black spot.

There was a shuffling close behind me. "What are you doing?" Hayden asked as he lifted another zombie by the ankles.

"There's something weird in its head," I told him. The blackness wiped away. I held up my fingers, looking at the dust that covered the gloves. Interesting. Right away I thought about telling Dr. Cara about this new discovery, even though I was mad at her.

I let the zombie fall to the ground, its open skull cracking like an eggshell when it hit the street. I bent over to pick up his ankles, dragging him away by his feet. I stepped a few paces back and over another body.

A hand stuck out through a gap between torsos. Fingers curled around my ankle and yanked me toward an open mouth. The zombie growled, pushing its way through the cleared off path to freedom...and food.

I dropped the zombie I had been dragging and yanked my foot up, breaking the grasp. But I moved too fast and slipped when my foot landed, my boot pushing through another zombie's stomach. I fell back.

"Riss!" Jason yelled. Hayden looked up and let go of the zombie he was moving. I scrambled away, bringing my leg up toward my chest. The zombie crawled out of the mangled mess of decaying bodies. A wrinkled flap of skin hung from his forehead, looking like a scalping gone wrong.

He let out a gargling roar, reaching for me with blood-crusted hands. I kicked him, heel connecting with his bottom jaw, breaking it and causing it to hang loose. I brought my leg up again and kicked him in the nose. The bones crushed in and thick brown blood slimed down his face.

Branches crashed against each other to my right. I whipped my head to the side. Fuck.

"Guys!" I yelled and kicked the zombie in the face again. My hands slipped, and I flopped onto my back, head cracking against the pavement. The pain rippled through me, ears instantly ringing.

The zombie pulled free from the hive of bodies. It was right there, over me, mouth open wide. My vision blurred as the pain radiated from the back of my head, banding around like a vice.

Then blood splattered my chest and the tip of a knife popped through the zombie's forehead. Hayden yanked his knife back, shoving the zombie to the side. He reached down. I took his hand and scrambled up.

"You ok?"

"Yeah," I said, rubbing the back of my head. "Fucker was alive the whole time, just hiding out."

"You hit your head," he said, moving his hand to feel for a lump. "I heard it smack."

"There's something about this location and head injuries," I mumbled. Leaves crunched. Hayden jumped back, holding his knife out, ready and in position. We heard her before she emerged from the trees, crashing into branches and tripping over the underbrush.

Hayden flew forward, swiftly moving his arm up, sending the knife into her skull. He yanked it out before she dropped. Blood sprayed up in the air. He kept his eyes on the trees for several seconds before turning and scanning the pile. "A few more and we can go."

I nodded, still feeling the effects of the fall, but rushed over to the pile. I dragged two more bodies to the side before we deemed it clear enough to drive over. I peeled the gloves off and threw them in the bed of the truck and shook my boot. Stinky, slimy stomach contents stuck to the material.

I looked at it, disgusted, when it hit me. There wasn't just undigested zombie food stuck to my laces. There were bits and pieces of chewed people. And for all I knew, it would be people I knew. The thought made my heart race and pound in my ears. I got in the truck, slamming the door shut.

Hayden gunned it over the few remaining bodies. They were dead, hardly even human anymore. Still, feeling the tires bump over torsos and limbs didn't sit well in my stomach. I let out a breath when the pile disappeared into the dark.

We were getting close. I wrapped my hand around Hayden's dog tags, moving them along the chain. I could feel Hayden's eyes on me. He didn't say anything, just put his hand on my thigh to let me know he was aware of my nerves.

"It's the next driveway," I told him. It had come up faster than I anticipated. I leaned forward. The truck slowed.

There it was, sitting far back from the road. No soft yellow glow spilled onto the overgrown yard. My grandpa's new Ford truck wasn't in the driveway. The house was empty and dark.

But it was home.

Hayden turned onto the driveway. The headlights illuminated the front of the house. I strained my eyes, looking over every window and door that I could see. It looked just as it did the day we left except the yard was exceptionally overgrown. My grandma would have thrown a fit to see it this way.

The driveway was almost hard to find since it was so overtaken by weeds. Granted, it was a mix of grass and gravel to begin with, even when my grandma was alive. The truck bumped along it, wheels dipping in the many potholes.

Hayden put the truck in park and waited. The low rumble of the engine drowned out the familiar sounds of wildlife.

"It doesn't look like anyone's been here," he said and I nodded. "Let's check it out."

I moved my hand to the release button of the seat belt, hesitating. I took a breath and pushed it. It was stupid to be nervous. It was a house—just a fucking house. I got out of the truck and slipped the quiver over my head, adjusting the strap so it rested in just the right position on my back, allowing me to grab arrows with ease. I flicked off the safety to the M9 that was strapped to my thigh and clipped a knife to my belt. Holding the bow against my side, I quietly closed the truck door and waited for the others.

"Just how I remembered it," Jason said quietly.

"Let's hope," I said. Hayden turned on his flashlight, holding it under his pistol. He and I stepped forward, pushing our way through the overgrown yard. Jason and Wade held back, keeping an eye on our surroundings.

I put my foot on the first step of the porch, knowing the wooden plank would creak as soon as my weight pressed down. Hayden shined the light across the wraparound porch.

"You guys weren't kidding about this place." Hayden turned his flashlight on the windows, the light reflecting off the metal bars. I shook my head. We hadn't been, not one bit. Hayden moved next to me, stopping when the beam of light illuminated a large spiderweb. "Ladies first," he said with a smile.

I raised my eyebrows. There was no way I was walking through that thing. It stretched from one post to another, blocking the entrance to the covered porch. I leaned in close. The web was new; the intricate system of lines and spirals was intact, each string glistening.

A large spider hid in the upper corner. I grimaced more than I liked when I saw it and took a step back.

"Really, Hayden, you should go first to make sure the coast is clear." I smiled innocently.

He pressed his lips together and raised an eyebrow. "No way. Not if I don't have to."

"You are such a baby," I teased and reached behind me, pulling an arrow from the quiver. I grabbed Hayden's wrist, moving the flashlight over the spider. "Great, it's one of those jumping spiders." Hayden moved away from the porch.

"You got this," he said encouragingly. I extended my arm, putting as much distance as possible between the web and my body and contemplated my next move. After deciding that throwing the arrow into the web and letting gravity do the dirty work was the best course of action, I tossed the arrow up and jumped back, scrambling away from the falling spider. The arrow clattered to the porch.

"Zombie?" Jason asked, springing around the truck, gun raised.

"No," Hayden said, turning around. "Spider."

"Just as bad," Wade muttered, shaking his head.

I nudged the arrow with my foot. I'd pick it up later...when the spider was long gone. I moved up the porch steps, my heart thumping in my chest. Hand prints—an indiscernible mix of dirt and blood—were smeared over the wood. Nails had scratched trails across the door. Zombies had tried to get in.

My fingers wrapped around the metal doorknob, slick with dew. I cast my eyes aside, looking at Hayden. He raised the flashlight, holding his knife out with the other hand.

"On three," I told him. One. My fingers tightened. Two. I flexed my wrist. Three. I turned the knob. And it was locked. "Well, shit," I said and let my hand fall, slapping against my thigh. There was no way anyone stopped to lock the deadbolt while we were running for our lives. Not even Raeya. Who had locked it?

"Can you pick it?" Hayden asked, moving down the porch. Siding along the front window had been pried loose. He shined the light into the house, looking in for a few seconds before turning back to me.

"No. Not this kind of lock." I turned around. "There's a hide-a-key." Or at least there used to be. I used it to get into the house when we first arrived from Indy. After that, I used the house key that was attached to the ring the truck keys were on.

Jason walked up the sidewalk, counting his steps as he went. "Seven," he said out loud and bent down, running his fingers over a loose piece of cement. To anyone else, the crack would have looked like it happened naturally. Jason had paid more attention that I thought he had the last time we were here. He knew exactly what he was doing. He pulled a knife from his pocket and slid the blade into the crack, slowly pushing the knife down.

The piece of cement came up and Jason grabbed the key. He stood and brought it over to me.

"Good hiding place," Wade said, still eyeing the sidewalk.

I rubbed the key against my pants, brushing the dirt off. "I wasn't sure if it would be there."

"Raeya put it back." Jason wiped his hands on his shirt.

"Of course she would," I said and stuck the key in the lock. Hayden moved close, ready just in case. Wade stood at the bottom of the steps, using the light on his high powered rifle to look around the yard.

I pushed the door open and stepped inside.

* * *

There was a chance something had come in through the back. I strung an arrow on the bow to be ready. Hayden stepped in behind me, shining the light around.

Jason entered the house next, running his hand up and down the wall to feel for the light switch.

"The generator's empty," I said quietly. I knew not even Raeya took the time to turn it off. I wondered if it would still work. It was kept out of the elements so I didn't see why it wouldn't, especially since all the gas had been used up and there was nothing in it to get sticky or corroded.

My eyes settled on the base of the stairs. I looked away, not wanting to think about it, not wanting to remember the shuffling thumps as Zoe tumbled down the stairs.

"How many exits?" Hayden asked.

"Two," I said. "That are operable. So the front door and then one in the kitchen. The sliding glass doors in the family room are completely boarded up." I was glad; those glass doors had creeped me out when I was a kid. There was something about them that made the house feel so vulnerable. The two big glass panes were easy to break and allowed anyone to see in. "Check the living room," I said to Jason and Wade. "We'll go in through the kitchen and meet in the breakfast nook, ok?"

Jason nodded and took the lead. Hayden and I went to the left, passing by the stairs. The breakfast table was still in the dining room, pushed up against the large dining room table. It was the only way our entire rag-tag group could fit. A thick layer of dust covered the dark oak surface of the tables. I swiped my finger across it. A plate speckled with hardened crumbs had been left out with a fork and knife alongside it.

We moved into the kitchen and I pointed to the door. Hayden shined the light across the room. A ball of tension eased—just a bit— when I saw that the door was still locked.

Dishes filled the kitchen sink. The floor was a filthy mess crumbs and dirt. Had it been that way before we left? I didn't think so. I looked at the floor, next to the fridge. Argo's food and water bowls were gone. A chill ran through me. I whirled around, opening a drawer that we had stocked full of candles and flashlights. It was empty.

"Someone's been here," I said quietly. My heart sped up. "This isn't how we left it."

Hayden tensed, moving his finger over the trigger.

"First level is clear," Jason said when he walked through the family room and into the breakfast nook. "Let's check the upstairs."

I looked at him, mouth slightly open and eyes wide. "Did you notice anything different from the last time?"

"Uh, not really." He looked around him. "It's kinda dark."

I breezed past. "The firewood's gone," I called from the living room. The guys hurried in behind me.

"We would stay here," Wade said. "On a mission. This place is perfect. It's not out of the question for someone else to do the same."

"Yeah," I agreed. "But how'd they lock the doors?"

No one had an answer for that. We moved on, checking the upstairs. I stopped at the top of the landing, looking down the hall. All of the bedroom doors were closed.

"S1s could be behind those doors," Hayden whispered. "Literally behind every door, waiting for us."

I swallowed and nodded, stringing an arrow along the bow. To the left was my old room and the bathroom. To our right were the other two bedrooms. The air was stale and thick, giving the entire house a dry musky smell.

"You two check down there," Wade suggested looking to the left.

"We'll stay here and watch the other side of the hall."

I moved to the bathroom door. Hayden moved to the other side, putting his hand over the knob. I pulled back the arrow.

Hayden threw open the door. I moved into the doorway just as Hayden swept the room with his light.

It was empty.

We crept down the hall, stopping outside my old room. Nothing jumped out when Hayden opened the door. I stepped inside, needing to check the closet. I pointed at it with the arrow. Hayden nodded and went past me and pulled the sliding door to the side.

It was just how we'd left it. I wasn't sure exactly how long my old group had stayed in this farmhouse, but over the weeks we had gone out on runs, bringing back food and supplies. On one of the trips into a nearby town, Raeya and I raided a fancy clothing boutique. I had never been able to afford anything in that stupid store before the depression hit. Given the huge clearance sale signs plastered all over the place, I guessed not too many other people could either. We had fun taking everything we could grab.

When I turned to leave, I noticed the bed had been made. I knew for a fact that we hadn't done it. My last memory of my bed was waking up next to Zoe who was cold and lifeless. We wrapped her up in the sheets and carried her outside.

We moved down the hall and looked in the other two rooms. When the coast was clear, we went down stairs and checked the basement.

I turned at the bottom of the stairs. The footsteps from my boots softly echoed off the cement walls. I stopped in front of a wide set of shelves. I could barely smell the scent of pine from under the dust.

"A train collection?" Jason asked, raising his eyebrow.

I smiled. "Didn't you ever wonder where all the weapons came from?" I asked him, running my fingers over a red boxcar.

"I figured you had a secret hiding place somewhere in the house." His eyes went from mine to the shelves. "No freaking way."

"Way." I flipped the boxcar up, revealing the hidden latch. I pulled the shelf away from the wall and opened the door to the secret room. Hayden held up the light. The guys looked around, salivating.

While they took in the guns still hanging on the wall, I looked at the empty spots. Half of the weapons were gone. While some had been missing from the start, I didn't think we had taken that many. Padraic had come down here during our frantic escape to collect more weapons. I couldn't be sure exactly what he had taken out and what had made it to the cars.

"I am so utterly confused by you," Wade said and picked up a box of bullets. "All that bullshit Jason made up about you being a government agent makes sense now." He shook the box, realized it was full, and set it down. "You're not, are you?" He ran his finger over a disassembled M2 Browning machine gun.

Hayden stepped forward. "How..." He shook his head, turning around to face me. "How the hell did your grandpa get some of these?"

"I can honestly tell you that I have no idea." I twisted the end of my braid between my fingers. "My grandpa had some *interesting* friends."

Wade raised an eyebrow. "Yeah. *Interesting* friends that can get you this beast." He patted the M2.

I knew my grandpa had dealt with shady people just as well as I knew he had done more than a handful of illegal things that could have earned him years in prison. But he had done everything with the intention of protecting his family. There was nothing wrong with that.

"People used to think he was crazy for believing the government was out to get us and sometimes I did too," I confessed. I shook my head, eyes focusing on an M4 Carbine. "But he was right all along." Hayden took my hand, his touch gently and comforting. He knew I was feeling guilty. I squeezed his fingers. I loved that he knew me well enough to sense even the smallest things.

"Why do I feel like I'm missing something?" Wade asked.

"Because you are." Hayden knew the truth. He knew what my grandpa had put me through and he knew why. It was a secret I kept carefully guarded. I loved my grandpa and understood that everything he did was with the best intentions. He wanted me to survive.

And I had.

Deciding it would be easier to sort through the weapons with the lights on, we went back upstairs to get our gear from the cars.

"It really bothers me to think that strangers slept in my bed," I grumbled. Hayden opened the front door for me. We stepped onto the porch and looked around before going to our vehicles.

"We've slept in other people's beds too," he said and unlocked the truck. "We've even had sex in other people's beds."

"Just one bed," I corrected with a small smile. I opened the truck, reaching inside for my bag. "And that doesn't matter. It's my bed. I don't want anyone but you in it."

"At least I'm allowed," Hayden said, slipping his arm through the straps of his own bag and then silently closed the truck door. We walked around to the bed, grabbing our bags of food. "It's nice here," he said quietly. "I can see why you like it so much."

"It is." I opened the Jeep, struggling to get a hold of Jason's bag while holding the rest of our gear. "The house is big for its age. But I think it's the memories that make it so special, as lame as that sounds."

"Not lame at all," he assured me and picked up another duffle bag. We headed back to the house.

"There's still gas in the barn, right?" Jason asked as soon as we came inside.

"There was when we left," I said and dropped the bags of clothing to the ground. "But I know for a fact that if I stayed here I'd take all the gas when I left."

"Should we go check? We could fire up the generator."

"We should wait until the morning," I said and looked past the foyer and out the breakfast nook's large windows. There were too many hiding places, too many shadows in the yard. We got lucky with the house. I had a nagging feeling this kind of luck wouldn't strike twice.

"This will do for now," Hayden said. "I'll take the lack of power if it means we are safe for the night."

"Me too," Wade agreed. "This place is perfect, Riss." He shone his light around the living room. Blankets were neatly folded on the couch. A mug sat on the coffee table, not on a coaster. There was on ring that would never come out. Boxes of board games were stacked alongside the fireplace. I couldn't remember the last one we had played.

"Hey," Jason called from the kitchen. "Come look at this!"

He sounded excited, not frightened. Hayden, Wade, and I hurried through the house.

Jason stood in front of the pantry. "All the food is still here!"

"What idiots," Wade chuckled. "They stayed here but left the food."

"They're loss," Jason said and reached in, grabbing a bag of potato chips. It was odd to leave the food, no doubt, but we had done it as well. Maybe whoever was here last had to run out just like we had?

I whirled around, compelled to check the rest of the house for supplies. I fished a flashlight from my bag and went back into the kitchen, opening cabinets and drawers.

"Yes!" I said when I opened a drawer. Hayden moved closer, snaking his arms around my waist.

"What?" he asked.

"Candles. This drawer was full when we left but look. We have about a half dozen left." I reached in, pulling out the tea lights. I set them on the counter; Hayden lit them with his own lighter. We dispersed them throughout the first level, then we were ready to settle in for the night.

I carried our heavy bag of sustenance into the kitchen, setting it on the counter. My stomach grumbled and I was tired. I had no idea what time it was but I guessed it to be after midnight.

"Is this you?" Hayden asked from the family room. I looked over my shoulder. He held his arm up, shining the flashlight on a photograph that hung on the wall. I smiled as I walked over.

"Yeah. It is." I looked at my eighteen year-old self, hair up in a mess of precariously placed curls. "Prom." My mom threw a fit about the low cut dress I wore. She wasn't home to take me dress shopping so my grandma, as sick as she was, dragged an oxygen tank behind her and took me to an expensive dress store. Knowing death could take her any day, my grandma had become rather rebellious in the end and said the cleavage showing, curve hugging dress was made for me.

"You look weird with makeup on," Hayden said.

"And I look ten years younger."

He looked at me then the picture. "Not really. You don't look like a teenager now but you haven't changed much."

"I'll take that as a compliment." I smiled.

"This looks like the Riss I know," he said, moving to another photograph. This one was only a few years old. I was tan and barefoot, standing along the edge of a lake wearing a tank top and jeans with a fishing pole in my hand.

I had to drag Hayden away from the pictures, telling him we could look through old photo albums during our watch. Jason and Wade were already eating, sitting at the counter in the kitchen. I smeared peanut butter over crackers and sprinkled raisins on top, then hopped up on the counter to sit while I ate.

"We totally could have stayed," Jason said with his mouthful. He finished chewing then continued. "We left because we thought the zombies were gonna bust through the door."

The thought had occurred to me as soon as I saw the front door still on the hinges. "If we were inside maybe they would have," I said. "And besides." I picked up another cracker. "I'm glad we left." My eyes flicked across the room to Hayden.

Jason made a gagging sound and rolled his eyes. I kicked him and he dodged away, laughing. "You know," he said, wiping his hands together and sprinkling more crumbs onto the floor. "I'm surprised this doesn't stink." He put his hand on the handle of the fridge.

"Ugh," I started, ready to tell him not to bother opening it. But he beat me to it and I almost fell over. Yellow light spilled from the refrigerator. Jason stood, transfixed. Wade sucked in a breath and pushed off the counter, striding over to the sink. His hand landed on the wall. He slid it up, flicking on a light.

"Holy shit," I said and jumped down. Hayden rushed into the room. I turned on the overhead light. "We have power."

The four of us stood there, dumbly staring at the light as if it was some sort of mystical source. I shook myself.

"I don't hear the generator." I didn't think about it; I turned around and opened the backdoor. Hayden called after me but I was already on the wraparound porch, eyes flitting to the large generator. It indeed was off and had even been pushed to the side of the porch. "It doesn't make sense." Hayden's hand landed on my wrist. Then I noticed the wires. I followed them down and off the porch. It was hard to see in the dim light.

"It's solar powered," Hayden said.

"That's fucking brilliant." I smiled, shaking my head. We returned into the house where it was safe. "Something bad must have happened to whoever stayed here," I guessed. "To leave all this."

"Unless they intended on coming back," Wade said casually. Then his words hit us. "Oh, shit."

"I don't care if they come back. This is my house." I crossed my arms.

"What if they say it's theirs?" Jason asked.

"It's not theirs. And I'm in the pictures to prove it. It was mine before the apocalypse, it's mine now, and I won't give it up."

Hayden held up his hand. "Let's not get ahead of ourselves. It's late; we need to spilt up and get some sleep."

Hayden and I took the first shift. I opened all the windows in the house. It was uncomfortably stuffy from being closed up in this heat. I went up to my room and hesitated in the doorway, eyes settling on my bed. Unable to take it, I strode in and threw back the comforter.

The mattress had been flipped and smelled faintly of bleach. Faded pink sheets stretched over the queen-sized bed, neatly tucked in. Even the pillow cases had been changed. I kicked off my boots and jeans and opened the dresser, looking for something comfortable to put on.

I settled for black yoga pants and a pink t-shirt that had a black print screen skull over the chest. I grabbed the scrapbooks my grandma had made for me, knowing Hayden would enjoy looking at them.

He had already found something to entertain himself with when I came back downstairs.

"Oh my God, no," I said, having to really try and suppress my smile. "We are not watching that."

Hayden sat on the floor in front of the TV stand with a shiny disk in his hand. "Yes, we are. I'm not passing up a chance to watch home videos of my future wife." He looked up at me, beaming.

"Fine. Just one." I rolled my eyes. Hayden plugged in the TV, dusted off the screen, and popped the DVD in. We settled on the couch. This particular recording was of me, only twelve years old, going through an obstacle course of sorts my grandpa had set up. He followed behind me with the camera as I moved through the course, shooting targets.

"You were raised like a warrior," he said and turned off the TV. He stood, extending his hand to me. I took it.

"Yeah, I know."

"I'm not saying it's bad."

I raised my eyebrows. "But you're saying it's not normal."

He smiled. "No, not normal at all. But in a weird way I'm kinda jealous."

I laughed and moved to the window. "That is weird."

"Just think of how good I'd be if I started young."

I turned to see him smiling. I rolled my eyes. He came up behind me, putting his arms around me. "This is weird too," I said and hugged him. "Having part of my old life back. I never thought I'd come back here again. I wanted to, of course. And now that you're here with me...I don't want to leave."

"We have to," he said gently.

"I know. I know we do. The compound is home. This...this isn't home anymore." I sighed and let go of Hayden. We made rounds around the house then sat in the living room going through the scrapbooks, getting up every few minutes to look out the windows until it was our turn to sleep.

Once in my room, Hayden stripped down to his boxers. I unhooked my bra, slipped it over my arms through my shirt, and took off the yoga pants. I threw back the comforter and settled under the sheets. Hayden put his gun on the nightstand and got in bed next to me.

I closed my eyes as he snuggled close, wrapping his arms around me and pulling me in. If I tried, I could pretend none of the bad shit had ever happened, that Hayden and I had met under different circumstances and that everyone I cared about was alive and well.

"You know," I said and pulled the sheet over us. "You're the first guy to be in this bed with me. My grandparents were very strict."

"No one ever sneaked up?"

"My boyfriends were scared of my grandpa."

Hayden laughed and kissed the back of my neck. A shiver rippled across my skin, goosebumps rising. "I like learning about you."

I turned around and hooked my leg over his hip. "Learning how messed up I am you mean."

He shook his head and brushed my hair out of my face. "You're not messed up, Riss."

"You do know you're a terrible liar, right?"

Hayden laughed. "We're all a little messed up. Some just hide it better than others."

I put my hand on his cheek, his day old stubble rough on my hand. I pulled his face to mine and kissed him, biting at his bottom lip. Hayden moved his hands to my waist, and in a quick movement, lifted himself up and on top of me. He deepened the kiss, grinding himself against me. I opened my legs, feeling his erection through the thin layers of fabric. Warmth tingled deep inside of me.

"We don't have to be quiet," he whispered, barely taking his lips off of mine. It was true. The only other people in the house knew about our relationship. We had nothing to hide. The thought of throwing all inhibitions to the wind turned me on even more.

I smiled deviously and stuck my hands inside Hayden's boxers, tugging them down over his butt. He kicked them off and moved back onto me, his cock pressing hard against me, begging to be let in.

I raked my fingers up his back, nails scraping at his skin. He shoved his tongue inside my mouth, his kiss showing his desperate desire to make love to me. I slipped my hand down and wrapped my fingers around his hardness. I slowly worked my hand up and down.

Hayden let out a sigh of pleasure and nipped at my neck. He reached his hand down, pressing his thumb over my clit. Warmth shot through me, tingling down my thighs. I let go of Hayden and grabbed his hand, sticking his fingers inside my panties.

I arched my back when he slid them inside of me. My heart sped up and desire wound in me, needing to be released. Unable to take the slow burn any longer, I yanked my panties down and took hold of Hayden's erection, guiding him to me.

But he wasn't done teasing me. He removed my shirt and trailed kisses down from my mouth, stopping at my breasts to suck on my nipples. My hands curled into fists, balling the sheet. He moved his mouth to my stomach, going slow on purpose. I put my hands on his head, wrapping my fingers through his hair, and pushed him down between my legs.

He wrapped his arms around my thighs and opened my legs before diving in. The hair on his cheeks tickled the inside of my legs. His mouth was against me, open and so warm.

I moaned, lifting my hips off the mattress just a bit. Pleasure was building up. "Hayden," I groaned, looking down at him. He flicked his tongue and I threw my head back as pleasure rippled through me.

He disentangled his arms from around my legs. Panting, I pushed myself up and grabbed him, flipping him over and onto the mattress. I climbed on top, slowly easing him into me. I leaned forward, my breasts in his face. Hayden put his hands on my waist, grinding me down on him.

I reached down and wrapped my fingers around his wrists. Forcefully, I pulled his hands off of me and slammed them into the pillow above his head. I held them there, slowly rocking back and forth, feeling him slide in and out of me.

He struggled to pull his hands free. I pressed down harder. I had no intention of letting him go. He opened his eyes, briefly looking up at me before closing them and turning his head to the side.

I moved faster, moaning in pleasure. Hayden's breathing quickened and he pushed against my hands. I let his arms free. He grabbed my waist and moved me back and forth in rhythm with each thrust.

The buildup erupted and I leaned forward, my hair falling into Hayden's face as I climaxed. Hayden's fingers dug into my hips as he came. Breathing heavily, I fell onto him.

"Mmhh," I sighed as he rolled us over, still holding me tight. Once my heart stopped racing, I got up, wrapped the sheet around myself, and hurried to the bathroom to get cleaned up. I could hear Wade and Jason talking, their voices softly floating up the stairs.

I returned to my bed, finding Hayden sprawled out with his eyes closed. I climbed over him and lay down, covering both of us. Hayden moved closer, his arms finding their way around me.

I was content, comfortable, and the most satisfied I'd felt in a long time. But that did nothing to keep the nightmares away.

* * *

By the time morning rolled around, I was tired. Hayden got up and told me to stay in bed to catch up on the sleep I missed. I didn't object. I got up to use the bathroom and then retreated to my room.

Thick gray clouds covered the sky, hiding even the slightest sliver of blue. Muted light filtered in through the window. I looked around the room. Other than being a bit cleaner than before, everything was the same as it was when we left. I grabbed the comforter from the foot of the bed and pulled it around me, snuggling back into bed.

I was almost asleep when I heard it. The distant whirling of tires on pavement seemed normal. But it wasn't, not at all. I froze, processing everything. Then I snapped awake, springing out of bed.

Chairs scooted on the hardwood floor below me. I tripped in my hurry to get out of the room. I landed on my hands and knees, feet tangled in the sheets. My palms started to sweat. I scrambled up, eyes darting around for my pants.

The rumble of the engine grew louder. Gravel crunched under the tires. Holy shit. It pulled into the driveway. My body was alive with adrenaline. I grabbed a pair of jeans from my bag.

"Riss!" Hayden yelled from downstairs.

"I know," I called back. My heart hammered. This was my house. I wasn't going to let anyone take it. My fingers trembled and I struggled with the button on my pants. I shoved my feet into my boots, not wasting time with socks. Maybe they would understand. Maybe they'd agree to come back to the compound with us and we could leave here skipping and holding hands and swapping zombie kill stories.

Yeah fucking right.

I flew down the stairs. Hayden was waiting, holding my bow. I took it, unsnapping an arrow from the holder. I looked outside through the dining room window. A large red SUV zoomed down the driveway, tires spinning on the loose gravel, narrowly missing Hayden's truck. It turned into the yard, pulling up close to the house.

Wade cocked his gun and stood by the front door. Jason pressed himself against the wall, across from him. His hands shook slightly. After meeting the people of Eastmoore, it was hard to trust anyone.

The door of the SUV slammed shut.

"All right you motherfuckers," he yelled from outside the house. I moved into the dining room. If I could get a clear shot from inside the house, I'd take it. "You have five seconds to get the hell out of my house."

My heart plummeted out of my chest and dizziness crashed onto me. The man moved, blocked by his SUV. His voice...no, no way. It couldn't be.

"Five," he started the countdown. He pumped his shotgun. "Four." He stepped forward, aiming his gun. Rain sprinkled down, pattering against the covered porch. I narrowed my eyes, looking through the SUV's windows. "Three." He moved again.

I caught a glimpse of his face. A thick gray beard covered his cheeks. My hold on the arrow faltered. I took a step back. Everything was spinning.

"Come out, come out wherever you are," he yelled and took another step. "We're getting close!"

I couldn't feel my legs moving, but I was getting closer to the door. I reached for the knob. Jason's eyes met mine as I twisted it. His look begged me not to open the door.

"Two."

I pulled the door back and stepped onto the porch. The scent of fresh rain was heavy in the air. Lightning flashed in the distance. "Riss!" Hayden whispered, making a mad dash for me.

"One."

The bow fell from my hands, clattering to the porch. My stomach dropped, the dizziness pressing in on me. My eyes filled with tears. I couldn't believe it. No, this wasn't real.

There was no way it could be.

PART TWO

CHAPTER FIFTEEN

"Grandpa." The word died in my throat. My bottom lip quivered and I shook my head. The old man that stood in front of me lowered his gun. He looked at me, wide eyed. He raised the shotgun again, not believing what he was seeing.

Hayden was right behind me, with his own gun raised. The old man didn't take notice. He lowered the shotgun and stared at me.

"Orissa?" he asked, his gruff voice breaking.

Tears slid down my face. I raced off the porch. My grandpa's arm fell to his side, the shotgun slipping from his fingers and thudding on the ground. He opened his arms, greeting me with a hug.

I couldn't help it; I started crying. I pressed my face into his shoulder, muffling the sobs. My grandpa ran his hand over my head.

"Is it really you?" he asked, his own voice tight with emotion. "Are you really alive?"

"Yes," I said with a sniffle. He let me go, taking a hold of my arms. He leaned back and studied my face. "Yes." I blinked away tears. "I listened to everything you said, did everything you taught me." I swallowed a sob and took a breath, steadying myself. "And you...you...you're alive too."

"Of course I'm alive," he stated his green eyes staring straight into mine. "I was prepared. And preparation is the key to survival." His eyes moved off me and his body went rigid.

"It's ok," I said quickly. "They're with me." I whirled around. Hayden stood on the porch with his machine gun at his side. I shivered, my exposed skin wet from rain. Jason and Wade stood next to Hayden, weapons half raised. I turned back to my grandpa. "I was here. I came back for you. We stayed...we waited until..." Tears filled my eyes again. I wiped them away. Fucking emotions.

My grandpa caught my left hand, bringing it to his face. He raised his eyebrows at the large diamond on my finger. "Did this happen before Armageddon?"

He called this Armageddon? I guess it wasn't too far off... "No," I told him. His eyes darted back to Hayden.

"That one?"

I nodded. I didn't know how my grandpa knew, but that was just him. He picked up on the littlest detail, the most minute of things. I was nowhere near as good as he was.

My grandpa picked up his gun, squared his shoulders, and walked to the house. "Better make sure he's good enough for my only granddaughter."

Still reeling from shock, it took me a second to turn around and rush after him. We moved into the house. Before my grandpa could even think about introductions, he went through each room, doing an obsessive safety check all the while muttering to himself. I followed him. Wade, Jason, and Hayden stood in stunned silence in the foyer.

"Guys," I said once my grandpa was satisfied the house was safe. I called them into the living room. "This is my grandpa."

"We got the who," Jason blurted. "Need the how."

I needed to know too. I looked at my grandpa. He was almost as tall as Hayden. He had lost a significant amount of weight but was still in considerably good shape for his age. His skin was a deep tan and he had a slew of scars on his face and arms that hadn't been there before.

"I came here, with Orissa," Jason went on. "And you weren't here." Jason's gaze darted to me. "She saved me. My sister too. And a crap ton of other people." He nervously gripped his rifle. "She told us she learned everything from you...so thanks."

My grandpa narrowed his eyes and leaned forward. He was good at looking intimidating when he wanted to. Jason swallowed and held his eye, cheeks reddening. Then my grandpa smiled.

"She did learn everything from me." He sat in the armchair next to the fireplace. Hayden and I sat close together on the loveseat, and Jason and Wade took a spot on the couch.

"Grandpa," I started. "These are my friends." I went over a quick introduction, saying only that we met while fighting zombies. It wasn't time to tell him about the compound yet. Subconsciously, I pulled on Hayden's dog tags. My grandpa saw and quickly put two and two together. He jumped up, pulling a gun from his waistband.

"You're military, aren't you?" he accused Hayden. I sprang off the loveseat, putting myself between the end of the gun and Hayden.

"Grandpa," I said calmly, holding up my hands. Great. Here we go. Only five minutes into meeting my fiancé and he was freaking out already. Hello reason number one why boys never came to the house. "Yes, they are. But they are *good* guys."

He grabbed the dog tags and pulled them to his face. My body jerked as the chain was yanked. Hayden stood. I knew he didn't know what to do. His eyes darted from me to my grandpa. I shook my head and flicked my eyes to the loveseat, begging him to sit back down.

"Marines," my grandpa growled and dropped the tags. "Did you know about this? Did they prep you?" He whirled around, hunching forward. "They're probably watching. They know where you are, they know where I am!" He flicked the safety off his pistol and went to the window. "The droids." He turned back around, gun raised. "Are there any droids? They could have followed you!"

"Hey!" I shouted. I closed my eyes and let out a breath. "There are no droids, Grandpa." I held out my hand. "Hayden and Wade served our country, just like you. They didn't know anything about the virus. We—"

"Didn't? What do you mean, *didn't?*"

Shit. He really didn't miss a damn thing. Crazy and paranoid...yes. Confused and forgetful...not so much. My shoulders stiffened with anxiety.

"Riss," Hayden said softly. "Want us to step outside?" His eyes were full of concern. Not for his safety or for my grandpa's sanity, but for me.

Something in my grandpa's face softened. He lowered the gun, looking at Hayden. I had seen him do a 180 before with lasting effects. My grandma was good at talking him down.

"If Orissa trusts you then I do," my grandpa said and put the gun on the coffee table. Thank the Lord. I dropped my arms to my side.

"Hayden was deployed when shit hit the fan," I started. "He had no idea what he was coming home to." My grandpa nodded, looking at Hayden. "And neither did Wade. Jason wasn't in the military."

It seemed to settle him enough to sit. "Where were you?" I asked and took my place next to Hayden.

"I went to get you and Jenny," my grandpa told me.

"Aunt Jenny. Is she ok?" I asked, hope rising inside me.

My grandpa shook his head and cast his eyes down. Hayden put his hand on my thigh. "Took me two days to get to that godforsaken city," my grandpa told us. "Found my sweet Jenny holed up in that tiny apartment she loved so much." He looked at me. "She told me where to find you. She tried to get to you but couldn't. We went looking but then that damn bus came, took us away." His fingers curled into fists. "They told us there was a shelter, a place with other survivors. But not me. I knew...I saw...and after all I had taught you."

I put my hand over Hayden's. I could tell by my grandpa's body language that this wasn't going to be good. I braced myself. "It was no shelter but a damn holding cell. Jenny thought you'd be there. She said you were sick, just had surgery but I knew better. I knew you wouldn't trust *them*. Once we were in, we couldn't get out. They started it, you know. Big Brother's not just watching. They're trying to kill us."

A chill crept over me. For once, his crazy theories weren't crazy...or even theories anymore. The rain picked up, blowing in through the open windows. I wanted to get up and close them before the water warped the wooden sills.

"I knew it would fall," he went on. "We spent our days getting ready. There was a group of us who wanted out. Once we had our chance, we took it." His eyes got misty. "Jenny...Jenny got lost along the way." He let out a long breath. "Those of us that made it didn't get here until after the winter. I knew it was you. The way the house was set up, the missing black bow, the jerky...I waited. You would come home eventually." He smiled, lines crinkling his face. "You always did."

Tears pooled in my eyes again. Dammit. Getting emotional wasn't going to solve anything. My grandpa stood, saying he was hungry, and scuttled off to the kitchen. I stayed in my spot.

"You ok?" Hayden asked softly. "This is a lot to take in."

I inhaled, forcing a smile. "Yeah. Fine."

He wiped away a renegade tear from my eye. "If you say so." He wasn't convinced.

"How the hell did your grandpa survive all this?" Wade asked. "No offense, Riss. You're great so he has to be, but to go it alone..." he trailed off, shaking his head.

"I have no idea." I rubbed my sweaty palms on my jeans. "I have so many questions too, trust me." I looked behind me. Dishes clanked together as my grandpa rooted around in the kitchen. A few awkward seconds ticked away.

"You know," Jason started, looking around the living room. "I missed this place. I didn't realize it until I came back."

My chest loosened. I leaned back on the loveseat. Hayden looped his arm under mine and took my hand. Our eyes met and suddenly everything was all right.

"I've been saving these for a special occasion," my grandpa said as he came into the room. "And I think this is as special as it gets." He set five beers on the coffee table. With no hesitation I leaned forward, extending my arm, fingers wrapping around the cool can. I handed it to Hayden and grabbed another for myself, leaning back and popping the top.

Jason's eyes widened, staring at the beer. Oh, right. He was underage...or at least he used to be. There were no rules anymore. He licked his lips, flicked his eyes to Hayden, who nodded an 'ok,' then grabbed it. For a moment, pure teenage excitement took over his face. His eyes flashed deviously, knowing he was doing something he wasn't supposed to be doing. He pulled the tab and put the beer to his lips, smiling as the first splash of alcohol washed down his throat.

Then the moment was over. We were sitting in the living room with my crazy grandpa while the living dead ruled the earth. There was no escaping reality.

"You treating my granddaughter nice?" my grandpa asked Hayden.

"Yes, sir," he answered right away. His muscles stiffened and his head twitched ever so slightly in my direction.

"He is, Grandpa. Hayden is...wonderful," I said and felt the tiniest bit of blood rush to my cheeks.

"Good," my grandpa said and took a long drink. He set the beer can down on the floor and leaned back in the armchair. "Remember that summer when Mr. Parker bought all those goats from the auction?"

"Yeah," I answered, not seeing where this was going. That happened seven years ago. Those goats were long gone now.

"And remember how they kept breeding? He had goats coming out of his ass."

I raised an eyebrow. "Yes, I remember. We took like a dozen. What does this—"

My grandpa continued. "I helped castrate them." His eyes moved to Hayden. Seriously? Some things will never change. "It's real simple, you see." He held his hand in the air. "You grab the testicles, like this, pull 'em down, slice open the sac and cut those suckers off." He chuckled. "Don't even have to stitch 'em back up. Sometimes they shiver from the blood loss but they make it. Sore for days as you can imagine."

The color drained from Hayden's face and the room fell silent. I could hear the ticking of my grandpa's watch. Some things never change...

"So," I began, playing with the tab on my beer. "What happened once you got out of the, uh, holding cell?"

"Assembled a group and got back here," my grandpa stated, making it sound easy. I nodded, knowing it took them a while to gather supplies, vehicles, and weapons.

"What happened to that group?"

"Lost most of them," he said with little emotion. "Got a group of five holed up in the school."

"Not here?" Wade asked.

"This is my house. There's no need for them to be here," my grandpa said and I felt embarrassed for him. My grandpa wasn't a bad person. He didn't do things to be an ass on purpose; he just looked at the world through blood splattered glasses. Everyone was a threat. He only trusted people who were family or who he'd known for years.

I knew my grandpa. He would help the others out of duty, of course, but he needed them as much as they needed him. My grandpa was capable, the most resourceful person I knew...but he was old.

"I come and go," he added, seeing the consternation on Wade and Jason's faces. "It's safer there. Brick walls, thicker windows, metal gates to block off sections of the halls. They're getting by. We went our separate ways." He finished his beer. "They do work around here for me in exchange for eggs."

My jaw dropped. "The chickens are still alive?"

My grandpa laughed. "Hell no. Had to get new ones." He stood, joints cracking. "Come on, I'll show ya. I need to let them out for a while anyway."

The four of us followed my grandpa out into the barn. He undid the latch on the metal door and slid it open, doing another safety check before he let us inside. The smell of chicken poop choked me. I almost preferred the smell of zombie over it.

"Wow. You thought of everything," Hayden said to my grandpa. And he had. A giant chicken coop was suspended from the ceiling of the barn, about ten feet up. My grandpa crossed the barn, risking getting pooped on when he went under the wire bottom, and grabbed a rope to lower the cage. He opened a door to let the chickens out.

"Rissy," my grandpa said. "Can you get the eggs? This old back isn't what it used to be and bending over is painful."

"Yeah, got 'em," I said and moved around the cage.

"I thought only Raeya called you 'Rissy'," Hayden said with a smile.

I looked up at him with an eyebrow raised. "Where do you think she got it?"

"Raeya?" my grandpa asked. "Your friend?"

"Yeah," I said and picked up two eggs. "I went to Purdue and got her." My grandpa proudly beamed at me like I just told him I got an A on a test. "She's at our camp."

"It's more than a camp," Jason started. I flashed him a shut-the-hell-up look. Luckily my grandpa was too interested in knowing how I rescued Ray to catch Jason's statement.

I told him the story while I gathered the rest of the eggs. Jason, who remembered where the tools were kept, took it upon himself to start cleaning the coop. Hayden jumped right in to help. Wade stood in the doorway, keeping watch.

Not too long after, we went back into the house. The four of us stood on the porch while my grandpa did another safety check. Being obsessively paranoid might be annoying, but it kept us all alive.

* * *

Six hours had passed since I had been reunited with my grandpa. We had spent most of those catching up: telling tales of zombie-kills, narrow escapes, and what we'd done to get by. My grandpa was curious about Hayden, and did his fair share to put the fear of God into my husband-to-be.

When they started swapping war stories, I got up saying I had to use the bathroom. I went upstairs. Too distracted with my grandpa, I had forgotten that I hadn't gotten properly dressed that morning. I grabbed what I needed from my bag and went into the bathroom, turning on the shower.

I studied my reflection while the water warmed up. My hair was a matted mess, a product of rough lovemaking followed by a restless night of tossing and turning. I pressed my fingers to my cheeks and pulled down, wondering if the dark circles under my eyes would ever go away. The red marks from being strangled were fading already, thankfully. I took my shirt off, stepping back from the mirror.

I took the rest of my clothes off and got into the shower, closing my eyes and tipping my head up. I took a deep breath and slowly exhaled, relaxing my muscles as I let the air out. I had a feeling that something bad was going to happen. Finding my grandpa—well him finding us, really—was too good to be true. Something was about to give.

"Just enjoy it while you can," I muttered to myself and ran my hands through my hair. I took advantage of the long lasting hot water, not getting out until my skin was red from the heat. I flipped my head upside down, rubbing my hair with the towel before wrapping it up.

I opened the medicine cabinet and grabbed a bottle of facial toner. Raeya had acquired a few beauty products during our trips into town. She'd be happy when I brought them back to the compound.

I rubbed lotion over my body and got dressed in jeans and a black tank top with a loose fitting ivory shirt overtop. I tucked it in on my right side, just enough to stay out of the way from my gun.

I hung the towel up on a hook on the back of the door then bent down, opening the cabinet under the sink, eyeing a hair dryer. I bit my lip. It was totally unnecessary to dry my hair but...I reached in and grabbed it, not able to remember the last time I dried it. Here, maybe once. With five people downstairs to guard and protect the house, I wasn't worried about not being able to hear death moans over the whirl of the hairdryer. I flipped my head over again and turned the blower on.

* * *

Later, I found Hayden and my grandpa in the family room. Both were laughing. I stopped, blinking and shaking my head. What was going on? And then I heard my voice, high pitched and childish, coming from the TV. Oh God, they had put in the old home movies.

My face was already set in a glare when I walked into the room. My eyes flew to the TV screen. My expression softened when I saw myself and Raeya as children, running around the yard with giant nets trying to catch butterflies. Raeya caught a moth instead and it flew out of the net and into her hair. Being the good friend I was, I tried to swat it away and ended up squishing it with my bare hand. We both started screaming.

My grandpa looked up, wiping his eye. Hayden paused the video, ready to spout off a cheeky comment, but he stopped as soon as he saw me and stood.

"Riss," he said, dropping the remote onto the couch. "You look beautiful."

"I wouldn't go that far," I said with a half smile. "More put together than you normally see me, heck yes."

He touched my hair. "I've never seen it straight."

"It feels weird, to be honest. After not doing my hair for months, all the attention I used to pay it seems extremely frivolous now."

Hayden laughed, little lines forming around his hazel eyes. My heart sped up, just a little. "Yeah, I guess it does."

My grandpa slowly stood to make sure Jason and Wade were doing a good enough job keeping watch on the covered porch. As soon as he was out of the room, Hayden put his hands on my waist, stepping in so our torsos touched. I wrapped my arms around his shoulders and looked into his eyes.

He bent his head down and slowly kissed me. His lips lingered close before he parted them, pressing his mouth to mine. I breathed him in, pushing my tongue into his mouth. The warm wetness of the kiss sent a pulse of desire between my legs.

Hayden lifted his lips just enough to talk. "I feel like I'm sixteen years old again, afraid of getting caught by my girlfriend's dad."

I smiled and let my hands trail down his back. "Oh please." I hooked my fingers inside the waist of his jeans, wanting at least one more kiss before we broke apart. Hayden looked over my shoulder.

"He threatened my balls, Riss."

I laughed. "No one but me is going to touch your balls." I moved my hand down, cupping them.

Hayden smiled and kissed me again. "I want him to like me."

"He will." I sighed and begrudgingly let go of Hayden. "I always knew he would. You guys have more in common than you'd think."

"Like we both have flashbacks?" he asked with a grin.

"That's not really what I meant but sure."

Hayden turned off the TV and looked over his shoulder at me.

"What?" I asked, seeing the glint in his eyes.

"Your grandpa wanted to make sure you were still saving yourself for marriage." He pressed his lips together trying not to laugh. "You?"

I pursed my lips. "It's not that hard to believe."

"As much as I'd like to be your one and only, I like the things you know how to do better," Hayden teased.

"What did you tell him?" I asked, suddenly nervous.

"That we were waiting." Hayden laughed again, shaking his head. "I don't think he believed me."

A commotion from the porch made my heart race. I ran to the door, scooping up my weapons as I passed through the kitchen.

"Damn coyotes," my grandpa grumbled, raising his gun. "Getting my chickens." He turned his head, eyeing my bow. "Ah, good. You can get him."

I didn't mean for the look of disgust to flash across my face. It was only there for a second, but my grandpa took notice. I was good at hunting...that didn't mean I liked it. I had no problem hunting when we needed food. It served a purpose.

My grandpa would argue that killing the coyote before it killed the chickens was as good a purpose as any. I pushed my shoulders back and raised the bow, unhooking an arrow from it. The coyote trotted through the field, ears back and mouth open. His fur was damp from the rain. He moved into a crouch, catching the scent of the chickens.

Dark eyes struck out from gray fur. His tail was held out behind him. He moved, slipping in and out of view. Every step eluded grace. His pace quickened. The chickens walked around, pecking at the ground unaware of the danger that lurked.

The coyote wasn't doing anything wrong. He was an animal of prey seeking his next meal. That was all. An innocent animal.

I could feel the heat coming off my grandpa as he leaned closer, waiting for me to let go of the arrow. I pushed aside my feelings and steadied myself. All it would take was one noise, one jump off the porch to scare the coyote away.

I couldn't disappoint my grandpa. The coyote turned, his beady eyes meeting mine. Then I let the arrow go.

"Shot through the heart!" my grandpa cried and clapped me on the back.

With a deep sigh I lowered my bow.

"She's always been my star hunter," my grandpa said and moved to the steps that lead off the back porch. He had a slight limp in his step. "Fast learner. Caught on to everything I taught her."

I moved my eyes to the ground. It was odd, this awkward feeling. Hayden stepped close and put his hand on my back, somehow sensing my indignation over killing the coyote.

"She's something else," Hayden agreed.

I walked around the porch to find Jason and Wade while Hayden and my grandpa went to drag the coyote back to the barn before it attracted zombies. I had no idea what my grandpa planned to do with it; he declined Hayden's offer to burn or bury it.

Later, the five of us went inside for a late lunch. My grandpa scrambled eggs while I smeared peanut butter over crackers again.

"Why weren't you home last night?" I asked him.

"Got caught up at the school. We don't travel after sunset," he answered. He looked out through the window. "Guess they'll have to wait."

"Who?"

"The people at the school. Came back to rest then bring them eggs. No time for both."

Jason took plates from the cabinet and set them on the dining room table. Hayden opened a can of peaches and dished them out.

"I can go," I offered. "So you can rest."

"Not alone," my grandpa said. I was tempted to bring up the fact he had come and gone alone.

"I'll go with her, Mr. Penwell," Hayden said right away.

"Call me Armand," my grandpa said. He came over to the table with the frying pan, serving the eggs then he sat down and turned to Hayden. "This one stays with me. I need to know more about the man who wants to marry my granddaughter."

"Yes, sir," Hayden answered. "It'll be nice to know Riss's family."

"You'll be part of it," my grandpa said with a smile.

I leaned forward, looking across the table at Hayden. "Sorry for that." I smiled and picked up my fork.

"You hear from your mother at all before this?" my grandpa asked. Like me, he wasn't happy about her going overseas with Ted. My grandpa didn't like him either, though neither of us could come up with good reasons why.

"No," I said, shaking my head. "She and Ted left for New Guinea at the beginning of October. She told me she'd try to call on my birthday."

My grandpa only raised his eyebrows. He had lost both of his children but would be dammed before he let his emotions show. I'd inherited his ability to suppress. I didn't want to think about my mother either.

* * *

After lunch, Wade and I got into the Jeep. I drove, since I knew where to go. I filled two empty Styrofoam cartons with eggs and set them inside a cloth grocery bag in the back.

"It's weird hearing about your past," Wade said as we drove down the road. "I forget people used to have lives before this mess."

"Me too," I told him. "It is weird to think about for some reason."

He looked out the window then quickly turned back to me. "Can I ask you something?"

"You just did."

"Something personal."

I took my eyes off the road for a second to look at him. "Sure. I'm pretty much an open book."

"No you're not," Wade laughed. "You're closed off sometimes, probably more times than not."

"No, I'm not."

He raised his eyebrows. "How long did it take you to admit you had feelings for Hayden?"

"That doesn't count," I said and tightened my grip on the steering wheel. "I was giving him the chance to admit it first."

Wade rolled his eyes. "And you never admit when something is upsetting you. And I still don't know why your grandpa has so many weapons or why you're so good at survival skills."

"Ok, fine. Maybe I'm not an open book. At all." We laughed. "So what did you want to ask?"

"Well..." he started, turning his head down, suddenly very interested in his pistol. "I was wondering about...uh, how you and Hayden, uh...you know."

"Have sex?"

"Yeah."

I turned, giving Wade an incredulous stare. "You want to know *how* we have sex? Like what positions?"

Wade's eyes widened and he leaned back. "No, no, God no. I mean like do you use protection because Gabby's too scared of getting pregnant to do anything without it," he blurted, cheeks glowing.

"Oh." I turned back to the road. "Sometimes we do, sometimes he just pulls out. Most times I don't even think about it until it's over. I get caught up in the heat of the moment don't realize it until it's too late. It feels better that way anyway."

"Over sharing, Riss."

"Hey, you asked." I smiled. "I didn't realize you guys were *that* close."

Wade's cheeks reddened a bit more. "Yeah."

"Good for you," I said. "Having someone makes this shitstorm livable."

"It does," Wade agreed. "I've never had a serious relationship before," he confessed. "I've dated, but got shipped overseas and didn't bother."

"Hayden's my first serious relationship too."

"Seriously?"

I nodded. "I've had a lot of boyfriends, don't get me wrong, but nothing lasted. I never felt...well anything really. As lame as it sounds you just know when you meet the person you're supposed to be with."

"You're cute, Riss."

"Shut up."

"Adorable," he teased, laughing. His smile faded and his eye widened.

"What?" I asked, feeling alarm prickle across my body. My eyes darted around the Jeep. Was there a zombie I wasn't seeing?

"Hayden," he stated. "He's infected, right? All the time but with no effect."

"Yeah, so—oh. I think I know where you're going." I wrinkled my nose. "I, uh, asked Dr. Cara about it. She said she needed a specimen sample from Hayden."

Wade laughed. "That's epic. I can totally see her asking for it and standing outside the door like a creep while she waited."

"And knocking and telling him to hurry up," I added, cracking up. "Don't tell him I told you. I think he'd get embarrassed."

"You have to be immune then too," Wade said seriously. "The virus is transmitted in saliva and blood. I have to assume it's in *all* fluids."

"Dr. Cara tested me and didn't see any traces of the virus." I shook my head. "I don't know. Honestly, I try not to think into it too much. It freaks me out." I swerved to miss a pothole. The roads were horrible with no one to take care of them after the winter.

"I get that." Wade looked out the window. "You grew up here?"

"Pretty much. I moved back and forth between my grandparent's and my mom's." I sped down a road with a thirty mile per hour speed limit. It had been a notorious speed trap and one of the town's few police officers used to hide behind the gas station. "But I definitely consider this home."

Wade nodded, watching the overgrown farmland go by.

* * *

Grades K-12 were all in the same building; the town wasn't big enough to warrant separate buildings for elementary, middle, and high school.

Sections of chain link fencing were pushed in front of windows and doors, secured to the building with pieces of metal and wood. A zombie lay on the ground under each window. What the hell?

I cut the engine to the Jeep and got out, swinging my quiver over my head and shoulder.

"That's fucking genius," Wade said and pointed to the zombies, "using zombies to mask the smell of the living."

Oh, that's what they were there for. It had my grandpa's name written all over it. "It is genius."

"Having your grandpa back at the compound is going to be a good thing. A very good thing." Wade grabbed his rifle.

It would be...if we could get him to come with us. An underground bomb shelter, kept hidden by the government then set up by a former commissioned officer with a crazy scientist making vaccines in the basement lab was a conspiracy theorist's worst nightmare. I couldn't think about that now.

"We need to get in through the back," I said as I picked up my bow and the bag of eggs. Wade stayed close to my side as we crossed the parking lot. "I haven't set foot in here since graduation," I muttered.

"Consider this an early ten year reunion." Wade playfully elbowed me.

"Hah, yeah. I wouldn't have gone regardless."

"Really? I loved high school."

I eyed him. "Really. I was a bad kid. I spent more time in the principal's office than I did in class."

"You have to be exaggerating."

"Maybe."

We stopped outside the back doors. More chain link was attached to the brick exterior on either side. The two pieces were held together with a bicycle chain. I spun the combination lock in the order that my grandpa had told me and pulled the chain free. Wade slid the panel away. We slipped inside, moving the chain link back into place.

"This place is very secure," Wade noted. "I never would have thought of some of this."

"Being a paranoid prepper comes in handy during the apocalypse."

"Really," he said. "Your house is impressive. I feel almost as safe in it as I do the compound."

"A few bars and boards doesn't compare to something that can withstand a bomb," I muttered. I didn't like admitting it. I wanted the farmhouse to be the safest place on earth. It would justify us staying.

"Safe from zombies, not bombs," Wade corrected with a smile. "Smartass."

I flashed an innocent smile. We stood right inside the doors, trapped between the glass behind us and a drop down barred barrier in the hall. We entered near the gym, in the high school section. There was a wall of classrooms on the exterior side of the building. Across the hall was an art room, music room, and the one and only lecture hall.

Wade slowly lifted the metal bars just enough for us to slip through. He set it down silently, keeping a hold of the metal so it wouldn't echo throughout the building.

"We need to go down that hall and turn left," I told him. "The courtyard is in the middle of the school." The group was staying in rooms around the courtyard. They had planted a garden in the small outdoor yard. I held an arrow up in the bow. Even though this place had been secured by my grandpa, the vastness of it made me uneasy. There were too many places to hide.

We passed by classrooms. The doors were closed and newspapers had been put over the windows. We moved slowly, crouched and ready. When we rounded the corner, we could hear voices. Wade lowered his rifle and nodded.

I relaxed my arms. "Hello?" I called. "Armand Penwell sent us. We're friends of his."

Whoever was talking immediately stopped. I waited, heart rate increasing just a bit. "What's the password?" someone called.

"Jackie-Jenny-Orissa," I said the password. My grandpa had two passwords: a safe one and an incase-I'm-tortured-to-tell password so this group would know what to expect. The latter password was 'I need a vacation.' My grandpa came up with the weirdest things...

"Armand sent us with the eggs. He's fine," I added quickly. "Just tired."

The end of a rifle came around the door. "That's far enough." The voice was deep and gruff. My muscles twitched as I resisted the impulse to raise my weapon as well.

"Are you armed?" he asked.

"Yes," I replied. "There are two of us. Both armed."

"Put your weapons down."

"No," I blurted. "Look, we came here with food for you. We know the password and the combination to unlock the chain. Armand *obviously* sent us, so cut the drama, ok?"

Several people spoke in hushed voices. Deciding it was safe, the man with the gun rounded the corner. He was younger than I expected, maybe early thirties at the oldest.

Dark jeans hugged his muscular thighs perfectly. A gray t-shirt covered his flat stomach and broad shoulders, and light brunette hair fell over his face, which was covered in dark stubble. He was good looking...and familiar.

He lowered his gun and took us in, his eyes running up and down my body, checking me out. Wade stepped in front of me.

"Can't be too safe now, can we?" the man asked and moved down the hall. Distressed cowboy boots softly clicked on the floor. "Didn't think Armand would send a woman."

"Excuse me?" I asked, fingers tightening around my arrow.

The man raised his eyebrows and shrugged as if he hadn't said anything offensive. He hooked his thumb on his belt loop, pushing his shirt up to reveal a large oval belt buckle. His lips pulled up in a half smile. He was charming. Dammit. "Though you do have that whole Lara Croft thing going on."

"You're going to regret that," Wade mumbled under his breath.

"And it's working for you, darling," he went on. "You almost look threatening."

I glared at the man in the cowboy boots. "What's your name?"

Wade asked and stepped forward, holding his rifle to the side.

"Bentley," he stated. "You?"

"Wade."

"Bent?" someone with a thick southern accent called from inside a classroom. "What's going on out there?"

"Armand sent some people with food," he said over his shoulder. "They passed the test."

"People?" she questioned. A middle aged woman with short blonde hair stepped out of the room holding a buck knife. "How?" She shook her head. "Where did you come from? Armand never mentioned other people."

"We crossed paths by chance," Wade answered.

Three more people came out of the room, crowding the hallway. They held weapons and looked just as suspicious as the woman. My grandpa had taught them well.

"Why didn't he come himself?" the woman pressed.

I looked at Wade and smiled. Would they even believe me? "He wanted to get some sleep before sunset," I answered. "So I offered to bring you the eggs."

The woman shook her head. "I know Armand. He wouldn't trust strangers."

"I'm not a stranger." I stuck the arrow back in the quiver. "I'm his granddaughter."

A few seconds ticked by with everyone staring at me. "Orissa?" the woman finally spoke.

"In the flesh."

She blinked several times. "Really?"

"She is," a younger woman said, pushing past the line of people. "She looks just like the girl in the picture." She stopped in front of Bentley and studied me. "And she has the same greenish-blue eyes that Armand has." She inhaled. "He swore you'd make it."

"I did." I took the bag of eggs off my shoulder.

Bentley moved forward to take them from me. "The old man said he had a granddaughter, but he never said she was hot." He winked.

"It would be really creepy if my own grandfather described me as 'hot'." I let go of the bag. Bentley was several inches taller than me, which made looking down my shirt easy. I pulled the quiver strap between my breasts, pushing the tank top in and blocking his view. "Do you guys need anything else?" I asked, backing away from Bentley.

"Company," he said and pushed his hair back from his face while biting his bottom lip. It was something he'd practiced, something he knew drove women wild. Just not this one.

The older woman took the bag from him and looked inside. "No, we're good, thank you. We just went on a run with Armand—your grandpa I mean—a few days ago." She didn't take her eyes off of me. "I just can't believe it. I almost didn't believe you were real. Well, I mean I knew you were from the pictures but the stories he told about you." She shook her head. "Look at you! You're here—alive. With a bow and arrows just like he said," she laughed. "You grandpa wouldn't stop talking about how good you were at archery."

Bentley laughed. "We don't know if she's *really* that good."

"She is," Wade said through gritted teeth.

Bentley held up his hand. "Settle down there, solider."

"I'm not a soldier," Wade said slowly. "I'm a Marine."

Bentley rolled his eyes. "There's a difference?"

I put my hand on Wade's arm. "There is," I said. "A big difference that you're obviously too ignorant to know." I wanted to leave before this Bentley guy pissed both of us off.

"Do you want anything?" the older woman asked. "We have running water."

It was hot in the school. And I was thirsty. Ever since I was intubated, a dry throat led to a sore throat, and I wanted to avoid that if possible. "Sure," I said. "But then we're gonna leave. I haven't seen my grandpa in a while."

She moved her head up and down. "I understand, honey. I'd love to hear your story if you don't mind." She turned, waving us into the room they'd emerged from. "I'm Marla, by the way. This is my sister Anne." The younger woman gave me a tight smile. Marla went on to introduce the four others in her group, but I didn't pay much attention. I wanted to get home.

We went into a classroom. It was set up like a studio apartment with different types of furniture making up little rooms. The back wall of the room butted up with the courtyard. Electrical cords came from a solar powered generator, powering lights, an MP3 player, and several fans.

The wall to our right had a doorway sized hole cut into it. A sheet hung above it, currently pulled to the side. Marla led us through it. The second classroom also had a view of the little courtyard. Students with perfect attendance or those who'd made the honor roll got to eat lunch in the courtyard on nice days.

I never did...

A garden had been planted where the picnic tables used to be. From the quick look I took, it appeared that the crops were doing well. Buckets had been set out to collect rainwater from the storm.

Beds were set up in the second room. There were more lamps

and fans in here and half the library. There was another hole functioning as a door. Marla lifted the curtain and went into the teacher's lounge.

"I always wondered what it looked like," I said out loud. Surely it had been rearranged since school permanently let out. It was set up very much like a living room, with couches and lounge chairs angled around a flat screen TV. Next to that was a little kitchen. Boxes and cans of food were piled on the small counter.

Marla turned the sink on, letting the water run for a few seconds before she stuck a glass under it.

"Thanks," I said when she handed it to me.

"Does your boyfriend want some?" she asked me, casting her eyes to Wade, who stood in the threshold.

"I'm sure he does," I said. "But he's not my boyfriend." I drained the glass and set it on the counter. The school wouldn't be my first choice to stay, but it worked. My grandpa had made it safe and these people had made it livable. I never would have thought of any of this.

I left the teacher's lounge, finding Wade talking to one of the guys, who had asked where we had come from. I went into the hall, compelled to keep watch in the halls. The last time the guys and I went into a school things ended badly.

His cowboy boots scuffed along the carpet in the classroom behind me. I pretended not to notice.

"Why so eager to leave, sweetie?"

I hated pet names. I hated them even more when a stranger used them. "Maybe it's because I'm eager to see my grandpa. It's been a while, ya know."

"It's been a while for a lot of things." Bentley leaned on the door, crossing his arms over his chest. His light brown hair fell into his eyes. He pushed it back, tossing his head up a bit. Why did he look so familiar?

"Are you from here?" I asked.

"Nope. Born and raised in Texas, baby."

"Ugh. Texas," I huffed. I could never go back and it would be too soon.

"You got something against the Lone Star State?" he asked, raising his eyebrows in a lame attempt to fake offense.

"Not the state but some people in it." I could still smell the charred flesh from the explosions. I blinked and tore my eyes away from Bentley. It bugged me that I couldn't remember where I had seen him.

"Ex-boyfriend?"

"Nope." I pulled on the quiver. Sweat beaded under it.

"Current boyfriend?"

"Why would I have something against a current boyfriend?"

Bentley laughed. "I'm just guessing here, lady." He moved closer. His eyes were blue. Not as vivid-blue as Padraic's. I felt suddenly homesick...homesick for the compound and my friends. I sighed and leaned against the wall, propping one leg up behind me.

"What?" I said, feeling Bentley's eyes on me.

He laughed and ran a hand through his hair again. "I'm sorry. I just haven't seen a good looking woman in a long time." He held up his hands. "Not that you're only good looking because of that. I'd hit on you anyway." He flashed a smile. There was something about him that was so familiar. It bugged me in the worst way.

"Now you're staring," he said, flashing that smile again.

"You look familiar." I shook my head. "But I can't remember where we would have met."

He straightened up. "I supposed I might." He stuck out his hand. "Bentley Owen."

I stared at his hand then back up at him, confused. "Is that supposed to mean something to me?"

Bentley's face dropped. "You've never heard of me? Seriously? Have you been living under a rock?"

His blatant distaste stuck a cord. "No rocks." I turned away.

"Then you must not like good music." He recovered fast, smiling again. Then it clicked. I had seen his face on an album cover from Hayden's iPod. Right. Bentley Owen was a country singer.

"The worse taste," I said sarcastically.

"I think I can forgive you."

"Great. I can sleep tonight." I pushed off the wall and walked down to the main door to check for danger.

"Mmm," Bentley said to himself, purposely loud enough for me to hear. "I hate to see you go but..."

I rolled my eyes. His one-liners and compliments might have worked on fan girls but would do nothing for me, even if my heart didn't already belong to someone else. I turned around, walking back to the classroom. "So," Bentley asked. "You really as good with that thing as your crazy grandpa says?" He pointed to my bow.

Big mistake, Bentley. *Big* mistake. "My grandfather is not crazy." It was a flat out lie. My grandpa bordered insanity on a regular basis. But I wasn't going to let someone get away with calling him out on it. "I can promise you, if it wasn't for him, you wouldn't be alive."

"Damn. You and your solider boy have quick tempers."

"He's a Marine," I repeated slowly.

"Hey now, I didn't mean to offend. You're right. Armand is a crazy son of a bitch but he's the reason we're standing here and I'm eternally grateful for that."

Wade walked out of the classroom. "Ready, Riss?" he asked.

"A world of yes," I told him.

Marla thanked us again, still a little flabbergasted with the whole situation. She said she'd walk us out, wanting to make sure everything was locked correctly after we left. She was smart.

Bentley followed, telling us about how many zombies he had killed and how awesome he was at it. Marla caught my eye and smiled, shaking her head.

"Be careful out there," she said and lifted the metal drop down gate. "And tell your grandpa we miss him."

"I will. You guys be careful too." My hand flew up out of instinct to grab an arrow.

"Will we see you again?" she asked then quickly shook her head. "Sorry, I know you want to see your grandpa. I have so many questions for you."

"Understandable," I told her with a smile.

Bentley rushed forward to get the door for me. "I hope we do see you again." He smiled at me, flashing those white teeth. I resisted the urge to make a gagging sound and walked out the door.

* * *

Hayden and my grandpa stood out in the rain, looking at the machine gun mounted on the bed of the truck. A smile crept up on me no matter how hard I tried to resist it. Hayden pointed to something and my grandpa nodded. He clapped Hayden on the back, smiling.

Was this really happening? I blinked. Of course it was. I meet the man of my dreams, someone my grandpa actually liked, when everyone around us was dying. It wouldn't happen any other way for me. I stepped on the gas, turning the Jeep off after it came to a halt.

I unbuckled my seatbelt and got out, holding my hand over my face to keep rain from splashing in my eyes.

"Hey, Riss," Hayden said, looking up at me. His eyes met mine and my heart skipped a beat. "Everything go ok?"

"Yeah," I answered. "Whatcha doing out here?"

"Your grandpa wanted to see the machine gun," Hayden said. He stepped away from the truck and pulled me to him, pressing his lips against my forehead.

"You guys getting along?" I asked quietly.

Hayden nodded, giving me a small smile. "We'll be in soon."

"Ok. I won't intrude." Wade and I went inside. I took off my boots and flipped my head upside down, fluffing my wet hair to help it dry faster. I could see Jason walking back and forth on the back porch, keeping an eye on things. Wade went outside with him, leaving me alone in the house.

I pulled my t-shirt over my head, leaving on my tank top, flipping it right side out to dry and wrapped a blanket around my shoulders and settled onto the couch in the living room, tucking my legs up under me.

Why had I missed the compound last night? My eyes moved around the living room. *This* was home. This was where I belonged. I closed my eyes and leaned against the arm of the couch. Raeya would be happy to come back.

Padraic too, maybe. I'd want the rest of my friends to come, and Jason would bring his sister and Olivia of course. And then there was Hannah... I sighed. It would never work. We were needed at the compound.

An odd sense of duty washed over me. The people at the compound relied on us to survive. No one had ever counted on me in that way before, not until the dead started eating the living.

I would never get my grandpa to leave home...and I didn't want to leave him. Not again. Hayden wouldn't leave me. My chest tightened. I saw no easy way out of this. I opened my eyes and stared at the fireplace. It was stupid but I felt like I was betraying this place. I wrapped the blanket tighter around myself and rolled over so I was facing the back of the couch.

"Tired?" Hayden asked when he came back in.

"Kinda," I answered. My body was exhausted and begged for sleep. My mind, on the other hand, was too distraught with conflicting feelings to shut off and let me rest. I sat up. "You're soaking wet." My grandpa stood behind him. "Both of you."

"That's what happens when it rains," Hayden said with a wink. "I'm gonna go change now."

My grandpa took off a long camo-print jacket, shaking little water droplets onto the floor. My grandma would have had a fit.

"Hayden told me about the compound," my grandpa said.

I didn't breathe. My muscles tensed and I stared wide-eyed at my grandpa. "Oh, did he now?" My grandpa nodded and sat on the couch next to me. "And?" I asked.

"I'll go back with you." My grandpa smiled. "Just to check it out."

I blinked. Had I heard him right? "You'll come with us? I needed to hear him say it again.

He nodded. "Not permanently. Hayden explained everything."

"Everything?" I asked, walking on eggshells.

"Government set up."

The air whooshed out of me, unnerved at how calm my grandpa was. Was this the calm before the storm? "Yeah. We just found out."

He looked at me, unblinking. One eye narrowed and twitched as he thought hard about something. Then he smiled. "I knew it. Knew it all along. Those sons of bitches were out to get us all the whole time. Listening to us through the radio. Watching, always watching. But they can't know about us now, no. The droids weren't made for this, Hayden told me. They can't make it this long."

I nodded. "Yeah, they can't," I agreed, having no idea what he was talking about. I didn't even know what he was envisioning when he thought of droids. "When do you want to go?"

"You have a mission to carry out. Swing by when you're done and I'll follow you"

"I'm not leaving you," I said, setting my face. "There's no way to promise you'll be here."

"I'm not going anywhere," he said with a wink. "You have a duty to your people."

I bit the inside of my cheek. Bringing my grandpa with us exposed him to unnecessary danger. He was smart, cunning, and was my teacher, my mentor...but he was also old. He had health issues before this all started, like high blood pressure. Leaving him here...no. I couldn't do it.

"I've been here all along," he said, knowing what I was thinking. "Go. Do what you gotta do and come back."

So many things ran through my head. What if something happened and I didn't come back? What if we were gone too long? Or came back to an empty house?

My grandpa put his hand on my arm, reading my mind. "Orissa," he said, eyes meeting mine. "You can do this." His face crinkled into a smile. "You've succeeded in everything I've thrown at you. On your own. Now you have a team, a good team." He tapped the engagement ring. "That boy worships the ground you walk on, as he should."

I couldn't help but smile. "He does."

"He'd do anything to keep you safe."

"That's what scares me," I confessed.

My grandpa took in a deep breath and smiled again, though this time there was something sad behind it. "Your grandmother used to say the same thing about me."

A twinge of sadness went through me. I twisted the ring around my finger. It felt weird and almost annoying to have the band between my fingers. I was scared of getting the diamonds caught on something. I was a little ashamed of that. The last thing I needed was a distraction. If I remembered, I should leave it here.

"What do you want to do about the people at the school?" I asked.

My grandpa shrugged. "Hayden is gonna tell them about the compound, let them decide if they want to go or stay." He took a breath and I notice his face had more wrinkles than the last time I had seen him.

"If you like it there, you can always stay until this is over," I offered. I twisted the ring. "We have to go back. We've set up a lot of stuff...people depend on us."

"You've done well, Rissy." My grandpa smiled. "I'm proud to say you're my granddaughter."

I waved my hand in the air. "Stop it." I smiled. "I only did what I thought you would do."

He put one foot up on the coffee table, knees cracking as it bent. "You really love him enough to marry him? You're not settling because it's the end of the world?"

"Not settling." I laughed and shook my head. My grandpa had never been one for subtly. "He's a good person and treats me well. Better than well."

Hayden came done the stairs. "Talking about me?"

I smiled at him. "I am."

My grandpa shakily stood. "I'll leave you lovebirds alone. There are lots of preparations to be made for an extended trip out."

Hayden took his spot next to me. "Ok," I said, sticking my arm under Hayden's. "How the hell did you do that?"

"Do what?"

"Convince my grandpa to come back with us." I shook my head. "I didn't even want to bring it up and you got him all agreeable. Explain this sorcery."

"He started asking questions," Hayden began. "I didn't want to go into detail since you said he'd be reluctant to believe me, but the man is smart. I couldn't lie and get away with it."

"Hah. Try growing up with him."

"So I told him the truth. About everything. He said he was curious and I offered to bring him to Arkansas to show in the compound. He didn't disagree so I asked if he could come evaluate for improvements."

"You're a genius."

"Maybe. I, uh, kinda made it sound temporary."

My shoulders moved up as I inhaled. "I know," I said with a sigh. "Is it naïve to hope that once he gets there he'll stay?"

Hayden shook his head. "Not at all. That's what I'm hoping too."

I put my head in my hands. "Why do things have to be so complicated?"

Hayden wrapped his arms around me. "Family is always complicated. It won't always be. Someday, I promise."

"We'll be dead by then."

His warm lips pressed against my forehead. "No. We'll still be kicking. If you take after your grandfather's side of the family you'll be fine. He's aging gracefully."

"Maybe I'll be crazy then too."

Hayden laughed. "You'll fit in just fine with the Underwoods then."

I tipped my head up, my chin rubbing against the stubble that covered Hayden's face. "I love you."

Hayden flashed a cheeky grin. "I know."

* * *

Hayden and I were on first the watch that night. I yawned and rested my head against Hayden.

"Don't fall asleep," Hayden said and put his arms around me.

I shifted on the wooden bench. "I won't. This isn't comfortable enough."

He kissed the top of my head. "Good." He pulled a blanket over us. We were sitting on the back part of the wraparound porch.

"It's funny how sixty seems cold when we're used to the heat." I said and leaned closer to Hayden.

He nodded. "I'll check around front."

I shivered as soon as he let me go. The porch vibrated under his weight as he walked around the house. My bow was by my side and a rifle rested on my lap. I had no intention of using the gun unless absolutely necessary. The night vision scope, however, was useful.

I pushed the blanket from my lap and stood, going to the railing and scanning the backyard. The night was dark. Thick rainclouds covered the moon. The outbuildings were black shadows. The chickens had been put back into their suspended cage for the night. When the wind was still, I could hear them shuffling around.

I was about to go back to the bench when I saw it, a flash of black behind the barn. I squinted. Yes, there was definitely something moving closer to the barn. Silently, I picked up the rifle and looked through the scope.

He was moving too fast to be a zombie; each movement planned and thought out. Crazy, maybe? I poised my finger over the trigger.

He ducked under the fence, pausing when he straightened up. He looked nervous.

Crazies didn't know fear. He slipped through the grass, heading to the barn. He kept looking behind him, worried he was being watched or followed.

Definitely not infected.

He was at the barn door now, trying to get in. I didn't think twice. I grabbed my bow and took off, jogging toward him.

"Hey!" I shouted. The guy looked at me and ran. Nothing says guilty like running away as soon as you're caught. I pushed into a sprint and was behind the guy in seconds. I jumped, sailing through the air, then tackled him.

"Get off me," he muttered, swatting at me as we wrestled. I shoved his face into the ground and positioned myself behind him, pulling his arms behind his back.

"Let him go," someone said, their voice cutting through the dark like a knife. I twisted the man's arm up until he yelped. "I'm warning you, girl." Clouds rolled over the moon, patchy light illuminating the face of a gruff man, dirt covering his face. He held a knife up, eyes flashing like his sharpened blade. "You have five seconds or I'll cut you."

"That'll be hard to do with a bullet in your head," Hayden said, pulling the hammer back on his pistol. He pressed the end of his gun into Knife Guy's head. "Drop the knife."

Knife Guy held up his hands.

"I said, drop it!" Hayden didn't give him another chance. He grabbed him, bending his arm back and taking the knife.

"Up against the wall," he told Knife Guy, using his gun to point at the side of the barn.

"You too," I snarled, yanking the guy I had tackled up by the arm. The back door of the house opened and slammed shut. Wade ran out, shirtless and wearing jeans with a rifle in his hands. He immediately raised it, looking through the scope. The guys moved to the barn, sitting on the ground with their backs pressed against the side.

"Are there any others?" I asked. Jason and my grandpa would be out in just seconds.

"Yes," the first guy said. He had bitten his lip when we fell. He licked at the wound, spitting blood onto the ground. "Just one more."

"Where?"

"Out there." He looked at the field behind me.

"Tell him to come here."

Knife Guy glowered at me. He planted his hands on the ground. "Don't even think about it," Hayden said, raising his arm again. "Tell your friend to get the fuck over here before we find him. Or we won't be nice."

Knife Guy inhaled. "Aubrey," he called, then looked at Hayden. "Please don't hurt her."

"I won't," Hayden said, expression softening. "As long as you don't give me a reason to."

"Aubrey," he called again. "Weapons down."

A young woman emerged from the field, coming toward the fence with her hands raised. Her arms trembled. She was crying.

"Don't hurt us, please," she begged.

Wade escorted her to the side of the barn. She rushed forward, falling into Knife Guy's arms.

The back door opened and shut again. "What's going on?" my grandpa yelled.

I looked over to see Jason helping him down the steps. He hobbled as fast as he could to us, huffing by the time he arrived.

"Not sure," I said, turning back to the three in front of us.

Hayden stepped forward. "Start talking," he said to Knife Guy, who wrapped his arms protectively around Aubrey.

"We didn't mean no harm," he said, his toughness gone now that he was out numbered. "We-we saw the chickens and were going to take them. We're hungry, that's all."

"Seriously?" I asked. I pointed to my grandpa. "Who do you think takes care of the chickens?" I glared at all three of them. "You knew *someone* put them in the barn. They're not wild birds just roaming around. It's not free game. You had all intentions of *sneaking* into someone's barn and stealing their chickens, right?"

"Yeah. We're hungry," he repeated.

"Did you even think to ask us?"

"No."

My ears were hot from anger. "And what about us? You have no issue taking our food source?"

"We didn't think—"

"Ugh!" I shook my head and held out my hand. "I have had it up to here with this end of the world, lack of hospitality bullshit! I'm not exactly a people person, but you don't see me going around being a dick. You know why? Because I'm a fucking decent human being!"

Knife Guy blinked. "I-I'm sorry, ok?"

I pointed his knife at him. "You know the funny thing? Had you had the decency to come to us, to *ask* for help we would have not only given it to you but we would have offered a safe place to stay for the night." I gave him a tight smile. "Blew it now, buddy."

"We're really sorry," Aubrey cried. "Shawn wasn't going to hurt anybody. I promise. Please! Let us go."

"I never took kindly to trespassers," my grandpa said, pumping a shotgun. He limped forward, gun raised. He wasn't bluffing.

"Grandpa," I said, holding a hand up. "Fresh blood attracts zombies," I blurted, needing to appeal to his rational side. I was pissed and thought these three people were assholes, but I didn't want them to die.

Hayden lowered his gun, eyes darting from me to my grandpa. He moved forward, putting himself indirectly in front of Shawn, Aubrey, and the other guy.

"We can figure this out," he said. "We obviously have a problem here."

"We do," my grandpa said through gritted teeth.

"Yeah we do," Jason agreed, rushing over. "We've got company."

CHAPTER SIXTEEN

I whirled around, heart jumping out of my chest. Weeds snapped, rustling back into place as someone crashed through. Their dark silhouette grew larger as they approached. And they were coming fast.

Was it part of this group trying to catch us off guard? We were all outside...easy targets in the dark. Shit! The house was empty! Someone could get inside and lock us out.

The smell hit me right before the gargling death groan filled the cool night air. Zombie. I let out a breath. How messed up was it that I was relieved it was a zombie? I took a few steps back and grabbed the bow.

The zombie was a few feet from the fence. I narrowed my eyes, trying to focus in the dark. I strung an arrow and aimed, zeroing in on his head. He was limping so much his head bobbed up and down, a difficult target at night. I released the arrow. It hit the zombie in the shoulder.

"Dammit," I muttered and grabbed another arrow. The zombie crashed into the fence. I let out my breath and the zombie became still. This time I got him, right in the head. His body slumped forward, toppling over the fence.

Jason walked over to retrieve the arrows. He used it as a spear, shoving it into the head of a gummy who had trailed behind the zombie. Thick blood and slushy brain splattered out when he yanked the arrow free.

We waited, looking out at the field. A minute passed and nothing else came. I lowered the bow and turned back to our unwelcome guests. I'd rather deal with the zombies.

My grandpa wheeled around with more speed than normal for someone his age. He pointed the gun at Knife Guy's face. "Who sent you?" he demanded. Great. He was at it again. "You were watching, waiting. How long have you been recording us?"

He lowered the shotgun and pulled a knife from a sheath that was hanging at his side. The handle was wrapped in electrical tape. I couldn't tell exactly what had been attached without more light.

My grandpa flicked a switch. A blue line ran down the blade, crackling and popping. I didn't need a light to know he had attached a taser to the knife. It was so crazy it was awesome.

"Did you get what you wanted?" He shoved the taser-blade in front of him. Aubrey screamed, burying her head in Shawn's chest. Blue light flickered over his face. His eyes were wide as he stared down my grandpa, who no doubt looked like a complete lunatic.

My grandpa lurched forward. "Is that information stored in the computer chips? They're not gonna get it." He shook his head. "No, I won't let them. I'll take it out. Destroy it like I did before. Can't find me."

He turned to me. "Get the hose. Have to use electricity. It's the only way to shut the cyborgs down."

"Grandpa," I said calmly. I licked my lips, debating on how to do this. Hayden stared at me, waiting for my signal. "They're people, not cyborgs."

"We won't know that until they pass the test."

I swallowed. "What's the test?"

"Give 'em a shock. Cyborgs malfunction."

I closed my eyes in a long blink and let out a breath. "And if they don't malfunction?"

My grandpa tipped his head, pressing the taser on the blade again. "Never made it that far before."

Oh my God. Had he killed innocent people? "I think there's a better way to test them."

My grandpa stiffened. He turned his head, eyes void of emotion. All rationality had left him. Armand Penwell had checked out and he was replaced by the shadow of a man who had seen too much. "How?"

"Heartbeats."

"The cyborgs could have computer chips. They can even increase the speed."

I cast a pleading glance at Hayden. We couldn't let him tase these people, not with his taser-blade at least. I could feel the electricity from it all the way over here. That thing had enough juice to stop a human heart.

"They can bleed," Hayden said, stepping forward. "Cyborgs don't bleed since they have no blood." My grandpa's arm started to relax. "And look at them," Hayden continued. "They're weak, thin...not built like cyborgs at all."

My grandpa nodded. Then his face twisted into a scowl. "It's a disguise." A blue line of electricity snapped down the blade. "They can't fool me. I won't let them. Not again. Not after they took my sweet Jenny." He raised his arm. "You have a mission. They're here to stop it."

"No!" Shawn pleaded. "We're not cyborgs I promise! Nobody sent us!"

"That's exactly what they want you to say!" my grandpa shouted.

I looked at the field behind me. We needed to get inside, out of the dark.

"If they were cyborgs they wouldn't have gone for the chickens," I said, exasperated. "They would have gone for us."

My grandpa looked at me, eyes narrowed. Then he slid the taser-blade back into its sheath. "You're right. Cyborgs don't eat. They *can't* eat. No stomachs."

"Right," Hayden said.

My grandpa crossed his arms. "So what I have is a couple of trespassers."

I stepped close to my grandpa "Yes. That's what we have. What do you want to do with them?"

"Your call, kid," he said. He was testing me and this time I didn't have the slightest idea what he expected.

"If all they wanted was food..." I looked at Hayden. "We should let them eat. Then question them."

"All right." My grandpa crossed his arms. "But under my watch."

* * *

They smelled like they hadn't showered in days...weeks maybe. Aubrey clung to Shawn. Her vivid green eyes stuck out from her dirty face. Her hair might have been blonde. I couldn't tell; it was too dirty. It fell in matted clumps around her shoulders.

"When was the last time you ate?" Hayden asked.

The man I tackled shook his head. "A few days ago...maybe. Everything blurs together."

That was something I could relate to. I was still pissed they were going to steal from my grandpa, but in a sense I felt bad for them. And as long as they weren't planning on stealing anything else or attacking us, I wanted to help.

My grandpa sat in the corner of the room, shotgun in hand, muttering about droids sending more cyborgs. The three strangers passed his test, but I knew he wasn't convinced they weren't brilliantly disguised cyborgs. The only way he allowed them in his house was to 'bring them in for questioning.' Once inside and in the light, he saw how ragged they were. The logical part of his brain began to surface.

"Take it slow," Wade said when he gave them each a can of peaches. "You can easily get sick if you eat too fast."

Aubrey cradled the can like it was the Holy Grail. Her face crinkled as if she was crying yet no tears fell from her eyes due to dehydration.

"Thank you," she said, her voice small. She stabbed a slice of fruit with her fork and put it in her mouth. I leaned against the table, giving them a few minutes to devour their food before questioning them again.

The man who I tackled was named Joel. He was Aubrey's brother. They were from Indiana and met up with Shawn several months ago. The three had stayed at a camp with nearly a hundred people. Food became scarce and tempers rose. The people were too busy fighting with each other when a herd came through.

They ran, and had been running ever since, scavenging for food and shelter. Joel admitted that he saw Wade and me in the Jeep this afternoon and followed us back. When he saw the chickens pecking the ground outside, he came up with the plan to sneak in at night.

"Why didn't you just ask us?" Jason stood, shaking his head. He waved his hand at me. "Like she said, we would have helped you. That's what we do."

"You've very nice people," Joel said.

"No shit," I said, frowning at a nick on my bow. "We'd be even nicer if you rang the fucking doorbell and asked for help."

"I'm sorry," he said, looking up from his can of peaches. "We didn't think about the people here...only the food."

"The past is the past," Jason said. "Just don't do it again."

I smiled, turning my head away from Jason. I kind of felt bad thinking he was cute trying to be authoritative. He tried so damn hard, and I was proud of him for that.

After Joel, Aubrey, and Shawn ate, they showered. Hayden and I pushed the coffee table aside in the living room and laid down blankets. Our plan was to let those three sleep here, under supervision of course, then drop them off at the school tomorrow before we left for our mission.

We went back to our posts. Hayden and I stayed inside this time, moving from window to window all the while keeping an eye on our houseguests. Around three in the morning Wade and Jason switched us out. I stripped out of my clothes and crawled into bed with Hayden, falling asleep almost immediately and not waking until around eight the next morning.

* * *

Hayden put the truck in park. A few zombies were in the school parking lot. They walked through the cars aimlessly, only turning their attention to us once we got out of the car.

"I'll take care of it," Hayden said. "Get them inside."

I did a quick count. There were two zombies and three gummies scattered across the lot. "Fine." I wasn't happy about leaving Hayden, but he could handle it.

"I want some practice," he said with a smile and reached for my bow.

I took the quiver off my shoulder, extending my arm. "Don't lose my arrows."

Hayden smirked. "If I do, I'll let you punish me."

I rolled my eyes, laughed, and pulled my knife from its sheath, holding it out in front of me. "Follow me," I told Joel, Aubrey, and Shawn. We hurried to the gate. I undid the lock, slid the panel of fencing away, and ushered them in.

I raised the drop down gate. "Hello?" I called. "It's Orissa again." I pulled the gate back down once we all were through. Boots echoed through the hall. Great. It was that douche bag Bentley.

"I knew you couldn't stay away," he said and rounded the corner. He stopped short, blue eyes narrowing. "More of your friends?"

"Not really," I said. "But they will be yours." I turned. "They're gonna—"

"Are you Bentley Owen?" Joel gushed.

Bentley flashed his brilliant smile. "Yes, yes I am." He ran his hand through his hair and winked at me, striding forward. He had a guitar strapped to his back and was wearing a black cowboy hat.

Seriously?

"Always glad to meet a fan." His eyes ran up and down my body when he walked past. He extended his hand to Joel.

I re-sheathed the knife and crossed my arms. It was stupid to get excited over a celebrity—if you could even call them that anymore. He was just one of us, a survivor, no different than anyone else. Actually, he was different. He had no training, no past that was helpful.

"They're going to be stay here for a while," I said.

"The more the merrier, I always say," Bentley said. "As long as it's not the undead," he added, earning laughs. He turned, waving down the hall. "Come on in, I'll show you around." They walked past me, following Bentley down the hall.

"You're not coming?" he asked me when I didn't move.

"Not yet." I looked outside. "Waiting for someone."

Bentley laughed. "I hope it's not that mysterious fiancé of yours. I see your ring disappeared."

I had left the ring on top of the dresser in my old room for safekeeping. I turned to Bentley, eyebrows raised. "Yes, it is him."

Bentley strode over, stopped next to me, and licked his lips. "He's a lucky guy." He stared at me so hard I could feel his eyes fucking me. "You look like a proper woman without that bow and arrows."

I took a breath. It wasn't worth it...it wasn't worth it.

"And by proper, I mean hot."

I whipped around. "Keep your boner-lusting eyes off me, asshole. I'm not interested in you. At all."

Bentley leaned back, eyes wide in shock. Then he laughed and put his arm on the wall. "And what if I don't?"

"You'll be sorry."

He leaned in more. He really thought he was hot shit. "You gonna sic your fiancé on me?"

I smirked. "Don't have to. I can take care of myself, thank you very much." The gates scratched against the cement sidewalk outside. I turned, opening the door for Hayden.

He was clean-shaven this morning, wearing a gray t-shirt and dark jeans. Blood had splattered across his face. His eyes went to mine, a smile subconsciously pulling his lips up.

"Everything go ok?" I asked, raising the metal gate.

"Yeah," he said and ducked under, holding his rifle to his side. "It was a piece of—Bentley Owen." Hayden straightened up. "You're Bentley Owen."

Come on, Hayden, not you too. I shook my head.

"I love your music," Hayden blurted. "You preformed for us overseas four years ago. I've been a huge fan ever since." His eyes lit up. I moved next to him, close enough to feel his body heat. I hooked my fingers under the strap of my quiver. Hayden's arm went slack as he let me pull it off him.

"Careful, sweetheart," Bentley said and winked at me. "Those sticks are pointy. Maybe you should leave the weapons with the big boys. You look much better without it."

Hayden blinked. "What did you just say to her?"

Bentley's cool smile faltered. Did he really think he could use his past star status on my Marine? I put the quiver over my head and took the bow.

Bentley laughed, tipping his head up so his hair fell back. "You gotta admit your woman is good looking. And those are few and far between these days."

Hayden's shoulders tensed. He stepped up, right in front of Bentley. Hayden was a few inches taller and more muscular. His body went rigid, ready for a brawl. "Orissa isn't my *woman*; she doesn't *belong* to me."

Bentley held up his hands, apparently *not* ready for a brawl. "Hey now," he said, trying to back away from Hayden's instant anger. "I didn't mean it offensively."

"Treating a woman like a piece of property *is* offensive no matter how you meant it." Hayden shook his head, eyes flashing in anger.

"All right," Bentley said. Fear pulled down his face. "Sorry, buddy."

"I'm not your buddy."

Bentley took another step back before turning to the stunned faces of Joel, Shawn, and Aubrey. I looked at Hayden, not meaning to smile as deviously as I did. I shook my head again, having to remind myself it wasn't worth is. Bentley hurried down the hall.

"Fucking soldiers," he muttered.

It happened fast: I grabbed an arrow, strung up the bow, and fired. The arrow sailed through the air right though Bentley's cowboy hat. It flew off his head and stuck to the wall.

"Riss!" Hayden exclaimed, eyes wide.

"Oops. Lost control of my pointy sticks," I said innocently. "And they're not soldiers. They're Marines."

Aubrey stared at me with her mouth agape. Between my grandpa last night and now me, she probably thought we were one headache away from turning crazy.

* * *

I wrapped my arms around my grandpa, burying my head against his shoulder. I closed my eyes to keep tears from spilling. We only planned to be gone for a few days, but damn this was hard.

"Be safe out there, kid," my grandpa said.

"I will," I promised. It wasn't us I was worried about. "You too."

He nodded and let me go. "I always am." He looked at Hayden. "Look after my granddaughter. Try and keep her outta trouble. It's a helluva job," he added with a wink.

I gave my grandpa one more hug before getting in the truck. My grandpa had crossed off towns on our map that he had already been to. It saved us a lot of time and trouble; that was for sure. Our current plan was to go east, beyond where my grandpa and his group had explored.

A traffic jam in Powell County forced us down a less-traveled back road. The trees were thick, blocking out the sun on both sides of the street. Undergrowth from the forest crept up along the pavement.

"I was thinking," Hayden began and turned down the music. He had skipped past every Bentley Owen song that came up on his iPod. "When we get back, want to stay an extra day or two?"

I tore my eyes away from the passing blur of trees. "Of course I want to." Hayden smiled and put his hand on my thigh. I laced my fingers through his. "What made you want to stay?"

"You." He squeezed my leg. "I like seeing you happy."

"I like being happy." I smiled and looked out the window. "It's been a while."

"I know," Hayden sighed. "I want that beach."

I closed my eyes and inhaled. "Yes. The fresh ocean breeze—no stinking zombie bodies in sight. Sand between my toes and a drink in my hand. I need it. Now."

"Wouldn't it be nice?"

"Yeah," I said. Signs for the state park flashed by. "It would—slow down!"

Hayden slammed on the brake then let off, not wanting to get rear ended by Wade and Jason.

"What's going on?" Jason's voice came over the radio.

"I saw something on that sign," I answered.

Hayden pulled over on the side of the road. I jogged down the pavement. Sunlight shimmered off the hot street in front of me.

"This!" I said, knowing the guys were right behind me. "All survivors welcome," I read the words that had been spray painted over a sign for the Red River Gorge campground. "Well that's just dumb. Let everyone know where you're staying."

"Should we check it out?" Jason asked, eyebrows rising with excitement. "There could be a ton of people there!"

"I suppose it's worth a look," Hayden said with reluctance. "Have you been here?" he asked me.

"A few times." I shook my head. "Wandered around in the forest more than once."

"So you know your way around?"

"Oh hell no. There are thirty thousand acres in this forest." I looked at the sign again. "We did come here, to this specific campground once. It was a *long* time ago, before my parents split."

Wade stepped up behind me. "I think we should drive down there, check it out at least." He tipped his head in Jason's direction.

"There could potentially be a lot of survivors."

Hayden shifted his weight. We couldn't take in a lot of survivors. Not only were we running out of room, there was no way we could provide enough food for everyone. He let out a breath and nodded. "We can't go by without checking. The sign says 'all are welcome' but remember, we have no idea what we're walking into."

The thought made sweat break out across my back. Part of me wanted to tell the guys to get in our cars and leave. It wasn't our responsibility to save everyone. It suddenly made me angry for taking on the role of zombie outbreak response team. Killing the undead and saving the living. Risking our lives to spare others.

But if we didn't do it then who would? There were hundreds of people back at the compound who had been saved because of our teams. The newfound sense of responsibility weighed on me. I got into the truck thinking about what life would be like if I had only run into Hayden and we were living in the farmhouse with my grandpa and friends.

We'd make it, that I was sure of. We could hunt and grow food for no more than a dozen people without too much of a problem. But what would be the point? Where would we go from there? Though the thought scared me, what if Hayden and I had a child somewhere far down the road? Would life in isolation be something I'd want for my children? They would grow up and then what? Live out the rest of their days alone because there was nobody else, no one to fall in love with, no one to cherish and hold onto every night?

"You ok?" Hayden asked.

I snapped back to the here and now. "Yeah, I'm fine. Just deep in thought, I suppose."

"Are you gonna tell me what you're thinking about?"

"Life," I laughed. "What it is now...what it would be like if just the two of us were together, well with some friends of course and we never went out on missions like this."

Hayden gave me a half smile. "I like the thought."

"We'd survive for sure."

"More than that," Hayden said. "With you, I'm not just surviving. I'm living."

I smiled, my heart speeding up. I turned in my seat to face Hayden. "I don't know how I'd make it through this without you, you know. You've keep me more than just safe during all this."

"I'm glad we stopped to save that crazy girl standing on top of a chicken coop, taking on a herd of zombies."

"I would have been just fine if you hadn't shown up," I said with a laugh. "I had a plan."

"You said that when we first met too. Did you really have a plan?"

I bit my bottom lip. "Yeah. I was going to run through the herd and try to get them to turn around. It would have given Padraic and Raeya time to escape."

"You couldn't outrun...oh." Hayden became silent. I snapped the band at the end of my braid. I had never told anyone my plan was to sacrifice myself. I hadn't exactly thought of it that way at the time either. I had lost hope and wanted to give up. I was ready to go out in a blaze of glory.

Then I met Hayden.

"There are tire tracks," Hayden said, leaning forward. "Not new but not that old either."

"Maybe three days ago?" I guessed. "It doesn't look like it rained as much here as it did back ho—at the farm."

The road gave way to a large slab of pavement. Tents and RVs circled around an enclosed picnic shelter. An indoor bathroom was off to the side. The entire area was enclosed with ropes. Pop cans, hubcaps, and other pieces of torn apart metal hung from the ropes.

A woman with short brown hair came out of one of the RVs. She looked to be in her thirties and was wearing broken glasses. She held a knife in one hand.

Hayden put the truck in park and opened the door. "Hello," he called as he got out. "We saw the sign," he added quickly. "We mean no harm."

A young girl with tight braids across her head came out of the RV. The woman waved her hand. "Get back inside!"

"He said they mean no harm," the girl said pointedly. The woman gave the girl a look, one that said we couldn't be trusted just yet. The girl whirled around and went back in.

"How many of you are there?" the woman asked.

"Four," Hayden said.

"You all armed?"

"Yes," Hayden said honestly and turned so she could see the pistol on his hip. "We won't hurt you. We came to see if you needed help."

The woman didn't seem convinced. I got out of the truck, holding my bow as casually as I could at my side. Her face softened a bit when she saw me, as if another female presence was proof Hayden really wouldn't hurt her.

"Hi," I said and gave her my nicest smile. "I'm Orissa."

"Stephanie," the woman said. Her eyes darted to the Jeep. Jason and Wade got out, hands held up to show they were not holding guns. "We don't have much," she said quickly.

"We're not going to take anything," Hayden assured her.

Stephanie swallowed, her grip on the knife tightening. "You're really here to help?"

I understood her apprehension. We were clean, well armed, and in capable vehicles. I would be wary of us too.

"Yes," I told her and took a step forward. "We know of a safe place."

She let go of the RV door. "Really?"

I nodded. "Yes." I moved my foot a few inches. "We can talk about it, if you'd like."

Still not trusting us—and rightly so—Stephanie walked away from the RV with her knife held out in front of her. How many people were hiding inside?

"You're not going to hurt us?"

"Has someone hurt you before?" I blurted before I realized it made me sound like a shrink. I shook my head. "No, we're not, as long as you don't hurt us."

She looked at me as if I was crazy, like attacking us was the last thing she'd do. "All right. Come in." She waved to a spot in the circle were only one piece of rope had been wound around two trees.

We ducked under the rope. The RV rocked as people moved inside. I saw the girl with the black braids peeking through the window. Someone put a hand on her shoulder and she stepped back.

We gathered in the center of the campsite. I looked around as Hayden went into his speech about the compound. At one point, this place offered real shelter. Now it was a shadow of that with slashed tents, dirty clothes hanging on a line, and an overflowing garbage can full of food wrappers. Buckets sat out to collect rainwater and their garden was dying from lack of sunlight.

The RV door creaked open. The little girl poked her head out. "Mom?" she called. I looked around; there was no one who looked like her mother out here. My heart sank and my stomach clenched. Shit. What happened to the girl's mom?

"Hang on, honey," Stephanie said. I looked at the girl then at Stephanie. Oh, right. She was probably adopted. She turned back to Hayden, listening to him as he explained everything in detail.

Not long after, Stephanie decided she wanted to come with us. We followed her into the RV. Her daughter, Daisy, sat beside another young girl and a twenty-something year old man.

She told us that four others from her group had set out last night, trying to hike through the woods to get to another campsite with a medical building in hopes of finding supplies. They never returned.

"How far is this medical cabin?" Jason asked.

Stephanie unfolded a map. "Not that far if you cut through the woods. There is a wildlife rehabilitation clinic in the back. I was so sure there would be antibiotics." She shook her head. "It would have been worth it...I swear."

"Maybe they're in there," the guy said, hope in his voice. "Maybe they had to rest or...or..." he shook his head.

Metal pop cans clanged together. The girls jumped. Stephanie flew to the door, locking it and drawing the shade.

"Crazies," Jason whispered. "They're dragging someone—something."

Stephanie moved over and gasped, her hand flying to her mouth. The tears in her eyes let me know she recognized the body.

"Stay here," Hayden said. He, Jason, Wade, and I slipped out of the RV. The crazy had enough sense to duck under the ropes. He was too busy yanking the body over a twisted root to notice us.

I shot an arrow into his back, severing his spine before he could even turn around. Stephanie came out of the RV, legs shaking.

"Pete." She quivered and sank down by the dead man. The crazy had torn open his abdomen and removed his stomach. After a minute of quiet grieving she stood. "The others could still be out there."

"Maybe," Wade said and put his hand on Stephanie's back. He flicked his eyes to me. "We could follow the trail, see if we find anything."

Hayden tensed then agreed. We helped Stephanie move Pete's body inside the circle, warning her it was a bad idea since fresh blood attracts crazies...and crazies attract zombies.

* * *

The trail was easy to follow. Bright spots of crimson were better than bread crumbs. We were maybe a mile and a half out when we heard the screams.

"Go!" I shouted to Hayden. "I'll keep on the trail."

"Not alone," Hayden said back.

"I'll stay," Wade said.

I shook my head. "I'll be ok. Trees," I said and swept my hand out. "I can climb." It was a bullshit lie and Hayden knew it. The trees were tall with no low hanging branches.

Another scream came from the direction of the campsite, this one long and high, sounding like a child. Hayden's eyes met mine in an unspoken goodbye. Then he and Jason took off.

Wade and I made good time, pushing through the thick vegetation as we followed the trail.

"Here," Wade said, several feet in front of me. "This had to be where it happened. There is so much blood and, uh, skin." He nudged something with his boot. "Is that a spleen?"

"I'm not sure what a human spleen looks like," I said and came over to look anyway. The weeds were smashed down, evidence of a struggle. There were two sets of prints. "I can't tell which is from the crazy. Both trails are even from walking straight."

"Pick one?"

I looked up at Wade. "Sure." I took the lead, following the trail through the woods. I wasn't sure how much time had passed when Wade grabbed my arm.

"What?" I whispered. He pointed to our left. A large, black tree stuck out of the ground, the greenery around it also dead. Something swung from the trees. I turned away, giving Wade a horrified stare. He nodded and moved through waist high bushes.

A breeze slipped through the forest, rustling leaves. We stopped a few feet in front of them. I slowly drew my eyes up. Bodies hung from nooses, dead and decaying. Something had been carved into the tree. I moved over to see past the skeletal remains and read it aloud.

"Here in the forest, dark and deep, I offer you eternal sleep." A tangle of rope sat under the woods, covered in moss. I reached out, fingers trembling, and touched the engraved words. My head was spinning.

"*The Poor Little Rich Girl*," Wade spoke, voice hollow.

"What?" I asked, turning around. I felt dizzy.

"It's a book. That's where they got the quote. I had to read it in school."

"If they wanted to be creepy, they succeeded," I said, stepping away. I stopped close to Wade, feeling safer already.

"For sure," he agreed. We moved back to the trail, neither speaking. We made it another few yards before a gun shot rang out, echoing through the forest. I froze, the hair on my back of my neck standing up. I whirled around, stomach dropping.

Stephanie didn't have a gun. Only Hayden and Jason had guns. And they wouldn't have fired unless something bad happened, something out of their control.

I didn't have to say anything. Wade took my hand, and we sprinted forward, running back to our friends. I held up the bow, using it to block branches from scraping my face.

I didn't see them; they blended in with the trees at first. Then the smell hit me, and I stopped, tripping over a log hidden by leaves. Wade rushed back to my side. We had run into a herd of zombies.

CHAPTERSEVENTEEN

"We have to get out of here!" I shouted over the death moans.

Wade nodded and took my hand, pulling me to my feet. "Come on, this way!" I pushed the bow back up over my shoulder. Leaves stuck in my hair and dirt smeared across my face. The knees of my pants were wet from the soft ground. "You can get us out of here, right?"

"I think so." Our eyes met in a fleeting moment of hope. Wade nodded and turned. We took off, tearing through the thick forest. I held my hand up, blocking branches and leaves from smacking me in the face as we ran for our lives. The ground was uneven and covered in year's worth of debris.

A flock of birds took off, their wings echoing throughout the forest for all to hear. My heart pounded. Sweat dripped into my eyes, but I kept running. I crashed into a feathery spiderweb. Tiny silken ropes pulled across my face. I didn't have time to brush them away.

"We came this way, right?" Wade panted, slowing down.

"Yeah," I huffed, hiking the quiver into place. The thing was heavy when it was full of arrows. I looked up. The blue sky was patchy under thick leaves. Everything swirled around me.

"They're ok," Wade promised me. My breath caught in my chest. Had that gunshot belonged to Hayden? "The herd is following us. We're going *away* from that camp site. Riss, it'll be fine!"

I swallowed hard. "If you say so."

Wade put his hand on my arm. "I know so. Come on," he said with a jerk of his head. "Can you find the tracks?"

I blinked back unwelcome tears. "Yeah. I can definitely do that." My heart thumped in my ears. Blood pooled in my face, making my cheeks hot. "Dammit," I swore under my breath. I dropped to my knees and gently brushed dead leaves away.

"What?" Wade asked, stepping close.

"Fucking zombies. They trampled everything."

Wade looked at the ground. "Yeah. They did. All I see is haphazard steps."

I stood and looked at the sun. "If there's one thing I'm good at it's finding my way out of God-knows-where woods in Kentucky." I smirked and shook my head.

"Uh...ok." Wade cast a nervous glance behind him. We had put some distance between us and the herd, but not enough to feel safe. "Am I ever going to know the truth, Riss?"

I rolled an arrow between my fingers, heart still racing. "My grandpa," I said shortly.

"Yeah...don't hate me but I noticed he's a little, uh, insane. Brilliant, but fucking insane."

I nodded. We moved forward in a brisk walk. "He's been like that for a long time. He was convinced something like this would happen so he started training me years ago."

"Seriously?"

I flicked my eyes to Wade. He was tan, his dark skin contrasted against his dark blonde hair. I often forgot that he was a few years younger than me. Mentally, I didn't feel any different. But when the sun filtered through the trees and illuminated his youthful face, I was reminded of the three year age gap.

I found myself telling him about my grandpa, his PTSD, the way he trained me, and his fear of government takeover. I did this as we moved and I sought the right direction.

"This way," I said, pointing. Wade nodded, smiling. Then the curve in his lips straightened. His hands flew to his knife.

Leaves crunched under their dragging feet. Branches swung wild as the zombies blundered forward. I strung an arrow and waited a beat before letting it go. Brown goop splattered the air. The zombie crumbled to the ground.

Wade turned around. "Riss, there's too many! We need to go!" He kicked a zombie in the chest, shoving the knife in its ear. Another zombie grabbed him by the shoulders, swinging him over. Wade stumbled back, hitting a tree.

I shot another zombie at the same time Wade stabbed the one that was advancing on him. He was right. The trees were too thick, too densely covered in leaves to see what we were dealing with. The zombies were close by the time we saw them.

The smell was overwhelming. Rotting flesh ripened in the hot summer sun. I lowered my bow.

"Wade!" I shouted, sidestepping around another zombie. Maggots dripped from its face. "Follow me!" We sprinted forward, pushing through everything the forest threw at us and them some.

My lungs heaved. I needed to stop, catch my breath. I stole a glance behind me. The zombies were still close. Too close to stop. I looked ahead and pushed on. Then I saw it: the beautiful break in the trees. Oh thank God. The road, the fucking road.

A smile broke across my face. "Only a few yards," I panted to Wade. I turned my head to the side, our eyes meeting.

He smiled, opening his mouth to talk. Then something snapped and he fell to the ground, crying out in pain. I skidded to a stop so fast my ankle rolled and I tumbled over the ground. A few arrows slid out of the quiver.

"Wade!" I screamed and stood. A steel jaw trap had closed around his ankle, the sharp teeth cutting through his jeans and into his skin. Blood dripped steadily. The death moans reverberated through the forest, reminding me of what little time we had.

I dropped to my knees, desperately pushing away the leaves. "There's a way out. There has to be a way out," I muttered over and over.

"Riss!" Wade yelled. He sat up, holding onto his leg. I pushed leaves aside until my hands became soaked in blood. The warm liquid sent a jolt through me.

"There's a way." I sucked in air fast—too fast. I was hyperventilating but I didn't care. I had to get Wade out.

I *would* get Wade out.

"Riss!" he yelled again in protest.

I kept pushing the leaves around until my fingers grazed a chain. I pulled it. The chain was staked in the ground. I crawled to the stake, tugging with everything I had. I screamed in frustration and pulled on the chain, moving the steel trap. Wade cried out in pain. "I'll get the pin," I mumbled, fingers trembling. Steel jaw traps had been part of my training...only my training involved setting them. Not getting out of them.

There was a way to unlock it, I knew it. There was something...a pin to press maybe, that would unlock it.

I heard the rattling death moan. I knew it was there, getting closer by the second. But I didn't care. I had to save Wade. My hands shook until they were useless.

"Riss!" Wade shouted and pushed me away. He pulled his gun from the holster and fired. The zombie dropped just inches from me. I snapped my head back.

Holy shit. We were surrounded. My heart hammered and my breath came out in ragged huffs.

"Go, Riss!" Wade pleaded, tears in his eyes. "Even if you get me out I'll slow you down."

"No fucking way," I mumbled, hands shaking as I felt along the inside of the trap. The rusted metal was slick with warm blood. "I'm not leaving you!"

"There's no time!" he shouted and fired his gun again. The walls of dead were closing in. I couldn't breathe. The rancid smell of rotting flesh choked me, gagged me. My eyes filled with tears.

"Stop it!" I screamed. "Just stop! I'm getting you out!"

Wade put his hand on my shoulder. "Riss. Please," he pleaded. "Save yourself. Finish the mission."

"Stop!"

My fingertip caught on one of the teeth, slicing through my flesh. I flinched. The death moans grew louder.

"Riss!" Wade yelled. I ignored him, busy feeling along the trap. There was a release. There had to be. "Behind you!"

I turned just in time to see snaggled, yellow teeth. Brown saliva dripped from her mouth and blood crusted over her lips. Her hands tangled in my hair, pulled my head back. I turned, bringing my arm up to hit her on the inside of her wrist, breaking the contact. I pulled an arrow from my quiver and jammed it in her eye.

I turned to see Wade struggling with a zombie. He had it by the shoulders, keeping its mouth just inches from his face. I sprang up and kicked the zombie in the head. It stumbled off him, rolling onto its back, unable to get up.

I flew back to Wade. He reached for me, trembling fingers taking hold of my arm. I pulled against him, going to the trap.

"Riss," he begged, his voice breaking. "Stop. Leave or we will both die!"

"No!" I cried, tears falling down my cheeks. I yanked on the chain. If I could pull it from the ground, I'd drag Wade away. Just a few yards. That's all I needed. I had to. I just fucking had to.

"Please." He sat up, face pale. "You don't know."

"What?" I turned my head, hair falling out of my braid and into my eyes. My entire body trembled. I pulled on the chain again, getting flakes of rusty metal embedded in my palms.

"You and Hayden."

"It doesn't matter!" I shouted. Wade wasn't making sense. It had to be from the blood loss.

"You two...you guys...your love," he panted. "It inspires us. All of us."

A chill ran through me. The chain went slack in my hand. I blinked away tears and shook my head. "It doesn't matter," I repeated. "I almost got it!" I lied, pulling on the chain once more. It wasn't budging a fucking inch.

Wade yelled again. A zombie grabbed me by the ankle and pulled. I slid away from Wade onto my stomach. I twisted, the quiver digging into my back.

"Get off me," I yelled, yanking my foot. The zombie was strong but with little festering flesh. He must have just turned from S1 to S2. He dragged me back another few feet. I planted my hands on the ground, getting the strength I needed to push him off. He fell and I kicked him in the head, slamming the heel of my boot down again and again until his brain oozed out.

Wade screamed. I grabbed an arrow from my quiver when another zombie came at me. I ducked out of its reach, swinging my arm and burying the arrow in his eye.

"No!" I turned. Wade's head rolled back, mouth open in a desperate painful scream. Two zombies were on him, teeth tearing into his stomach. My heart pounded in my ears. I turned around, loose strands of hair flying into my face, sticking to my sweaty skin. My hand moved up behind my shoulder, fingers closing around the blood crusted fletching of an arrow.

I could hear every beat of my heart. My breath left me, whooshing out too loud. I bit the inside of my cheek, the metallic taste of blood filled my mouth. The string on the bow groaned. I let the arrow go.

The zombie fell forward, knocking the other to the side. I rushed forward, kicking it away. I grabbed the other zombie, pressing my thumb into its eye.

Wade screamed in pain, tears running down the side of his face. I jammed my thumb deeper into the zombie's brain. It snapped yellowing teeth, its mouth glinting with Wade's blood.

Rage filtered through me, empowering me. I twisted my hands, turning the zombie's head all the way around. I shoved him away.

"It's gonna be ok," I spoke, not even realizing that words were coming out of my mouth. I couldn't catch my breath. My head shook and I wasn't able to focus on anything. Wade's eyes met mine and his hands moved to his abdomen.

Vomit rose in me, burning my throat. Wade's stomach had been ripped open. His intestines spilled out, scattered around him.

"It's gonna be ok," I repeated and rocked forward. Wade's breathing labored. He wheezed. I knelt down, putting my trembling hands on his bleeding abdomen. His large intestine had been severed. Something thick oozed from it. "Padraic will fix you. You're gonna be ok." Fat tears rolled down my face.

I pressed my hand to his stomach and pushed the intestines back into the gushing cavity. Wade's eyes closed and his body went rigid.

It was so warm. Everything that spilled out of him was warm. Wade's hand closed around my wrist.

"Riss," he wheezed. I shook my head. I couldn't talk now. I had to save him, had to put what was outside back in. He brought his leg up, jangling the chain that held the steel jaw into the ground.

I pushed my hands down. If I could just get everything back in…I couldn't breathe. My vision filled with black spots. My fingers were too slick with blood. I couldn't pinch the skin closed, couldn't keep everything inside.

Something heavy landed on my shoulders. It pushed me forward, sending me into Wade. My hand slipped inside of him. He yelled and I screamed.

Hot, dead breath was on the back of my neck. My ragged breaths turned into sobs. I fell forward, one hand still inside the hole in Wade's stomach. I felt something hard under my fingers, something sharp that felt like bone. Oh god, it was his spine. Wade cried out again.

The zombie pushed me down, opening his mouth to get a taste of the fresh blood. I was paralyzed, stuck under his dead weight. My cheek pressed into Wade's stomach. The zombie reached his hand in, pulling something up that stretched and snapped. Blood splattered my face.

I couldn't move. I didn't want to move. Somewhere inside of me, I knew this was it. There was no coming back. Wade was dying and I'd be next. Ripped apart by savage beasts.

Another zombie dropped to her knees. Her dead hands closed around Wade's face, fungus covered fingernails digging into his skin. He screamed. The zombie on top of me leaned in, pushing me down even further.

Time had no meaning. I could see everything. Hear everything. Each slurp. Each splash. The smell of blood and death wrapped around me, pulling me down into a murky hole of despair.

Then I blinked. I planted my hands on the ground and pushed up. No. This isn't ending like this. I wasn't going to lie there. If I went down, it would be fighting.

I pushed up, knocking the zombie off of Wade. Tears ran down my cheeks. I turned, twigs snapping under my weight. My hands, red with blood, pulled the knife from my waist. I rammed it into the zombie's skull. I pulled my arm back and turned on the female zombie. She snatched her head up when I grabbed a handful of her hair. A large piece of Wade's flesh hung from her teeth, torn off of his cheek.

I tackled her to the ground, shoving the knife into her forehead over and over. The groaning echoed off the trees. Somehow I got to my feet. This wasn't how it ended. I wasn't giving up.

They came, attracted to the noise and the blood. And I went after them, one by one until there was nothing left to fight, nothing left to kill.

My knife clattered to the forest floor.

I dropped down. "Wade," I murmured, crawling to my fallen friend. His stomach was ripped open. Half of his organs were out, splayed across the ground next to him. His chest rose and fell unsteadily. Skin and muscle had been torn from his face, exposing his cheek bones. Tears blurred my vision. I wrapped my arms around him, crying.

"Tell..." he started.

I sniffled and sat up, face just inches from his. He opened his eyes, gaze locking with mine.

"Tell Gabby..." Then his eyes rolled back. One final breath left him.

"Wade?" I swallowed. "Wade! Wade!" I shook his shoulders. "Wade, please. No!" I fell forward, sobbing. My entire body shook, pain rippling through my soul.

* * *

Time passed—minutes or seconds. The forest was still, suspended in a red pool of death. I stayed, clutching Wade's body and crying until he became stiff. I sat up, eyes swollen and took in a breath, hiccupping down a sob.

I looked at Wade's face. The blood had stopped dripping down his cheek. His eyes were halfway open, cold and lifeless and already losing color. I reached up. I needed to close them.

My fingers touched his skin. It was cold and hard. I jerked my hand away. Trees swirled around me. I closed my eyes and fell to the side, unable to hold myself up. I was on a ride, a horrible ride, spinning around gruesome death. There was no way off. It could only go faster, getting bloodier with each pass.

My face pressed into the forest floor. I could feel bugs crawling beneath me but was too numb to care. My heart hurt. Each beat shoved the knife in further and further. I closed my puffy eyes. Be still. I needed to be still, needed to disappear from this.

Wake up. This was all a dream. A nightmare. If I could wake up things would be different. Better. Wade would be alive. Not lying in a puddle of blood, body dismembered.

A gunshot echoed in the distance. I jumped, opening my eyes. A tangle of Wade's small intestine came into view. I pushed up onto my elbows and threw up. I wiped my mouth and stood, collecting my arrows as if I had switched on the auto pilot.

I stood in the middle of the carnage, barely breathing. What was I supposed to do? I couldn't leave Wade here, alone in the forest. I couldn't drag him and destroy what was left of his body.

My eyes burned. I had no tears left. I moved back to Wade and dropped to my knees.

"I'm sorry I couldn't save you," I whispered, choking out the words. I closed my eyes, silently crying, and pushed leaves over his body. "Here in the forest," I whispered and put a handful of leaves on his chest. "Dark and deep." I flattened a large green leaf and held it over his face. "I offer you eternal sleep." A single tear found its way down my cheek as I laid the leaf over Wade's torn apart face. I picked up his gun, cradling the M9 to my chest. It was all I had left of him, the only thing I could take back with me.

The rustling of the leaves I was placing on Wade's body masked the sound. I didn't hear them coming until one was right behind me. Anger flashed through me. I sprang to me feet, turning around. I thought I'd see one or two zombies: the stragglers. I hadn't expected another horde.

CHAPTEREIGHTEEN

I didn't move. I eyed down the zombie closest to me. His gray eyes were focused on Wade. I pulled an arrow and shot him. As soon as he fell, another took his place. I stepped over Wade's body. I wouldn't let them have it. I shot two more but they kept coming.

I heard my grandpa's voice telling me to run, to get out while I could, that there were too many to fight.

"No!" I said out loud.

His voice was in my head again, screaming at me. Wade was dead. It was just a body. I needed to leave. Turn around and run.

So I did.

The road was close. If I made it there I could get back to my group, back to Hayden. I could warn them about the zombies and we could get out of here once and for all. I sprinted forward, dodging around trees, and sliding down steep hills and drop offs.

My ankle twisted and I fell, rolling down the hill. My bow smacked me in the face and my arrows jostled around, falling out. I scrambled to my knees, gathering my arrows. The road stretched out in front of me. I was so close.

And so were the zombies. They crashed through the forest, hurdling their bodies down the ravine. I watched them rise like ghosts from the mist. Terror plagued me, but somehow I managed to get to the road.

Panting, I looked up and down it knowing right away this was not the road we had come in on. The hills on either side were too steep, too densely wooded. Zombies blundered through the forest. There were so many. Too many. I needed to move. One look at the sun in the sky and I knew which way I needed to go. I hooked the bow over my shoulder and gripped Wade's gun in my hand.

A massive rocky hill loomed in front of me. It was straight, like a giant stone wall. I slowed, heart racing. Did the road come to a dead end? Zombies milled through the trees above me, snapping and snarling. Every few seconds one fell, tumbling down the steep embankment.

They were getting closer, with no intention of giving up until they ripped me to pieces just like Wade. My boots pounded on the pavement. If the road suddenly ended, I'd be forced to trek back up the hill and try to make it through the forest and past the herd.

Then I saw it. The opening in the rock wall was just large enough for a car to get through. The road continued, going right through the rock in a man-made tunnel. My chest tightened. Anything could be in there.

I stopped, breathing heavy. Zombies closed in on me. I couldn't turn around, couldn't go back into the trees. I had to go forward. I looked into the black tunnel. I had no choice. I was going in.

I closed my eyes, giving myself a head start on adjusting to the dim light, and picked up the pace. Just a few feet in and the air was different, cooler, stale. I felt like the walls were closing in on me the deeper I went, just like they did when Olivia and I got stuck in the haunted house.

Only this wasn't set up for fun. This wasn't supposed to be entertaining. My heart pounded so fast it hurt. I kept running, my lungs burning and begging for air. Each footfall reverberated off the tunnel walls, echoing loudly like a beacon for the zombies.

Finally, when I wasn't sure if I could take it anymore, the tunnel curved and I saw the light at the end. I pushed forward, mind blanking out, and kept running.

* * *

My feet hurt. Each step was painful. I concentrated on that, the physical pain. It kept me from thinking about anything else, anything that would hurt worse. The string from my bow had rubbed me raw, eating away a line of skin between my neck and shoulder.

I turned down the road, staring at the tire tracks. Something in me wanted to stop and turn around. I didn't want to come back alone. I kept going, trudging along, somehow finding the strength to put one foot in front of the other.

Their voices floated through the air. I was almost there...maybe. My head was down. I couldn't bring myself to look up. Someone gasped.

"Riss?" Hayden asked. Pop cans jingled as he ducked under the rope. "Shit, Riss."

I was covered in Wade's blood. Dirt and leaves clung to my battered body, leftovers from the forest that had swallowed us whole. I stopped walking and lifted my head. Hayden's hazel eyes were full of worry. "What happened?" he asked, afraid of my answer.

I shook my head, tears blurring my vision.

"Where's Wade?" His voice cracked as he asked the last question. He already knew.

My hands trembled. I held up Wade's gun. Then it slipped through my hands, thudding to the ground. My heart broke, bringing my body in on itself. I fell forward, crying. Hayden's strong arms caught me, and he gently lowered me to the ground, holding me tight against his body, rocking me gently while I cried.

"What's going on?" Jason asked, voice tight. I opened my eyes just enough to look at him. "No," he said, shaking his head. "No, no!" He turned away from me, hands on his head. "No!" he shouted and pulled at his hair. He whipped around. "He's fine. He's out there, and we just have to get him."

I sniffled and opened my mouth to talk but failed. No words came out, only sobs. Jason sank to his butt, head in his hands.

"Jason," I said and reached for him. "I'm sorry."

"Don't be sorry," Hayden said, fighting back his own emotions. "This isn't your fault, Riss."

"I couldn't get it out," I mumbled. "I tried. It was stuck. But I couldn't. Couldn't get it out." Hayden ran his hand over my hair, soothing me. I clung to him, knowing that if I let go my entire world would collapse even deeper into darkness. When my tears turned into sniffles, Hayden gently said, "Let's go."

He helped me to my feet, taking hold of my hand. I didn't object to anything, didn't ask where we were going. He led me to the truck and removed my weapons before gently peeling off my blood soaked shirt. He was so gentle, careful, hands moving slow as he took care of me, wiping off blood and cleaning my wounds.

He pulled a clean t-shirt over my head. I stuck my arms through the sleeves and pulled it down to my waist. He handed me a new pair of pants. I blinked, realizing how filthy I was. I changed then got into the truck, feeling numb.

Jason and Hayden quickly removed the supplies from the Jeep, transferring them into the truck. Jason got in the back with us, giving Stephanie and her friends the keys to the Jeep.

I sat in the passenger seat with my hands on my lap. Hayden got in and fired up the engine. He stepped on the gas and the truck lurched forward. I stared straight ahead, not blinking until my dry eyes burned.

I rested my head against the window. If I closed my eyes, I saw the decaying bodies swinging from the tree. All I could do was think about the pain in my feet. When they stopped hurting, I pressed them down onto the floor of the truck. I needed to feel it, to be distracted by it. I couldn't handle thinking about anything else just yet.

An hour passed before Hayden and Jason spoke. I heard their voices, knew they were forming words, but nothing made sense to me. I stared at the window, realizing that we were headed toward the farmhouse. The sights were familiar, but it did little to comfort me.

"Stop," I said suddenly, startling Hayden. "Stop the truck!"

He pulled over. "What?"

I pointed to a large building we had just passed. Hayden's eyes widened.

Jason leaned forward, thinking I was close to a breakdown.

Hayden followed my gaze and knew what I was thinking. "Oh." His hands fell from the steering wheel. "Riss, we don't have to. Let's just go home."

"No," I spat. "No. We set out on this mission for a reason. It can't be for nothing. I'm not going home empty handed."

Hayden took a breath and ran is hand over his head. He was hurting too, as was Jason. But we couldn't stop and just go home. Not after all we'd lost. "Ok."

"What?" Jason asked, eyebrows furrowing.

Hayden nodded in the direction of the building behind us. "A food pantry."

Jason's mouth opened slightly. "It could be full of nonperishables. Boxed up too. Sonja and I used to volunteer at one in Indy."

Hayden made a U-turn. Stephanie followed behind in the Jeep. "I had to do community service here. Multiple times," I said before they guys had to ask. "There is a freezer in the back to avoid. Everything up front should be good to go...as long as no one else took it first."

"I'm guessing it's still there," Hayden said. "I never would have thought to look at a food pantry, but it's brilliant. Like Jason said, everything is nonperishable and boxed up for delivery."

I sat up straight. I could to this. Carrying out a mission gave me something to focus on. We pulled into the parking lot. Hayden gave Stephanie a walkie-talkie and told her to radio us if she saw anything.

I went first, hoping for zombies. I channeled my grief into rage and needed to take it out on something. With my bow held to my side, I pushed the door open onto a small lobby. Dust covered everything. Cobwebs clung to every corner. A plastic Jack-o-lantern filled with cheap candy sat on the front desk.

I took the guys through a hall, past a bathroom and volunteer lounge, emerging into the large warehouse.

"Holy shit," Jason swore, his hands drooping. Cardboard boxes were stacked as tall as me, all full of presumably edible food.

"Bring the truck around," Hayden said to Jason, fishing the keys from his pocket. Any other day, Jason would have held the keys up like the fucking holy grail, like his role model big brother had finally let him drive the cool sports car home from school. But today he just nodded and left the warehouse.

I remembered from my time here that almost every box was identical in supplies, making it easier for mass shipping. This place had once been full of donated food and boxes. When the depression hit, more people needed the help and fewer people were able to donate.

Pick box up, take it to truck, put it in bed. I repeated that over and over in my head, keeping any and all thoughts away. I lost count of how many boxes I moved. My body was so sore. The cuts on my hands broke open, bleeding through the bandages Hayden had wrapped around them.

I moved further into the warehouse, seeing if there was anything unboxed to look through. I walked through a narrow hall that connected two warehouses and pushed open a door. There was a body in the corner, nothing but clothes, bones, and bits of leathered flesh.

It was a woman, I guessed from the pink jacket. She died curled up, with her hands wrapped around her torso. Part of a name badge stuck out from the wrinkled material. I swallowed hard.

"Gillian," I read out loud and touched her name tag. I remembered her. She was one of the few employees of this place. I always seemed to get stuck with her during my community service hours. She was quirky and upbeat and never got annoyed or bothered with my constant teenage sarcasm and bad attitude. Eventually, I started to like her. I took some of her advice to heart, though not enough to keep me out of trouble.

I pulled my hand back. The name tag got caught on my bandage. Her skeleton slumped over, landing at my feet. Hers wasn't the only body. A teeny little skeleton was curled up inside of her, resting on her spine. That's why she died holding onto herself. She was pregnant.

Tears stung the corners of my eyes. I remembered her talking about wanting a baby ten years ago. My last stint of community service was a few days after my eighteenth birthday. She came in crying, telling us that her doctor told her the chances of her getting pregnant were slim to none. I didn't get it back then, didn't understand why it was so upsetting.

I couldn't look away from the tiny bones. My lip quivered. Was this her first baby? Had she finally gotten pregnant just to die?

"Riss?" Hayden called. No matter how hard I tried, I couldn't move. His footsteps came up behind me. I could sense him looking at the body, taking in the fact that two lives were gone. He slipped his hand into mine and turned his body in. His other arm went around me.

Then I broke into a flood of tears. I sucked them back in, shaking my head. "I'm fine," I said and pushed off Hayden. He didn't let me go.

"No, you're not. I'm not."

"I am." I waved my hand at Gillian and her unborn baby. "It doesn't matter. She's already dead." Suddenly, I couldn't breathe. Every inhalation was pushed out before I had the chance to get the oxygen.

"Riss," Hayden said, holding onto me. "Orissa," he repeated, voice breaking. "You're hyperventilating."

I shook my head. No I wasn't. I didn't do that. There was no point, it didn't solve anything. I needed to stop, stop crying, stop caring. I had a job to do. I leaned forward, chest tightening to the point of pain.

Hayden cupped his hands around my face and kissed me, soft lips pressing into mine. He opened his mouth, sliding his tongue inside mine. Then I did stop, stopped panicking, stopped repressing my feelings. I melted into Hayden, tears streaming down my face.

He pulled away, gently biting at my bottom lip, and pressed his forehead into mine.

"I act like I'm tough, like I know exactly what to do all the time," I whispered. "But I don't. I wasn't prepared for this." I closed my eyes, fat tears falling steadily. "Caring about people and then losing them." I shook my head. "I don't know how to handle this, Hayden. I...I can't. I just can't."

"Riss," he said gently. "It's ok." He took my hands in his. "We shouldn't have come here. Not after..." he couldn't finish. "Let's go. We're not far from the farm and it's not like we can fit all this in here anyway. We can come back."

He gave me a gentle tug. I didn't want to go home. I'd have to face reality there, have to deal with the fact that Wade wasn't coming with us, that I was never going to see him again.

"Riss?" Hayden's hazel eyes got misty. He looked down and blinked. Darkness started closing in on me. We'd have to go back to the compound at some point, have to tell Brock and Ivan and oh

God...Gabby.

I wiped away my tears and went with Hayden. Jason's eyes were red. He ducked his head, embarrassed, and loaded a final box into the bed of the truck. In silence, we got in and headed home.

* * *

The sun set. Brilliant orange clouds stretched across the purple sky, reflecting off the glass of my bedroom window at the farmhouse. The front door opened as soon as we pulled into the driveway.

Hayden got out, waved to my grandpa, and opened my door. My chest tightened when I saw the house.

"Back already?" my grandpa asked and limped down the porch steps. He stopped short. "Four of you left."

My hand froze on the seatbelt release. I had to remind myself to inhale. Jason got out of the truck and went around to the Jeep, telling Stephanie to stay inside until someone directed them to the school.

My grandpa rushed through the overgrown yard. Hayden met him halfway, explaining what few details he knew about Wade's death. I hadn't told him what happened and he hadn't asked. I never wanted to think about it again. Ever.

I got out of the truck, not really processing what I was doing. My grandpa hugged me and ushered me inside. I took off my boots. They were spotted with blood. Fresh, red blood. Wade's blood.

"She was with him," Hayden whispered, thinking I couldn't hear him as he spoke to my grandpa. "I don't know what happened."

"She needs you," my grandpa said. "Don't worry about the others. I'll take them."

"I'll go with," Jason offered.

My grandpa didn't object. He felt bad for us. "All right, kid," he said. "Tell them to hang out for a few." He came into the living room, carrying a glass. Ice clinked on the sides. "I believe this is your choice in poison," he said with a wink. He couldn't fool me. I could see the desperate worry behind his eyes.

I took the glass and put it to my lips. It had been a while since I'd had a cold Jack and Coke. It was strong, much stronger than anything I'd make for myself. I've must looked like I was losing it. I certainly felt like I was about to. I tipped my head back and tossed down the drink.

"Easy," my grandpa said.

I put the glass on the coffee table, waiting for the spinning to set in.

"Want to tell me what happened?" Grandpa asked.

I shook my head. I hadn't cried in front of my grandpa since I was eleven years old when they picked me up from my mom's apartment. She had been passed out drunk on the living room floor for hours in a puddle of urine and vomit.

"Did you see it happen?" he asked slowly.

I nodded. "I tried..." Tears rimmed my eyes. "I wasn't fast enough." My arms wrapped around my torso. I swallowed back a sob and bit my lip. My grandpa sighed and put his hand on my shoulder.

"You did everything you could," he said definitely. "I know you did. We...we can't beat them all. Jenny," he started. "I wasn't fast enough with her either."

I blinked. The tears I struggled to hold back ran down my face. My grandpa gave me another hug. The room spun when he let go. Good. I needed it to dull the pain.

"Why don't you take a shower then lay down. We'll talk about this after you've rested." He tipped his head, looking into my eyes. "You need to talk about this, Rissy."

I nodded, scared that if I opened my mouth the entire truth would come out, retelling everything that happened. My grandpa waited until Hayden was in the room to leave. I heard the jingle of keys and Jason's voice. The front door closed.

Silence rang in my ears. Hayden sat next to me, unmoving, not speaking for several minutes. I took in a ragged breath and stood, walking out of the room. Hayden stayed close behind me, only hanging back when I went into the bathroom.

"Do you want to shower?" he asked when I came out. I shook my head and went into the kitchen, making a beeline for the sink. I sank down, opening the cabinet to get the bottle of Jack. My grandma didn't think my grandpa should have drunk when my mom became an alcoholic. My grandpa argued that he didn't have an issue and should still be able to. Why should he suffer for someone else's mistakes? Nevertheless, he started hiding bottles of booze in the far reaches of the cabinet.

I went to the cupboard and grabbed a glass. I filled if halfway with whiskey and took a swig, shuddering from the taste. I found a box of Coke cans in the pantry and poured one in.

Hayden stood behind me. He was likely thinking that I had overfilled the cup. He sighed and put his head in his hands. Then he took the glass from me and took a drink. I had already chugged nearly half of it.

Instantly I felt sick. I put the glass down, feeling the effects of the alcohol pull me under. I hooked my arm through Hayden's and closed my eyes.

Red.

It was everywhere. Red blood, seeping out of Wade's eviscerated stomach. Digested food leaking from his torn open intestines. My body went rigid. I felt like throwing up. I couldn't handle this. I reached for my glass.

"You've had enough," Hayden said.

"No!" I argued. I closed my eyes and saw Wade's lifeless face. The skin had been torn off his cheek, exposing the bone. "I can still see it when I close my eyes!"

Hayden's eyebrows pushed together. "What, Riss, what do you see?"

"Him!" I hunched forward. "I was right there, Hayden. I tried to save him and I couldn't. I tried." I shook my head, tears falling. Red spots floated in my vision. I needed to sit down before I fell. I clung to Hayden for support. "He was stuck and then they came. They pulled him apart and I tried, Hayden I tried. I couldn't get it back in."

He wrapped his arms around me. "Riss..." he trailed off and looked away. His eyes were red and full of tears. Hayden brought me to the floor and into his lap. He held me, rocking us back and forth while I cried.

"I'm so sorry, Riss," he whispered. "I wish I could fix this...fix everything."

I moved my head up and down, listening to his heartbeat.

"Seeing someone die." He stopped, getting his emotions under control. "Seeing someone you care about die...it changes you. When Ben..." He stopped and put his head down against me, pulling me closer. I was warm in his tight embrace and was scared that I would unravel if he let me go.

My head was spinning. I was drunk. Good.

"Let's shower," he said. "Together. I'm not leaving you."

I nodded. My body itched from the dried sweat and blood. Hayden pulled me to my feet and I wobbled. I brought the drink with us and ended up needing more help that I thought with going up the stairs and washing my body.

We dressed in pajamas and got into bed. Jason and my grandpa were back now; I could hear their voices coming from the kitchen. I downed another few gulps of the drink, feeling sicker by the minute.

Hayden spooned his body around mine, stroking my hair. Silent tears rolled down my face, soaking the pillow. I couldn't close my eyes. If it wasn't Wade, then it was the hanging tree or Gillian's dead baby. When I thought I got past that, Rider showed up.

Finally, in a twisted haze of alcohol and visions, I fell asleep.

I woke up screaming.

"Riss," Hayden said, hands landing on my shoulders. He gave me a gentle shake. "Wake up, Riss."

My eyes flew open. "I'm awake," I panted, blinking. Images from my nightmare flashed before my eyes. "The trees are bleeding." Blood poured out of holes, holes made by my arrows that stuck out of them, arrows that missed zombies, zombies that ripped apart my friend before my very eyes, feasting on his body until there was nothing left.

My face crumbled into tears. Hayden pulled me to him. "Riss," he said, his own voice tight with emotion. He sharply inhaled and pressed his head against me. His chest tightened and his body shook. I clung to him, shaking.

It was dark outside. The window was open and a warm breeze blew into the room, sending the curtains flying. My heart raced. I held onto Hayden, making myself aware of everything about him.

His heart beat fast too and his skin was clammy from a cold sweat. His chest rapidly rose and fell. Light from the hall spilled into my old room. I wrapped my arm around Hayden's left arm, tracing his tattoos over and over until I was calm enough to let go.

I finished my drink. It instantly went to my head. I stumbled to the bathroom before coming back and passing out, letting the heavy darkness pull me into an abyss.

* * *

I didn't wake up until the morning. I took a breath, blinking in the bright sunlight that streamed through the open window. For a second, everything was ok. Then reality crashed down on me.

Physically, I felt like shit. My throat was dry, head throbbed, and my body ached from running and falling the day before. But it paled in comparison to the pain of the heartbreak.

I ran my hands over my face, rubbing my eyes. I took a deep breath and pushed myself up and out of bed, stumbling into the bathroom. I was going to go back into my room and sleep some more but stopped. Hayden's voice floated up the stairs. I paused at the top to listen.

"I don't know," he said. "It's a gamble."

"Of course it's a gamble!" my grandpa spat, fire in his voice. "That's what they want."

"We can't just pack up and go."

"Of course you can!" My grandpa hit the table. "They wouldn't expect it."

What were they talking about? I held onto the railing and leaned down. "You said it yourself," my grandpa went on. "You don't know what it's like in New York. It could be fucking utopia for all those politicians. They might be watching us. But they might not be."

Hayden sighed. "I know. We don't know we—"

"That's why you have to go, get in, make them see what they did to us, to you. To *Orissa*. You need to make them pay. Or, at the very least, make them know you exist."

"They meant to kill us."

"Of course they did! They've been trying to kill us for years—decades! But you also said not everyone there knows the truth. If you could infect one of them..." he trailed off laughing. "What's more contagious than the virus? The *truth*."

There was a few seconds pause. "It could start a riot," Hayden said.

"What do you mean?" Jason asked.

"When a group of people believing a lie find out the truth," my grandpa explained. "They're not happy. To say the least."

Hayden said, "How would you feel if you were living in perfect safety, thinking that the people protecting you did everything they could to save the country when really, they went out killing everyone in sight?"

"Oh, right. Yeah..." Jason let out a breath. "I'd be pissed. Really pissed."

"And," Hayden went on. "That's not to mention telling them the virus was created on purpose and set loose on the public with the intent to cause this."

"How do you know people inside these safe places don't already know?" Jason asked.

"I can't be sure. It was something Fuller said." I could imagine Hayden's eyes clouding with self doubt as he shook his head. "He made it sound like not everyone inside knew what was going on. And those people have to have family and friends out there somewhere that didn't make it."

"That's why you gotta go in," my grandpa said, speaking fast like he did when he was excited about one of his crazy theories. "Expose 'em. And kill Samael."

A chair creaked as someone leaned back. "It's something to consider," Hayden said.

"You gonna make it through the winter?" my grandpa asked. "All those people you got back in Arkansas?" When Hayden didn't answer he continued. "No, they're not. You're going to run out of food and then what?"

"It's going to turn into the Donner Party," Jason mumbled.

"No it won't," Hayden said. "We'll figure it out."

"Time for that is gone. Sure you might be able to scavenge, take everything in that food pantry back, but it won't last long. How many people you got back there?"

"Well over three hundred," Hayden answered. I hadn't realized there were *that* many people at the compound. No wonder I couldn't remember anyone's name.

Pots and pans clanked around. "And you're responsible for food for all of them?"

"Yes, sir," Hayden said.

"You should start sending them out, make 'em fend for themselves."

Hayden didn't say anything, not wanting to offend my grandpa. The smell of eggs churned my hung over stomach. I snuck down the stairs and went outside.

Thin grays clouds covered the sky, trapping in humid air. I walked barefoot through the yard, dew soaking my pajama pants. I stopped by a pile of rocks. Weeds stuck out through the gaps.

"Hey, Zoe," I said, clasping my hands together. My bottom jaw began to tremble. I sank to the ground, crossing my legs. I closed my eyes and leaned forward, putting my head in my hands, not moving. I needed to be still.

The grass rustled behind me. I opened my eyes, face still covered with my fingers.

"Riss?" Jason said softly. My shoulders relaxed. He came closer. "Hayden's looking for you. I thought you'd be here."

I nodded. "Yeah."

"You ok?"

"I don't know," I said honestly. I was trying hard not to feel anything.

Jason sat down next to me. "I miss him."

"I tried." I closed my eyes, blocking back the tears. "But I couldn't save him."

"It's not your fault, Riss."

I nodded. Somewhere in me I knew it wasn't my fault, just like Rider. But I couldn't push the crippling feelings of guilt away. He put his hand on my shoulder.

"When we saw those people die in that parking lot...you know, when you, Padraic, and I went out for supplies?" He shook his head. "It gave me nightmares for weeks. So...I don't know. This sounded better in my head. I'm sorry, Riss. But at least you were with him. He wasn't alone."

I looked up at Jason. I hadn't thought of it that way. "Thanks," I said.

Jason hugged me. "I'm gonna tell Hayden you're here. He was worried."

I nodded again but didn't get up. I watched spiders crawl in and out of the crevices of the rocks until Hayden came. He stopped behind me.

"We should go," I said without turning around.

"Where?" He knelt down.

"I heard you guys talking."

Hayden looked straight ahead. "It's a crazy idea, Riss. Crazy and stupid."

"You know what's stupid?" I asked, temper rising. "This!" I waved my hand at Zoe's grave. "All of this! This world..." I trailed off, shaking my head. I turned to Hayden. "I don't want to live like this! Do you?"

"Of course not."

"Then what other choice do we have?" Anger burned inside of me. "Our time *is* running out. We haven't grown enough crops to get all three hundred of us through the winter. Going to warmer weather isn't an option. Hayden, what will we do?"

He sat down and took my hand. "I don't know, Riss." The line of worry was back between his eyes.

I curled my fingers around his. There was one thing I did know for certain: I loved Hayden more than I ever thought I could love anyone. I would make him happy in any way possible.

I looked over the stones at the field behind the house. I wanted to stay here with Hayden. I exhaled. That wasn't an option. The sun came out from behind a cloud, warming my skin. We couldn't stay...but we could come back.

I turned to Hayden, squeezing his hand. "Hayden," I started. "I never knew what to do with my life before. I was lost—so lost. I had no idea what I was doing or what I wanted. But now I do. I want to be with you. I want to grow old together. I want to live in a world where we don't have to worry about surviving the winters or getting attacked and eaten if we step foot outside the fences. I want to laugh and have fun and spend all day making love because there is nothing better to do. And I will do anything to get that. If that means going to New York then we have to do it. We can't do this on our own."

The line of worry faded and a small smile pulled up his lips. He drew me in. "Then we'll go."

CHAPTERNINETEEN

My heart sped up when the gates came into view. Seeing the gates to the compound always had that effect on me. I still remember my apprehension when we first came here, worried that maybe I'd made a mistake in trusting Hayden. I never doubted him for a second. From the moment we met I trusted him. I couldn't explain why, even looking back now I couldn't find anything logical that made me trust his word. I just did. And I was damn glad that I had.

Hayden let off the gas, letting the truck slow down on its own. My stomach flip flopped. I was so nervous to go inside, to have people see us come home without Wade. Hayden flicked his eyes to the rearview mirror, meeting mine for a few seconds. My grandpa sat shotgun and Jason and I were in the back.

We had quite the entourage. The four of us were in the truck, leading the way. Bentley, Marla, Anne, and two more from their group piled in the Jeep. Aubrey, Shawn, and Joel drove a truck with my grandpa's chickens in the bed. Stephanie, her daughter, Daisy, and the other young girl drove a minivan full of supplies, and the remaining people crammed into the SUV my grandpa had been driving.

To be safe, we cleared out the farmhouse of weapons and supplies. The same day Hayden and I decided to leave, my grandpa went overboard on locking up the house and the barn. Hayden and Jason went outside to help. I stayed in my room, curled up in bed. Now I felt slightly ashamed of that. But at the time, I couldn't get the horrendous images of Wade's disemboweled body out of my head.

I saw him every time I closed my eyes. His cries of pain echoed in my ears. Even now, as we passed through the gates of the compound, I could smell the death around us mixed with the metallic scent of Wade's blood.

I caught sight of Jason out of the corner of my eye. He was close to falling apart. Though he wasn't with Wade at the time of his death, he felt guilty. Wade was his partner. Jason didn't have to say it out loud; I knew he felt like he had failed Wade by not being there.

I didn't want to tell him that I felt even worse. I *was* there. And I still failed him. I reached across the bench, putting my hand on top of Jason's. He turned, giving me a forced smile and gave my fingers a squeeze.

The normal chaos of bringing new people into the compound buzzed around us. Things always moved fast, whisking the newcomers away to the quarantine barn as soon as they set foot outside of their vehicles.

I got out of the truck, standing by my grandpa. It became apparent, right away, that something had gone horribly wrong. Not all of us had returned.

There was no way I was letting my raw emotions go uncloaked in front of anyone except those who had been in the truck with me. I took a deep breath and buried my feelings.

After a moment of stunned sadness, the A3s in charge of getting everyone into the quarantine barn snapped back into action. Jones, an A3 who took care of the dogs, got in the truck that had the chickens, asking Hayden if it was ok if he took them to the farm.

Hayden nodded, forgetting he was technically in charge of everything. Hayden, Jason, my grandpa, and I went into the estate, entering through the front doors.

"Rissy!" Raeya exclaimed. She raced down the stairs, followed by Ivan and Brock. A huge smile was on her face, disappearing as soon as her eyes met mine. "What..." she started. Then she saw my grandpa and almost fell down the stairs. "Holy shit!" she swore.

"Hello, Raeya," my grandpa said, giving her a warm smile. Raeya stood, stunned, looking back and forth from my grandpa to me. She was too busy taking it all in to notice that Wade wasn't with us. But Ivan and Brock did.

I started shaking. A tear escaped, rolling down my face. Raeya saw and strode over. "Riss, what's wrong?" She looked around, taking in Ivan's somber expression. Then it all clicked. She wrapping her arms around me. I hugged her back, pressing my face into her shoulder to hide my tears.

Everything happened in a blur. We moved into the living room on the first floor of the estate, a room we rarely used. Raeya stayed close to me, holding my hand and telling me it was going to be ok. My grandpa sat on the other side, explaining what he knew about Wade's death to Ray.

Hayden reported the mission to Ivan and Brock, who said they would make the official announcement, giving us time to get cleaned up and rest. Everyone was ok with that plan, even my grandpa. I knew he was bursting with questions but kept them in for my sake.

To keep the peace, Raeya offered to show him around, leaving Hayden, Jason, and me time to deal with everything now that we were back. Sometimes Ray knew me better than I knew myself. There was no way I could deal with it all at once, no matter how much I tried to convince myself I could.

* * *

I woke with a start, shooting up and throwing the blankets back only to see that I was covered in blood. A small cry of horror escaped my lips. I blinked, eyes not focusing in the dim dawn light that came in through the curtained window of our room.

Heart racing and unable to breathe, I scrambled out of bed, my feet getting caught in the sheet. I tripped, falling with a loud thud to the floor. I blinked, pulling myself out of the nightmare. I untangled my feet and sat on the floor, panting. I wasn't covered in blood. It was all in my head.

I rubbed my eyes and stood, going to the closet to grab clothes and my bag of shower supplies. I wasn't sure where Hayden was or when he got up. He had taken a few days off when we got back, giving himself time to grieve and time to deal with my constant nightmares.

I'd showered last night and had braided my wet hair. I went to the bathroom to brush my teeth and wash my face then went back to my room and dressed in jean shorts, boots, and a white t-shirt. I unbraided my hair, running my fingers through the wavy locks. I didn't feel like putting forth the effort to braid it again so I left it hanging down my back.

I slowly walked back to my room, looking in the other rooms to see where my friends were. Jason's door was closed. He had yet to get a new roommate. I paused by the door, listening. When I heard nothing, I assumed he was asleep and moved on. Ivan and Brock weren't in their room; they were probably in training like I should be, but no one pushed the issue.

The new A1s had moved upstairs and were at training as well. I dropped my stuff off in our room and put my shoes on to go downstairs and look for my friends. I ran into Hannah on my way down.

"Morning, Riss," she said.

"Hey, Hannah." I looked at the room she had just walked out of. "What are you doing?"

"I stayed with Gabby," she said, crossing the hall into the bathroom. "Getting her through her grief." She winked at me.

"Gabby's into girls?"

Hannah sighed. "No, she's not. Or not yet," she added with a smile. "But she really needs someone right now."

I gave her a tight smile. "I'm glad she has you as a friend then."

"Thanks. How are you?"

"Fine," I said quickly. Too quickly. Hannah pressed her lips together and smiled, able to see past my lie. She didn't pester me though and I was grateful. I hurried downstairs.

Hayden was in a meeting with Hector and the overseers. I didn't feel like being around anyone but my friends so I kept walking down the hall, planning on swinging by the cafeteria, grabbing food, and going back to my room.

Lauren stood at the end of the line in the cafeteria. I rolled my eyes. Of course I'd get stuck behind her. She annoyed me as much now as she had when we first met in college.

"Orissa," she said, pursing her lips.

"You know my name, good for you," I said and crossed my arms.

"What's this I hear about you wearing a diamond ring?"

I blinked. Oh, right. "Maybe I am wearing a diamond ring." My left hand was hidden under my arm. The line moved and we stepped up. Lauren grabbed a tray.

"There are rumors about you, you know."

"That's nothing new, *you* know."

She flipped her hair and laughed. "People think you and Hayden are an item. Some even say you two are engaged. Can you believe it?"

Her petty comments used to get under my skin. But with everything else going on and the hell we had gone through...it just didn't matter. I suddenly felt free in a way I never knew I could. I had always said that I didn't care what people thought about me, but deep down on some level, I did. Now I saw it didn't matter. What Lauren said or thought about me wasn't going to make my situation any worse or any better.

"We are engaged," I said and reached for a tray. The bright lights sparkled off the large center stone on the ring. "We have been for a while but didn't want to make a big deal about it."

"Why would he propose to you?" she scoffed.

I just shrugged and picked up a fork.

"I mean you're so...so..." she scrambled for an insult, trying to get a reaction out of me. "So not his type."

I looked at Lauren, curious instead of angry. "You have no idea what life is about, do you?"

"I know I would never be caught dead in those hideous cut offs and dirty boots."

"Don't talk to me about being dead," I snapped, not hungry anymore. I turned around and instantly regretted it.

"Well hey there, lady," Bentley's smooth voice came from down the hall. "Long time no see." He walked over, cowboy boots clicking on the tile. "Funny, isn't it? This place isn't all that big and I haven't seen you for days."

"Hilarious," I said, my voice monotone.

He ran his eyes over me. "You could have been in one of my videos, ya know."

I bet he expected me to swoon over that line.

When I didn't say anything he leaned toward me, purposely making his hair fall into his face. "You're kinda famous in this joint."

"Yes. And for a good reason."

He laughed. "Sure you are. Listen, if the fame gets to be too much for you to handle, you know where to find me."

I didn't know where his room was and I had no intention of finding out. My mind whirled with snarky remarks but I stopped short, turning my head. "I have someone for you to meet." I smiled sweetly. "Hey, Lauren!"

She whipped around, scowling at the sound of my voice. "You two will get along just fine," I said and walked away. I didn't pay attention to where I was going. I needed to get away from Bentley, who was so wrapped up in himself he couldn't see the world for what it really was.

I jogged down the stairs and headed for the hospital ward. I pushed the doors open, hoping to see Olivia at the desk. I sighed when I saw another B3 but went in. Now I wanted to find Padraic.

But what I saw instead shocked me even more. My grandpa and Dr. Cara sat in the lab, deep in conversation.

"They both think the government is spying on them," Padraic said from behind me.

I turned around to see his smiling face. "I've been listening to this for days."

I returned his smile. "I'm not jealous of you. I can only imagine the crazy fest that's going on between those two."

He nodded. "Cara swears the CIA hacked her computer during her undergrad research and planted bugs in her dorm room."

"They're going to get along just fine then," I laughed. "You working today?" I asked Padraic.

He looked at the clock. "Just passed off a report to Karen so I can go to the meeting."

"Meeting?"

Padraic narrowed his eyes. "Yes. The big meeting we're having about our fate in the winter."

I rubbed my forehead. "Oh."

"Are you all right, Riss?"

"Yeah, fine." I blinked then forced a smile. "Just tired."

"Funny," he said, taking off his lab coat. He was wearing blue scrub pants and a gray t-shirt. Padraic was tall and lean, but firm. His wavy dark hair was in need of cutting and he hadn't shaved for several days. "Because you've spent a lot of time sleeping since you came back."

I pulled my lips over my teeth and turned away. It was true. If I wasn't spending time with Hayden, my grandpa, or Raeya, I was in my room, dealing with the guilt...or not dealing, I suppose.

"Have you had breakfast yet?"

I shook my head. "I'm not hungry," I said at the same time my stomach growled. Padraic gave me a worried frown.

"We have some time before the meeting. I'll get you something to eat and we're gonna talk, ok?"

* * *

Padraic's room was bigger than Raeya's, but still resembled a crammed dorm room. Everything was neat and organized. When I went in, Argos wagged his tail. I looked at Padraic's clothes that were folded on a shelf across from the bed. A laundry basket sat next to it, filled to the top with dirty clothes. I almost didn't notice it.

I leaned forward, smiling when I saw the purple lace nightgown. I knew Padraic had been spending some time with a woman named Maya—who I thought was fucking nuts. She believed zombies were possessed by demons. But no matter, it made me happy to know Padraic wasn't lonely at night.

I sat on the edge of the bed, petting Argos until Padraic came back and handed me a plate of scrambled eggs, one tomato slice, and a cup of powdered milk. I choked it down.

"I'm really sorry, Riss," Padraic began. "I hate that you go out there. You don't have to, you know."

"I do," I said, taking a drink of milk. "I can't really explain it...but I do. I have to try to make things better."

"I get it," Padraic said. "I think, at least. After all that's happened you should give yourself a break."

I nodded and finished my food, setting the plate on the floor for Argos to lick clean. I put my head in my hands. "I wish the nightmares would stop," I blurted.

"What are they about?"

I closed my eyes. Everything was so clear, like I was there. "It's a replay of everything that happened. Over and over again. But the end is different...worse than what really happened."

"Want to tell me about it?" He gave me a lopsided smile. "I spent some time studying sleep and dreams. I find it very fascinating."

I looked up at Padraic. I did want to tell him. I wanted his professional opinion to tell me that I wasn't losing it and that I'd get over it in time. And I wanted to open up to a friend, one who could make me feel better.

"I was with Wade when it happened," I started. I closed my eyes again. The bodies hanging in the tree swung before me. "We were running from a herd. He stepped in a steel jaw trap. I...I couldn't get it off before—" I sharply inhaled.

Padraic put his hand on mine. I fiddled with Argo's chipped name tags.

"In the dream, I grab a zombie, one that's eating...eating him. I pull it back and stick a knife in its head. Then I realize it's Rider. I watched my friend die and killed another...again."

"Why do you say again?"

Padraic didn't know. I looked down at Argos, tears stinging my eyes. "Because I really did."

Padraic's eyebrows pushed together. "No you didn't. Those guys did."

I couldn't help the tears that went down my cheeks. "No. That's just what we told everyone. When we were leaving I...I found him."

Padraic leaned away. "Riss, what happened? What aren't you telling me?"

I ran my hands over Argos's fur. "He had been bitten."

"Rider was a zombie."

Padraic hugged me, pulling me into his chest. I let him wrap me in a tight embrace. "I am so, so sorry, Orissa."

"Will the nightmares go away?" I didn't want to be plagued by them for the rest of my life. I saw how hard it was for Hayden.

"I can't promise you anything," he said. "But you're the toughest person I've ever met. I know you can get through this." He loosened his hug. "You've got plenty of people here that love you."

I smiled at that. "Thanks for being one of them."

He put his hand on my cheek and pulled me to him, kissing my forehead. "I'm always here for you, Riss. I'll help any way I can."

"I know you will."

I wiped my eyes with the back of my hand, hitting myself with the engagement ring. "Ow," I said and we both laughed. I stood, stretching my hands above my head. "Maybe we should start looking for a therapist," I joked.

Padraic raised an eyebrow. "That's a good idea." He stood. "We should go, but only if you're ready."

"I am," I said, rubbing at my eyes again. I didn't want anyone to know I'd had a moment of emotion. "Thanks again."

* * *

"Bottom line," Hayden said, an hour into our meeting. "We do not have enough food to make it through the winter."

Raeya squeezed my hand. We were sitting on the floor in Hayden's office, leaning against the wall as he spoke. Ivan, Brock, Jason, Padraic, Hector, and my grandpa were crammed in as well. All the bodies made the small room get hot fast despite the constant blast of cold air from the air conditioner.

"Our gardens are doing well," he went on. "But we won't have enough by the time the first frost comes."

It was scary, hashing out the details like this. We had spent the last half hour trying to come up with ways to up our supply. Nothing could be guaranteed. Really, it came down to having so many people here. If we had started the garden earlier and planted more, we might have a better chance. But then we ran into the issue of medical supplies.

"I'm telling you," my grandpa said for the fifth time. "We storm into New York, kill those bastards, and take everything they got. And start an uprising in the process, if we're lucky."

As crazy as his plan was, it was becoming the only one that seemed feasible for getting this many people through the winter. Whoever was in New York was prepared to keep a large number of people alive. They had the resources to do so. Resources we needed.

Hayden pushed that idea aside, saying it was too dangerous and not worth the risk.

"Isn't the risk what makes it worth it?" my grandpa countered. "The riskier something is, the more it's worth taking."

"Now I see where Riss gets her daredevil side," Padraic whispered to Raeya. She smiled and shook her head.

"We get there and then what?" Ivan asked.

"You tell those motherfuckers the truth," my grandpa went on.

"And her potty mouth," Ray added.

I glared at her.

My grandpa said, "Tell 'em the truth and see how obedient they are."

"You want to cause a riot?" Brock asked.

"Hell yeah, I do."

Hayden put his head in his hands. "I don't know."

"I am curious to see what it's like," Ivan added. "We could just check it out. No harm no foul."

"That term doesn't apply to this world anymore," I said dryly. "But I'm kinda with you. Maybe we should..." I shook my head. "No. We can't."

"I'm telling you," my grandpa said. "It's the only way. With this many people you should have been prepared." He leaned forward. "This is what you were supposed to do."

"What do you mean?" I asked when silence took over the room.

"Why else do you think Colonel Fuller didn't start preparations? He knew about this, all of this, from the beginning. He wanted you to go to New York and end this."

His words hung in the air, the quiet buzzing in my ears. Raeya shivered. Why hadn't Fuller better prepared us? He knew how many people were capable of living here. He knew we would face hardships in the winter...and yet he kept the secret to himself.

"He wouldn't do that," Hayden finally spoke.

"He wouldn't?" my grandpa questioned. "He knew everything and didn't tell you until after he died. Think about it."

"It makes sense," Hector said, surprising us all. "Fuller never had long term plans. He said we had to live each day in the moment, see what it brings. His views made sense then but now...I don't know."

"He didn't leave us very prepared," Brock said. "If he wanted us to go into the government's safe house you'd think he would have left us instructions."

"Maybe he did," my grandpa said, excitement rising. "Where's that letter? It might be coded."

Hayden's eyes flicked to mine. We both knew the letter wasn't coded. I moved my head up and down in a small nod. Hayden unlocked the desk and got out the letter, giving it to my grandpa, who stood.

"I'll get to work on this, right away." Then he left, presumably going to his room. He had moved into Fuller's old room, which turned out to be the largest bedroom in the whole compound. It worked out well in my grandpa's favor.

"I think this is enough for today," Hayden said, putting his arms on the desk. Raeya and I stood.

"I got lists to make," she told me and left. Hector went to check on Gabby and Padraic needed sleep since he had been on duty all night. Ivan, Brock, Jason, Hayden, and I stayed, not quite done with the meeting just yet.

* * *

"We can't just charge into New York City. We have no idea what it's like or how secure their perimeters are. We could get shot on sight." Hayden put his hand on his back, pressing between his shoulders, and rolled his neck.

I pulled on my braid and looked at the map of New York City. I had always wanted to go and see it. But not anymore. Not like this.

"Can't we scope it out from a distance?" Jason asked.

"Ideally, yes," Brock answered. "But who knows what it's like? Measures have been taken to ensure the safety of everyone there."

Jason nodded. "I'm imagining a giant wall, like the Wall of Berlin."

Brock tipped his head. "Could be for all we know."

Hayden picked up his coffee cup, realized it was empty and set it back on the desk with a sigh. "We need to question somebody from the inside, see how they operate like what we did with Jon and Eastmoore...though it didn't work out exactly as planned. And we aren't going to get lucky enough to find an abandoned greenhouse to stash our vehicles and supplies in." He shook his head. "For all we know, there is one way in and out of the city. We'd never get through unseen."

Ivan crossed his arms. "I'm not seeing a way to win this one, guys."

Something clicked into place in my head. "Wait." I held up my hand and looked at Hayden. "What did you just say?"

"There might only be one way into the city."

I shook my head. "No, before that."

"Uh...we won't be able to get inside information or hide out in—"

"Greenhouses," I interrupted, mouth opening in a broad smile.

Hayden's eyes narrowed in question. "Riss, what are you—oh. Oh! You're right. And brilliant!"

"Did I miss something?" Jason asked, leaning forward in his chair.

I spun around to face the guys. "We found those greenhouses, real working greenhouses, remember? Someone was running them, obviously. Who else would have the resources to do that?"

Ivan's lips pulled up in a devious smile. "You are a smart one, Penwell."

Jason bit his lip, still not completely understanding. "Someone from the government has been going there, daily, weekly...I don't know. But they're there, taking care of the crops and taking them

THE TRUTH IS CONTAGIOUS

back to the city," I explained.

Jason's jaw fell open when it clicked. Brock said, "It makes perfect sense, and now I know why Fuller never sent us back."

"We go," Hayden said. "Camp out for a few days until the groundskeeper comes and question him, feel things out before we make the next move." His eyes went to mine, almost sparkling with excitement. "We're doing this."

His words sent a chill through me. It was what I wanted, what we needed. But it terrified me.

It was the most dangerous mission we would ever attempt.

CHAPTERTWENTY

A month had passed since we had made our decision to go to New York. We had spent the time getting the compound ready for winter as well as an extended time without some of its best protectors. We made sure Hannah had her medicine, too. Three cabins were complete without electricity. Their construction had been put on hold—again. Getting enough food, medicine, and supplies became our priority.

Having my grandpa, however crazy, had proved to be more helpful than anyone could have imagined. Anyone but me and Raeya, since we knew him and his crazy ways. He worked closely with Hector, making the tough decisions when Hector was unable.

We kept the truth about the virus from the others. Hayden thought it would be best to not get anyone's hopes up...or make anyone so mad they would do something crazy. We could very easily trek halfway across the country for nothing and come back empty handed.

Our plan was being executed tomorrow. Since we were driving to the greenhouses, we might as well make the most of it. Brian and Bryan—the two new A1s in my group, were driving with Brock, following us to the greenhouses. As long as we were able, we planned to take as much fresh produce as possible, load it up in a truck and then turn around and have them drive it back home.

Ivan, Jason, Hayden, and I were going to continue on to New York. It was a battle to get my grandpa to agree to stay behind. He wanted to go, to fight, to tell the president he was onto him the whole time. Finally he agreed to stay after we told him that we needed him to take over Hayden's role as leader of the compound. In all actuality, my grandpa and Hector balanced each other well. Plus, Raeya and Padraic were on board for making any big decisions.

Everything we needed was loaded into our cars, ready and waiting for us to leave the compound for what could be the final time. It was getting late but none of us could sleep. The guys crammed into Ivan and Brock's room to play video games, trying their best to act as if tomorrow would be an easy mission.

I had already said my goodbyes to Raeya, my grandpa, and Olivia. Sonja had spent the night crying, not wanting her brother to leave. In all honesty, I didn't want him to go either. I had grown to care about him as if he was my own brother. He should stay here, where it was safe.

I stood, weaving through the guys, saying I had to go to the bathroom. Hayden looked at me as I left Ivan and Brock's room. He narrowed his eyes ever so slightly in an unspoken question. I nodded and gave him a small smile, letting him know I was ok. I love how he can read me like that: one quick look and he knew exactly how I was feeling.

I twisted my engagement ring around my finger and walked into my room. My heart was beating faster and faster the more I thought about going to New York. I had a bad feeling about it...a feeling worse than my normal bad feelings about missions. I tried to convince myself it was because I had spent several hours alone with my grandpa last night, listening to him spit out theories in a paranoid haze. He was convinced whoever was in New York was alive and well, completely prepared to ride out this shitstorm.

I stopped in the middle of the room and put my hands over my head, letting out my breath before I bent over and touched the floor. My grandpa's words replayed in my mind.

He'll be there...that conniving joke of a president. Samael will be there. And when you see him...stick an arrow through his eye.

I knew it wouldn't be that easy. Certainly the president would have some sort of protection around him. Let's just say we were able to get inside this safe house. It's not like I could bring my bow and arrows. A pistol...maybe. I needed something smaller, something lethal that could be concealed.

I walked my hands up on the floor, stretching out my back. I closed my eyes and concentrated on breathing. I didn't want to go in without a backup plan, without some sort of weapon I could keep on me at all times. The thought made my stomach turn to the point of feeling sick.

I opened my eyes. "Holy shit," I whispered and popped up. I left my room, padding down the hall and down the stairs, not stopping until I was in the hospital ward.

"Is Dr. Cara working tonight?" I asked the B3 at the desk.

"Yes, she's in the lab is everything alright?"

I just nodded and breezed past, needing to get to Dr. Cara. I pushed open the lab door without knocking. Dr. Cara was sitting at a microscope when I came in. She jumped, knocking into the table.

"Do you still have the isolated virus?" I asked, getting right to the point.

"Of course," she said, blinking. Then she turned back to the microscope.

"Can I have it?"

That got her attention. She flicked the light off to the microscope and turned around. "Why?"

"I want to use it as a weapon."

Her eyes might have lit up just a bit. She gave me a rare smile and got up. I followed her to the back of the lab. She put on gloves and opened a mini fridge and pulled out a baby food jar filled with a nectar-thick, translucent green liquid.

"Does it have to be refrigerated?" I asked.

"Not at all." She set the jar on a plastic plate. "The cold slows the virus down. It does best at body temperature. That's why when a body reaches the S3 stage—"

"Give me details later. Do you have any smaller jars?"

"Of course I do. Hang on." She turned, opening a cabinet above us. "Will this do?"

I nodded, looking at the little vials. "It'll be perfect."

"How many do you want? Just a few drops of this stuff is enough to infect someone with the Contagium Virus."

I had forgotten Padraic had haphazardly come up with that name. "Then just one will do."

CHAPTERTWENTY-ONE

"I've never been inside one of these," Jason said, his voice echoing throughout the large pole barn. He took a deep breath. "It smells so...so...fake."

I nodded. "Exactly my thoughts. You can taste the chemicals in the air." I propped the door of the green house open behind us. We drove straight through, not stopping until we arrived at the greenhouse. Hayden, Jason, Brock and I were going to New York. Ivan, and the two new A1s, Bryan and Brian, were taking the food back to the compound.

"But the strawberries taste good," I said.

Everything looked the same as it did the last time we were here, which was unnerving. Months had passed...the plants should be in a different phase in their growth cycle now. I reached out, touched a bright red strawberry, so large it bent the plant down.

Jason and I walked through the greenhouse, finding wheelbarrows at the end. I tipped one up and shook it, sending dried leaves and shriveled strawberries to the ground. I wiped my forehead, sweaty already from the humidity in this building. We went right to work, picking strawberries and tossing them in the wheelbarrow, eating a few along the way.

When that wheelbarrow was full, I took it outside where Ivan and Bryan stood, keeping watch. They dumped the strawberries into boxes and loaded them into the truck. I went back in, getting another load before moving on to the next greenhouse. We worked feverishly, afraid someone would come back and catch us in the act. It would mess up our current plans, through not enough to keep us from following through with going to New York.

Several hours later, we were done. My back hurt from bending over and the tips of my fingers were stained from twisting fruit and vegetables off their steams. Everything was loaded in the armored car, ready to go. Hayden filled a bag with fresh produce for us to take with us on the rest of our mission.

Ivan hugged me goodbye, making me promise to come back in one piece. I made him promise to look after Raeya and my grandpa in case I didn't. He got in the car with Brian and Bryan, turned around, and headed for home.

Brock, Jason, Hayden, and I feasted on fruit, sitting in the bed of the truck.

"I don't think anyone's coming," Hayden said, looking at the sinking sun. "Not this late." He should his head. "Though it really wouldn't matter, right?"

"Not really," I answered.

"They have to drive in the dark at some point," Brock said. "Unless they stopped along the way. But I could see waiting to harvest until daylight."

"How many people do you think will be here?" Jason asked, tossing a pear core on the ground.

"Hopefully no more than four," Hayden said wryly. "And they won't be as armed as we are."

"Hah, yeah," I agreed. I peeled a banana and took a bite. "They have to know, right?" I looked at the greenhouses. "They have to know that not everyone is dead. Think about it." I bent my legs up under me, shifting uncomfortably in the truck bed. "They drive here all the way from New York. I know it's not super far, but it's a long enough drive to have seen something."

Hayden said, "I'm assuming whoever takes care of this is in on the whole thing."

Brock nodded. "They'd have to know. Why else would everything be set up?"

"What if they're not from New York?" Jason asked, eyes widening. "What if it's just a bunch of random people, kinda like us?"

I took a deep breath. "I suppose it's possible."

We continued to come up with theories, some of them so out there my grandpa could have thought them up. When the sun was almost done, we moved into the strawberry greenhouse for the night.

There were walkways above us, going between each row of rotating produce. We walked up the metal stairs, went down a walkways and into a small room that overlooked the entire greenhouse.

Hayden stopped short, blocking the entrance to the room. My heart skipped a beat, thinking that maybe the groundskeeper had been up here all along, watching us through the large window.

"There's a computer," he whispered. "And it's on."

"It's not going to jump up and bite you," I said and put my hand on Hayden's side, gently nudging him forward. His skin was hot and the fabric of his shirt was damp with sweat. "Don't tell me you think it's a droid," I said when he didn't move.

He shook his head. "No, I don't. There could be a camera."

"There's only one way to find out," I said. Hayden nodded and went in, waving his hand in front of the screen. "I don't see a webcam built in," I said quietly, feeling paranoid as well.

Hayden turned, waving to Brock, who knelt down in front of the desk. He inspected the wires, knowing exactly what he was looking for. He sat in the faded rolling chair and wiggled the mouse. The black screen gave way to a green box. The curser flashed.

Brock bit his lip. Then he entered a password. His shoulders tensed as he tried again, typing so fast I couldn't keep up.

"Are you hacking in?" Jason asked, voice full of awe.

"Kinda," Brock said. "I used to do this when I was on active duty." He shook his head. "Though I never tried to hack our own government. And I had internet connections."

"There isn't a connection?" I asked, though I knew the answer. There couldn't be. The satellite signals to Padraic's built in GPS stopped working within weeks of the virus hitting. It never made sense to me. It shouldn't have gone out that fast. Eventually...yes. But not in mere weeks.

"There is," he said, shocking us all. "But I can't tell you what it is. I've never seen it before." Brock continued to type away. He hit enter then leaned back, a smile on his face. ACCEPTED flashed across the screen.

"No fucking way," I said, moving closer.

Brock shrugged. "I just bypassed the login password. I won't be able to get on anything else."

Hayden narrowed his eyes, thinking. "It has to be some sort of satellite transmitter, right?"

Brock let out a breath and shook his head. "That's my best guess. One that's heavily encrypted." He clicked something and files popped up. "I'm not attempting to get on. I don't want to alert anyone that we're here."

"Good thinking," Hayden said.

My head swam. Encrypted signals...hidden computer files...it was like we were living my grandpa's nightmare.

"This is just a log of upkeep and harvests," Brock said as he scrolled through the files. "Nothing useful." He was about to close the files when he said, "Hang on."

"What?" Hayden, Jason, and I all said at the same time.

"This is interesting," Brock said and tapped the screen. "This pulled up all the files. Look at the numbers from two years ago. They stay consistent...until July of last year. Production tripled, dropped to almost nothing in October and increased in November, going back to normal in February."

"They were preparing," Hayden said and another chill ran through me. "Our own government had planned this months in advance." He shook his head. "Wow."

"It looks like the watering and rotating system is run electronically through this program," Brock said as he scanned through the files. "And someone comes to harvest once a week. Every Wednesday."

I had no clue what the date was let alone what day of the week today was. By the sudden increase in tension I could only guess.

"Tomorrow," I said. "They're coming tomorrow."

"Yeah," Hayden said. "At least we know."

Brock closed the files and put the computer in standby, like it was before. We set up a camp for the night, unrolling sleeping bags and getting our weapons ready just in case.

Hayden and I took first watch and spent the hours walking up and down the greenhouses. I was tired by the time we switched. Hayden draped his arm over me, raising my body temperature even more. I closed my eyes, feeling the stress of *needing* to get some shuteye. After an hour passed and I still wasn't asleep, I wiggled out of Hayden's embrace and stood.

"Fuck it," I said and kicked off my boots and jeans. Stress was building as each minute passed where I wasn't asleep. I pulled my t-shirt over my head and neatly laid it out, ready to throw it on if need be. Really, I just needed my boots. If it came down to it, I'd fight zombies in my underwear.

Much more comfortable, I moved close to Hayden again. Even in his sleep he responded to me, running his hand down my naked thigh. His touch was comforting and helped me relax. I closed my eyes and focused on taking steady, calming breaths until I fell asleep.

I had rolled over onto my stomach in my sleep. Hayden's hand slid and was resting on my butt.

"Rise and shine," Jason said, opening the door to the small room. I stretched my arms and pushed up. Jason stared at me, mouth hanging open. "Sorry!" he said and whirled around, closing the door. I couldn't help but laugh. I never understood why I was considered indecent in a tank top and underwear but perfectly ok in a bikini.

Hayden snaked his arm around me and pulled me close. "Don't get up yet," he whispered, his breath hot in my ear. "Who knows the next time we'll get to do this."

"That's what you said yesterday," I whispered back, smiling as I thought of our last night together at the compound. I pressed my face into his chest, running my hand up his shoulder. Carefully, I traced over the scar tissue from the bullet wound on his left shoulder. That horrible day seemed so long ago. So much had happened since.

Begrudgingly, we broke apart, got dressed, and rolled up the sleeping bags. Brock and Jason were outside, using the greenhouses as shade while they ate breakfast. Hayden and I put our stuff in the truck, grabbed several pieces of fruit, and joined them.

"It should be you and Jason," Hayden said, looking at me. He sat on the ground, peeling an orange. "You two are the least intimidating-looking, no offense."

I glared at him but knew it was true. I was female, and as much as I hated it, I knew how a lot of men—and even some women—thought of females in situations like this. Jason was young, only eighteen years old, and had one of those faces that exuded innocence.

Hayden was tall, muscular, and tattooed. There was a stigma against him as well. Brock wasn't as tall, but he was just as well built from all our time working out. His face carried sadness, something he got during the war. He would have a hard time playing victim.

"Fine," I said and looked at Jason. "You're my brother and we've been wandering for weeks. Just act hungry and scared."

"You sure you don't want to be my hot cougar girlfriend?" he asked with a wink.

"Shut up," I said. "I'm not that old."

"At least he said you're hot," Hayden teased.

"So," I said and looked around. "Where are we gonna hide the cars? There's nothing close."

"I already thought of that," Brock said and pulled a map from his pocket. It was hand drawn but incredibly neat. "Here," he said and pointed to a cluster of trees. "Logically, whoever comes here will drive down this way and not come anywhere close to us."

I nodded. It was quite a hike but it wouldn't kill us. "And you guys will be?"

"Roughing it in the weeds behind the greenhouses."

I wrinkled my nose. "You could be there for hours."

Hayden shrugged. "I've been in worse for days."

I nodded, momentarily forgetting that he had been through hell before this.

"I'll tap three times on the walkie," he said. "No talking in case they have radios on the same wave."

Once the details were worked out, we went into out positions. Jason had fun smearing dirt over our packs and then our faces, making it look like we were as ragged as we were going to claim to be.

I sat on the tailgate of the truck, swinging my legs. Anxiety wrapped around my heart. I didn't like not knowing what was going to happen. And I really didn't like Hayden being so far away.

"Should we talk with accents?" Jason asked.

"Huh?"

"You know, as a disguise."

"I don't think they'll recognize us at all." I shook my head. "Let me hear your accent."

Jason looked up, thinking about which accent to do. "What about this?" he asked in an Irish accent. "I can say my name is Padraic."

I laughed. "No, that's horrible!"

"Top of the morning to ya, lady!"

"Stop!" I said, doubling over from laughter. "You sound like an evil leprechaun!" Amidst the laughter, we almost didn't hear Hayden's signal. The smile left my face right away. I took in a deep breath and held a hand out to Jason. "Ready?"

He nodded, taking my hand. We emerged from the trees, hurrying to the road. A cloud of dust hung in the air. My heart beat faster. They—whoever the hell *they* were—were there.

"Shit," Jason muttered under his breath.

I followed his eyes. Two zombies staggered through the field. My arm twitched, wanting to reach up and grab an arrow. I hated not having my bow. I felt naked. But that was part of my barely-getting-by portrayal.

"This could work, actually," I said. "Just follow my lead."

We continued down the road, slowing enough to give the zombies a chance to catch up. They were only yards behind us when we came up to the greenhouses. I looked at the weeds, hoping Hayden could see me. If he heard the screams, heard me begging for help, would he come running? I couldn't be positive he'd know it was all an act.

I pressed the button on the walkie and tapped it three times, just like he had. I hoped that was enough. Jason squeezed my hand and turned to me. I nodded and let go. Adrenaline rushed through me, making my hands shake. I dropped my knife in the street and turned, waiting for the zombies to catch up.

Jason and I went for the faster of the two, knocking it down and off the street. He went to it, keeping it in the grass. I turned and waited.

This could end badly, very badly. One wrong move and zombie teeth could ascend on me, tearing open my flesh. I swallowed and let out a breath. He was close. I resisted the urge to close my eyes. Just feet away. He stretched out his arms. I turned my head. His hands landed on my shoulder. I kicked his legs out, keeping a hold on him, and lowered both of us to the ground.

I fell faster than I planned, thudding on the street painfully. But the zombie was right on cue, pressing his hands against my body, pinning me to the ground. I took a deep breath and screamed.

"Help me, please!" I turned my head and screamed again. I cast a look at Jason. He dodged back, barely missing his zombie's grasp. The one on top of me pushed harder. "Someone, help!" I screamed again, wondering if it was too obvious. We weren't supposed to know anyone was in the greenhouses.

I struggled to hold the zombie away. Brown goo dripped onto my neck. Repulsed, I flinched and my hand slipped off his shoulder. Shit. The zombie came at me, teeth barred. I wasn't pretending anymore. I needed to get away. Now.

I stuck my hand up, pushing my palm into his chin as hard as I could in an attempt to keep his mouth shut while I squirmed out from under him. He was strong. And heavy, so heavy, pinning my legs underneath him.

I opened my mouth to call to Jason, to tell him that I needed help when a gunshot rang through the air. Bits of rotten brain splattered my face. I pushed the zombie off me and sprang up. Then I remembered I needed to act weak and scared.

Scared wasn't hard. I was scared. I turned my head and saw a man rushing out of the greenhouse. Another stood at the edge of the street, holding up a gun. Jason shoved the zombie in front of him down and pushed his knife into his skull.

The man on the street lowered his arm and came over to me, extending his hand. I took it and let him pull me to my feet.

"Th-thank you," I stuttered. I wrapped my arms around myself.

Jason rushed over and hugged me. "That was a close one, sis," he said. I ducked my head down against his shoulder and squeezed my eyes shut, generating fake tears. I pulled away, wiping at my eyes with my wrist.

"Thank you," Jason said, turning to the man who shot the zombie. "Thank you for saving my sister."

The man just nodded, gray eyebrows flat and face void of emotion. "Where did you two come from?" he asked. The second man moved closer. He was younger, and looked scared.

"We've been wandering," Jason said.

"Wandering?" the older man questioned.

"We had a camp," I said before Jason could speak again. "It got overrun." I blinked, causing fat tears to roll down my cheeks. My lip quivered, and I took in a ragged breath. I held onto Jason's hand. "We ran...I-I think we're all that's left."

The older man nodded, then looked at his partner. "Good day." He turned to leave.

"Wait!" I called, not having to fake the desperation. "Do you have somewhere safe? Can we come with you? Please! We're so hungry!"

The younger man's face softened. "Cal, come on, we can give them some food."

"No!" Cal growled. "We have no camp. It's just us and we don't take on strangers. Be on your way."

"Please, mister!" I begged. "We know you have food in there." I swept my hand in the direction of the greenhouses. "You have enough to spare just a little."

"There's nothing in those buildings!" Cal growled. "Nothing!"

"I can hear the machines running," Jason said, sounding startled. "Are they working? Should we check?"

"No. You be on your way," Cal snapped. "And leave us be."

"That's not gonna work," I said, dropping my act just a bit. "We're hungry."

Cal narrowed his eyes. He was angry, but I could see the panic he hid. He hadn't expected to run into anyone. He wasn't prepared for this. "Stay here," he grumbled and went to his truck.

"How many were in your group?" the younger guy asked. He kept his distance, looking at us like we were covered in the virus and could pass it on with just a touch.

"About fifty," I answered.

His eyes bulged, giving away the only clue I needed to know that he had been fed a lie. He had no idea what was going on. Cal, on the other hand...he knew exactly what he was doing.

"Louis," Cal called. "Keep your mouth shut." Cal came back, holding a sandwich. He ripped it in half and offered the pieces to Jason and me. We had to eat if we wanted to keep up our act but there was something about it, something that seemed off...too off.

But before I had the chance to warn Jason, he took a bite, acting as if he really hadn't eaten in days.

"Thank you," he said with his mouth full. I picked off the crust and took a bite.

"Eat and be on your way," Cal said, grinning. He put his hand on Louis's arm and guided him away. They walked down the road, going into the greenhouse at the end, as far away from us as they could get.

"Spit it out," I said to Jason. "Don't eat any of it." I opened the sandwich, looking for zombie blood.

"It's actually good," Jason said. "I miss lunchmeat." He stared at his sandwich. "Is it just me or are those guys super shady?"

"The shadiest," I said and sat on the ground, pretending to eat. Jason sat next to me. "Cal's not going to talk, I can tell you that now. Fuck. Give me a minute and I'll think of something."

I slowly picked the sandwich apart, scattering the pieces in the tall weeds. I looked across the street near the shed where Hayden and Brock were hiding. Maybe they'd have a better idea of how to get info out of Cal and Louis. Everything I thought of involved violence.

Jason's body slumped forward, shoulders hunching and head drooping.

"Jason?" I asked. The rest of the sandwich fell from my hands. I reached out for him, wrapping my fingers around his forearm.

His skin was hot. "Jason!" I said and pressed my hand to his forehead. He was burning up, like he had a high fever. Nerves painfully tingled through my body, I scuttled up to my knees, shaking Jason. "No, no, no!" I shook him. His head flopped back. I pulled him to me to keep him from falling.

My heart was pounding. There was something wrong with Jason. Had they poisoned him? If they had, with what? I hadn't seen anything on the sandwich. Carefully, I laid him down. His breathing was shallow. I grabbed the walkie from the back belt loop on my pants, ready to tell Hayden I needed him. I wasn't fast enough.

Jason sprang up, eyes bloodshot and teeth pulled back in a snarl. He let out a harrowing growl and lunged at me.

CHAPTER TWENTY—TWO

I screamed, for real that time. Horror paralyzed me. Jason snarled, saliva dripping from his mouth. He came at me, teeth bared. I blinked, snapping back into action. I moved away, getting to my feet. Jason sprang up, gargling growls as he reached for me, fingers splayed as if he had claws.

I didn't think. I balled my hand into a fist and punched him in the throat. His hands flew to his neck, and he fell back, wheezing.

"Hayden!" I yelled. "Hayden!"

Jason dropped to his knees, still wheezing. His head flopped down, drool seeping from his open mouth. Then he looked up at me, bloodshot eyes narrowed. His lips pulled up in an evil smile and he laughed.

"Jason!" I called to him. "Jason, please, no!"

He collapsed onto the street, rolling onto his back. "Hot...hot," he mumbled and started pulling at his clothes. He kicked his legs in the air, as if he was seeing something that wasn't there. "Get away," he panted and pulled at the hem of his shirt.

"Riss!" Hayden said as he ran over. Brock was right behind him. Hayden stopped next to me, arm going around my shoulders.

"Fuck," Brock said, moving next to Jason. "What the hell happened?"

I spun around, staring at the last greenhouse. Could the guys even hear us? "They did it! They infected him!"

"Get him off the street," Brock said. It took all three of us to grab Jason's arms and legs and drag him out of sight. He writhed around on the ground, reaching for us and snarling.

"No," he mumbled, swatting at nothing. "No!" He rolled onto his stomach and pushed himself up, charging at Brock.

"What do I do?" Brock asked and caught Jason by the arm. He twisted Jason's arm back and pushed him away. Jason stumbled, laughing manically. He wildly looked around before turning his head up to the sun, staring at it unblinking. Then he started pulling at his shirt again.

"He's infected," Hayden said, voice flat. He pulled his gun from his hip, shaking his head. "There's nothing we can do."

Jason had his shirt around his head, unable to pull it free. He was blinded and stumbled, falling down in a patchy spot of weeds and gravel. He moaned in pain, hand flying to his injured knee.

"Get them off me!" Jason yelled, thrashing around and clawing at the shirt that was over his head. "Get off, you motherfuckers. Get off!"

"Wait!" I said and moved closer to Jason. "Crazies don't feel pain or fear." I put my hand on Jason's exposed chest. "His heart is racing." I turned up to Hayden. "He's been drugged!"

"Drugged?" Brock asked and knelt down, taking hold of Jason's legs so he wouldn't kick me.

"Yes." I grabbed one of Jason's arms, unable to keep a hold of it. He was unusually strong . "PCP or bathsalts or something."

Hayden holstered his gun and yanked the shirt off of Jason's head. Jason looked at Hayden and screamed, calling him a demon.

"Holy shit, you're right." He pushed down on Jason's arms. "What do we do?"

I shook my head, tears blurring my vision. "I don't know. The few times I've seen this it always ended with a trip to the ER." I put my fingers on Jason's neck. "His heart is so fast. He's going to have a heart attack!"

"No he won't," Hayden said. "We'll do something."

There was nothing we could do except wait this out. And those guys inside the greenhouse could come out at any second. I stood and took my belt off. Brock and Hayden struggled to flip Jason over.

"Please," Jason begged. "The fire is hot. Don't take me to Hell. Not to Hell!" Then his fear twisted into laughter and his body contracted as he rambled about spiders.

"Jason," I said, hoping to reach something inside. "It's Riss. We're going to get you help."

"Riss," he repeated and relaxed.

"Yes, Riss."

He laughed again and swung his arm, his nails scraping the skin off my chest. I pushed back, reeling. Then I jumped up, flying to Jason's side. Hayden and Brock flipped him over. I straddled him, using my weight to keep him down while I wrapped the belt around his arms.

We flipped him back over. Jason screamed and was talking nonsense. Brock used his teeth to yank a braided cord bracelet off his wrist.

"It's a survival bracelet," he told me. I grabbed it and immediately started to unwind the red and blue nylon cord, using it to bind Jason's hands and feet to his sides. I took my belt back, quickly looping it around my waist without bothering to feed it into the loops.

Jason started pounding his head against the ground and thrashed his legs around. Brock slid his hands under Jason's head to lessen the blow.

Hayden was wearing my quiver and had dropped the bow several feet away. I scrambled over to grab it and took the quiver from around Hayden's arm. He looked up at me, pleading with me not to go. But we had no choice. We couldn't leave Jason alone, and it took more than one person to control him in this drug induced mania. I snapped the quiver into place and sprinted down the road, rage fueling me.

The door to the last greenhouse was locked. I stood back and kicked it, breaking the frame. The door swung open and I stepped inside, looking for Cal and Louis. They were in the little room that each greenhouse had. Having heard the door break open, they looked up, stunned and scared. Had they expected Jason and me to kill each other while high?

I didn't give them a chance to explain. Nothing they could say would make things better. I grabbed an arrow and shot the window. It crashed down in a rain of broken glass, tiny shards flying everywhere. Cal and Louis ducked, covering their heads.

"What did you give him?" I demanded and moved inside, stringing another arrow. Cal had a gun. Would he try to shoot me? I let the arrow go, hitting a corner of glass that had remained in the window. I ran up the metal stairs and kicked the door to the little computer room. Both men had ducked under the desk. The gun rested on top.

Cal's muscles twitched. He was thinking about making a mad dash for the gun. It was out of his immediate reach, but he could get it. And if he did, I'd be dead. His eyes met mine. Gray eyes, full of hate and loathing. I was a fly in the ointment, annoying and in need of purging.

He jumped. And I shot. My arrow hit him in the shoulder, just below his neck. I was aiming for his arm and I missed.

He slumped to the ground, crying out in pain. His body trembled and blood poured out before he went still. I hadn't meant to kill him but I did. My blood turned cold and I stared at Cal's lifeless eyes, still harsh and full of hate.

"What did you give him?" I asked, turning back to Louis.

He held up his hands. "I don't know!"

"Bullshit!"

I couldn't look at Cal. I stepped to the side, blocking him from view. I leaned over the desk and grabbed the gun, tossing it down onto the greenhouse floor. I nocked another arrow and turned on Louis. "I will ask one more time," I threatened, able to hear Jason's screams from outside.

"I don't know!" Louis repeated.

I pulled the arrow back. The string groaned, wanting to be released.

"I don't know what it is. It's...it's what they told us to use if anyone found this place!"

My arm drooped. I shook myself and refocused. "Who?"

"Samael!"

My heart skipped a beat. "What?" I asked, my voice too shrill for my liking.

"W-we have to keep it a secret. But he said...he said there was no one left. He said they searched!"

"I won't shoot you," I said calmly. "As long as you tell me everything."

"And then what?" he asked with a sharp laugh. "Then what do I do? I can't go back...he won't let me, not after this. Not after I screwed up."

"You didn't screw up. You ran into a horde of zombies." I lowered the bow and released the pressure on the string. "Samael lied. There are plenty of us left. And *nobody* came looking."

Louis shook his head like he couldn't believe me. "No. He wouldn't do that. We're all that's left. They told me they spent weeks." Tears filled his eyes. "My wife...my wife and kids were out there, but he said there was no one left...that it wasn't worth looking."

"I'm sorry," I said honestly. "But there was a chance they were alive. Samael lied," I repeated. "He's nothing but a coward, hiding in safety while the rest of us are fighting to survive, barely getting by."

Louis shook his head, tears falling from his eyes. He reached into his pocket. I pulled the arrow back, raising my arm.

"Don't!" I shouted, thinking he was reaching for a gun. He held up a picture—faded and worn from being folded—of his family.

"They would have waited for me." He shook his head. "They would have waited!" he yelled. "But I never came." He sniffled. "They told me everyone was dead."

"No, not everyone. A lot of us made it. Even after Samael dosed us with the second round of the virus."

"What?" he asked incredulously.

"You don't know?"

He shook his head. "What are you talking about?"

I lowered the bow again. "How about this?" I asked, wincing over the sound of Jason's screams. "You answer one of my questions, and I'll answer one for you."

"Ok," he said and took a breath. He stared at the picture of his family.

"Where is everyone hiding?"

"The Regency Hotel. What is the second dose?"

"The zombie virus. We were hit with it again to try and kill everyone."

"What do you mean?" Louis begged.

"That's two questions," I said and shook my head. "How many people are at the hotel?"

"A thousand, maybe more." He put the picture of his family down. "The virus was meant to kill everybody?"

"Yes," I answered. "How is the hotel guarded?"

He shook his head. "You didn't answer my question."

"I told you yes. That's an answer. My turn. How is the hotel guarded?"

My words didn't sink in. Louis slowly shook his head as the truth revealed the lies he had been living. "I gave up everything for this. My home...my job...my-my *family*. They told me it was an accident...it wasn't supposed to happen."

"Again. Lies. When are you going to get that? It wasn't an accident. Not at all. Everyone was supposed to die. The accident was that we lived."

"My family." He looked up at me, eyes wide and brimmed with tears. "Do you think they could still be alive?"

"It's possible."

"My kids...they are young. Oh God...to think what Laura went through." He fell back, shaking his head. "The kids are all right, don't you think? They have to be all right."

I almost told him yes, there was a chance the kids were just fine. But I had just preached about lies. I wasn't going to spread any more. "In my experience, young kids don't do well in this world." I looked out the window at the door. "Do you even know what it's like out there?"

He was silent for a few seconds. Jason had ceased screaming. My heart sank and cold fear wrapped around me. Had something happened to him?

"How do I know you're not lying?" Louis asked me.

"You don't," I told him. "But why would I make this up? What good would it do for me?"

He shook his head. "I...I don't know. Are you telling the truth?"

"Yes. I am. If you come outside with me, I'll explain." I needed to get out, see what was going on with Jason.

"Ok," Louis agreed and wiped his runny nose. I had him go first, still not trusting him at all. "I'm sorry about your friend," Louis said as we walked across the suspended walkway.

"He's going to be ok," I told him. Jason had to be ok.

Louis nodded, doubting what I had said. He left the greenhouse and turned, gasping.

"What?" I asked and pushed past him. Shit. I broke into a run, pulling an arrow from the quiver on my back. I hadn't thought about it but it made perfect sense. The screaming and yelling...it had attracted zombies.

CHAPTER TWENTY—THREE

"Hayden!" I shouted and ran toward my friends. Hayden and Brock were fighting off zombies. Jason lay on the ground, hands and feet bound. I shot a zombie that fell just feet before it got to Jason. I scooped up the knife that I had purposely dropped before and tossed it to Louis. He reached for it, catching the blade and slicing open his hand. "Kill them!" I yelled and turned back around.

I fired off arrows, dropping zombies left and right. Hayden pushed through the herd, knifing zombies in the head.

"Get Jason out of here!" he called over the death moans. My heart raced. Zombies circled Hayden. Blood sprayed in the air as Hayden brought his knife up, making a perfect reddish brown arch. Then he disappeared from view.

"Hayden!" I screamed. I shoved a zombie down, stomping in his skull with my boot. "Hayden!" I stopped, fingers trembling so much it was hard to focus. I shot three zombies, each falling on top of the another. And then I saw Hayden, in the middle of the herd, fighting not only for his life but for ours as well.

I turned, stealing a glance at Brock, who was dragging Jason toward a greenhouse. I pulled the machete from my quiver and ran forward, slicing off heads as I went. They kept coming.

"Riss," Hayden said, stepping over a body. "We have to get out of here."

"Help Brock with Jason," I said and turned to shout to Louis. All I saw was his hand, on the ground and still grasping the knife. Zombies crowded around him, pulling him apart.

A vision of Wade lying on the forest floor flashed into my head. I blinked but it was still there. I shouted in frustration and pushed a zombie off of me before bringing the machete up and down into his brain.

Hayden kicked open the door to the nearest greenhouse. He and Brock carried Jason—who was still thrashing around—up the stairs and across a walkway. I shut the broken door, sliding a wheelbarrow in front of it to keep it in place. We went into the suspended room and closed the door.

Jason had been gagged, which explained his sudden silence. His hands were torn and bloody and his right eye was stained red. I slumped against the door, panting.

"They'll pass," Brock said, catching his own breath as well. "When they do, I'll get the truck. We have to take Jason home."

Hayden pressed his hand to Jason's forehead. "He's burning up. We have to get him back soon."

"Fuck the mission," I said and knelt by Jason. "I'm not losing another friend."

"We won't," Brock said.

"Those guys..." Hayden started.

"Dead." I blinked and looked at the door to the greenhouse, suddenly thankful for the strong chemical smell. It masked our scent from the zombies. "But I got some info." I swallowed hard and told Hayden and Brock what I knew.

"We can't stop now," Brock said. "Not after all this. And someone will come looking for those men. This is our chance."

"But Jason..." I started.

Hayden said, "Brock's right. We can't stop. Jason has to go home, he needs medical treatment. I have no idea what the detox is gonna be if he...when he gets to that point."

Jason was drenched in sweat. He struggled against his restraints and chewed on the gag. "What are you going to do? Keep him tied up the whole way?"

"As long as he needs to be," Brock said. "How long does it last?"

I shook my head. "I have no idea. I don't even know what he had." I leaned against the wall. "Do you think he'll make it? I mean, isn't he going to get dehydrated from being so hot and sweating?"

When neither Brock nor Hayden answered, I knew it to be true. I stared though the window, watching shadows flicker by the door as the zombies passed. Hayden held onto Jason, keeping him from kicking the walls and making noise. He was exhausted by the time he let Jason go.

"I'm going to be bruised tomorrow," he mumbled, rubbing his arms.

"Hah, tell me about it," Brock said and took his hands off Jason's legs. "I'll get the Jeep."

"Make sure the herd is gone," Hayden said. "Completely. It's not worth it."

Brock nodded and took the walkie-talkie from Hayden. "I will."

He silently slipped through the door and down the walkway, taking the stairs two at a time. He held up his gun and peered through the window of the broken door. Then he left.

"There's a hose down there," Hayden said, eyeing the ground level. "We should try and cool Jason down."

I nodded, feeling a stab of pain. Wade had gotten overheated not that long ago. It was terrifying. And now he was gone, his body torn apart in the bellies of zombies. Parts of him were all over, constantly on the move. I shuddered.

"Yes, we should." I flicked my eyes to Hayden. "And you should wash your face. It's covered in zombie blood."

"Yours is too."

"When isn't it?" I mused.

We waited until Brock pulled up with the Jeep to move. The three of us struggled with Jason but were able to take off his jeans, leaving him in just boxers, and spray cool water over his body. Hayden removed the gag and offered Jason water. To our surprise, he drank it. I kept expecting him to act like a crazy and had to remind myself he wasn't infected...just drugged.

Brock, Hayden, and I took turns washing blood and grim from our bodies. I rinsed off my clothes, planning to change as soon as we got to the truck. Day one and I was already in my spare outfit. Great. I hadn't packed enough, though having clean clothes wasn't a priority.

We situated Jason into the passenger seat, keeping his hands and feet bound, and buckled him in. Brock gagged him again, feeling guilty, but we all knew the screaming and loud jabbering would attract more zombies. Hayden and I got in the back. Brock drove us to the truck. I got out, going around to the front of the Jeep.

I put my hand on Jason's cheek before they took off. His skin was still hot, though having removed most of his clothes and spraying him with cold water had helped lower his temp for now.

"You're gonna be all right," I told him, looking in Jason's dark eyes. They were rimmed with red as if a vessel had burst. "And when you are, you tell Olivia that you've been crushing on her, ok? She'll be happy to hear it."

I took in a breath and stepped back, closing the door. I walked around the Jeep to where Hayden and Brock were talking. I wrapped my arms around Brock, giving him a goodbye hug.

"I'll see you two again," he said with a forced smile. He gave Hayden a one armed handshake-hug and got in the Jeep. I turned to Hayden. His hair was still wet and dripping with water.

"Well," he said and pulled his shirt over his head, tossing it in the bed of the truck. "Ready to go to the Big Apple?"

* * *

"I've never heard of the Regency Hotel," I told Hayden after he said it was the perfect place to hide out during the apocalypse.

"Really?" he asked, taking his eyes off the road to look at me. "It was a huge deal seven years ago."

I lifted my shoulders and shook my head. "Must not have been that huge since I never heard of it."

"I was twenty-two and had been enlisted for a few years by then. You were...what, only eighteen? Fuck that makes me feel old."

"That was a bad year for me," I confessed. "The freedom of college made me a little, uh, too free."

"Oh. Maybe that's why," he suggested. "Anyway, that's when the economy starting tanking and the healthcare system went through that reprise that didn't do shit. State hospitals lost funding."

I nodded. "I remember that. A lot of them closed and the patients were turned out, ending up in jail or homeless." I mostly remembered being angry with my mom and Ted for going to China that year. So many people in our own country needed help from their mission group. Why did they have to go so far away and leave me?

"The Regency Hotel is on Wards Island. There used to be a state hospital on that island. Once it closed, a private buyer—don't ask me who cuz I don't remember—bought it out and heavily renovated the building into a fancy hotel for high rollers. Only three years later, it closed. No one could afford that shit."

"Oh. And it's been abandoned ever since?"

"Supposedly. The whole island was abandoned. The last I remember was that the bridges were blocked off to keep gangs out." He drummed his fingers along the steering wheel. "I wonder how long Samael has been setting this up."

"Me too." The thought made my stomach bubble with anxiety. What exactly were we going to find? I closed my eyes in a long blink. "It's so...weird to think that our government is out to get us. I never thought it would happen."

Hayden stiffened. "I know. I spent how many years risking my life for them? And Ben..." he couldn't finish his sentence. I reached over the center console, putting my hand on his thigh, knowing that Hayden was thinking his childhood best friend lost his life overseas for nothing.

He put his hand over mine and held his head up, focusing on the road. About an hour later, we made a pit stop. We were a little over two hours from New York City. I walked away from the truck to go to the bathroom and came back to find Hayden leaning on the hood, looking over the map I had taken out of Louis and Cal's delivery truck.

"Their path isn't clearly marked," Hayden grumbled. We figured they were familiar enough with the journey to not need a map anymore. "All it shows is this bridge," he said as he pointed to the map, "is closed. It looks like we have to go through Manhattan."

"That seems like a horrible idea." I stopped next to Hayden, putting my arm around his waist, fingers resting on his hipbone. "Indy was so overrun we could barely get out alive. Even Bowling Green had too many zombies. Can you imagine what Manhattan will be like?"

"Oh, I can." He shook his head and folded the map. "But if those guys came through that way then..." He sighed, running a hand through his hair. "There has to be a way, right?"

I nodded. "I guess." I didn't see how there could be could be. Even if half the population of Manhattan had died instantly from the virus, that still left too many crazies and zombies.

"If it's overrun, we leave," Hayden decided. He took my hands in his. "I'm not stupid; I know our limits. Yeah, we need something big to get us through the winter but dying won't solve anything."

I took my hands out of his and wrapped my arms around his shoulders, stepping close so that my hips brushed against his. "I hate that you're in harm's way," I started, looking into his hazel eyes. "But I won't want anyone but you on this trip with me."

"Trip?" he questioned. "I think we should call it a quest. I always wanted to go on a quest, you know."

I laughed. "You're such a nerd."

Hayden smiled and kissed me. We ate and got back in the truck. I calculated our time and the daylight we had left. If everything went smoothly, we'd get to the outskirts of Manhattan with two hours until total darkness, giving us just enough time to find somewhere safe to spend the night.

* * *

"Don't worry, baby," Hayden said. "I'll be back as soon as I can. You know I hate leaving you."

I tapped my foot, impatiently waiting. Our daylight was fading fast.

"You'll be fine, I promise," Hayden went on. "You're safe in here."

"Do you want me to get you a jar of Vaseline and leave you and the tailpipe alone?" I asked.

Hayden patted the truck hood and scowled at me. He pressed the lock button—again, and looked at his truck as he joined me. We had just made it through the Lincoln Tunnel. Anxiety still prickled through my body. If I never went through another dark tunnel again, it would be too soon.

Only one entrance to the tunnel was open. The others were blocked off with cement walls. A large chain link gate blocked the only opening to the tunnel. Hayden dragged it away and in we went. We stashed the truck in a warehouse a few blocks away, thinking it would be best to hoof it the rest of the way and not risk being seen until we were ready.

Hayden picked up his heavy pack and put it on his back. He insisted we combine everything we needed into one pack so I could wear the quiver. We didn't want to use guns unless absolutely necessary.

I put my hand on the warehouse door, looking at the rusted metal sides. My heart thumped so loud I could hear it. Sweat beaded around my hairline and adrenaline made my knees shake. Hayden put his hand over mine, his skin warm, his touch reassuring.

I took a deep breath. Together, we twisted the knob and stepped out. The city was alive with birds. Weeds grew along the sidewalks and into the street. The strap from the quiver dug into my shoulder, the rubber coating sticking to my sweaty skin. I debated stopping and digging my button up shirt out of the pack, but it was all the way down at the bottom and not worth the effort.

"It's quiet," Hayden said, stepped off the curb. Grit crunched under his feet. Dust coated the windows of cars, stopped randomly along the road with doors ajar. The skeletal remains of a woman rested against the steering wheel of a Volkswagen.

"Seriously?" I said, pulling the ball chain of Hayden's dog tags out from under the quiver strap.

"What?"

"Never say that unless you want the opposite to happen."

Hayden shrugged. "I almost want it to. This is unnerving."

I bit my lip and looked around. "It kind of is." The fronts of businesses were boarded up with CLOSED spray painted on them in big letters. "I thought New York was doing well."

"Not all of it, apparently." Hayden held his knife at his side. "I'm starting to think the whole thing was a lie to cover up the preparations."

"It makes sense," I agreed. We made it another few blocks into Midtown before stopping. My heart thumped in my ears. My fingers tightened around the bow and I licked my lips, looking at the blackened buildings and broken windows. "What happened?" I asked out loud.

"Bomb," Hayden said, voice tight. The word was like an icy dagger to the heart. "This place has been bombed. That's why there's no one around."

I turned my head up to Hayden, eyes wide. "They blocked off the exists and bombed Manhattan."

"Yeah," he breathed. "Fuck." He shook his head, staring at the mangled body that had been blown halfway out a second story window. "We're still blocks away from ground zero."

"What kind of bomb?" I asked. Were we at risk for radiation? Would it mutate the zombies into something worse than what they already were?

Hayden shook his head. "Not sure. Nothing nuclear," he said, sensing my fear. We stepped over twisted metal. "I'm assuming the waves weren't meant to hit Wards Island either." He tipped his head. "It's fucked up to think like this, but if it were me, I'd plant several small bombs around the city. It would ensure destruction without damaging the shelter."

"Not fucked up at all," I said. "It's what I would do to. Kill the survivors who could fight back. It kept them from turning into zombies," I added with a grim smile. "I'm thinking our chances of working things out are slim to none."

Hayden agreed. "And our chances of getting shot on sight..."

"Shut up," I said, fear rippling through me. I jumped onto the hood of a car, needing to get around a pile of wreckage. Bits of brick from ruined buildings, overturned cars, and a broken bus stop shelter blocked our way. When we made it over, I stopped, laughing.

"What on earth is funny?" Hayden asked.

I pointed to the intersection. "The street signs are gone. I have no idea where we are."

Hayden put his hand on his forehead, wiping away sweat. "Neither do I." He got the map of Manhattan out of his back pocket. "This is useless." He let the map float to the ground. "We need to go northeast. We'll find the island eventually."

"It's bound to stick out among this mess," I said. Hayden and I stayed close together as we picked our way down the rubble filled streets. Every now and then we came across a body, strew across the street or huddled behind a wall. I inspected one as we walked past.

He had died with his arms wrapped around another person, shielding them from the blast. It was a moot effort, but his last actions were heroic. Unwelcome images filled my head, reminding me of Hayden, throwing his body over mine when I fired that arrow at Cutter's car in Eastmoore.

He was so willing to die for my sake...and that terrified me.

* * *

Time's Square hadn't been anything spectacular in years. The Depression reduced the entertainment industry to almost nothing. Movie posters and advertisements were something nobody could afford. I expected it to be empty, with peeling posters and empty store fronts.

I didn't expect it to be ground zero.

"Come on," Hayden said, holding out his hand. We booth stood, transfixed, eyes running up and down the tall buildings. Entire parts had been blown off. Everything was charred, blackened beyond recognition. Parts of a taxi lay in jumbled tangles of metal along the street. I blinked and took a step. Hayden shook himself and followed.

We went around the block, stumbling over ruins. The debris slowed us down. The sun would be down soon, causing a desperate anxiety to fuel us forward. There was nowhere safe to stay.

We were forced to veer off the road and cut through an alley. Immediately, we realized it was a bad idea. Bodies had been piled, left to rot.

"They died after the explosions," Hayden stated. His hand slipped into mine. "Someone killed them after they made it through this war zone." His grip tightened as his anger grew.

I didn't know what to say. The truth was worse than the lie. Worse than anything I could have thought of. Suddenly, I longed for the days at the compound where we worried about gathering supplies. Life still sucked, but things were simpler, more black and white. It was the healthy versus the infected with no political shit thrown in.

There was no going back. Not after what we'd seen, not after all we knew. I turned around, tugging on Hayden's hand. We picked our way through a building, ducking under fallen beams. I hurried to get out, afraid one gust of wind could knock the thing over.

We continued north east, using the quickly sinking sun as a guide. I had lost count of how many blocks we had gone, but judging by the lessening rubble, we were more than a few away from Time's Square.

"What about there," Hayden said pointing to the remnants of an art museum. "It might be a good place to stay the night."

I nodded. The front had been damaged from the bombs, as had everything around here. We needed off the streets before night came and this place seemed as good as any. We were in the middle of the street when I suddenly stopped, realizing at once that everything was wrong.

The birds, that had been busy singing and flying around the city in the pale dusk light, had disappeared. Eyes pressed into my back, running a cold finger down my spine. I grabbed an arrow and whirled around. I couldn't see into the shadows but I knew it was there.

Hayden moved, putting his back to mine. We circled around, waiting for the crazies to come out of the dark. My chest rose and fell and my fingers trembled. I took a deep breath, forcing myself to focus.

A low hiss emanated from the dark shadows. I pulled the arrow back, looking, waiting. But I couldn't see anything. I didn't know where the crazy was.

Then one of them screamed, the drawn out war cry reverberating through the ruined city. They moved as one, their presence suffocating, and the dark mass of crazies crept forward. Another let out a harrowing yell. Then another...and another, until the entire group of crazies was shouting and yelling.

I wanted out of there. Now. They were everywhere, slinking back in the shadows unseen. How many surrounded us? Did we even have a fighting chance? The battle calls were terrifying. Each screech curdled my blood, and I struggled to keep breathing. I stepped back until the quiver pressed into Hayden. The crazies kept screaming and growing, waiting to make their move until we were fully paralyzed with horror.

Hayden's hand wrapped around my wrist right as the mob lurched from the shadows.

"Run, Riss. Run."

CHAPTERTWENTY—FOUR

I didn't pay attention to where we were going. I just ran, making sure Hayden was next to me. We sprinted away from the museum, turning down another street. A crazy, horribly disfigured from the bombs, jumped down from a building, landing in front of us. The height from which he jumped would have splintered bones or hurt enough to cause a normal person to fall to the ground in agony.

He walked forward, ankles shaking but blind to the pain, swinging a baseball bat at us. The end had been wrapped in barbed wire. I slowed to shoot with an arrow.

"Come on," Hayden yelled, a few paces ahead of me. He yanked the arrow from the crazy's chest and turned, waiting for me to catch up. The pack was behind us, gaining speed. They knew where they were going, knew how to avoid the pile ups of broken buildings and overturned cars.

Hayden and I rounded a building. The light was almost gone and we had no idea where to go...if there was even a safe place. But we didn't let that slow us down, not one bit. We pushed forward, turning down another street. Then I saw it: the dark outline of trees. The familiarity of nature among this concrete jungle sent a flash of hope through me. I cut in front of an overturned park bench and pointed. Hayden, too busy gasping in air to speak, nodded.

We only slowed enough to jump over the fence. My feet landed in packed dirt and the smell of the forest brought instant comfort. Hayden held out the arrow, panting. I took it and shoved it into the quiver and pushed my shoulders back, trying to get in as much air as possible.

That few seconds of a reprieve was too much. The crazies barreled down the street. Hayden straightened up and extended his hand. I reached out but didn't take it. There was no time. We turned, pushing into the dark trees.

The woods were alive with wildlife. I crashed into a spiderweb, the thin strings sticking to my face and neck. I desperately pawed at my face as I ran forward. Hayden was a few feet ahead. He turned to make sure I was ok, taking his eyes off of what was in front of him.

He collided with a fence, toppling over. I slowed, boots skidding on fallen leaves. Hayden sprang up in just seconds. I hadn't slowed enough. In my haste, the bow got caught on the fence, causing me to slip off. I landed on my feet but bumped into Hayden. He dropped his knife.

We stopped, panting. Hayden made a move to keep going, not bothering to look for his knife in the dark. I grabbed his arm.

"Listen," I said, my voice breathy. He looked behind us. The crazies were still growling, threatening us. But they hadn't followed us into the woods.

"They're not coming after us." Hayden shook his head and laughed. "Why the fuck not?"

"I don't know." I turned him around, patting along the pack for the flashlight. "Maybe because they can't see in the dark?"

"Maybe." He picked up his knife when I turned the flashlight on. "Stay on the path. There might be a map posted along it." We took a second to catch our breath before pushing on, following the path through Central Park. "If we make it to the other side, Wards Island is almost a straight shot across."

"Easier said than done, right?"

"I'm sure."

I hooked my bow over my shoulder. It was pointless to fire off arrows in the dark. I pulled the machete from the quiver, keeping it in my right hand. I held the flashlight in the other, shining it back and forth across the path. I expected crazies to jump down from the trees, landing on us and tearing us apart.

We crossed a street and passed a statue of Shakespeare. Lawn chairs, coolers, and tattered clothing lay strewn across the path. The remnants of a tent was in a shredded mess a few feet from us.

"I don't even want to think about being trapped inside the city," Hayden said under his breath. "This place seems huge but really..."

"I know. Just think of all the places we've been to get food and supplies. They had to have run out so quickly. How long do you think they lasted?" We passed another ruined camp site.

"Not long, even if the bombs didn't go off right away."

"I almost hope they had," I added ruefully, knowing how twisted that sounded. "It would have ended this nightmare instantly for a lot of people."

Hayden only sighed, shaking his head. We pushed into a jog, wanting to get the hell out of Central Park. The trees thinned a bit, letting moonlight spill onto the path. Tree branches snapped. Hayden and I came to a stop. I clicked the flashlight off, shoving it into the top of the quiver and held up the machete.

Another branch flew back from someone pushing through the woods. Then the ground shook and we realized why the crazies stayed out of Central Park: It was full of zombies.

"This way!" Hayden said and took off down the path, his head turned to make sure I was right behind him. We tore down the path, jumping over fallen trees and failed campsites. Clouds rolled over the moon and suddenly we couldn't see. I reached my hand out, feeling for Hayden. My fingers grazed the heavy pack.

"I don't hear them," I huffed. Hayden turned, his arm out stretched. When he found my arm, he ran his fingers down it until he held my hand. I laced our fingers, holding onto him tightly. I had no intention of letting go.

"Not yet," Hayden whispered. We didn't dare turn on the flashlight. Zombies couldn't see in the dark any better than we could. Unless they followed the scent or caught sight of our movements, we were safe...for now.

Silently, we inched along the dark path. Each step was agonizingly slow. The clouds moved off the moon and natural light illuminated our way again. But it was brighter this time. I looked up. There were no leaves on the trees. The faint smell of burned wood hung in the air. Had a fire ripped through Central Park?

I didn't have time to think about it. The death moans came from deep inside the trees, a ways off the path. Hayden and I took off again, not stopping until we heard the lapping of water. Moonlight reflected off a still lake, sparkling in the calm of the night. It seemed out of place, way too ethereal in a world filled with walking corpses.

"I think we're halfway through," Hayden whispered.

"Halfway?" I asked, looking behind us. "That's it?" How big was this place?

"Yeah. Maybe. I know there's a lake roughly in the middle. This might be it." His fingers tightened around mine. "Only about four hundred more acres to go."

My breath whooshed out of me. "Should we get back onto the streets?"

"Crazies or zombies...take your pick."

"'Neither' isn't an option?"

"I'm afraid not," he said. He looked down the path. "I don't know where we are."

"Ditto." My heart was still racing. "Isn't there a running path around this lake?"

Hayden shook his head. "I have no idea."

I looked at the water. "I've only seen it in movies. Let's follow it and see where it goes?"

"Sounds good enough for me," Hayden agreed. "And we only have to worry about zombies coming from one side."

"And only having one side to run off to in case of emergency," I added with a shake of my head. Seeing as we had little option, we took off. The pack rattled a bit with each step and I hoped Hayden was doing all right carrying the weight.

We veered off the running path and onto a road, emerging from the park near a hospital that lay completely in ruin. I only knew what it used to be by the damaged logo that lay on the ground.

"Look," Hayden said, letting go of my hand. I pressed my hand over my chest, willing my heart to stop racing. My legs ached from the constant running and adrenaline made them shake. I followed to where he was pointing.

"Holy shit," I breathed and felt chilled all over again. I swallowed, taking it all in. I stepped closer to Hayden, tightening my grip on the machete. There it was, in the distance, lights glowing in the dark. "It's real."

Hayden shivered. He put his knife in his other hand and held onto me, looking into my eyes. "Part of me hoped we would get here and find nothing."

I tore my eyes away from him to stare at the distant glow of the Regency Hotel. "Me too." We were so close, a little over a mile probably, from the people who'd started this whole thing. It scared me more than the park full of zombies. "Now what?"

"I don't know," Hayden blurted. He let go of me and wiped sweat from his forehead. "We need to find somewhere to hide out until morning. We should get some rest, but I know it'll be hard to sleep."

"You're telling me." I readjusted the bow. "Maybe the crazies will stay away from this area," I said, sweeping my hand in front of me. "Since there are zombies behind us."

"Yeah, there are," Hayden said. "We can't stay here. We got a good head start but they'll catch up to us eventually." We picked a street and went down it, going as fast as we dared through the rubble.

"There's someone up there," I whispered. To our left was a large, multi story building. It had been blown up; half was gone, leaving walls and floors exposed as if the building had been messily chopped down the middle. "I saw shadows."

"Crazies?" Hayden suggested.

"Yeah. They're watching us." Hayden switched his knife back into his right hand. "I can feel their eyes."

"Me too," he said. "Let's get out of here."

We picked up the pace, moving down the street. The crazy went through the building, staying parallel to us. Something heavy clunked inside the building. I jumped, turning to face the ruined structure. I clenched my jaw together, ears ringing. Another black shadow moved across a broken window.

Then, like spiders descending upon a fly trapped in their web, the crazies poured out of the building.

* * *

We turned around, prepared to hightail it back into Central Park. But the crazies were one step ahead and blocked our path. I couldn't tell how many came out of the building. It was just too damn dark. We didn't know where they were or what kind of weapons they had. It wasn't worth the risk. We ran.

We went down another street, going away from the yellow glow. Anger flashed through me, making me skid to a stop. There were people in that building, enjoying all the comforts a luxury hotel offered. Sure, they had to go without cable and their fancy sports cars, but they were safe in a building that was no doubt impenetrable. On a fucking island.

"Riss!" Hayden yelled, realizing I wasn't following him anymore. "What are you doing?"

I brandished the machete. Shoes scuffed on the littered streets. I brought my arm back. "I'm not running anymore!" The crazy was just a dark silhouette. I swung the machete down, the blade hitting the crazy in the shoulder. She hissed at me, fingers bent like claws. I put both hands on the handle of the machete and brought the blade down, dragging it back as it sliced through muscle and skin.

She took another step forward before she collapsed. Blood sprayed on my face when I yanked the blade up. I turned and swung again, catching another crazy in the stomach.

"I'm sorry," I said as he fell, intestines spilling onto the street. "It's not your fault." I glared at the Regency. "It's *theirs*."

Hayden pulled his knife out of the brain of another crazy, turned around, and kicked another away from him. He moved with speed and grace despite wearing the heavy pack.

Then they moved around us, circling like a pack of wild dogs, chattering to each other in some sort of primal language. I looked over my shoulder at Hayden. He tipped his head down in a curt nod and moved his eyes to a break between dilapidated buildings. We slashed our way through the pack of crazies, climbing over jumbles of broken walls.

The crazies didn't follow us. For a split second, I thought we got away, narrowly escaping like we had before. I was wrong. The herd of zombies had followed us out of Central Park. There was an incoherent murmur among the crazies. Some turned to fight off the zombies.

And others continued to pursue us. Hayden and I ran, ducking under fallen beams. The roads were almost impassable. Buildings had fallen into each other, creating dangerous obstacles to go through.

Wires hanging down from a beam, caught on my hair as I raced under it. Bits of drywall speckled my face, getting in my eyes and making them burn and water. It wasn't like I could see in the pitch black anyway. I squeezed them shut for a few seconds, waiting for the tears to wash the dust away.

"Riss!" Hayden called, his voice getting cut off by debris sliding down a slab of concrete wall. "Look out!"

I whirled around, opening my eyes expecting to see a crazy behind me. My vision was still blurry and everything was just a dark shadow. I turned around, ready to push forward when I heard the creaking. The crazy wasn't behind me. He was above me.

Hayden saw him before I did, reacting twice as fast. He dove for me, knocking me out of the way just in time for split beams and pieces of floor boards to crash down upon us. I landed hard on my back, whacking my head on a sharp edge. I sat up, head spinning.

"Hayden," I called into the dark. The crazies clicked and chirped to each other, struggling to get through the rubble. "Hayden," I said again, fear rising inside of me. I swallowed hard, my heart beating so fast I could feel it pulsating in my neck.

My wrist turned in, keeping a hold on the machete. I pushed up, pain shooting along my arm. A broken desk had fallen on my legs, pinning them down. "Hayden!" I called. He didn't answer. I yanked my foot up. My boot got caught. I pulled harder. I didn't care if my boot came off. I needed to find Hayden.

"Hayden!" I shouted. "Please, say something!" Fear prickled through me, making more tears well in my eyes. I screamed in frustration and finally pulled my foot free. I didn't have the chance to stand up before a crazy flew at me. I gripped the machete and almost let go, the pain was so intense. But nothing was bad enough to keep me from him, to keep me from finding Hayden.

I slashed the blade through the air, slicing the crazy below the belt. He hissed, hands flying to his crotch, not in pain but in anger. I wildly waved my arm, making contact with his chest. He dropped to the ground in just seconds.

I scrambled to my feet. "Hayden." My voice shook. He wasn't responding. I looked at a pile of ruin, squinting in the dark. He was nowhere to be seen.

* * *

I reached behind me, sticking my hand into the quiver for the flashlight. It had fallen in too deep to reach and I wasn't going to waste time getting it.

I stumbled over a beam and saw the pack, covered in dust. The machete fell from my hands, clattering against pipes and chunks of wall. Hayden lay face down, half of his body buried. I flew to him, shoving broken beams and parts of wall off of him.

"Oh God, Hayden," I cried. My hands shook. I gently cupped his face and tipped his head up. Blood streamed down his forehead. His eyes were closed. "Hayden!" I shook him. He was completely unresponsive.

"Hayden!" I crumpled down, crying and buried my face in his hair. Then I felt it. A heartbeat. He wasn't dead, just knocked out. "Hayden, come on. Wake up. We can't stay here. Please, Hayden!" I stuck my arms under him and dragged him out of the pile. I tripped, falling backwards. The bow dug into my spine, crunching against the bone. Hayden toppled onto me, his head landing on my stomach.

He groaned. I scurried up, hooking my arm through his. "Hayden," I said, fighting back tears. "Hey, baby, come on. Please. *Please!*" The death moans echoed off the crumbling high rises.

"Riss," he muttered. "You ok?" He struggled to his feet, unable to open his eyes. He held onto my shoulders needing support. So much blood dripped down his face. I kept a hold on him to keep him on his feet.

"I'm fine. Hold onto me. We have to get out of here. Now!" Hayden took a few steps before he was overcome with dizziness and slumped to the ground. I dropped down with him, pulling his arms through the straps of the pack.

"No," he said, his voice breathy. "I...I got it."

"Shut up." My teeth chattered together I was so terrified. "You're concussed." I put the pack on not caring that it caused my bow and quiver to dig into my back. I went around to Hayden. He took a deep breath and shook his head. He stood with minimal assistance. He wrapped his arm around me, hobbling a few paces. Then he let go and was able to continue on his own.

We made it another block before Hayden stopped, his gait faltering. He had one arm around my shoulders and I had one wrapped around his waist. He sidestepped, tripping over his feet. I struggled to keep a hold of him. Then he doubled over and threw up.

"Fuck," he panted.

"It's bad," I said, referring to his head injury. "We need to find somewhere to stop."

He nodded, wiping his mouth. I pulled him to me and trudged forward, going to the first building I saw. The lobby was a mess and the stairs were blocked. I turned, defeated. There was nowhere to go. The crazies were going to catch up to us. I couldn't fight them myself and Hayden could barely keep his eyes open. I didn't see a way out of this.

Then I saw the fire escape on the outside. The metal was bent, but it was still in place. I took the pack off and jumped, having to make several attempts to get the ladder down. Flakes of metal rained down on me, letting me know that no one had pulled it down in a long time. I put the pack back on and had Hayden go first in case he stumbled. I knew I couldn't catch him, but I would try. I would always try.

We made it up. I lay on my belly and reached down, pulling the ladder up. We continued going up, until Hayden couldn't make it any farther. He leaned against the side of the building while I went in through the door that had been blown off from the blast.

Glass crunched under my feet. I took the pack off, dropping it to the ground. Then I removed my bow and quiver. I reached inside, getting the flashlight. Wallpaper hung in tattered sheets and bits and pieces of the building crumbled along the floor. The hallway was blocked, caved in on itself. Only two doors could be opened. I held my breath and waited.

Nothing came running out at us. I went back to the door and helped Hayden inside, going into the first room, not daring to venture too far from the fire escape. Wind blew in through the large window that was missing all its glass. It offered a good view of the city below.

The furniture had been tossed around from the explosions. The carpet smelled like mildew from being rained on. But it had to do. Hayden put one hand on the doorframe, fighting to stay awake.

I flipped a leather couch over, brushing off dirt. The cushions were slashed and slightly damp. "Sit," I told Hayden. He pursed his lips, wanting to object. "Please," I added and the desperation in my voice caused him to obey.

I looked around the room we were in, guessing it to be a living room and kitchen all in one. There was a door on the far wall, blocked by a broken table. Once Hayden was situated, I moved the table and went through the apartment, surprised to see some of the furniture in good standing...but buried under rain rotted ceiling tiles.

The bedroom was tiny; there was hardly room for the twin bed. I pulled the mattress off and dragged it out, bumping over debris. I yanked the sheets off, flipped it over, and put it in the middle of the room. I held the flashlight in my mouth as I opened the pack. I tossed the sleeping bag onto the mattress and grabbed the first aid kit.

Hayden and I were covered in cuts and scrapes. The only one I was worried about was the gash on Hayden's head.

"I'll be fine," he said, opening his eyes for a few seconds as I dabbed at the wound with an alcohol swab.

I took in a ragged breath. "You hit the same side not that long ago when Hannah drove off the road."

"Yeah, so?"

"I'm no doctor, but even I know repeated head trauma is bad." I finished cleaning the wound to the best of my ability then wiped down his remaining cuts, using most of the alcohol swabs.

Hayden took my hands in his. "Let me take care of you."

I took my hands out of his and put them on his cheeks. I pressed my lips to his. My heart finally took a moment to stop racing. My eyes closed, and a second of warmth passed through me, calming my mind. Then I opened my eyes and was terrified again.

"No. You need to lay down. I got a bad concussion not that long ago and it took me days to get better. Start resting now." I stood, helping him up. The movement made Hayden sick again. My chest tightened. Hayden was going to be all right. He had to be.

I removed his weapons and helped him lay down, loosely draping the sleeping bag over his body. I wanted to collapse onto the mattress, curl up next to him, and cry. Instead, I bent down and unclasped his watch, pressing a button to light up the screen to tell me the time. "I'm going to wake you up every hour," I told him. That's what Padraic had done for me, right? Maybe it was every half hour? I doubted I'd be able to wait that long. Every ten minutes seemed more likely. I'd worry too much if more time passed.

"Ok," he mumbled and reached for me. I squeezed his hand and got up, moving the broken table in front of the door. It did little good since the frame had been damaged. The door didn't even latch. Still, it made me feel better. And the only way up was from the fire escape. The chances of someone else being in here were slim to none...well, anyone being in here that posed a threat. Any zombie would be a melted gummy by now.

I put a cushion on the floor and sat, the bottom of my pants soaking up the moisture that was locked inside the old padding. I got up, tossing it to the side and sat on the edge of the mattress, quietly going through the pack.

We both needed to eat. The thought of chewing food seemed too tiring, but I forced myself to eat a banana and granola bar anyway. The fruit was bruised from being jostled around in the pack. I set some aside for Hayden and downed half a water bottle.

I checked on Hayden before going out in the hall to look through the other door. I couldn't open it. The frame had been smashed down, pinning the door to the floor. I sighed, relieved. Unless something came up the fire escape, we were safe for the night. I went back into our small shelter and sat at the end of the mattress again.

"Hayden?" I whispered. I didn't want to fully wake him since he needed sleep. A simple response was enough...I hoped. "Hayden."

"Mmh," he groaned and lifted his head. "I'm ok, Riss."

I nodded, forgetting he couldn't see me in the dark. "Ok." I checked the time, watching each minute tick by until I could check on Hayden again. My heart never stopped racing. As soon as I'd start to relax, the wind would blow through the open window, causing debris to noisily blow throughout the building. Crazies moved throughout the city, their calls floating up here in the most chilling echoes.

I wrapped my arms around myself. I had already put my button up on and was still cold. Exhaustion tugged at me, begging my eyelids to close. I checked on Hayden and bent my legs up, resting my arms and head on my knees.

Anxiety consumed me and I couldn't turn off my mind. Had Ivan and the Brians made it back to the compound with the food all right? And what about Brock? I could easily rattle off ways his trip back home could go wrong. Then there was Jason...the detox from whatever the hell he was given had to be awful. If he went into withdrawal before he got back to Padraic...I shook my head.

"No," I whispered. Brock would get him back in time. Somehow, someway, he would. And if anyone could, it was Brock. He was always prepared for anything and everything.

I pressed my trembling hands into my legs, trying to take slow, steady breaths. When the anxiety pulled me under, I got up and went out of the room, crawling through the broken door onto the fire escape.

I bit my lip and looked down, unable to see much in the dark. I inhaled and looked up, blinking back tears. I stared at the Regency until my vision blurred. How in the hell were we going to get on that island? I couldn't tell from this far away just how well guarded it was. It looked like a palace, shining bright in a sea of evil, offering safety and shelter. I imagined it to have a large steel drawbridge of some sort.

A feeling of foreboding bubbled inside me. The wind blew and goosebumps broke out over my arms. I pulled the button up closed, my fingers catching on the scratch marks on my chest from Jason. The tears I was holding back spilled over, running down my cheeks. Pulling on the scabs hurt, but I wasn't crying from the pain. I sniffled, shaking my head. Crying didn't help. It wasn't going to solve anything or make this mess of a journey any easier.

I wiped my eyes and went back inside, rousing Hayden every twenty minutes to make sure he was ok. Around 4:00 AM I sat near the broken window, leaning against the wall. I bent my legs up, wrapping my arms around them and resting my forehead on my knees. I only meant to close my eyes for a little while.

I woke up over an hour later to the loud chatter of birds flying around in the twilight haze that held the city in a suspended state between night and day. I gasped when my eyes went to the window. It was the first thing I saw when I woke and had forgotten how high up we were.

Then I jerked my head to the other side, stiffly scrambling to my feet. "Hayden," I whispered. He didn't move. "Hayden," I said louder. He still didn't move. I hurried to him, dropping to my knees. I stuck my hand out, grabbing his arm. He was cold and stiff.

"Hayden!" I screamed, my fingers pressing into his skin. He took a shaky, labored breath and moved his arm, his muscles trembling. The sleeping bag had fallen off of him. "Fuck. You're freezing!"

I yanked both shirts over my head and kicked off my boots, struggling to yank my feet out without unlacing them. I unbuttoned my jeans and hastily pulled them down, almost tripping when I stepped out. I lay down next to Hayden, pressing my body to his, and pulled the sleeping bag over our heads.

"Hayden," I whispered, wrapping my legs over his. I pulled up his shirt so our skin touched. "Can you hear me?" He wasn't shivering. That was bad...very bad. This was my fault. I had fallen asleep and didn't check on him. Hayden got injured saving me. *Again.* I ran my hands up and down his arms. "Hayden," I cried, unable to hold back my tears any longer.

"Riss," he mumbled.

I swallowed a sob and stopped moving. "Hayden?"

He inhaled and moved his arms. "You're warm," he said.

"I'm so sorry," I said and started crying.

Hayden embraced me, pressing his head against my neck. "Don't cry. It's ok."

"No, it's not ok. I fell asleep and didn't check on you and now you're cold and hypothermic along with the concussion."

"I'm not hypothermic," he said, his voice thick with sleep. "And you needed sleep. You didn't have to—are you naked?" His hands ran over my bare back.

"Not completely. You need body heat."

Hayden softly laughed. "It's not cold enough to be hypothermic, is it?"

I shook my head. "It's windy up here."

Hayden hugged me tighter, keeping the sleeping bag over our heads in a cocoon of warmth. "It is. But I'm not freezing to death. One life threatening injury at a time, I promise."

"That's not funny."

He kissed my forehead. "I feel a little better, not so sick anymore."

"Good," I said. "But you still need to rest. You need your strength for whatever the hell we run into and of course I want you better." I pressed my hand over his chest, feeling his heartbeat. "I really thought you were dead," I said and felt emotional all over again.

"I'm sorry, Riss. I know how scary it was when I thought you were dead before. It's the worst feeling."

"It is," I said, sliding my hand up his chest and over his shoulder. I gently ran my fingers over the bullet wound scar. "Don't ever leave me."

"I won't. I promise, Orissa. I never want to live a day without you." He kissed me again then put his head down, quickly getting sucked back into a deep sleep. We stayed there, wrapped in each other's arms. I finally fell asleep myself, not waking for several hours.

I gently shook Hayden; he opened his eyes and said my name then went back to sleep. Sunlight poured in through the broken window. I got dressed, ate breakfast, and went out onto the fire escape, bringing a pair of binoculars with me.

The Regency had to be well guarded. I held the binoculars up to my face as my mind whirled with the possibilities. They were on an island, so the perimeters wouldn't have to be as closely watched as ours were at the compound, but they would be fools not to have some sort of lookout.

It was hard to see around buildings; we had to get closer to get a better look. How would we do it? Pretend to be crazy and hope not to get shot? Judging by the amount of crazies left in the city, I didn't think whoever was at the Regency cared. They probably felt untouchable. I hoped it had gone to their heads.

I went back in, waking Hayden for breakfast. Despite his protests, we stayed in that cruddy apartment for another day. Hayden had gotten hurt badly and needed the time to heal. His movements were slow and jerky at best. There was no way he could fight yet.

We sat on the fire escape that night, each eating an apple. We had just enough food to last us one more meal since we hadn't planned on a delay like this. Hayden felt bad about it. I argued it gave us more time to come up with a plan though really, until we were closer to the Regency, we didn't know what we were dealing with.

The wind brought in rain, blowing a cool mist in through the broken window. We moved as far back as we could, putting the mattress behind the couch which blocked some of the wind and rain.

In the middle of the night, the rain turned into a thunderstorm. We huddled together under the sleeping bag, watching clouds swirl around when the lightning flashed. The building groaned and swayed in the gusty wind. My stomach was in knots and we both feared another tornado.

Hayden rolled over, covering most of my body with his. "Are you cold?" he asked.

"I'm ok," I told him, running my hand up under his shirt. "You?"

"No, I'm good." Thunder boomed; the crackles resonated against the ruined building. "I'll be glad when this is over." He pushed up, looking over the couch. "I never minded storms before this."

I sighed. "Me neither."

Hayden laid back down, resting his head against me. "As long as this doesn't turn into a zomnado, we'll be ok."

"Ugh. Flying zombies. Thanks for the nightmares, Hayden."

He chuckled. "I'll wake you up."

"You better." I stretched my legs, sore from being crammed together on the tiny mattress. I didn't dream about zombies being hurled through the air from wind. Instead, they came out of the water surrounding Wards Island and pulled us down, ripping us apart under water.

We were woken by a stentorian chopping. Hayden stiffened, his eyes glazing over the way they did when he had a flashback. The deafening noise shook me. I hadn't heard it in months, but I was able to quickly identify it as a helicopter.

"Hayden," I said over the chopper. "It's ok!" But was it ok?

Wide eyed, Hayden stared at me. Then he blinked. We stayed hidden behind the couch until the chopper was gone. "I know I'm going to sound like your grandpa," Hayden began. "But I really hope they didn't have thermal imaging on that thing."

"We could be crazy for all they know," I added quickly. Hayden nodded. We went to the window, looking out at the sky.

"It makes sense they'd have one," Hayden said, peeling the bandage off his head. The wound had scabbed over nicely. "How else would they get out of the city? The roads aren't drivable."

"Yeah, you're right. I hadn't even thought about it."

"I bet they're going to look for those guys at the greenhouses, wondering what happened."

"At least it will just look like zombies," I said.

"Ready?" he asked me.

"If you are."

He stretched his arms over his head. "I am. I feel back to normal."

I nodded. We moved away from the window to pack up our stuff. Then I turned and swung at Hayden. He caught my fist, twisting my arm away. I pulled back and came at him again.

"See?" he said when he deflected my blow. "I'm fine."

I smiled at him. "Ok. I believe you now."

We brought only what we needed. If we hadn't gotten in by nightfall, we were coming back here to hide out the dark. We carefully picked our way down the fire escape, keeping an eye out for crazies. We made it one block before we ran into company.

Hayden and I stopped, watching the zombies that had followed us out of Central Park struggle to get over the debris in the street. One caught sight and reached forward, blundering into a mess of pipes and broken walls. He impaled himself on a rusted piece of metal. Stuck, he wiggled his arms in the air, growling and groaning. We sidestepped around him, crossing to another less occupied street.

Wards Island loomed ahead. If we wanted to look like real crazies, then we couldn't carry so many weapons. I took the quiver from my shoulder and carefully stashed it along with the bow in a nook of demolished cement. I covered my gun with my shirt and held my knife flat against my thigh.

I looked over Hayden, who had done the same with his weapons. We were dirty and disheveled enough to fit the bill. My heart sped up, beating so fast it pulsed in my ears. I gripped the knife, afraid it would slip out of my sweaty hand.

The city smelled like fresh rain, and birds hopped in and out of puddles, fluffing their feathers in the water. We moved through a ruined building, stopping at the edge of FDR Drive. Only the East River separated us from them.

Right away we could tell things had drastically changed on

Wards Island. Hayden scanned the island through the binoculars, hiding behind an upside down taxi.

"The hotel is the only building," he whispered. "The rest has been leveled and planted over. There are...uh, I think cattle."

"Fuckers," I said to myself. They had greenhouses with endless supplies of food *and* sources of meat and dairy.

"The bridge is gated," he said as he moved his eyes down the island. "Three gates that I can see. And people are there." He squinted, closing one eye. The sun wasn't helping. "Heavily armed. I'm guessing that's the only way in and out by foot."

He stepped around the taxi. I tensed, afraid he was going to be seen. My breath whooshed out of me. I whirled around, checking for crazies or zombies. "The north side of the island where the East River is the thinnest..." he started. "...looks funny. I think they made it wider. And that bridge is gone."

"They thought of everything."

"Seems that way," Hayden said and lowered the binoculars. He came back to my side, crouching down. "We need to go that way," he said and pointed north. "To see the bridge."

"Can we do it without being seen?"

"I think so. We'll just act crazy, remember?"

I bit my lip. "Let's go back a block or two and then come out. Less risk of being seen but more risk of being eaten."

Hayden agreed and we slipped back into the city, grabbing our stashed weapons. We climbed into another blown-apart high rise that had bits of crumbling walls clinging to its damaged frame. This time I took the binoculars.

Hayden was right. Three large gates blocked the bridge to Wards Island. The one closest to the island was a single layer of chain-link fencing with rolled barbed wire along the top. Three solar panels were stationed on top of the fence. I traced my eyes along them, going down to the electric wires that were woven throughout.

The second fence was made of chain link and cement. A tank was stationed close to it, and half a dozen men with large guns walked up and down. The last fence was several yards away and was a stockade of cars stacked on top of each other, held in place with thick wire mesh on either side. There was a small opening in the middle to allow vehicles in and out.

My breath caught in my chest. Zombies were tethered to it, tied up like dogs. Needless to say, no one was walking onto Wards Island. I lowered the binoculars, shaking my head and reported the findings to Hayden.

We were at a loss. How the hell were we gonna get on that

island? There was no way we could walk to it. Pretending to be lone survivors wasn't a feasible story either since it made little sense to venture this far into the city after seeing it in ruin. I looked through the binoculars one last time and noticed a marina on the other side of the bridge.

Suddenly, I had an idea. It was a crazy idea, like everything I seemed to come up with. But it had worked once before. Would we get lucky enough to have it work again?

CHAPTERTWENTY-FIVE

"Are they taking the bait?" I asked, nervously pulling on my braid.

Hayden looked through the scope of his rifle. "Yes. I'm giving it another minute...or less."

I inhaled and quickly nodded. It had taken the rest of the day to carry out our plan but things went as smoothly as we had hoped. I felt a little guilty, coaxing out the crazies to use as zombie bait. They were infected, all traces of humanity gone. But they were still human.

Now their death would mean something, we had decided. They were going to provide the distraction we needed to get onto the island. I pulled an arrow from the quiver, rolling it between my fingers.

"Get ready," he told me. I put the arrow back in the quiver and pushed onto my feet, prepared to spring up and race across FDR Drive and down to the bank of the East River.

Hayden pushed off the car we were hiding behind. "Go," he whispered at the same time the shouts filled the night air. The image of the crazies tearing into the zombies that were chained to the fence flashed into my mind. The guards would run down to see what was going on, hopefully distracting them just long enough for Hayden and I to make our move.

We raced through tall weeds, splashing into the river. I threw my bow into the old boat and jumped in, grabbing an oar. I took Hayden's rifle and moved back. He pushed the boat a few more feet before getting in himself. I tossed his oar to him and turned my head to the side, watching the bridge, waiting for gunshots.

We stuck the oars into the water and a few frantic seconds went by before we found a rhythm and moved forward. Come on...shoot the crazies. They couldn't get through the gates. Maybe it wasn't enough of a threat. I turned back to Hayden, only able to see his black shadow in the dark. He kept his eyes focused on the glow of the hotel in front of him.

Then they fired. The echoing bangs were like music to my ears. My arms stopped moving and the boat spun in a circle. I snapped my attention back to the water and continued to paddle.

The fire broke out and my heart skipped a beat. It was a gamble, going back to the warehouse where the truck was stashed. It cost us half the day and a bit of trouble fighting our way there and back. But it was worth it. We had coated the crazies with explosive liquids that ignited from the rapid gun fire.

They wouldn't burn for long. Just long enough for us to make it across the river. I tore my eyes away from the flames and looked behind me, watching the hotel come closer. When the shore was just feet away, I dropped my oar and stood, carefully balancing in the rocking boat. I jumped out, feet splashing in the water, and dragged the boat onto the shore. We grabbed our weapons, flipped the boat over in a tangle of weeds and jogged away from the river, taking shelter under a tree.

We stopped close together, not having to speak to know what we were each thinking. We were here. On the island. This was it...there was no walking away from this. We would either leave successful or not at all.

A large, stone fence surrounded the hotel, which rose like a fortress in the night. It was beautiful, built to look like a 1920s grand estate on steroids. I could see how it was marketed to the rich and famous. And I could see how no one could afford it.

We pressed forward, not knowing what the hell we were going to run into. We had a plan, a very vague plan. I tried to take comfort in that. We continued on, not daring to relent now. We ran through an overgrown field, past a cluster of abandoned buildings, and through an empty parking lot.

Only a small lawn lay between us and the stone fence. It was dotted with trees and not kept up at all. Weeds and wildflowers had taken over, twisting around the foliage. A path had been worn through, pushed down from foot traffic. We stopped, huddled next to a tree while we thought up our next move.

Then she walked through the weeds. Hayden's eyes met mine and we jumped into action. I sprang forward, pulling back an arrow and aiming for her face.

"Relax guys," the woman said, holding up her hands. "It's just me."

I didn't let off the arrow. I kept my hold, creeping closer. "Don't move," I said, my voice tight.

"I know, I know," the woman sighed. "You have to go by

protocol." She waved her hand in the air. She moved under a dim solar powered light. "See. Just me, Valencia."

I took a step closer. The woman's eyes widened when she realized I wasn't who she thought I was. "Oh my God," she exclaimed. "Don't shoot me!" She turned around to run and let out a yelp when she saw Hayden just feet behind her with a rifle aimed at her head.

"I'll scream!" she threatened.

"And I'll shoot," I said.

She turned back to me, trembling with fear. "Please, don't kill me!"

"I wont," I told her. "As long as you come with us."

Her eyes flicked to the stone fence. Tears rolled down her face. "Ok. I'll go." She took two steps when something rustled behind her. Hayden whipped around, ready to fire.

"Mommy!" A young girl skipped out of the bushes. "I found those white flowers!" She came to a halt, taking in the sight of Hayden. The flowers fell from her hands. "Mom?"

"It's ok, Elizabeth," Valencia called, her voice wavering. "Come here, baby. This is a drill."

Fuck. I looked at Hayden. This changed everything. He shook his head, telling me we couldn't stop now. We were already in. Elizabeth took her mom's hand, staring at me with curiosity rather than fear. What kind of drills was she used to?

"I won't hurt her," I said when we crossed the lawn. "I just want to talk."

Valencia swallowed. "Ok." She clung onto her daughter. "Baby," she said, biting back tears. "I have to talk to these guys about the drill. Go pick me another flower. There is a patch of them right over there." She pointed, her arm trembled. The girl skipped off, believing her mother about this not being a serious situation. "Who are you?" she asked, turned her face up to me. She spun around to look at Hayden and shuddered.

"My name's Orissa," I said, not seeing the point of lying.

"What do you want?"

"Justice," I spat. Then I shook my head. "We want safety. And shelter."

"What are you—wait, where did you come from? How did you get here?" She looked at her daughter, likely regretting sending her away.

"Kentucky," I said. It was our agreed upon location. Valencia opened her mouth, mirroring the same shock that Louis had when he found out there were survivors. "A lot of us are there," I added.

Valencia shook her head. "That's not possible. There's no one left out there. We...we're all that survived."

I snorted a laugh. "Sorry, sweetie, you've been seriously lied to."

"No...no, no, no. This isn't possible. They went looking. They told us they spent weeks."

"Did they tell you when they found survivors they rounded them up and killed them?" Hayden asked, his voice a low growl.

"No!" she shouted. "They said...they promised us..."

I lowered my bow. "You really have no idea what's going on, do you?"

"Bioterrorists," she started. "Broke into the lab and stole a virus...it made everyone mad or killed them. People from the military saved all the survivors and brought them here."

"That's not what happened," I said, taking the arrow off the string. "Sit," I told her, seeing that she was close to hysteria already. Valencia was a delicate woman, with her blonde hair pulled up in a fancy twisted bun. She was wearing a knee length dress and sparkly sandals and her jewelry cost more than most people made in a year. I wondered who she had married to make her worth saving in the eyes of the government.

Valencia was at a loss for words when Hayden and I were done telling her the truth. She sat on the ground, pulling at the grass. She kept shaking her head, muttering 'no' over and over. She liked thinking that she was part of the group of underdogs, the last of humanity just barely getting by.

She looked up at me with tears in her eyes. "I should get back," she said. "My husband will be looking for me."

"Who's your husband?" I asked, extending a hand to help her up. I needed Valencia to trust me.

"Robert," she said, not realizing his first name meant nothing to me. "He...he's a scientist." She burst into tears. "He created the virus."

CHAPTER TWENTY-SIX

Valencia took the news of being married to a mass murderer responsible for the genocide of our country better than I expected. Really, she was in shock. After a few minutes of hysterical sobs, she muttered over and over that this couldn't be right.

"You're here," she finally said, snapping her head up. "So it has to be true, right?"

"I can't make you trust us," Hayden said gently. "But why else would we risk everything coming here?"

She shook her head, wiping at her eyes. Mascara ran down her cheeks. "Right...right." Her daughter came over, giving us each a bouquet of flowers. "If it's true," she shook her head. "It can't be true. Rob would never...all those people. So many are dead." She looked at the flowers her daughter gave her. "My sister. She lived in Indiana. She had three kids and took care of our mom." She started crying again.

"Don't cry, Mommy," Elizabeth said. She looked like a mini version of her mother, wearing designer clothes that looked odd on a child. Valencia wrapped her arms around her daughter with a distant look in her eye.

It was one I recognized—the realization of the truth setting in. Valencia hugged her daughter then stood. "How can I help?" she asked, looking from me to Hayden.

"We need to talk to Samael," Hayden said but didn't explain further.

Valencia nodded. "He doesn't come around too often. But in two days we're having a dinner party." She said the last word as if it was offensive. Now that she knew what life was like outside the island, a party was embarrassingly frivolous. "He'll be there." She looked me up and down. "You won't hurt anyone?"

"Not unless they hurt me first," I said and Hayden nodded.

She took a breath. "Come with me."

* * *

Hayden and I sat on a velvet sofa in Valencia's hotel room. It was more than a room, really. I tried not to look around in wonder. Even before the zombies, I would have been impressed. I had only seen suites like this in movies.

We had just recanted the story to Valencia's friend, Heaven, who was sitting in an arm chair next to us. She pushed her long, wavy dark brown hair behind her ear. Her sapphire earrings sparkled in the light.

"I knew it," she said, shaking her head. "All along. I said something didn't add up, didn't I, Val?"

Valencia nodded. "You did. That's why I had to tell you."

Heaven put her hands over her mouth and shook her head. Her nails were long and painted bright red. She was wearing heels, skinny jeans, and an off the shoulder blouse. It was weird to see someone look so normal. She blinked, long lashes coming together over her bluish-green eyes.

She stared at Hayden, hardly taking her eyes off him the entire time. "I told Val the timelines didn't match. That this place was set up before things really got crazy."

Valencia sunk into her chair, looking ashamed. Her hand shook, making the ice in her glass of rum clink against the side. She took a drink. "I didn't know," she said again. The poor woman was in shock from guilt.

"I'm not the only one who thinks it either," Heaven said, her words bringing more anxiety to Valencia. "There are a few of us...we've talked. This doesn't all make sense. And there was no way the *entire* country was searched. People would have survived. And obviously, you did."

"Why question a good thing?" Valencia asked, not able to look at us. She traced her finger down a line of condensation on the glass.

"This isn't a good thing," Heaven said, temper rising. "We're living under the same roof with murderers! God, Val! If they did that to the country they supposedly love, then what's stopping them from offing us, huh?"

"They wouldn't do that!" Valencia hissed.

"How do you know? Besides, do you want to live with them? I don't want any part of it." She turned back to us. "We're supposed to start over. If our leaders are willing to do that to their own people..." she trailed off, shaking her head.

Valencia downed her drink and stood. "I need to talk to Robert," she stated. "I won't tell him anything about you two, I swear. I need to know." She looked away, tears filling her eyes again. "He's a good person, a good husband. He wouldn't..." she cut off, overcome with emotion.

Heaven got up, hugging her friend. "Hun, there's no way you could have known," she soothed.

Valencia turned, throwing Heaven's arms off of her. "No! He wouldn't do that! He'd never hurt anyone. They made him...threatened him or something!"

Heaven just nodded and refilled Val's drink. She sat down, running her eyes over me again.

"I expected you to look..." she started and shook her head, laughing.

"What?" I asked.

"Different, that's all. You know, like how they dress in movies."

I rolled my eyes. "You mean wear a gas mask, tight leather pants, and a shirt that only covers half my torso, right?"

"Pretty much. And black platform boots with lots of buckles."

"What the fuck good would that do? Do you realize how impractical that is?"

She smiled. "I never thought of it before." She put her finger on her right cheek, subconsciously rubbing at a fading scar. Heaven stared at Hayden again, her eyes taking in every feature of his face. "I'm sorry," she said and blinked. "You look like my cousin. He's been gone for years."She blinked and the seriousness came back to her face. She bit her lip as she thought. "You want to talk to Samael?"

"Ideally," Hayden said.

"And then what?"

Hayden's shoulders tensed. "Honestly, we don't know."

"We want to make things right," I said, pushing my hair back.

"So do I," Heaven said. "I had this nagging feeling." She took a deep breath and shook her head. "And I wasn't the only one. We all said if we found out the truth...I don't know. We hadn't gotten that far because the idea was too scary to discuss any further. But I promise you, you're not alone in wanting to make things right."

I sat up, eyeing my bow as it rested at my feet. I wasn't ready to give up the weapons just yet. "No offense, but why do you want to help us?"

Heaven stood, going to the window. "My uncle was in the Marines," she started. "He always stood for the right thing. He would want me to help." She turned back around. "He raised me after my mom skipped out. And he introduced me to my husband, who's a politician. He instilled that in me, doing the right thing." She looked down at her large diamond ring. Then she bit her lip and shook her head.

"He didn't want to stay here," she blurted. "My uncle, I mean. He told me it didn't feel right. He said he was going to check something out and come back for me and Danny once he found out the truth." She heavily sighed. "He never made it back."

"What?" Valencia asked. "You never told me."

"What was there to tell?" She shook her head. "My uncle is a good man. He followed his gut and it got him killed." She turned back to the window. "He would have come back if he wasn't dead. I know it."

Hayden stood. "Is your uncle Henry Fuller?"

Heaven whipped around. "How do you know that?"

My heart skipped a beat as everything clicked into place. The glass slipped from Valenica's hand, spilling all over the carpet. Heaven stood by the window, eyes pushed together in shock.

Hayden swallowed. "Fuller set up our camp. He's the one who told us the truth."

Heaven leaned against the wall to keep from falling. "Oh my God," she muttered. "He's alive?"

Hayden's brow furrowed. "No. He had a heart attack not that long ago," he said gently. "I'm sorry."

"He was right," she whispered to herself. "Oh my God, he was right." She stared at the ground for a few seconds before flying to Hayden's side. "He saved all of you?"

Hayden nodded. "He did. And he would have come back for you," he added. "But he couldn't. He told me that since he knew the truth, he would be killed if the government found him."

Heaven turned around with tears in her eyes. "Val, we have to do something! We have to end this!"

"How?" Val said as she bent over to mop up the spilled drink.

"We have an idea," I said.

"Tell me," Heaven said. "I will do whatever I can. You have my word. And yours too, right Val?"

Valencia shook her head. "I...I don't know. If your uncle..." She sank in the chair with her head in her hands. "This is too much."

"You said other people doubt Samael, right?" I asked Heaven.

"Right."

"Can we talk to them?"

"Yes. Yes, of course! They'll want to see you." She lowered her voice. "We've met a few times before. Everyone is scared of getting caught. If you break the rules here or question Samael you get thrown out."

"Fuck that," I said, pushing my eyebrows together. "That wasn't enough of a clue for you that something was horribly wrong?"

Heaven shook her head. "I know. We're all scared. I didn't think we had a choice."

"You always have a choice," Hayden told her.

"I know that now. I'll get my friends." She stood, then realized it was late. She turned back to us. "I can get a meeting set up tomorrow, but not until the evening. It has to look discrete. I don't think you'll mind waiting, right? By the looks of it, you two need some rest."

"That's an understatement," I said.

"There's an empty room at the end of the hall," Heaven said. "It's nothing fancy but it will do. I'll bring you clothes."

* * *

Heaven's version of 'nothing fancy' was my version of living it up. The room she took us to was set up like a typical hotel room with one king size bed, a little table and chairs by the window, a mini fridge and a desk. The bathroom was a glorious sight: a counter with double sinks, a shower and a whirlpool tub. I set my bow on the counter and looked at myself in the mirror.

My hair was crusted with blood that I was sure wasn't mine. My face was speckled with red and my tank top was stained from sweat. I unbuttoned my shirt and pulled the tank top over my head just as Heaven knocked on the door.

Hayden let her in. She was holding a fabric shopping bag full of clothes. "I wasn't sure what you'd like," she said. "Or what sizes you'd need." I stepped out of the bathroom in just a sports bra and jeans. "Whoa," she said when she saw me. "You are incredibly physically fit. Maybe I should get chased around by crazy people," she joked.

Hayden and I didn't laugh. She apologized and said she'd be back later with food. Hayden and I stripped down and got into the shower. I didn't realize how nicked and scratched I was until I scrubbed myself with a bar of soap. I winced, but didn't stop. I wanted to be clean.

I ran a wash cloth over Hayden's face, gently scrubbing away the blood that had dried on his head. He turned up the temperature of the water and put his slippery hands on my waist. Even though hot water poured down on us, a shiver ran through me. I dropped the washcloth and wrapped my arms around his neck, reaching up to kiss him.

His hands slid up my back, crushing me against his slick chest. I ran my hands down his arms, feeling all the bumps and bruises.

"I love you," he whispered.

"I love you, too."

We finished showering, carefully cleaning our wounds and got out. I gave the whirlpool a look but was too tired to do anything besides collapse into bed. I got as far as putting on a pair of cotton shorts and a loose fitting t-shirt when Heaven came back.

"Is this ok?" she asked as she came in. She was carrying a tray with sandwiches, salads, yogurt, cookies and a bottle of juice. "It was all I could get. You can't order anything past eight," she said with annoyance.

"We can order food?" I asked, feeling like a kid on Christmas.

"Uh, yeah. We have a limit though. Tell me what you want too. This room is supposed to be empty. I happen to know where they keep the master key." She smiled and set the tray down. "I know you're tired so I won't bother you." She moved to the door. "In the morning can you tell me more about my uncle? I want to know everything he did."

"Of course we will," Hayden said. He was dressed only in plaid pajama pants.

Heaven ran her eyes over his muscular torso, looking at his scars a few seconds too long. "I don't think the shirts I brought you will fit." She blinked and looked back into his eyes. "My husband isn't as built as you are. I'll bring something else in the morning when I bring you breakfast."

"Thanks," I said and felt slightly awkward, like I had my first day at the compound. We were used to helping others, not having the help given to us.

"You're welcome." She smiled. "I'm in room three twenty-one if you need anything. Danny will be in there some time tonight when he decides to leave the bar but don't hesitate if you need anything, ok?"

"I think we'll do fine with what we have," Hayden assured her. As soon as she left and the door was locked, we brought the tray of food to the bed. I devoured the salad like it was a freaking piece of cake.

We ate everything Heaven had brought us and collapsed onto soft pillows. I pulled the fluffy white comforter over my shoulders, snuggling close to Hayden.

"This is weird," I said, hardly able to resist sleep from having a very full belly combined with being extremely exhausted.

"It is," Hayden said. "Everything is so normal. It's unnerving. I never thought I'd get used to camps and shelters."

"I know. I miss bars on our windows...almost."

He wrapped his arms around me. "Your grandpa has to be right."

"About what?" I asked and let my eyelids come down.

"Fuller wanting us to do this."

That opened my eyes. "I think so too. His niece was here the whole time. He knew she would help us." I closed my eyes again, rolling over and putting a hand above my head. "He didn't know we'd find her."

"Maybe he thought she'd find us."

"How? She doesn't really seem like the kind of girl who could make it out there."

"I have no idea, Riss. We'll never know."

He was right. We wouldn't and there was no use playing the guessing game. A certain amount of fear stayed in my heart, so deep I wondered if it would ever leave. Things could go wrong, terribly wrong in the blink of an eye. But for right now, I needed to believe we were safe.

We didn't wake up until someone knocked on the door at seven in the morning. Heaven had a tray heaping with waffles, pancakes, bacon, fruit, and eggs. I salivated at the sight of it. Valencia followed behind her with another shopping bag. She slipped into the room unnoticed.

"We talked last night," Valencia told us, eyeing my M9 on the nightstand. Her discomfort around guns was obvious. "Heaven was able to get the message to the others who questioned, uh, this place." She shifted her weight nervously. "There is a woman named Martha who started the secret meetings. She's arranged for one tonight at seven o'clock. All you have to do is get into her room unnoticed."

Heaven gave me a piece of paper with a hand drawn map of the hotel floor we were on. Martha's room was at the opposite side of the building from where we were, and a floor below.

"Once the coast is clear, we will get you," Heaven said, glancing at Valencia, who gave a tight smile and nodded like she was eager for this to pan out, but she wasn't able to fool anyone, even with the layers of perfectly applied makeup. She had spent the night crying and was close to coming unhinged even now.

"How's she doing?" I asked Heaven when Valencia went back into the hall, saying she had to find her daughter.

"Not good," Heaven told us. "She talked to her husband last night and he denied the whole thing. He's looking guiltier by the minute."

"Have they been married long?" Hayden asked, taking a plate of pancakes.

"Almost ten years." Heaven shook her head. Her hair was pulled up today, revealing large hoop earrings encrusted with diamonds. "You think you know someone and then find out they're responsible for the end of the world."

She clasped her hands together, nervous. She sat with us while we ate breakfast, asking questions about Fuller. She brought a family photo, showing her, Fuller, and Fuller's son who looked like Hayden. Seeing Fuller's face smiling up at me as he stood beside Mickey Mouse at the happiest place in the world brought a bit of relief. There was no way this Heaven girl was lying.

* * *

I fell back into the pillows, clutching a bowl of salad. "Would you judge me if I ate this with my fingers?" I asked Hayden.

"Not at all," he said with his mouth full. He picked up another cookie and a glass of chocolate milk. "As long as you don't judge me for making myself puke so I can eat more."

"That's disgusting," I said, wrinkling my nose. "But almost a good idea. I forgot how much I love food." I ate several more forkfuls of salad before I put the bowl down. "I feel sick but in a good way."

"Yeah," Hayden agreed and finished his milk and cookies.

* * *

We had spent the whole day eating and soaking in the whirlpool. It was immensely satisfying.

Then, in the evening, we'd sneaked downstairs into another resident's room, an older woman named Martha, per Valencia's instructions. She was a doctor and told us that her suspicions rose when she was instructed by the CDC to contact them when patients who had been admitted with headaches died. Padraic had said something similar. Martha was also threatened to keep everything quiet. Like me, she didn't respond well to threats. But unlike me, she hadn't fought back...yet. She had been waiting for hard evidence, and that evidence couldn't be clearer than Hayden and me.

Since she had witnessed crazies first hand, fear kept her quiet when she first arrived at the Regency. Then she started talking to a man named Gorge, a horticulturist. The more they talked, the more they realized things didn't add up.

Once they realized that the whole thing was a set up, they wanted off the island. But there was no way. And they had no way to survive even if they did get off the island. They were stuck, living in terror under the same roof as their blood-thirsty political leaders. She told us she tried to be grateful that she was among those worthy of saving, but guilt got the best of her and she'd been carefully adding more to her group ever since.

We met a few other members of her group within the hour.

We went over our options, coming to the conclusion that Hayden and I must speak to Samael. If he wouldn't agree to let all of our survivors come here, then everyone in Martha's group who wanted to leave would come to our compound. Things had changed, but the president was still heavily guarded. The only way we would get the chance to talk to him face to face was at the dinner party tomorrow night. Now we had to figure out a way to crash it.

Heaven had led us back to the room. She looked down the hall and waved us on. She pressed the button to the elevator repeatedly as she waited not very patiently. The doors opened and we got in. Hayden pushed the button for the seventh floor. When the number six lit up, the elevator slowed. Hayden and I turned into each other, standing in the corner behind Heaven.

Two young women got in. They said hello to Heaven and pushed the button to go to the eleventh floor. One turned around and obviously checked out Hayden. The other looked at me.

"Hey...aren't you Elle Wilson?" She patted her friends arm. "Oh my God, it's totally Elle! I had no idea you were here!"

The friend waved her hands in the air. "They said they were bringing in entertainment for tonight! You totally should have won, by the way."

I smiled. "Uh, thanks. Don't tell anyone I'm here and ruin the surprise."

"We won't," they said in unison. When we got out, my heart was racing. None of us spoke until we were safe inside our room.

"Told you you look like her," Hayden said, face white from the close call. Heaven tipped her head. "You do kinda look like her. She's been out of the spotlight for a while now; no one could say for certain she hasn't changed." A smile broke out across Heaven's face. "It will work. I can get you in."

* * *

I felt a mixture of nerves and excitement as I remembered it all: the meeting, being accused of being Elle, and Heaven's plan to get us in. I brushed cookie crumbs off of Hayden's chest and lay down, resting my head against him. I listened to his heartbeat until I fell asleep.

CHAPTERTWENTY-SEVEN

I closed my eye, trying for the second time to get the false eyelash to stick. I used to be good at this. Now, my fingers shook with anxiety and I couldn't help but think the whole thing was stupid. Zombies roamed the world and we were dressing up to go to a dinner party. Looking pretty wasn't going to make life better.

"Finally," I muttered when I got the stupid fake lashes to stay in place. I touched up my eyeliner and took the curlers from my hair, flipping my head upside down and gently running my fingers through the spirals before spaying them with hair spray.

I took off the white bathrobe and tossed it on the counter. I grabbed a garment bag that hung on the door. The bag was heavy, making me wonder that kind of dress Heaven had picked out for me. I unzipped the bag and pulled out an evening gown out, holding it up in front of me.

I put it on, struggling to get the zipper up in the back. Then I turned around, looking at myself in the full length mirror.

"Who are you?" I asked my reflection. The woman in front of me looked elegant and beautiful, not like the zombie hunting killer I had become. It was odd to see makeup on my face again.

I had to admit the dress was gorgeous. It was light blue chiffon and lace with tiny little beads sewn along the bodice. The hem fell to the floor and a split ran up the side to my hip. The neckline was low and the dress clung to my body, hugging my curves then falling to the floor like a waterfall of expensive fabric.

I picked up a jar of concealer, carefully dabbing at the many scabs and bruises on my arms. Then I put on dangly earrings and a matching bracelet. I took Hayden's dog tags off, coiling up the chain and sticking them inside the quiver. Heaven had brought me a gaudy necklace of alternating sapphires and diamonds. I held it up to the light, watching the sparkles dance off the cut stones.

I set it down. I still wore my grandmother's necklace. The simple silver leaf hung from a thin chain. It wasn't flashy in the least, but I liked it. I sat on the edge of the tub and stuck my feet into silver heels, tightening the straps. I stood and wobbled a bit. There was a time when I wore heels regularly, back when I frequented bars, looking for a distraction from my unfulfilling life.

I walked to the door, getting my sea legs back in no time. I cast one more look in the mirror, shocked again by my own reflection. I put my hand on the doorknob and twisted, emerging into the hotel room.

Hayden stood by the window, tugging at the collar of the dress shirt he wore under a black tux jacket. He turned when he heard the door open. His jaw dropped then he smiled.

"You look beautiful," he said and walked over.

"You're not looking too bad yourself," I said, taking him in. His hair was styled and his injuries covered up. The tux fit perfectly and looked good on him, making me want to rip it off and throw him on the bed.

Hayden put his hands on my arms. "I feel fucking ridiculous."

"You don't look it, I promise." In heels, I didn't have to reach up to kiss him. I kinda liked that. "This does feel weird, though, I'll agree with you there. It's like we're playing dress up."

He nodded. "These people have no idea what it's really like. I'd say they're living in a fantasy world but this is their reality."

"Makes me sick," I said, putting my hands on Hayden's chest. He looked good, downright hot in the black jacket and white dress shirt. Was it odd I preferred him in jeans and a t-shirt?

He gently touched a tendril of curls and let his hand run across my collar bone. "Seeing you like this is...weird," he said shyly. I smiled, glad I wasn't alone in liking my fiancé in normal clothes. "It makes me feel very out of your league. You're like a model or something." He smiled.

I slipped my hands under his jacket. "You have no idea how good you look, do you?"

He just smiled and gave me a quick kiss. "I am looking forward to getting you out of this fancy dress."

"If this dress is too fancy for you, you're gonna hate the black lace I have on under it," I said coyly.

Hayden wiggled his eyebrows and pulled me in. All this talk was fun but neither of us were feeling it. Tonight was the night, the moment that determined the rest of our lives...as well as the lives of hundreds of others.

* * *

I picked up a glass of champagne and put it to my lips. It was tempting to down the whole thing and calm my nerves. But I had a fake reputation to uphold. It was easy—fun, even—to make up lies about what I'd been up to the last few years. The life of a sorta-famous singer wouldn't have been affected by the Depression as much as mine had.

Hayden stood close to my side, protectively keeping an eye on everyone in the room. A group of people milled about a hall, eating, drinking, and laughing while they waited for the dinner to start. We were in a small room outside the large banquet hall, acting as if we were enjoying the cocktail hour before a reception.

Many of the people we had talked to yesterday were here, which offered some comfort. Their support was the only reason we were following through with this. We still had no definitive plan. It felt like we were here, at this party on a Hail Mary...our last resort and final chance to make things right.

Valencia was nowhere in sight. I scanned the room and spotted Heaven. She raised her glass to me and smiled. Anyone else would have seen it as a friendly gesture. It offered a bit of reassurance. I took another sip of champagne and stabbed a toothpick in a piece of cheese. I also had to show restraint and not go to town on the finger foods. I freaking loved cheese.

Hayden put his hand on my back. "I thought this was a party for everyone," he whispered, his breath hot on my neck.

"That's what Valencia told us."

He looked up then stepped in close, making it appear as if he was whispering naughty things to his used-to-be-almost-famous fiancé. "Then were is everyone?"

I swallowed the cheese before I was done chewing. It lumped down my throat, making me cough. I took a gulp of champagne to wash it down. He was right. Only about a hundred people milled around the hall, all dressed to the nines sipping on drinks completely unaware. I moved my eyes to the buffet table. There wasn't enough food to feed more than who was here. And there was no staff serving us.

"Something is wrong," Hayden said, fingers pressing into my back. Nerves prickled down my spine. "We need to get out of here."

I put my glass down and took his hand. Hayden stuck his other hand inside his jacket, flicking the safety off his gun.

"Heaven!" I shouted over the laughter and chatter. She was at the other end of the room. Keeping a tight grip on Hayden's hand, I pushed through the small crowd. My heart started pounding. My heel caught on the hem of my dress and I stumbled, recovering before anyone even noticed. *Stupid, impractical shoes.*

I madly looked around. The doors we had come through were tall, at least ten feet, and made of solid wood. They had ornate carvings along the top, little swirls and loops. They swung shut with an echoing boom. It shook the room, causing everyone to cease talking and turn. Only seconds passed before the room filled with noise again, some people laughing at their surprise. The doors had closed by accident, of course.

"Heaven!" I shouted again. Anxiety brewed inside. I squeezed Hayden's hand, whirling around. "We need to get these people out of here," I told him.

He nodded. "We're boxed in."

I followed his gaze. The doors to the banquet hall were closed as well, as they would be before a big party. It hadn't raised any suspicions; that was the way to do it, right? Keep the decorations out of sight to build anticipation and then have a big reveal. It was something Raeya would have just squealed with excitement over.

We moved through the sea of people. Why was everyone so calm? Couldn't they see what was happening? Martha caught my eye. I stopped, pushing Hayden on to try the doors. She looked grand dressed in a gray evening gown with a black wrap.

"Orissa?" she said, putting her hand on my arm. "You look alarmed."

"Yeah," I said, whipping my head back. Curls flew into my face. "I am. Just a little."

"What's going on?"

I blew the loose strands away and turned to the older woman. "Isn't this party supposed to be for everyone at the Regency?"

"Yes. It's a celebration for making it through the season. Everyone was invited."

"Then why aren't more people here?" I looked around, easily spotting half of Martha's intelligence group. I waved my arm at the buffet table. "This isn't enough to feed everyone here. Not at all. I could eat all that myself."

Martha laughed. "What does that—oh. Oh my!" She grabbed my wrist, face white.

"You need to get everyone out of here. Have them...have them go to their rooms or back into the meeting room. I don't think we have much time." I looked through the crowd, barely able to see Hayden. He was at the banquet hall doors. Our eyes met and he shook his head, telling me that the doors were locked.

"What about you two?" Martha asked.

"Don't worry about us. Get your friends out of here. Now!"

I pulled my arm back, spinning to get to Hayden. The lights shut off and a hush fell over the room, attention turning to the banquet hall doors. But they didn't open.

The small door that led into the kitchen opened, spilling an arc of light into the hall. Whispers filled the room, full of wonder at what was going on. But something else floated through the hall, drowning out the whispers.

The gargling death moans of zombies shook me, sending red hot fear down my legs. I was too shocked to immediately react. A high pitched scream rang out, and the zombies staggered forward, drawn to the noise.

Speakers, mounted high on the wall, crackled to life and classical music rang forth, so loud it coved the sounds of the full fledged panic that broke out across the room.

"Hayden!" I screamed, to no avail. The music was too loud. There was no way he could hear me. The only light came from the spotlights outside. I closed my eyes to help them adjust. So this was Samael's grand plan? Everyone who questioned him was in this room...and he wasn't going to let them leave and risk spreading the truth.

"Damn it!" I cursed. If only we had noticed it sooner...maybe, just *maybe* we could have stopped this. The smell of walking death permeated the air mixed with the coppery scent of fresh blood.

Someone had already died.

"Hayden!" I screamed again. I reached inside the slit of my dress, pulling out the knife I had concealed on my inner thigh. I shoved a hysterical woman out of the way. "Go to the back!" I screamed. "Get the doors open!" my instructions were lost in a sea of Beethoven and terrified shouts.

The people ran away from the zombies like I had wanted. I just hadn't counted on getting knocked over and nearly trampled. I pushed up, grasping the knife. The hem of my dress caught under my heels again. I grabbed it and sliced into the fabric with the blade, unevenly tearing off a good two feet.

I turned, moving through the chaos. "Hayden!" I yelled. He had been there, right next to the kitchen door. He was ok...he had to be. He promised me! But I hadn't heard any gunshots...

I got an elbow to the eye. "Ugh!" I felt like thrashing the knife just to get people out of the way. I needed to get to Hayden. A zombie grabbed a woman, sinking its rotting teeth into her shoulder. He pulled back, stretching her skin until it ripped. Blood sprayed in the air, showering down on more dinner guests. I rushed forward, stabbing the knife into his head. The zombie slumped down. I extended my hand to the bleeding woman, pulling her to her feet. "Go!"

She pressed her hand onto her shoulder, hysterically crying and scrambled away, disappearing into the frenzied crowd.

"Hayden!" I yelled again, refusing to give up on him. I grabbed another zombie by the back of his shirt. The material stuck to his skin, ripping a layer off his rotting body. I pushed the knife through his open mouth.

Hands landed on my leg. I yanked my foot up and brought my heel down on another zombie. The stilettos turned out to be useful after all.

Then a gunshot rang out. The music crackled then fizzled to silence. Hayden! He shot the speaker. Adrenaline fueled me. He was alive. And he was taking out the music. Everyone would be able to hear the screams now. Samael couldn't cover up the carnage anymore.

People banged on the doors, trying to get out. I kept pushing through, fighting off zombies. A herd swarmed by the kitchen doors, dropping to the ground to tear into their next meal.

Four more gun shots rang out, ringing in my ears. The sound was wonderful, letting me know that Hayden was alive and fighting. I stepped over a body, blood soaked through a gray dress jacket. Zombies dove for the man, ripping at his clothes in a desperate attempt to get to his flesh.

"Orissa!"

I whipped around. In my desperation to get to Hayden, I had forgotten about Heaven. She stood behind a table, holding a chair in front of her. I made a move to go to her.

"No!" she cried. "Get him. Make him pay for this!" She swung the chair, hitting a zombie.

I swallowed, eyes watering from the foul rotting bodies.

"Go!" she said.

I took a step back, slipping on blood. My hands flew out, catching my balance. I didn't want to leave Heaven. I didn't know her very well, but I couldn't leave her. Not after knowing that she was Fuller's niece. And not after all she'd done for us, for getting us in here.

Then it hit me. I had to go. I needed to get Hayden and sprint out of this room. If we didn't find Samael, all these people would die for nothing more than the silence he wanted and the lies he meant to conceal.

I swung my arm, shoving the knife into another zombie's face. I yanked the blade back, blood spraying in the air. I heard another gunshot and followed the noise, fighting past two more zombies. There was so much blood, so may bodies on the floor. The zombies were grouping together to eat those already fallen.

It gave those still alive a fighting chance. They continued to pound on the door and rattle the handles. Someone picked up a chair and started beating against doors that led into the hall. Their screams were deafening.

I blinked and time stood still for a second. I took it all in. Bodies, ripped apart and dripping with blood, lay strewn across the hall. Their intestines and organs pulled from their torsos and shoved into festering zombie mouths.

Martha was among them. Her lifeless eyes stared into me. Zombies crowded around her, tearing at her gray dress and shoving their fingers into her open stomach. A female zombie stuck her hand in the hole, pulling up and peeling her skin back. She dove down, slurping at the blood and stomach contents that rolled along Martha's side.

I looked up at the kitchen door where Hayden had been standing. "Hayden!" I yelled. He didn't answer. I pushed a zombie away from me, shoving its head into the wall over and over until his skull cracked and brown brain matter oozed out. "Hayden!"

I looked back and didn't see him. Five zombies knelt on the ground by the door, ripping apart another body. Oh God, was it Hayden? I looked around the room again, heart beating in my throat. Where was he? Why didn't I hear any more gunshots? I was on the verge of panicking.

I gripped the knife so tight my fingers hurt. I couldn't find Hayden anywhere. I stood, rooted to the spot with horror. No, he didn't die. He wasn't getting eaten. Not him.

Then the doors opened. I turned, seeing Hayden jump out of the way. Terrified people flooded the hall, their screams echoing throughout the entire fifth floor. Zombies followed them.

I doubted if Samael had counted on that.

"Riss!" Hayden called. He kicked a zombie in the knee, causing it to fall. Then he stomped on its head.

I fought my way over. "We need to get Samael," I told him.

He nodded and took my hand, pulling me into the hall, shooting two more zombies and emptying his clip. He put the gun back in the holster. We made it into the hall before a zombie grabbed me, blood tinged saliva dripping from its mouth. I turned, raising my foot to kick it in the stomach and shove it away.

My leg caught on the dress and I teetered back on my heels. Hayden caught me, giving me a push and getting me back to my center of gravity. I outstretched my arms, wrapping them around the zombie's grimy head. I twisted it around and slammed him into the wall. It wasn't enough to kill him, but it let us get away.

The bloody chaos gave us time to slip into the stairwell unnoticed. I stopped, panting, as soon as the door shut. Hayden bent over, catching his breath. He reloaded his gun. His hands were stained with blood and his white dress shirt was covered in red spray. He took off the jacket and untucked his shirt.

"You need to change," he said to me.

"No time for that. I just need our weapons."

Hayden nodded and started to jog up the stairs. I stayed just a few steps behind him, too pumped on fear and adrenaline to let the pain in my feet register. We didn't stop until we reached the seventh floor landing.

The screams could barely be heard up here. Hayden ran down the hall, going into our room. I held my breath, waiting until he returned with my bow and arrows and, thankfully, my boots.

"Good thinking," I said and frantically pulled my heels off. I shoved my boots on without socks, fingers trembling. Hayden held up the quiver, putting it over my shoulder. I snapped the buckle around my waist and took the bow.

Hayden attached his knife to his belt and threw his rifle over his shoulder.

"How are we going to get to him?" he asked.

"I don't know," I breathed. "He's on the top floor. I say we just go." I blinked, wiping blood off my forehead. "He's probably waiting for this to end and come in, saving everyone else and looking like a hero."

"Fuck him," Hayden spat. "I got an idea." He started up the stairs. "I think. You go. I'll distract everyone."

"Hayden, no—"

"I got this," he pressed, turning around. "We have to do this, Riss!"

I nodded. "We do." I took a breath and went up the stairs, out of breath by the time we reached the top floor, which turned out to be a private floor set up just for Samael. The stairs emptied into a narrow corridor.

We peered through the narrow window. Two guards stood in the hall, looking stricken. Were they ok with what Samael was doing? Had they agreed to come to the Regency? Or were they simply the muscle, forced to do his dirty work. I couldn't think about who they were. They were in our way...in the way of the greater good.

"Here goes nothing," Hayden said and took his rifle off. "Get an arrow ready."

I nodded and reached into the quiver. Hayden closed his eyes for a second then pounded on the door, frantically yelling for help. He rattled the knob. I stood back going up a few stairs, arrow at the ready.

One of the guards opened the door. "Sir, calm down," he said, using his body to block the doorway. I leaned over the railing and let the arrow go. I didn't want to kill the guard when he might be innocent. The arrow hit him in the arm, pinning him to the door frame. His gun clattered the floor. Hayden scooped it up and pushed past him.

The second guard ran forward. In a swift, graceful movement, Hayden swung, twisting his body and grabbed his gun, yanking it from the guard's hands. Stunned, the guard backed up, raising his hands into the air. Hayden hit him over the head, knocking him out. I grabbed Hayden's rifle from the stairwell and used the butt to conk out the guard who was stuck to the door. I yanked the arrow free, letting his body slump to the carpet.

We hurried down the hall, stopping in front of the only door. I stood back, arrow strung up in the bow. Hayden knocked on the door. Another armed guard answered it, eyes going immediately to Hayden. He never saw the arrow coming.

Hayden stepped in over the guard. One more rushed forward, gun drawn. Hayden shot him and aimed his gun at another. I came in, face set and arrow drawn.

"Impressive," a voice came from inside the room. A chill ran through me. I knew that voice, remembered it from the endless ad campaign commercials I was subjected to. My eyes trailed into the room, feeling like I was walking into deep, icy water.

Samael sat at a desk, watching something in black and white on a computer monitor. He looked just as he did in those stupid commercials: perfectly groomed dark blonde hair framing his youthful face. He was wearing jeans and a polo shirt, leaning back in a leather chair as if it was just another day at the office.

"You can put your weapons down," he said and waved his hand at us like he was batting away a pesky fly. "You do realize how easily I can have you killed, right?" he laughed. "Though I can honestly say I'm surprised you made it out of the party."

"You have a lot of nerve," Hayden said through clenched teeth and edged forward. The remaining guard flinched.

Samael laughed. "Some call it initiative."

"You murdered millions of innocent people," Hayden snarled. "You're nothing more than a lazy coward, killing everyone instead of fixing the problem."

Samael rose from his seat. Hayden and I tensed. Hayden still had one gun on the guard and another aimed at Samael. I had an arrow pointed at Samael's chest. He looked me up and down. "You're not what I expected," he said, putting his hands on the desk. "But I like it." He pushed his chair back, not taking his eyes off the tip of the arrow. "War is no place for a woman," he said with a smile. "Just look what happened to your friend Martha."

I lunged forward. Samael held up his hands. "Easy there, killer. All I have to do is say the word and you're dead."

"Go ahead," I snarled. "Shoot me. I can't hold the arrow back when I'm dead."

Samael's smirk wavered. "I'll tell you what," he started, looking from me to Hayden. "Put your weapons down, and I'll send out the guards. We can talk this out like adults."

"Why would we trust you?" Hayden asked.

Samael smiled, dark eyes glowing. He tipped his head. "You don't have a choice, do you? You're pawns in my game. I determine your next move and right now I'm curious. Who are you? How did you get here? Who did you talk to? We took careful measures to keep this place hidden."

"What difference is it to you?" I snapped.

Samael shrugged casually. "Not much. But I like to punish those who break the rules." He narrowed his eyes. "Lower your weapons, and I'll send out my men."

I looked at Hayden, chest rapidly rising and falling. Samael had the upper hand...for now. Hayden tipped his weapon down and I lowered the bow. The guard stepped back and another came from across the floor. As promised, Samael waved them out of the room.

He moved away from the desk, going to a thin table. He picked up a glass pitcher. "Lemonade?" he asked. "Freshly squeezed." He poured some in a glass and drank the whole thing. "Reminds me of summer." He set the glass down and smiled. "Which is something you'll never see again." He crossed his arms. "I'll make you a deal. Tell me *exactly* what you know about this place and your death will be quick. If not..." he plucked a grape from a vine and popped it into his mouth. He raised an eyebrow and looked at Hayden. "I'll kill her first, nice and slow. And you'll watch."

Hayden sprang forward. I put my arm out, catching him. Samael chuckled.

"Just as I suspected," he said. "Love makes you weak, makes you not able to do the things that need to be done."

"Funny," I said. "Because you love yourself an awful lot."

He pointed at me. "I like you. Maybe I'll let you live for a while, see what other tricks you got up your sleeve while I dismember your lover."

I swallowed hard. Sweat dripped down my face, rolling over the splattered blood. My eyes went to the lemonade. I still had a weapon, one more deadly than my bow, one Samael hadn't taken away from me.

Samael clapped his hands together. "Where are my manners? Please, introduce yourself."

"Orissa Lynn Penwell," I said proudly.

"Soon to be Underwood," Hayden added.

"Oh!" Samael sat on a couch, putting his feet on a marble-topped coffee table. "I love a good love story. Tell me, did you meet before or after I released the virus? And speaking of the virus, the zombies...couldn't have planned that better myself!" he laughed. "We had no idea, you know. *That* wasn't supposed to happen." He wiped a piece of lint from his pants. "Ironic isn't it? America's youth was obsessed with the undead. Little good that did."

My heart sped up. I had to do it. It was my only option. "I want some lemonade," I said, my voice too tight for my liking. I crossed the room, taking the little vial from between my breasts. I twisted the cap.

"It's great!" Samael said. "Be a doll and pour three glasses."

I hesitated, having second thoughts. No, I had to do it. I thought back to all the times I had been exposed to the virus. I knew I had gotten blood in my mouth when the crazy holding the Molotov cocktail exploded. There was no way I *hadn't*. I had just been too scared to entertain the thought. I blinked and thought of Hayden. My heart thumped in my chest. I had to do it. If I died, Samael would too.

I dumped the vial in the pitcher, making sure to be discreet and fast. The green liquid dispersed in the lemonade, its color unnoticeable. I gave it a shake and poured three glasses. I set the glasses on a tray and carried it over, grabbing a glass and giving it to Samael.

He took it, smelled the drink, and laughed. "Nice try sweetheart." He extended the glass to me. "Just can't play with the big boys." Then he thrust the lemonade to Hayden. "Go on, bottoms up."

Hayden's eyes flicked to mine. The slightest smile flashed on his face. He put the glass to his lips and took a drink. Samael made him take drinks from the other two glasses. Then he turned to me.

Hayden tensed, and even I felt a little nervous. But it was ok...it had to be. We had already talked about it. Hayden wasn't convinced when I'd told him Wade's theory of me being resistant too, even though the more we thought about it, the more it made sense. Hayden was infected, and I'd been exposed to the virus from him more times than we could count. And I was still okay. I was resistant, just like Hayden.

I finished my lemonade, a little annoyed that it was really good, the perfect balance of sweet and sour, reminding me of the lemonade my grandma used to make.

"There," Samael said and picked up a glass, taking a drink. "Now tell me. Who told you about this place."

"A brave man," Hayden said.

Samael didn't look amused. "Who. Give me names."

"Colonel Henry Fuller of USMC. Remember him?"

Samael's face flashed. "Henry? No. He died."

"Sure about that?"

Samael pressed his lips together and leaned back. He took another drink of lemonade. "What did he tell you?"

Hayden spent several minutes telling him everything we knew so far, all the while keeping the location of the compound a secret.

Samael rubbed his forehead. He blinked several times, glaring at the lights above us. I inhaled and ground my jaw. It was working.

"Now you tell us something," Hayden said. "When everyone finds out you're a mass murderer, how will you rebuild the country?"

"They won't find out. I'll send my guards in—my own personal guards—to kill the zombies that got in. And I'll tell them the unfortunate story that one of our very own double crossed me, trying to get off the island. It will show them what happens when they doubt me."

"They will never buy it," I said.

Samael rubbed his temples, blinking several times. He wrinkled his nose and shook his head. He finished his glass of lemonade and set it on the coffee table, flicking his eyes to me. "Maybe I underestimated you."

Hayden turned to me. "You should never underestimate her."

Samael's face went white. "You both drank it," he reasoned, thinking there was no chance it had been poisoned.

"How much do you *really* know about the virus," I asked, running my finger over the lip of the glass.

"I know that it did exactly what I wanted and then some," Samael said. He was being completely honest with us thinking we would soon be dead. Why lie to a corpse? "This country will start over and I will rise to power again. I'll bring the United States back then go to the aid of the other struggling countries. They will worship me."

"Do you have a cure?" I asked, still making circles on the top of my glass.

Samael leaned forward, bringing his hands together. "It was purposely made to be incurable. Once infected…"

Hayden finished his lemonade and set the glass down, smiling at it. He shook his head, and chuckled. "You'll be sorry about that."

Samael gave him a half smile. "I doubt that."

It was my turn to smile. "Want to bet?" I slammed the little vial on the coffee table. "I'm sorry to tell you, President Samael, but you're infected."

He took the vial, face drained of color. "No…no you-you both drank it."

"I poured it in the pitcher," I told him. "All three glasses were contaminated the whole time."

"Then you…you're infected too," he stammered.

I looked at Hayden. "No. We're immune. Didn't come across *that* in your controlled studies, did you? Not everyone can get the virus. Serious flaw in your plan, isn't it?"

Samael stood and faltered. "You…you poisoned me!" He reached out, grabbing the vase of flowers on the coffee table. His fingers wrapped around the stem of a tulip and he tipped back, pulling the vase over. "Guards!" he yelled. "Guards!"

Three men burst into the room, guns turned on us. "He's infected!" Hayden shouted, taking my hand and jumping back. "Look at him!"

Samael's face was white and red spots covered his cheeks. He struggled to get up. The headache intensified. He shut his eyes, unable to stand the light. "No…no," he said, holding up his hand. "There's a cure."

"No sir," one of the guards said. "You just said it yourself." He was young, staring down at Samael with disgust. "And I have orders— strict orders from you—to shoot anyone infected."

Samael fell to the ground, pulling the table runner off the coffee table. The glasses of lemonade fell across him.

I stepped over, looking down at him. "You're right, President Samael. This country is going to start over. Just not with you leading it."

EPILOGUE

I pulled the arrow back, narrowing my eyes in the bright sun. I let out a breath to steady myself, aimed, and fired. The arrow hit the gummy right between the eyes. He fell to the ground, lifeless and still. He was so deteriorated that he was nothing more than skin—flesh so old it looked like antique leather stretched over brittle bone. He didn't pose a threat; I shot him to put him out of his misery.

I turned, looked at Hayden by the water's edge, and smiled. I set my bow down and grabbed the hem of my t-shirt, yanking it over my head. I unbuttoned my jean shorts and shimmied out of them, having already kicked off my flip flops. I skipped on my tip toes through the hot sand.

"Nice shot," Hayden said, reaching inside a cooler.

"Thanks, baby," I said and took the cold beer from his hands. I popped the top and settled down, stretching out my legs on the towel. Hayden lay down next to me with a satisfied sigh, closing his eyes and tipping his head to the sun.

He held his arm up and I knocked my beer against his then took a long drink. I was unable to keep the smile off my face and set the beer down, pushing it into the sand. I put my arm across my face, blocking the blinding sun from my eyelids.

We were here, at that beach. Granted, it wasn't the sunny ocean beach we had always imagined, with white sand and crystal clear water. What we were at was nothing more than a glorified swimming hole in Kentucky. But my ass was in the sand, a cold beer was in my hand, and the love of my life was next to me. I couldn't complain. We were at that beach. *Our* beach.

"Don't let me fall asleep," I said, turning to Hayden. "I want to get an even tan."

He tipped his head, grinning. "You should take your top off then."

I smiled and rolled my eyes. "Well, I do hate tan lines."

He rolled over, playfully pulling at the bikini top strings. "You could use some sleep too, Riss."

"I know," I said, closing my eyes. "Wake me up in an hour then."

"I will if I don't fall asleep," he laughed and stretched out.

We left the beach around sunset, pulling into the driveway of my Kentucky farmhouse. We paused on the front porch before we went inside, looking through the screen door.

"Put that down!" I heard Raeya shout. "You do not eat dog food!" I took a step closer as she chased a rowdy four year old boy through the room, holding a sleeping baby in her arms. "You're going to wake up your sister!"

I couldn't help but smile. I wanted to rush in and help her, but she was determined to do it on her own. The little boy let out a shriek of joy and tipped the dog bowl, sending pieces of kibble rolling across the floor. I put my hand over my mouth to keep from laughing.

"Benjamin Rider Underwood!" she scowled. "What did you do?"

"You said put it down," Ben told her. "Sorry, Aunt Ray. Are you mad?"

I moved up the remaining stairs and knew the *exact* innocent smile he was giving Raeya...and I knew it would work on her. Ben was the spitting image of Hayden, from his defined cheekbones to his hazel eyes. We hadn't meant to have him. Finding out I was pregnant was one of the scariest events of our lives, even with all we'd been through.

* * *

It had only been six months since we'd returned from New York. Nothing had been fixed yet. The world was still the same, still just as dangerous as before. We were still at the compound, desperately working on expanding our little community into a real village.

I hadn't felt well for days and was just so damn tired all the time. I knew, deep down, but held off on taking a test for another week. It terrified me, right down to my core, to bring a brand new, innocent life into this harrowing world. Hayden was nervous but excited. Ever since we had Pastor Jim marry us, he had been dropping hints that he eventually wanted a family. I just hadn't expected 'eventually' to come so soon.

Everyone shared in Hayden's excitement. Raeya openly admitted that she had been hoping for this for a long time. My grandpa was over the moon knowing he would get to meet his first great grandchild. He confessed he wasn't sure he'd live long enough for that day to come.

He did, and was the doting great grandfather he had always wanted to be. Holding that sweet baby eased my grandpa's paranoia. Two years later, my grandpa passed peacefully in his sleep. It had always been his wish to be buried next to my grandmother. When we brought his body back here, Hayden suggested we stay. So we did.

No, Ben wasn't planned...but he was the best thing that ever happened to us.

* * *

"Rissy," Raeya whispered so she wouldn't wake the baby in her arms. "What are you doing back so early? I told you guys to spend the whole day together!" She used her foot to push the dog food into a neat pile.

"I wanted to make sure Ben wasn't driving you crazy," I said. Really, I missed my children too much to be away from them for that long.

"I got this, really," she pressed, going to the closet for a broom. Ben ran wild through the house, stomping with each step. "You need some time for yourself." She turned around, raising an eyebrow. "You and Hayden haven't been alone since Zoe was born. And that was what...five months ago?"

I looked at the little girl in Raeya's arms and smiled. "I know. I miss Zoe when she's not with me." I crossed the kitchen and took my baby from Raeya. "She's just so cute." I kissed her forehead, causing her to stir. "When are you gonna have one?" I asked Raeya.

She looked up from the spilled dog food and laughed. "This is enough for me. You know I do not ever want to be pregnant."

I looked at Zoe. "I loved being pregnant with her since it was planned," I laughed.

"Riss, you threw up every day for twenty weeks then became anemic. Why on earth would you enjoy that?"

I laughed again. "Because you get something like this out of it!"

"No thank you," she said and put the broom away. "Ivan and I are quite happy being the cool aunt and uncle. Just don't tell Hannah that. She thinks she's the cool aunt."

The front door opened and closed. Ben jumped off the couch, screaming for his dad. Hayden scooped him up, flipping Ben upside down. The boy cracked up then wiggled out of Hayden's arms to pester Ivan. Ben jumped up at him, trying to entice him to play. Ivan jerked forward, giving Ben a head start. Then he chased him around the house. Hayden took Zoe from me, cradling her against his chest.

"How was it?" Raeya asked, opening the fridge.

"Good," Hayden said, gently rocking his daughter in his arms. He smiled down at her. "Saw one gummy. Wasn't even a threat."

"Maybe they're finally melting," Raeya said. That's what seemed to happen to them. Their skin hung from their bodies, dripping off with each step. It was rare to come across zombies now. But rare wasn't good enough to feel completely safe.

"It seems that way," Hayden said. "We haven't seen a crazy in, what, seven months now?"

The packs of crazies were thinned now as well. Every once in a while we came across one, alone and wandering about, close to the next stage. Thanks to the vaccine Dr. Cara and Padraic were able to perfect, a bite no longer posed as much of a threat. There was still a chance of getting ripped apart and eaten...that hadn't changed, not yet.

"Go upstairs," Raeya instructed to both of us. "You can get a few hours of sleep before they get here."

"Ok," I said, giving Zoe one more kiss. "If she's hungry, come get me."

"There is milk in the fridge," Raeya reminded me. "Like there has been all day. Get some sleep or take a shower. We'll watch Ben and Zoe." She took Zoe from Hayden and shooed us up the stairs.

Padraic, Brock, Olivia, Sonja, and Jason were driving here from Arkansas for Ben's birthday. They had stayed in Marbles Falls at the compound having risen into new roles in the village we had built.

After we had infected President Samael, the truth had spread across everyone at the Regency. Some wanted to stay and continue on as they had been, and other wanted to leave. Gorge, the horticulturist who was friends with Martha, came back to the compound with Hayden and I when we returned. Several hundred others wanted to leave New York too, but had to wait until things were safe.

Gorge helped up set up more greenhouses that were only two hours from the compound. In just a few months, we had our own endless supply of fruit and vegetables. It eased a lot of tension for Hayden.

Over the next few months, my grandpa rose to the role of leader. Being busy kept his paranoia away—well, if you could call it that. Everything he was worried about turned out to be right. It allowed Hayden and me the time we desperately needed to be alone and cope with everything we had been through together.

In the spring, construction on the cabins was back in full force and a little village slowly grew, being added to year after year. We still had to go on supply missions, and Hayden never wanted to give up looking for survivors. Things weren't easy: we lost people on missions, zombies made their way into the fields and got several of our cows before we battled them away, and a nasty case of the stomach flu swept through the compound, claiming the lives of one young child and several others.

No, it wasn't easy. But everyday we were getting closer and closer to what we had before. Moving to Kentucky was something Hayden and I wanted to do. After all we'd done, all we'd been through, we had to get away. Especially once we became parents. We were ready to pass on the roles of leaders, ready to just be a family. And with Padraic, Jason, and Brock still there to oversee things, the compound was in good hands.

They chose to stay, continuing to spread what Fuller had started and what Hayden and I had worked so hard to continue, the thing that made life worth living. It was a word... a concept. And it was dangerous, infecting one person to another with little contact. Once you got it, it was hard to get rid of. It sank into you, affecting every decision you made. It was something we all wanted, something we all needed to keep going.

After all...what's more contagious than hope?

ACKNOWLEDGEMENTS

There are so many people I would like to thank. First is my family, for not only supporting my love of writing and obsession with zombies, but for ensuring I got the quiet time I needed to make this story happen. Second is my editor: you are a rock star! It's not everyday I come across someone who "gets" my books as well as you do. Thank you for caring about Hayden and Orissa as much I do and making the series reach its full potential. Thank you Lori, Lindsay, Elyse, and Stephanie. You guys are my go-to beta readers and my biggest cheerleaders. I love you all. Thank you to Michael at Permuted Press for working so closely with me to give the series all it deserves. Dean Samed, thank you for four amazing covers that represent the books perfectly. And of course, last but certainly not least, thank you so much to my fans. You guys have made the Contagium Series what it is today. I couldn't have done it without you. Thank you.

OTHER BOOKS BY EMILY GOODWIN

The Guardian Legacies Series:
Unbound
Reaper
Moonlight

Beyond the Sea Series:
Beyond the Sea
Red Skies at Night (releasing 2015)

Dark Romance standalones:
Stay
All I Need

The Contagium Series:
Contagious
Deathly Contagious
Contagious Chaos
The Truth is Contagious

ABOUT THE AUTHOR

Emily Goodwin is the international best-selling author of the stand-alone novel STAY, The Guardian Legacies Series: UNBOUND, REAPER, MOONLIGHT (releasing 2014), The Beyond the Sea Series: BEYOND THE SEA, RED SKIES AT NIGHT (releasing 2015) and the award winning Contagium Series: CONTAGIOUS, DEATHLY CONTAGIOUS, CONTAGIOUS CHAOS, THE TRUTH IS CONTAGIOUS (Permuted Press).

Emily lives with her husband, daughter, and German Shepherd named Vader. Along with writing, Emily enjoys riding her horse, designing and making costumes, and Cosplay.

www.emilygoodwinbooks.com
facebook.com/emilygoodwinbooks